Greig Beck grew up across the road from Bondi Beach in Sydney, Australia. His early days were spent surfing, sunbaking and reading science fiction on the sand. He then went on to study computer science, immerse himself in the financial software industry and later received an MBA. Today, Greig spends his days writing, but still finds time to surf at his beloved Bondi Beach. He lives in Sydney, with his wife, son and an enormous black German shepherd.

ALSO BY GREIG BECK

GORGON

GREIG BECK

momentum

First published by Momentum in 2014
This edition published in 2014 by Momentum
Pan Macmillan Australia Pty Ltd
1 Market Street, Sydney 2000

A CIP record for this book is available at the National Library of Australia

Gorgon

EPUB format: 9781743342800
Mobi format: 9781743342848
Print on Demand format: 9781760080488
Print format: 9781760081652

Cover design by XOU Creative
Edited by Nicola O'Shea
Proofread by Laura Cook

Macmillan Digital Australia: www.macmillandigital.com.au

To report a typographical error, please visit momentumbooks.com.au/contact/

Visit www.momentumbooks.com.au to read more about all our books and to buy
books online. You will also find features, author interviews and news of any author
events.

To the men and women of the allied armed forces – thank you for being there as both our sword and shield.

None shall behold the Gorgos and draw again the breath of life.
From Greek pottery shard, 1050 BC

Gorgon – the name derives from the ancient Greek word gorgós, which means 'dreadful.'

PROLOGUE

Psychro Cave, Crete, 1500 BC

Ducetius kneeled to grab a handful of coins. He rose slowly, his eyes fixed on the magnificent golden discs. Below him, the red marble street was so polished he could see his grin reflected in its burnished hues.

He blinked away the sting of perspiration and wiped an arm quickly over his brow. Ignoring the stifling heat he glanced about, still grinning. It was true – the hidden city of stone with its streets of red marble, majestic houses, elaborate statues, and black rivers of oil, some of it afire, existed. And there was the treasure, so much of it, piles and piles of precious stones, metals, and mountains of gold coin.

The single long street was abandoned, silent – but it was like the silence that grew from the holding of breath rather than that of solitude. Ducetius felt he was being watched. The statues were so lifelike and their details exquisite, but their visages were nightmarish. It was if the sculptor had captured a terror that had befallen the models in life.

He drew the sack from his shoulder and bent to scoop up more coins. It had all been worth it. He had followed the clues, paid bribes, cheated men, and stolen maps and scraps of information wherever he could, and at last he had found it – Hades. An underground city filled with riches beyond reason.

He threw his head back and whooped, the sound bouncing away into the enormous cavern's depths. Ducetius listened to his voice grow softer the further it traveled in the stygian darkness. He grabbed at more coins, then froze. A noise.

He spun and let his eyes travel over the street – there was nothing save the blank stares of the statues who stood mutely weeping, screaming, or tearing at their own faces. He bent again to his task, but hurried now, feeling the desire to be out in the sunlight again. The sack was heavy and beginning to drag. He wished his son was here to help, rather than waiting for him at the surface.

Another soft sound. A footstep? He whirled.

His mouth gaped and his eyes went wide as a white-hot shock ran through his entire body. The thing loomed over him, taller than anything he had ever witnessed.

In the ancient scrolls there had been a warning about the Cursed Ones who walked the pits of Hell. In his haste and lust for wealth, he had chosen to ignore them. He had been selective in what he believed, impatient, foolish. Now he could see, too late, that the warnings were true.

He didn't want to look but felt compelled to. His eyes traveled up the body until he came to its head. Ropey outgrowths coiled over each other in constant movement, parting to reveal a ghastly white face and the red-slitted eyes of a snake. A shocking pain like a thousand daggers started in his head.

Before he knew what was happening he found himself running, climbing, scrambling toward the light. Thick paste-like vomit spewed from his gut. Still he moved upwards, but was slowing now with every step. His body felt numb.

Ducetius squeezed through the tiny opening in the cave wall, into daylight. He was only barely conscious of the sun's warmth on his torso, and his vision was misting as if behind a layer of gauze. He was finally out of the creature's lair but he knew he was not free.

The coins fell from his fingers that stiffened to stone. He lifted his head on a creaking neck and tried to stand, but managed only to get to one knee before the joint seized. His son's voice sounded distant yet he should have been only a few dozen feet from where Ducetius had exited the hidden cave.

A shadow fell across his face and his son's voice came again. He could just make out the boy's features as the ashen veil closed around him. He would have wept, but there were no words, no tears, no moisture at all left inside him. He lifted an arm to reach out to that familiar, beautiful face, but his hand fell from his wrist like crumbling chalk.

His son's voice rang out again, this time in a long, tormented scream, but for Ducetius the sound receded as if into the dark cave he had just climbed from. The sunshine disappeared too, and Ducetius became another stone monument to the gods.

CHAPTER 1

The Sunken Palace, Istanbul, Turkey; yesterday

The guide walked slowly ahead of the forty tourists, turning now and then to glare at an individual who looked like he or she was considering taking a photograph. There were magnificent pictures for sale at the café on completion of the tour – end of discussion. His nasal monotone bounced around the cathedral-sized chamber, followed by a hollow echo, as he ticked off facts and figures in the autonomous manner of someone who had spoken the words a thousand times, displaying an enthusiasm as dulled as the once polished marble surrounding them.

He waved an arm toward the forest of enormous columns that had been colored moss-green by the centuries, and were now illuminated by lights suspended thirty feet above them and extending hundreds of feet into the distance. 'The Yerebatan Sarayi, also known as the Basilica Cistern or Sunken Palace, was built in the sixth century by the great Emperor Justinian. It is 105,000 square feet in area, and can hold nearly 3 million cubic feet of water – that is about 250 Olympic-sized swimming pools. It is also –'

'I understood that it was built by Emperor Constantine.' The American woman's voice was grating in the hushed interior of the underground chamber.

The guide groaned – there was always one who thought they knew something. 'An uninformed misconception. Emperor Constantine built the Great Basilica on this site several hundred years before, but it was a place of commerce and for gathering – more an open garden with some underground vaults for storing things he valued. It was Justinian I who in 532 AD made the Great Basilica Cistern what it is now.'

'Where was Sean Connery standing? Was it around here?' asked another overly loud voice.

The guide rolled his eyes and exhaled. Here they were, within one of the wonders of the Middle East, and all these people cared about was where one of their movie stars had once stood. *These are the true Western values*, he thought. Aloud, he said, 'It is true that the 1963 movie *From Russia With Love* was shot in these very chambers, before the walkways were constructed – that is why Mr. Bond had to travel by boat. And no, he was a half-mile further down in the waterway. Now please, keep moving as there is more to see before the cistern is closed for the day.'

The guide motioned with his arm and led the group of garishly dressed tourists further into the enormous chamber. He stopped on the walkway and turned to face them, his back to what looked like a small island in the center of the cistern's lake. Here, the water had become shallow due to silt build-up, but the deeper pools still bubbled and splashed from time to time with large carp that had been introduced to keep the algae levels down.

'The Medusa Columns,' the guide said, and pointed over his shoulder with a flat hand.

The group turned as one to stare at the giant heads at the base of the columns. The faces, all showing the unmistakable countenance of the dreaded Gorgon from Greek mythology, were stained green with age, and either lying on their side or upside down. Snakes wove thickly through their carved hair.

A teenager bent and turned his head sideways to look into a face. 'They say they were turned sideways and upside down to reduce the power of her stare.'

The guide grunted; *at last, a semi-intelligent comment*. 'That is one interpretation. There are other suggestions, such as the head placement is part of some long-lost puzzle, or the heads were carved in Constantine's time and used by Justinian's stonemasons because they were the right size for a base for the columns.'

The teenager sagged slightly at the more mundane explanation.

The guide waved the group on again. 'If we can move along – hurry, please.'

They moved like a single mass toward some wooden stairs. The guide didn't bother to take a headcount. If he had, he would have noticed that his group of forty tourists now numbered thirty-nine.

*

Janus Caresche waited as the sounds of the group retreated into the distance, followed by the clang of a heavy door being pulled shut. One by one the overhead lights drummed out. A wall of darkness stepped down the chamber toward him, then passed over him to chase the remaining lights further along the ancient cistern.

Caresche was one of the new breed of archeologists – just as much entrepreneur as historian. They tended to avoid traditional work in museums or universities, instead acting more like mercenaries for the highest-paying collectors around the world. Janus Caresche was young, arrogant, and liked to think of himself as an antiquity detective. He got results, but he was expensive.

He kneeled down, removed his small backpack, and pulled out a plastic lunch box. After popping the lid, and removing several wrapped sandwiches, he lifted free a fake bottom to reveal a set of night-vision goggles, six large button-shaped objects, and a ball of blue putty. Caresche shrugged the pack over his shoulders, slipped the goggles over his forehead, and stepped into the shallow water to make his way to the first of the Gorgon heads.

'*Ma belle.*' He ran his hands over the large face. '*Gorgos.*' He used the ancient Greek name, meaning "*dreadful*", for the monster, and spoke softly to the flaring green-enhanced image of the cruel stone face. 'May your gaze turn me not to stone but instead make me rich.'

Caresche knew that the three statues weren't, as many amateur archeologists believed, different artisan's representations of the Gorgon, but in fact one each of the famous sisters – Medusa, Stheno, and Euryale.

He laughed softly and patted the broad forehead, before placing a small ball of putty over the baseball-sized pupil of each stone eye. He took two of the buttons and pushed them gently into the center of the putty, then turned the casing on each. A thin red beam shot out from both, neither overlapping nor hitting the same object in their path. Caresche quickly moved to the next head, conscious of the time, even though it would be more than twelve hours until the next tour party arrived. By then, he, and any trace of his exploration, would be long gone. He went through the same procedure with the second head, and then the third. He stayed low for a few seconds, tracing the path of the lasers with his eyes. As he'd expected, each head faced a different section of the ancient Sunken Palace.

Such was the fear of the Gorgon's gaze that her image was often used as a deterrent to invaders, even in many modern Greek bank vaults. Caresche guessed it was the same here: the Gorgon's gaze was guarding something of value to the Emperor Constantine; something that needed all three of the sisters' power to keep it secure and hidden away from the world.

Caresche ticked off in his mind the historical myths about the possible treasures that could have been hidden in Constantine's vault. They ranged from lost texts from the Great Library of Alexandria, to the body of the boy king Caesarion – the only child of the brief relationship between Julius Caesar and Cleopatra – supposed to be wrapped in a golden web of Indian rubies and African emeralds. There was also the legend of the death mask of Magera, the fourth sister of the Gorgons, erased for unknown reasons from the ancient Greek tales. Whichever treasure was hidden here didn't matter to Caresche – any one would be worth a hundred king's ransoms. And he didn't even have to remove the items, just provide proof of their existence and their location. For Caresche, a picture wasn't just worth a thousand words; it was worth a million bucks.

He waded through the ankle-deep water to where the six beams intersected and looked up at the chamber's roof. He twisted a dial on his goggles to enhance their vision, but still there was nothing; and no further clues on any of the other columns.

Undeterred, he began to feel around with his foot – *there*, a lump or extrusion. He pulled up one sleeve and reached down to trace the outline of the object – it seemed to be a stone crucifix, roughly a foot long, stuck to the brickwork on the bottom of the cistern floor. He was lucky he was here in the dry season – the water was low now, but originally the cistern would have been filled to the ceiling, and this part of the chamber could have been accessed only with scuba equipment, or not at all.

The archeologist traced the cross for a moment longer, before pushing the goggles up on his head, and pulling a headband flashlight from his backpack. He slid it over his forehead and switched on the beam, squinting at the harsh white light. Though the water had been stirred by his movement, it quickly settled, and he could see that the embedded crucifix was at the center of two large rings – the first, some five feet across; the second, at the far edge of his water-refracted beam, more than twenty.

Caresche straightened and looked up at the ceiling, then at each of the Gorgon heads. This was where the lasers intersected; this was the meeting of the Gorgons' gaze that his research had indicated he should seek out. *But what now?*

He frowned, standing still and listening to the sound of the carp softly stirring the water in the darkness. He shook his head, kneeled in the water and gripped the cross with both hands, and pulled, then pushed, then turned it one way, then the next. It didn't budge.

'*Merde!*'

He sucked in a breath, grabbed the long end of the crucifix and yanked it toward himself, straining his shoulder muscles. The crucifix moved an inch, like the long hand of a clock. Encouraged, he yanked some more – and was rewarded with another inch.

Silt swirled up, dislodged from the ancient stone cross. Caresche readied himself again, taking a few seconds to suck in some deep breaths. He yanked, and this time the stone cross grated heavily before lifting and turning freely like a giant door handle.

Almost immediately, there was a grinding all around him from the very edges of the cistern walls. Caresche stood as fish darted past him like miniature rockets in the now turbulent water. The grinding noise increased, as though some huge stone machine was starting up under his feet, and he could feel the vibrations in the stonework surrounding him. Dust rained down, and he was contemplating running for the exit when the floor seemed to judder, and then drop a few inches.

Caresche backed up against one of the columns. The grinding turned to a roar as the water level lumped higher, and then started to drop.

He quickly removed his backpack and pulled free another large flashlight. As he aimed the beam at the walls and the source of the noise, he saw that huge blocks of stone had slid aside at the water line, revealing drains now filling with millions of gallons of water rushing to escape. He moved his beam further along the wall – the drain vents seemed to have opened the entire length of the ancient cistern.

In what seemed like minutes the water had gone, leaving stranded carp flopping miserably in muddy puddles. The inner and outer ring carved into the floor around the crucifix were now clearly visible. As Caresche traced them with his eyes, they started to hiss, as if pressure was building beneath them.

The archeologist's mouth opened in a smile as the larger outer circle spun and then dropped … and kept dropping, until it disappeared completely. It wasn't a freefall motion, but more a lowering, as the stone seemed to split and then reassemble itself into spiral steps that dropped deep down into the lower cistern chambers.

Caresche stepped forward quickly and stared into the darkness. He coughed. The chamber must have been sealed for many long centuries, and the air smelled of damp, decay, and something that reminded him of fish putrefying at the high-tide line on a beach.

The archeologist glanced at his watch, its face large on his slim wrist. He lifted his head to listen – there was a constant dripping and a few gasps from dying fish, but no shouts or sirens, and the chamber's lights remained off.

Janus Caresche grinned. 'All mine', he said to the dark hole before him.

He reached into his backpack for a small hammer and metal spike. This time, if he came to another barrier, he'd go through it. He slid the tools into his belt, took one last look around, and started down the black stone steps into a stygian darkness.

He counted the steps as he descended, finishing at one hundred – the *centum*, an important number in ancient Rome. The twin beams from his flashlight and headlamp barely illuminated the large vault-like room. The ground and walls ran with moisture and dripping mosses.

Caresche kneeled and wiped his hand across the floor – polished mica, still shining like glass after all the centuries. Behind the slime, the walls were covered in beautiful mosaics made from abalone shell, more mica, and semi-precious stone shards, showing images of serpents, faces screwed up in agony, or night-time scenes with chalk-like figures shielding their eyes. In one, a large figure sat in an ox-drawn cart with a covering concealing its head. The detail of every mosaic was exquisite, and even now, centuries later, the faces seemed to take on life in the light of his beam.

Every few panels showed a large staring face, like a ghastly death mask, its eyes orbs of metal. Lifting his light, Caresche saw the metal was silver, and he knew that it would once have been polished to a mirror-like sheen. Viewers of the panels would have seen themselves reflected back in all the silver eyes.

He held out his arms. 'All shall bathe in the gaze of the Gorgos.'

He grinned and threw his head back, then frowned. He lifted his flashlight to the vaulted roof. In *trompe l'oeil* style, which created an almost 3D effect, the magnificent painted ceiling depicted a noonday sun, soft clouds and birds flying across a blue sky. Someone had gone to great trouble to ensure this room would forever seem bathed in perpetual sunlight.

Caresche lowered his light toward an ornate doorway. He immediately recognized the design – a Roman triumphal arch, used to signify victory over an enemy, or even over death. A wall had been erected across the arch, sealing it. He placed a hand on the brickwork – typical Roman fire-hardened clay. Strong, but the mortar would be weakened by nearly a millennium of moisture.

He wedged the sharp metal spike between two bricks and struck it with the hammer. The hammer clanged and bounced back, causing minimal damage to the wall but jarring his shoulder.

'Fuck you too,' he said, and replaced the spike.

This time he swung hard, and the bricks separated. It took him another ten minutes to remove the first brick, but from there, most came out like old teeth from loose gums. He kicked at the last few blocks, which crumbled inwards.

Janus Caresche flicked sweat from his face, placed a hand over his mouth and nose, and stepped inside. '*Oof*.' It stank … of something unidentifiable.

The space was small, no more than twenty feet around, and plain by Roman standards. It seemed to be a fortified storeroom, which he had expected for something Emperor Constantine had wanted to keep hidden away.

There was a single object in the center of the room – a huge urn of age-darkened bronze, as tall as he was. It reminded him of the pots whalers used in the 1800s for rendering whale blubber down to oil. He walked slowly around it, flicking his light up and down its sides. It stood on three ornate clawed feet, its sides adorned with horrible faces crowned with what looked like writhing snakes. There was writing on the vessel and on the walls nearby – a strange script he didn't recognize, even though he spoke and understood a dozen languages.

He rapped against it with a knuckle; the sound was deep and hollow.

'*Bonjour*, beautiful. Anybody home?'

He smiled and was about to step back when he froze. *What was that? A sound?* He put his ear to the urn – listening, waiting. *Nothing.*

He snorted softly and shook his head. 'Let's get this done.'

He ran a hand along the top to feel a manhole-sized lid held in place by huge clasps and chains. Caresche had seen many Roman chests and many ornate locks in his time, but this was a first – probably purpose built. The signs were good: it was a significant strongbox with plenty of locks and a lot of chains, and to someone like him, that meant whatever was inside was of enormous value.

Payday, he thought as he placed the metal spike against one of the bronze clasps. He tapped it once with the hammer for alignment, then raised the hammer high and swung down hard.

The first lock broke away.

CHAPTER 2

Twenty miles north of Fort Detrick, Frederick, Maryland, USA

Medical officer Lieutenant Alan Marshal groaned under another onslaught from his immediate superior, Captain Robert Graham. He kept his hands tight on the wheel, hunkered down in the driver's seat, and let the man vent. He knew Graham was a man under pressure, and besides, the guy had a temper like Satan himself.

Graham headed up the Alpha Soldier Research Unit at Fort Detrick's Medical Command Installation; its goal to create physically and mentally superior soldiers for the US military. Graham had had only one real success in nearly five years – Alex Hunter, their first subject trialed on the experimental Arcadian treatment.

Hunter was brought to them following a catastrophic battlefield trauma, more dead than alive. The treatment wasn't expected to do more than deliver some cerebral stimulation for enhanced cognizance and muscular mobility. After all, the man was little more than a vegetable. But Alex Hunter had recovered – with massively increased strength and abilities. No one had ever seen anything like him – and they'd let him simply walk away.

Neither Marshal nor Graham had realized at the time that Hunter was a biochemical fluke, an aberration. Since then, countless Arcadian test subjects had been mutilated and destroyed, often by their own hands. Graham's recent batch had proved to be little more than brutal automatons with a metabolism that cannibalized their own morphology: they melted down as their internal core temperatures burned through their flesh and sanity.

Marshal had to hand it to Graham for persistence – he never gave up. He always had something new to try, and was constantly on the verge of a breakthrough. Marshal knew if it were up to him, he would have tapped the mat ages ago.

He sucked in a deep breath and looked at the dashboard clock: only 10pm in another fourteen-hour shift. You certainly didn't join the ASRU for the social life.

'How?' Graham said angrily, his frustration still simmering.

'Huh?' Marshal half-turned. 'How what?'

'How does Hunter's system provide the thermoregulation necessary to balance the huge rises in core temperature? What extra factor does he use or possess? What was different about him?'

Marshal groaned. *Here we go again – more self-flagellation.* 'Bob, we've been over the treatment notes countless time. There was nothing –'

'We missed something – we must have. Was there some sort of impurity or contamination? Something already in his system that interacted with the compounds?' Graham shook his head and folded his arms tight across his chest.

Marshal chanced another look at the clock, counting down the minutes until he could get his boss home ... and bring himself some peace and quiet. He decided to steer Graham back to the science; that always seemed to refocus him.

'Well, we know that the human body's thermal output is primarily generated in the liver, brain, and heart, and also in the contraction of skeletal muscles. So perhaps he –'

'Bullshit, Marshal. I don't believe it has anything to do with his body. The preoptic area of the anterior hypothalamus manages thermoregulation. It's his brain, it's always been his goddamn unique beautiful fucking brain.'

Marshal sighed, and glanced at the clock again. The run through Cunningham Falls State Park took about ten minutes, and the winding road through the darkened forest with the headlights lighting the road lines and little else was almost hypnotic. At least Graham's bellyaching served to keep Marshal awake, even if it did make the drive seem to go on forever.

'What's that?' Graham leaned forward and put his hands on the dashboard.

Marshal slowed. 'Someone hurt, is it? Or had an accident?'

He flicked on his high beams. Immediately the figure of a man hunched over a bicycle was lit up like an actor on a floodlit stage. The man kept his back to them, fiddling with the bike. He lifted one arm and waved, but didn't turn.

'For Chrissakes, can't he do that by the side of the road? We could have run him over.' Graham wound down his window as Marshal pulled the car up about twenty feet from the crouching man. 'Can you move, please?'

The man ignored him and continued to tinker.

Graham pulled his head in. 'Drive around him.'

Marshal shook his head and pointed to the side of the road. There was a high embankment on one side and a steep drop into the forest on the other. 'It's too steep, we'll roll. Besides, he could be hurt.'

'Doesn't look hurt.' Graham leaned out the window again. 'Excuse me, sir, are you hurt? Do you need help?'

The man nodded but still didn't turn.

Marshal sensed Graham looking across at him, but he kept staring straight ahead. It was cold out, he was tired, and knew nothing about fixing pushbikes. He really hoped Graham didn't order him to get out and help.

'Fuck it. Times like this I hate being a doctor,' Graham said, and pushed the door open. He paused to look back into the car. 'Keep the motor running. I'll see if we can't get this guy out of the way. Maybe we can call the local police to come and give him a lift.' He paused again. 'If we give him a lift, you drop me home first.'

Marshal watched Graham saunter toward the man, who didn't stop working on his task or acknowledge the approaching doctor in any way. *Arrogant prick*, Marshal thought.

Graham reached the man and bent forward over his shoulder to see what he was working on. At last there was a reaction – the man turned and began to rise. One large arm shot out like a striking snake and a huge hand wrapped around Graham's bicep. The cyclist rose to his full height, and seemed to unfold. Marshal's eyes widened. Captain Graham was a tall man, standing six feet, but this ogre towered over him by at least another eight inches, and was more than twice as wide. The man's dark beard glinted in the car's headlights, and Marshal caught a reflection from one of his eyes. Marshal knew prosthetics and recognized it as glass.

The big man pulled Graham close, said something, then shook him violently as if to get an answer. Graham nodded meekly, keeping his shoulders hunched as if expecting a blow. He got it. The giant swung a huge fist into Graham's face, knocking his head backward on his neck and causing him to drop to the ground unconscious.

Marshal was momentarily frozen with disbelief and shock, then he leaped from the car. 'Hey!'

He regretted the action instantly. He wasn't armed, and the man outweighed him by more than 150 pounds. Further, a small black pistol magically appeared in the big man's hand.

Marshal dived and rolled as bullets started flying toward him, then got to his feet and sprinted back down the dark road. He was picking up speed until a mule-kick to his shoulder threw him forward onto the pavement. He immediately got to his feet and ran again. The devil himself couldn't have stopped him now.

He kept running, and didn't stop, even when he heard his car start up and drive away.

*

Hammerson read the report again, his eyes lingering over the physical description of Marshal's assailant: large frame, bearded, possible glass or synthetic eye. He had no doubt it was Uli Borshov, one of Russia's most effective assassins and the man who had originally put Alex Hunter into a coma. He shook his head in disbelief, his lips pulled back, teeth clamped together in fury, and slammed the report down on his desk.

'How the hell did that big bastard get into my front yard?' He rubbed his forehead hard, breathing deep. 'And how does someone the size of a grizzly bear stay under the radar?'

Seated beside him at the desk was an enormous man in black military fatigues. He shrugged, and stood up smoothly, accompanied by the small whine of electronics. 'He's good – we knew that. The guy's ex-Spetsnaz and a psychopath. If anyone can get inside our tent and stay invisible, he can.'

Hammerson leaned back in his chair and assessed First Lieutenant Samuel Reid. The big HAWC soldier's arms and shoulders bulged, and the knuckles of his hands where he gripped the seat arms were raised and callused, testament to years of brutal action. The big man looked fit – the benefit of the extensive upper-body physical work needed to compensate for his legs being useless. A recent mission had ended with Sam shattering his L1 and L2 spinal plates, and worse, severing the cord. Hammerson had needed Sam back in action – and Sam had wanted it double. Advancements in bionics and battlefield armor had moved to field-test phase, so six months ago Hammerson had authorized Sam for a trial of the new MECH suit – or part of it. The Military Exoskeleton Combat Harness was designed as the next-generation heavy-combat armor. On Sam, the half-body synaptic electronics were a molded framework built onto, and into, his body. A metal bracing belt fit around his waist, comprising a power pack and supportive base for the banded ribbing up the back, which then dropped additional struts down each side of his waist, hips and thighs to attach to the hyper-alloy-composite exoskeleton framework covering his legs and feet. It was light, flexible and a hundred times tougher than steel. The bands weren't just fastened to the outside of Sam's body; electrodes had been surgically inserted directly into his muscle mass – in effect, moving and working his muscles exactly as before his accident. It was still Sam's brain sending the signals, but they were now relayed via the computer's fiber optics instead of his broken spinal cord, and the MECH's exoskeleton provided the support his own bone mass couldn't.

'A psychopath, but a damned clever one,' Hammerson said slowly. 'There are too many coincidences – the Arcadian shows up back home, and then the assassin who left him for dead in Chechnya reappears from the other side of the world and either kidnaps or kills Captain Robert Graham, the doctor who originally saved Hunter's life.' He shook his head. 'Coincidences? Bullshit!'

Sam leaned forward over the desk. 'Sir, Graham's Arcadian program couldn't remain a military secret forever. It was already compromised by the Israelis; it's not surprising that

Russia, China, North Korea, and every other nation with an enhanced weapons division are suddenly taking an interest.'

Hammerson ran one large hand through his iron-gray crew cut. He was the person who had sent Alex Hunter, near death, to the Israelis, hoping they could revive him after he'd been infected by the Hades virus. They had, but it had cost the young HAWC his memory, and even now it was unclear exactly what had been rebuilt or rewired in the man's brain. But Sam was right: the genie was out of the bottle, and getting it back in would be impossible.

'Well, looks to me like some asshole decided to leapfrog the hard yards on R&D and go straight to the source – steal the creator.' Hammerson exhaled long and slow. 'Fuck it. We dropped the ball.'

Hammerson picked up the phone and called through to the US military's electronics surveillance factory beneath the Offutt Airforce Base in Nebraska. He was after Major Gerry Harris, a friend and the man responsible for coordinating the constellation of orbiting birds that fed back high-altitude intelligence from over the United States mainland, and also much of the globe. Harris and his team had been immediately set to work to find Captain Graham or Uli Borshov.

'Gerry – anything?'

'Sorry, Jack, nada. It's as if the pair of them just walked off into thin air. I've got every bird in a favorable orbit looking down over every shoulder. We're peeking out of every ATM, CCTV, traffic camera and surveillance scanner on or off the grid, and there's absolutely nothing.'

Hammerson growled. 'Christ. Okay, put the recognition programs into overdrive – I want Captain Graham found, all of him. I know Borshov – that monster won't go to ground. He knows we'll eventually find him, so he'll be on the move somehow, and fast. He's got to be trying to get back to Russia.'

Hammerson looked at his watch. It'd been ten hours. Graham was probably already out of the country by now, sealed in a wooden crate and on his way to the Kremlin's deep interrogation rooms. Hammerson shook his head and rubbed a knuckle against his brow. He'd had his differences with the sonofabitch – a lot of them – but he wouldn't wish that on anyone.

He knew Graham would give up the Arcadian program, and he didn't blame the man. Advanced physical, chemical, and psychological torture meant everyone talked in the end … or died. The only upside was, the man's work wasn't so much a success as an ongoing concept. Still, it belonged to the US, and Hammerson didn't take fondly to people taking his stuff.

'Gerry, put some extra eyes on it. This is a priority.'

'Don't worry, Jack, I'll find them. Harris out.'

Jack Hammerson sat back again, and turned to the large picture on the wall beside his desk. It was a black and white photograph of a granite-jawed man in full dress uniform. Arthur 'Bull' Simons had been one of the first commanders of the US Rangers, and Hammerson's first mentor. Hammerson read the inscription on the small brass plate on the lower rim of the frame: *Go hard or go home.*

Sam cleared his throat. 'There's one more thing to consider, sir. Borshov might have another target. Some unfinished business with Alex Hunter.'

Hammerson narrowed his eyes. If he could find the Arcadian, then the Russians could as well. He didn't want that happening on home turf – the confrontation would be damned messy. A lot of civs could get killed. He tapped his fingers on the desk for a few moments and stared into the lieutenant's broad face.

He sat forward. 'The world's turning under our feet, Sam. Time to bring our boy in.'

CHAPTER 3

Terrorism and hostages – they were trigger words that immediately called in Kemel Baykal. That morning forty tourists and a guide had entered the Sunken Palace, and none had returned. The site manager had then entered, and also failed to return. A single scream had stopped any other management or security personnel from going after him. The police had been next, and they had also vanished. It was if the caves were consuming people, and not even throwing back their bones.

After a frustrating hour with no contact from the police officers, another squad was sent in, with the same results – no return, no contact. Once again, the cave had eaten them.

The severity of the incident was escalated immediately. Now it was Kemel Baykal's turn. Baykal was an Atsubay, or commander, of the Special Forces Command. The Turkish military was NATO's largest armed force after the United States, and included two fully functional Special Forces groups. The first, the Askeri Komandos, numbered over 30,000 soldiers, and were used in frontline insertions and higher-grade operational activities. The second group were the elite Special Forces Command, or SFC. This group, Baykal's group, comprised the most professional soldiers, the best of the best, drawn from the ranks of the Turkish army, navy, air force, and gendarmerie. And counterterrorism was one of their specialties.

The big man stood with his arms folded in the darkened truck, listening to the agitated police komiser give his report of the situation. Baykal's unblinking eyes were a bottomless black under his bushy eyebrows, and a brush-thick moustache jutted from his upper lip. His large bulk filled the interior of the mobile command center.

When the police chief had finished, Baykal saluted and turned away, thinking over the information. Turkey had twelve active entities on its significant terrorist list that sought either to destabilize the region through a political process, or, more crudely, to blow as many Turkish people as they could into atoms every chance they got. In the last twelve months alone, Baykal's unit had engaged twenty-two times – and twenty-two times they had stopped an attack before it occurred. His negotiations were short and simple: total surrender, or death. The political agitators ended up in jail, and the fanatics who wished to die for their cause ended up in bodybags – everyone got what they wanted.

He watched, his concentration hawk-like, as his six men split into two teams of three and moved up the left and right flank of the now drained cistern in a standard insertion V-pattern, M4 assault rifles at their shoulders, mounted flashlights throwing long pipes of light into the gloom. Communication and visual relay equipment was built into the men's helmets, and though most dialogue was performed with short and sharp hand signals, they also listened for Baykal's deep and calm voice.

Baykal leaned forward on his knuckles and stared hard at the screen that was split into six individual frames. As his two teams came to the dark pit, their torchbeams illuminated circular steps leading down into the near impenetrable darkness. There was some sort of debris at its edge.

'Hold it there.' Baykal squinted at the objects on the screen. 'What's that?'

A soldier advanced and zoomed the focus on his small camera, and the object increased and clarified. He spoke briefly back to his commander. 'Broken statue.'

Baykal grunted. There shouldn't be that sort of debris on the chamber floor, but it may have been submerged. After all, there should have been millions of gallons of water in the cistern, and no access to some secret lower chamber.

'Proceed,' he ordered.

There was complete silence as the men darted forward, the images onscreen sweeping back and forth, the barrels of their guns up and visible. The soldiers fanned out around the pit, swung around the area briefly, then looked over the pit's edge. 'No bodies,' reported the insertion team leader.

For Kemel Baykal, that wasn't good news. Nearly fifty people had entered the cisterns, and if there were no bodies, warm or cold, that meant they must have been taken down into the hole in the ground. They had no information on what was down there, what the terrain was like, or why the hostages had been taken there – or, for that matter, where the opening had even come from. It also meant a blind firefight with terrorists was probably unavoidable, which in turn increased the likelihood of civilian deaths.

'Break formation,' Baykal ordered. 'Mizrak team to lead in. Çekiç team's one and two, in after ten seconds. Çekiç three, hold at rim of pit. Acknowledge.'

The instructions were repeated back immediately, and the first trio entered the dark hole, followed exactly ten seconds later by two members of the second team, leaving the remaining man down on one knee at the edge of the circular pit.

Baykal watched Çekiç three's camera image as it moved from the inky blackness of the pit to the surrounding chamber, then back down to the pit's depths. Already the other team's lights were being swallowed by a darkness blacker than Hades.

Baykal's eyes moved to the other five image feeds that showed what his men were encountering as they descended into the pit. They traveled downwards for approximately one hundred steps until they came to the damp floor of a large vault-like room. Though the walls were thick with slime and moss, the men's flaring pipes of light picked out mosaic images and what looked to be Roman script, as well as several other languages.

The Mizrak team leader signaled his men to spread out. The five images moved slowly forward, each soldier's light beam cautiously sweeping left and right. As the men came to the end of the circular room, Baykal could see arched stone doorways leading off into more velvet-thick darkness. For a fleeting moment, he imagined the Colosseum of ancient Rome, where slaves huddled in the center of the arena, waiting for savage beasts to spring upon them from arched doorways just like these.

The men were drawn to one central doorway, larger than the rest, which looked as if it had once been bricked up. Bricks lay scattered before it, evidently roughly chipped and pulled out of position. The Mizrak team leader pointed to new cuts and breaks in the stone, revealing the paler granite beneath.

A hundred questions sprang into Baykal's mind, but now was not the time to ask them. Distractions could be lethal.

A boot pushed aside some of the debris, to reveal a metal chisel and hammer. *Modern tools*, Baykal thought. Someone had pulled those stones out recently. *The tourists? Why?*

The five onscreen images came together, and a hand went up flat in a *hold it* gesture. All five images froze.

'Proceed?' the team leader asked.

Baykal responded quietly. 'Affirmative.'

The flat hand came down to point at the broken-open doorway. Baykal stared with fierce concentration as his men stepped cautiously forward, careful not to stumble over the broken stone and bricks, careful not even to nudge the rubble and make a noise. The images jumped as the soldiers looked down for foot placement, then quickly back up at the doorway. On the ground, Baykal saw more pieces of what looked like broken statue – multiple statues – and also, strangely, piles of dusty clothing.

One camera focused in on the closest carved figure and Baykal saw that the detail on the face was exquisite. The artist had truly captured the emotions of pain, agony, fear, and a sort of hellish torment. He could only wonder at the artisans' intentions as they crafted those tortured visions. He frowned; there was something at the back of his consciousness bothering him. Being a former Special Forces soldier himself, he was trained to miss nothing – but he felt he just had.

The five images onscreen coalesced as the men reached the doorway and stood before it. Baykal leaned across and put his arm on the technician's shoulder. 'Rewind the last thirty seconds.'

The man's fingers leaped forward on the keyboard, and immediately the dark images raced backward, then replayed at normal speed.

There – he knew it. On the slender finger of one of the broken statues – a gold ring. Baykal knew Roman statues had often been adorned with laurels of gold and other embellishments, but the ring didn't look right given the antiquity of the tunnels. He straightened and reached up to pinch his chin.

A soft noise drifted around the chamber.

The team leader moved the barrel of his gun slowly across the space. 'Are you picking that up?'

Baykal leaned forward and the technician amplified the sound. Baykal frowned – it sounded like weeping.

'We got it,' he said. 'Maybe one of the tourists. Proceed.'

The images moved forward again, slow and controlled. Baykal was about to get the technician to play back footage of the statues' faces when the tomb-like silence exploded into chaotic sound. Shouts quickly turned to screams, followed by gunfire, and the images on all five screens bounced and jerked. On each appeared a fleeting image of something large and mottled – *a face?* Frustratingly, the image refused to clarify and become distinct. It was well over the tallest man's head, hanging there for a second or two, motionless, but not still. Its edges seemed to boil with movement, like coiling ropes thrashing in fury.

Baykal felt like his brain was being squeezed, and he turned to throw up. He wiped his mouth and spun back. Around him, the technicians vomited, or fell from their chairs unconscious.

The screens were a chaos of light and movement, then transformed into a snowstorm of static. Only noise was being relayed now from the pit's depths – that same cacophony of screams, shouts, and rapid bursts of full automatic gunfire.

Before Baykal could give his instructions, the remaining Çekiç team member flew down into the darkness to support his comrades. For the first time in years, Baykal's calm exterior burst and he pounded the table, roaring into his handset – but no one listened, no one responded.

As the last man reached the deep chamber floor, his screen turned to static and new screaming started.

*

'Someone's coming up!' The shout immediately quietened the frantic movement and chatter of the command center.

An unmanned drone used for bomb disposal had been sent into the cisterns. Its tractor wheels had easily navigated the sludge and small pools of water, and it was perched at the top of the pit, its single eye on the end of a crane-like structure that reached out and down, scanning for the slightest movement on the dark circular stairs. For hours there had been nothing.

Kemel Baykal had been joined by the head of the local police and his counterpart from the Askeri Komandos, as well as dozens of local security personnel and a growing army of media that had to be corralled and kept well back from every entrance to the Basilica Cistern. It was proving to be a frustrating and enormously distracting job when all Baykal wanted to do was get back in and find his men. He was convinced they'd been attacked by an unknown number of assailants with access to superior weapons technology. He would have staked his men against any unit in the world, and knew there was not a chance in hell they would have allowed themselves to be ambushed and either killed or incapacitated so easily.

Just as he was contemplating sending in a larger force with more firepower, the shout had come from the technician monitoring the robotic camera.

There was complete silence as the technician zoomed and refocused the lens. Someone was coming up the stone steps on their hands and knees, crawling in the agonizingly slow manner of the heavily fatigued or mortally wounded.

Baykal pushed police and commandos out of his way to get back in front of the screens. His eyes still watered after glimpsing the floating face and he had a headache like he'd been hit with a sledgehammer, but he concentrated on the image. As the figure came closer to the rim of the pit, the camera was able to pick out further features. It was a man, and he was entirely gray, as though he'd been painted or showered in plaster dust.

At last, he placed one hand on the rim of the pit and pulled himself out. In agonizing slow motion, he rose from his knees to his feet.

Baykal could see that it was his last soldier, the man who had been stationed at the pit's rim. He whispered the man's name softly. 'Zeren.'

Finally on his feet, Special Forces soldier Zeren Yanar opened his eyes and blinked several times. He slowly lifted one arm in front of himself and waved it about, as though blind, then let it drop it as if it was too great a weight for him to sustain.

The technician telescoped the camera upwards, level with Yanar's face, and zoomed in on the man's eyes. They were completely white, from sclera to pupil, blank orbs.

Zeren Yanar opened his mouth wide, as if to scream, and revealed a tongue and throat that were also chalk-white. Though the sound was being fed back to the communications command center, they heard nothing. All that emanated from the man's ghostly white lips was a small cloud of powder that twinkled in the harsh light of the robot's cyclopean eye.

As Baykal and the dozens of other military and security personnel watched, the Special Forces soldier tried to raise his arms again. They appeared even heavier than before, and showered more of the powder to the cistern floor, before cracking at the elbows and shoulders. The cracks became fissures, and then the wretched man simply fell to pieces before their eyes.

There was complete silence in the command center. It was nearly a full minute before Atsubay Kemel Baykal realized his mouth was hanging open. For the first time in his life the Turkish Special Forces commander had no idea what to do.

He finally spoke just two words. 'Seal it.'

CHAPTER 4

Allandale Woods, twelve miles south-west of Boston, Massachusetts, USA

Within the overgrown thicket, the grass moved. A manhole-sized 'door' lifted an inch. From the darkness, unblinking eyes followed the woman as she ambled slowly through the parkland. Allandale Woods was eighty-six acres of oaks, maples, pines, and peppermint trees. There were also deep ponds and cattail marshes fed by underground springs. It was beautiful, secluded, and where Aimee Weir had come every other day for the past eighteen months since she had returned home.

After she'd passed by, the grass trapdoor lifted further and Alex Hunter slid out. He rose to his feet, keeping behind the trunk of a mature oak. Since finding Aimee again, he'd been at war with himself over whether he should reveal to her that he was alive, or stay hidden. Indecision racked him, short-circuiting his ability to think clearly. Seeing her both electrified and tormented him.

He watched her, knowing where she'd stop – the same place every time. There were very few formal monuments in the woods, but this one had stood there since the end of the Great War in 1919. A single sandstone block, rough carved and dedicated to a solder who had never returned home. Aimee bent to place a single flower on the ground in front of it. He wondered if she ever questioned what had happened to the previous flowers she'd left. Alex put his hand in his pocket and drew forth a single crushed bloom. He held it flat in a hand that was black with dirt and grease, looking down at its fading beauty. His eyes traveled further down his body and took in the decrepit clothing. His hair hung to his shoulders for the first time in his life, and he also had a long beard, probably stuck with twigs and debris. He only ever thought about his appearance when he saw Aimee.

He looked at her again – she hadn't changed. She was still beautiful, and still haunting him, as he obviously did her.

You got nothing to offer her. You're dead, and you look it, a sneering voice whispered in his head.

His jaw clenched and he took a half-step out from the tree, but, like a dozen times in the past, he stopped. What would he say to her? What *could* he say? She *did* think he was dead. He'd let her think that, everyone had let her think that.

You'd end up killing her.

Never. He shook his head, anger flaring.

The Other One would. You can't control him.

I can, I know how now. Alex sucked in a breath and stepped out further.

'Mommy.' It was the boy – about two years old, with black hair and gray-blue eyes.

Alex retreated into the shadow of the huge tree trunk.

Aimee kneeled to gather him to her, and stayed down as they looked at the inscription together. A man joined them. He bent to kiss Aimee's head and ruffled the boy's hair. Alex leaned his head back against the tree and watched. It was such a normal and comfortable scene, so unlike his own chaotic life. He shut his eyes.

I told you. You're nothing but a memory now. Nothing but a ... ghost.

Alex's eyes watered. They looked so happy – the perfect family unit.

I could win her back, he thought with little conviction.

The man put his arm around Aimee and together they walked slowly away. She called the boy to follow, but he stood for another few seconds staring at the monument.

You'll never win her back, the voice sneered.

A snake slid out of the long grass into the warm sunlight, and moved quickly toward the boy. Alex recognized the brown triangular banding and powerful short body – a copperhead, venomous, and deadly to a child. He tensed, judging he could make the several hundred feet in a few seconds. But before he could move, the snake reared up.

The boy's hand shot out, grabbing the snake around the neck. He showed no fear as he held it, turning it one way and then the other. The snake's mouth opened and its long fangs reared forward. The boy squeezed, and squeezed, until the head fell to the side, the flesh compressed within the scaly skin.

'Joshua.' It was Aimee calling to him, and he dropped the snake and scampered after her and the man.

Alex's mouth curled into a smile. *He's like me*, he thought. *So it can be passed on.*

He stepped out from behind the tree again. He had so much to tell the boy, so much he could show him. He could help.

Help? You can help get him killed.

Alex paused.

When they know what he is, they'll cut him up – like they tried to do to you.

I won't let them – I'll tear them apart. Alex's fingers came together, gouging a chunk of bark from the trunk.

You can't even protect yourself, the voice said. *Look at you – you have to hide like an animal. You couldn't protect him all the time. Once they know, they'll snatch him up, and he'll end up in a hundred pieces – an experiment, a lump of tissue under a microscope. That would be your legacy. What would Aimee say if you brought that to her door? A disdainful laugh. You know what she'd say, don't you?*

He closed his eyes and ground his teeth, knowing that everything the voice said was true.

Aimee lifted the boy and placed him on her hip. He looked back to where the snake's body lay, then up to the tree. He stared, seeming to see through its trunk, and Alex knew the boy saw him.

Joshua waved.

Alex lifted a hand and waved back slowly.

After another few seconds, he rolled away around the trunk, his eyes watering.

Get the fuck out of here, dead man.

Alex nodded, and started to walk.

*

He jacked a car, and drove without a plan, cap pulled down to hide his face from the many cameras he knew were watching. Alex had been a HAWC, a Hot-Zone All Warfare Commando, and he'd been the best of them. He had lived off the land, slept under snow, hidden under burning sands and in more urban environments than he cared to remember. He knew how to make himself invisible if circumstance demanded it.

He also knew who, and what, he was. He was capable of things that other people couldn't hope to accomplish. He was different, very different, and because of that people either wanted him dead, or wanted to dissect him to see what made him tick. His own military science division had tried to take him down, then the Israelis. The memory of Adira Senesh, the Mossad agent who had saved his life, and nursed him back to health, made him frown. She had turned out to be no better than any of them. Trust was the one thing he missed, and without it he felt truly lost and alone.

His memory had slowly returned, but there were still some gaps. When he pushed hard to see into those dark places, he got tattered images of freezing caves, and loathsome jungles inhabited by creatures that should only exist in nightmares. The headaches still kicked his ass, but given he'd been almost liquefied by a black bacterium from the center of the Earth, he counted himself lucky to be alive.

The endless lines on the road were a tether, dragging him forward. His face was blank, but his mind was a cyclone of emotions – and the sneering voice was always with him. *You're a coward, a hobo, a dead man. You got nothing left, no purpose, no hope.* As the voice sounded again, he screamed his fury and banged the steering wheel until it broke in his hands. He held the single remaining spoke and put his foot down, his fury matching the machine's speed, until the engine popped and spluttered, then died.

As the car rolled to a stop, he blinked, conscious that he didn't know where he was. It was dark, and after midnight. He looked at the shopfronts – Omaha, Nebraska. Over 1200 miles from Boston. He'd been driving nonstop for two days, without sleep.

He pushed open the door, grabbed his duffel bag, and started to walk, keeping his head down. He had to believe he'd done the right thing, that he'd saved Joshua. By fleeing he'd made him safe.

What makes you think they're not watching the kid now, waiting to scoop him up?

Alex shook his head and kept moving.

You certainly can't help him now, huh, tough guy?

He placed a fist to his forehead and pressed hard. 'Leave me alone!'

His voice echoed down the dark streets. He was on the outskirts of town, in an industrial area. He'd been walking as if in a trance. The place was rundown, with graffiti all around. There would be no cars worth stealing here.

I just need to rest, he thought as his mind churned.

He only heard the men as they hurried to catch up to him.

'Hey, Jesus ... creeping Jesus ... what's in the bag?' one of them called.

Alex kept his head down and kept moving, his fatigued mind trying to make plans where none existed.

The three men jogged to come abreast of him and watched him for a while, eyes sharp and hungry. They exuded a sense of menace, like a pack of savage dogs preparing to circle their prey. To them Alex would have seemed a drifter, with his long hair and beard. The duffel bag over his shoulder and dirty longshoreman's jacket completed the image of a traveler who'd been down on his luck.

Alex allowed his eyes to flick over them: two solid, one whip-thin, all dressed in the uniform of the disaffected – dirty jeans and hooded tops. One of the tops lumped slightly at the belly – the unmistakable impression of a handgun. He had to assume they were all carrying something. But it didn't matter.

'Hey, asshole, I asked you a question. What's in the fucking bag?'

Alex kept staring straight ahead but he heard the footsteps quicken. They were close. A cigarette butt bounced off his shoulder.

'Hey, creeping Jesus – give to the poor.' The man laughed cruelly. 'Give every fucking thing you've got to the poor.'

The laugh came again, confident, and closer. They were fanning out behind him, moving into a simple attack position. Alex automatically assessed their assault pattern and picked up speed, quickly scanning the street. There was no one else around – *good*.

More yelling, and an empty bottle exploded against his shoulder. His hands curled into fists, and he ground his teeth. *Parasites* – he hated them; these ticks on civilization that burrowed in and then corrupted it from the inside out. So many good and decent people had died – family, friends, comrades – so these ... *men* could replace them. Life's transaction was all wrong.

They were nearly on him now, their footsteps rapid, almost dancing in anticipation. They hooted and catcalled with the exhilaration of the hunt. They didn't really care about what was in his bag or pockets. They wanted to rain hell down on someone, and tonight he'd been chosen.

'Stop, or we'll fucking stop you!'

So be it, Alex thought, and quickly shifted sideways into a small alley. It stank of urine and was almost pitch-black and tomb-quiet.

The men sprinted after him, screaming their annoyance, thinking he was attempting to flee. 'You sonofabitch – we gonna want some skin now.'

They careened around the corner, and skidded to a stop. Alex hadn't run deeper into the gloom to hide among the mounds of soggy newspapers and rotting garbage. Instead, he stood with his back to them, hands down at his sides, as immobile as dark block of stone. His body was relaxed, ready, but his mind burned; his pent-up fury was like a tidal wave smashing against a rock wall, the pressure building.

He felt the trio's soft footsteps on the wet asphalt as they approached. They slowed, wary. He closed his eyes. He heard and sensed everything – their breathing becoming quicker as excitement accelerated into nervousness. There was a slight ruffle of clothing, then the click of a hammer being drawn back on a small caliber revolver. He automatically identified the weapon from the sound: a .22 snub-nose Smith & Wesson J-Frame – a toy.

A snigger as the men's confidence returned, and then an almost imperceptible movement of air behind his head.

Kill them all, the voice whispered deep inside his brain. *Let me.*

He spun, and grabbed the man's gun hand just as it was coming up behind his ear. He bent the hand around and back on itself, forcing the gun under the shooter's chin, crushing both his finger and the trigger at the same time. The bullet entered his skull and probably ricocheted around a few times in the cranium, not able to escape and turning an already addled brain to mush.

The man's face retained a look of surprise even as life's spark left him. Alex released his body, but before it had fallen to the ground he'd turned and swung his closed fist backhanded like a sledgehammer into the face of another attacker, who was holding up a greasy blade. The blow came so fast and hard, the man's skull crumpled like an old soda can. Alex flung the body into the wall behind him.

The third attacker dropped the metal bar he held and turned to run. He didn't get half a dozen paces before Alex had him by the collar and was flinging him to the slick ground. It was the whip-thin one, scrabbling backward, babbling now.

'I didn't know … sorry, man … I didn't know.'

Alex lifted him again and slammed him into the wall. The thin hands tore at his captor's grip, but he might as well have tried to break steel chains.

Alex brought his face in close. 'You have no idea what's really out there.'

'I didn't know. Please ... don't.' The eyes that had been aggressive and confident were now wide with terror. The predator had become prey. He clawed at Alex's hands and then at his bearded face, babbling and sobbing. 'Who the fuck are you?'

Alex felt nothing for the man. No, that wasn't true; he did feel something. He felt good. He drew his fist back.

CHAPTER 5

Special Forces Mobile Command Center, Istanbul

Kemel Baykal's frustration showed in the volcanic glare he turned on the team of local police who were tasked with monitoring the image feeds from the cisterns. He had requested a twenty-four-hour watch on the cameras placed in both the inner and outer chambers of the deep tunnels. But sometime during the night, one of the image feeds had gone dead, and no one had noticed for several hours. Whoever was supposed to have been watching, wasn't.

Baykal noticed a young policeman's eyes darting back and forth, refusing to meet his own. *You*, he thought. He leaned his large frame toward the young man, his moustache a black shelf of bristles and fury.

At last the young man's eyes slid up to his, and he dry-swallowed. 'I just stepped out for –'

'Go.'

The policeman's mouth snapped shut. He looked like he was about to plead his case, but then must have thought better of it. He got to his feet and left the room.

Baykal turned to a seated technician and spun his finger in the air, indicating he wanted the relay feeds backed up so he could look at the information prior to the image whiteout, for the tenth time. He folded his arms, but one hand crept up to pull at his moustache. There was always something, a tiny speck that might seem insignificant but gave a clue as to what had taken place, he thought.

Concentration drew his brow into deep clefts on his forehead as he viewed the footage. Like all the other times, the cameras showed nothing – all was quiet, dark, no motion. However, the mobile unit still stationed over the pit had picked up some sound: initially, a sighing, or low weeping. Then a soft padding, like slow heavy footsteps, followed by a noise like ragged breathing – as if someone or something large was moving around in that pitch-black of the pit.

Baykal waited while the technician tried once again to focus in on the pit's depths, but just as a slow-moving lump began to take shape, the camera's lens clouded, as though steam had risen in front of its electronic eye, and then the image changed to static. The breathing turned to a soft hiss, a sob, and then something indistinct. If a language, it was impenetrable.

'*Kahretsin!*' Baykal's curse bounced around the small room. He stood straighter, feeling an angry tension from his feet to his furrowed brow. His fist came down on the benchtop. 'Again.'

The technician rewound the recording. The answers were there – they had to be. Baykal had had the place locked down, no one had gone in or out, and his guards were stationed at all known entrances. But he knew that for every entrance that was on a map, there could be a secret passage into the enormous 1500-year-old tunnel system that hadn't been used for centuries.

Again the recording played; again, nothing. Baykal dragged his fingers through his hair. He couldn't afford to sit on his hands any longer. His request for orders from his superiors had placed him in an operational suspended animation, but enough was enough. He needed information; he needed to know what happened to his men, the tourists, and the first police teams. There was a knot in his stomach that tightened every minute he delayed. For all he knew, there was a terrorist cell down there, releasing some strange gas or plague into the cisterns, which would slowly seep out to infect the whole of Istanbul.

He couldn't send in another team; not after seeing Zeren Yanar literally crumbling to pieces before his eyes. Kemel Baykal had risen through the ranks of the elite Special Forces to become an Atsubay, and though age had ground down his stamina, his spirit remained as strong as ever. He wouldn't ask a man to do anything he wasn't prepared to do himself.

He picked up a phone. 'I'm going in.'

*

Nobody spoke as Baykal kneeled beside Yanar's remains. He held a long heavy flashlight up at shoulder level, and with his other hand reached out to touch the man's shoulder. He hesitated; even though he and his team wore fully sealed level-1 biohazard suits made of toughened PVC, he had no idea if what he was seeing was the result of biological, chemical or radiological assault on the young man's system. He shrugged and placed his gloved fingers on the body anyway. His first impression was of coldness, and a density more like concrete than flesh. There was no blood, just a dry and powdery residue, and chalk-like debris close to where Yanar's body and head had separated.

He rolled the detached head toward him. Yanar's face was literally frozen in a mix of agony and surprise. Baykal remembered the statue with the gold ring on its finger in the lower chambers. He had a growing suspicion about what might have happened to the missing tourists.

He half-turned to one of the men standing close behind him. 'Bag it … him; all of it.'

He got slowly to his feet, wiping his hand on the biohazard suit's trousers. He knew it was a futile gesture, but it was instinctive to want to shake off something so horrifying. He turned to his three soldiers waiting patiently and cradling skeletal M16s with illuminated flashlights on their barrels. He pulled his own pistol from the holster nestled in the middle of his back, nodded toward the pit, and walked to its edge. He stared down into the inky blackness for a few seconds, waving the flashlight's beam back and forth.

Baykal was the first to descend. He eased down the slick steps, finding the thick PVC suit restrictive and counterproductive for any sort of stealthy approach. The faceplate was front-facing so he had no peripheral version; and the suit's oxygen cells gave off a constant whine, like having a mosquito trapped inside with him, which meant any small external sounds were lost.

The deep chamber at the bottom of the steps was exactly as it had appeared on his original team's monitors. Baykal waved his men toward the large archway, cautiously stepping over the tumbled stones and dislodged bricks scattering the floor. A few pieces of the statues were strewn about, and Baykal no longer thought their tortured expressions had been created by long-dead artisans with an eye for the macabre.

The SFC commander raised his hand and his small team halted mid-step. Something about the tunnel before him, the impenetrable darkness that refused to be illuminated by his pipe of yellow light, made his animal instincts scream. *Fight or flight.* His heart rate must have been close to a hundred beats per minute; he could feel the pulse from his stomach to his neck.

Baykal swallowed, and carefully placed one foot in front of the other until he passed under the arch of the doorway. His three men immediately followed, fanning out to either side of him. Baykal moved his flashlight around the room: it was no more than fifty square feet, and octagonal in shape.

'Temple room.' His voice sounded loud inside his suit.

The walls were decorated with mosaics of serpents and hideous faces either screwed in torment or with something like blue ropes writhing around their heads. Baykal stepped toward one of the faces and saw that its eyes were filled with a dulled orb of metal. Lifting his light he realized that it was solid silver. He rubbed his gloved thumb back and forth across one of the orbs, and revealed his own ghostly reflection. *Pure*, he thought, *to remain intact and without corrosion.*

He turned and moved his flashlight around the room; each set of eyes glowed momentarily as the beam passed over them. When his light came to the farthest wall, it fell into more depth – there was another small room. He motioned for two of his men to approach from one side, as he moved up from the other.

The vestibule was undecorated, suggesting it was a vault rather than the antechamber of a place of worship. In its center stood a vessel made of age-darkened bronze. It was huge, six feet across, and stood on three ornate clawed feet. On the side was a horrible face, crowned with what looked like writhing snakes.

There was a manhole-sized cover resting on the floor, and bronze chain-links strewn about nearby. Judging by the fresh scars on the side of the huge urn, Baykal assumed the cover had only recently been removed. Whatever had been inside had been sealed in tight and then the lid further locked.

The Special Forces commander walked forward and then stopped, frowning. He looked around the vestibule. It didn't make sense. The urn was large, and certainly could have held several people, but it wasn't big enough to conceal the thirty-plus that had gone missing.

Baykal stared at the urn, concentration making his eyes burn. All he heard was his own breathing and the whine of his suit's air-conditioning unit. Though he was thankful for the insulation, he wished he could have turned it off momentarily, so he could listen, or smell the air, or use any of his other senses, rather than having to rely on the narrow focus of vision the faceplate afforded him.

His men held their positions, waiting for him to make a move or issue an order. Any of them would have been willing to peer inside the vessel first, but Baykal never asked his men to do anything he wouldn't consider doing himself. He sucked in a deep breath and stepped forward, his flashlight in one hand, the other gripping a gun held defensively in front of his face, his finger already putting pressure on the trigger. If someone, or something, unfriendly leaped out, it would take a point-blank slug to the head.

He edged over the rim ... and then exhaled, long and slow. He hadn't even realized he'd been holding his breath. Relief flooded his muscles as the oxygen inflated his lungs. Whatever had been inside the huge vessel was gone, or had been dust for over a thousand years.

'Empty,' he said.

One of Baykal's men lifted his M16 to shine the barrel-mounted flashlight into the urn. He craned his neck forward. 'Almost ... I think there's something down at the bottom.'

The soldier motioned to one of his colleagues, who pushed his own gun up over his shoulder and made a cradle with his hands. Putting his foot into the interlocked fingers, the first man stepped up over the side of the bronze urn and dropped down inside. His boots clanged against the heavy base as he landed.

The two remaining soldiers crowded forward, but Baykal held up his hand. 'Taluz, keep watch.'

The man nodded, and went to stand at the entrance to the vestibule.

'What have you got?' Baykal kept his voice hushed.

The man inside the pot straightened; he was holding something in his hand. He shrugged. 'Flakes ... like scales or fingernails, I think.'

'Scales? Of what?' Baykal asked, his voice rising slightly.

The soldier shrugged again, and Baykal motioned with his thumb for him to climb out. 'Whatever was here has long gone. Let's get back topside.'

The soldier went to drop the material to the floor, but Baykal stopped him. 'Bring it with us. I want to take Yanar's remains too. We still need to find out what the hell killed him.' He looked around. 'And everyone else that came down here.'

'Sir.' It was Taluz, still in the doorway. He waved Baykal over. 'You've got to see this.'

Baykal followed him out of the chamber and around the corner. Behind a mound of debris and shattered wall tiles, there was another exit – or at least a huge hole smashed through the wall.

Taluz crouched beside it. 'Looks like someone found another way out.'

Baykal got down beside him and ran his hand around the edge of the hole – new stone. He shook his head. 'No, not another exit. It looks like someone made their own exit.'

By the look of the gouges and smashed and pulverized debris, something had literally torn a hole through the wall, at great speed.

Baykal cursed. 'Whatever was trapped in here has got out. And it's now somewhere in our city.'

CHAPTER 6

Jack 'The Hammer' Hammerson sat in his darkened office watching the feed from the VELA satellite. His face was an emotionless mask as his fingers pressed several buttons on a keypad recessed into his desk, causing the image to dive down and enlarge and then clarify the moving figure. The man was tall and bearded with long hair – a typical drifter, like thousands right across the States. Anonymous, invisible – but not to all. Not to Jack Hammerson. He'd been tracking his former Special Ops soldier ever since he'd given the impression of stepping off the side of a mountain in the southern Appalachians a year back.

Alex Hunter, the Arcadian – Hammerson would know him anywhere. He'd been tracking him for months. Many times he'd sent clean-up crews to deal with the damage Alex had inflicted on some person or group determined to interfere with him. Just recently, Hammerson had watched Alex pursued by three men just outside of Omaha. He'd entered an alley, and men had followed. Hammerson had known what the outcome would be even before he'd hijacked an adjacent CCTV feed to watch Arcadian dismantle the men in under seventeen seconds. *Community service*, Hammerson had thought at the time.

Alex was nearing a phone booth. Hammerson paused for a second, but his hand moved without him even thinking about it. He slid an onscreen bombsite over the phone box and pressed another key – the phone's number appeared over the box, with two highlighted options: *Call* or *Cancel*. He pressed down, and the number flashed green as the call was initiated.

The tall bearded man slowed as the phone rang, and stared at it. Hammerson could have sworn the face behind the beard twisted into a smile.

'Pick it up,' Hammerson said.

Alex started walking again, past the phone, then stopped and looked up ... almost directly into the lens of a satellite hovering more than 20,000 miles overhead.

Hammerson waited, looking back into the young man's face. Time seemed to stretch as he remembered the remarkable warrior Captain Alex Hunter had become. Severely wounded in a black ops mission in Chechnya, Alex was expected to live out his existence in some sterile hospital wing, with just the beep and hiss of artificial respirators for company. Hammerson had intervened and personally authorized administration of the experimental Arcadian treatment – and it had worked, sort of. How, was a mystery – a fluke of circumstances; a thousand variables colliding at just the right time to see the man revived. But the Alex Hunter that woke was different – vastly superior in strength and stamina, with senses more acute than any other human being. As unique an individual as he was an enigma to both the US military and the USSTRATCOM Science Division's Alpha Soldier Research Unit.

Hammerson had told his young soldier that the startling and unnatural changes he was experiencing were 'gifts' – but some gifts came with a price. For all the advantageous changes to his physicality, Alex had also been afflicted by psychological tempests – a beast within him. Conditioning had taught him to manage his furies, and sometimes control them, but they were never fully suppressed. Instead, they waited inside him, growing stronger each time, until they burst forth in a rampage of obliteration. Alex Hunter was like a high-powered weapon: a military game-changer, but one that if not handled correctly could destroy those trying to wield it.

Alex strode into the phone booth and lifted the handset. 'Jack.'

The single word made Colonel Jack Hammerson sit forward in his chair, his mouth momentarily dry. 'Hello, son,' he managed, then waited for Alex to speak again.

'I know you've been following me.' Alex's voice had an edge to it.

Hammerson shook his head even though he knew Alex couldn't see it. 'Not out of malice or intent, just . . . looking out for you.'

'I don't need a minder; I don't need anyone. I'm not safe to be around, remember?'

Hammerson smiled. 'We're HAWCs, we're not supposed to be safe to be around.' He paused, steeling himself. 'We want you to come back in.'

The silence that followed felt like it had physical weight. Hammerson knew what he was saying wasn't wholly true – he needed his soldier to come in from the cold, but he wasn't ready to bring him back onto the base. Quite simply, Alex Hunter, the Arcadian, was supposed to be dead. Incinerated in a chemical furnace in the bowels of the military's disposal centers; turned to ash to destroy the lethal bacteria that was overrunning his system. And also to throw off some pretty pissed doctors in the medical division who wanted him back to work out why he'd survived the Arcadian treatment when all other subjects had turned into self-destructive psychopaths. Captain Robert Graham had found out about Alex's survival, which was another reason to leave him out in the wilderness; but the game had changed. Graham had gone missing, which gave Hammerson an opportunity.

'I'm tired,' Alex said, his tone flat and emotionless.

'You? Hard to believe.' Hammerson concentrated on the young man's movements, his body language and facial expressions, his voice, assessing his operational status.

Alex looked over his shoulder, as if concerned about being overheard. 'Not physically. I get bad dreams still.'

'We all have them,' Hammerson said calmly. 'Can't outrun them, so best to embrace them, try and understand them, determine which are real and which aren't. We can help you. We're ready now.'

'What about Graham?'

'Not an issue any more, but there are others still looking for you. You need to keep eyes in the back of your head. Look, Alex, there's too much to bring you up to speed on now. Let's discuss it over a coffee. Where can I find you?'

Hammerson knew exactly where Alex was, but wanted to check whether the man was aware of his own location. Or was he wandering aimlessly along endless highways?

There was more silence, then. 'Lincoln. But you know that.'

Hammerson smiled. Only about fifty miles or so southwest. He split his screen and called up a street map.

Alex spoke again. 'I'm close to the Capitol Building – I can wait.'

Hammerson traced some gridlines on the streetscape. 'No, there's too much surveillance there. Stay indoors or out of sight – we'll find you. I can be there in a few hours. Do you need anything?'

'No, just to talk is fine. I'll grab something to eat.' There was a pause. 'Come alone, Jack,' Alex said.

'I only ever bring what I need,' Hammerson said, and disconnected. He kept the phone in his hand, then dialed again.

'Reid, suit up. You're taking a trip with me to Lincoln ... to meet an old friend.'

*

Alex reached up to feel his face – he was clean-shaven after carrying a full beard for months. It felt good. He'd rented a room for the shower, then cut away his beard and long hair, and discarded most of his old clothes. He was wearing the last clean shirt he owned; he'd get some new ones later. First he had more pressing needs – his body craved food, again; a side effect of a blistering metabolism. It was eleven ten in the morning – late for breakfast, and early for lunch. He crossed the road to a small red-brick restaurant and sat down in one of the outside tables, close to the wall, sheltered by some potted palms but facing the street.

A tall thin waiter pushed out through the door and stared at Alex with a mix of disdain and concern. 'I'm sorry, sir, we're not open yet.'

Alex pointed with his thumb over his shoulder. 'That's okay, I can wait. It says on the wall that you open in twenty minutes.'

The waiter pursed his lips, obviously contemplating whether he was going to allow Alex to sit there, in or out of business hours. Alex smiled again, trying to appear as harmless as was possible for a large stranger with intense eyes.

The waiter rearranged his features to feign sympathy. 'There's a nice little café down the road that's open right now. Why don't you try there? '

He went to pull the menu from Alex's hands, and suddenly Alex was gripping the man's wrist a little too tightly. He wasn't even aware he'd moved; the response was automatic, like someone else was controlling him for that split second.

'Let go ... please.' The waiter's voice rose in pitch.

Alex fought an overwhelming urge to bring his fingers together and crush down on flesh and bones.

'Please.' The man used his other hand to pry at Alex's fingers. 'Please!'

Alex blinked, finally hearing him, and let go. 'Sorry ... just tired. I only want something to eat, coffee to start, and then I'm gone.'

The waiter held his hand up in front of his face, recoiling from Alex's gaze. Alex smiled again, sat back and tried to look relaxed. He knew he could be frighteningly intimidating; hell, his glare made other soldiers take pause. He breathed in and out slowly, easing the anger back into its cage. He didn't want to become some kind of bogyman that dogs barked at and people crossed the road to avoid.

The waiter looked up and down the street. Alex could tell he was wondering whether he was going to need assistance from the local police – exactly the sort of attention that Alex wanted to avoid. He put his hand in his pocket and pulled out a roll of notes, peeled off two hundred-dollar bills and laid them on the table.

'Just a steak, rare, and keep the change.'

The waiter's eyes darted from the money to Alex, then back to the money.

'Just a rare one, then I'm gone,' Alex said again, and slid the notes across the table.

The waiter's lips pursed for a second before pulling up into a smile that didn't reach his eyes. 'One rare steak, very good, sir. Would you like fries and salad?'

Alex shook his head. 'Just the steak, and make it a big one – half a cow.'

The waiter laughed obsequiously, and backed away into the dark interior of the restaurant.

Alex exhaled, sat back and rubbed a hand through his hair. He kept the hand up, examining it as he curled it into a fist.

The knuckles popped and stood out, raised and callused. They looked hard enough to break rock – which they could. He dropped his hand, slid down a few inches in his chair and reflected on his coming meeting. He wanted to trust Colonel Jack Hammerson, and for the most part he felt he could. He had saved Hammerson's life in the Appalachians, and in turn the tough old soldier had had his back more times than Alex could remember. But there was a seed of doubt that urged caution.

Before he'd seen Aimee and the kid, Alex had wanted to disappear; he'd even wished for death. But seeing them had changed everything. They made him want to live again. But as long as he suffered these uncontrollable rages, he was a danger to them. He couldn't protect them if he was far away, but he couldn't guarantee he wouldn't hurt them if he was close. There had to be an answer. If Hammerson wanted something from him, then he would need to trade for it.

The waiter put a coffee down, and Alex drained it in one. Next came the steak. He looked at it and nodded. 'Nice.' The thick and bloody slab of meat hung over the sides of the plate. Alex ate slowly, savoring every bite.

As he chewed, he watched the surrounding area. Half a mile down the road, Antelope Park's manicured lawns and memorial displays were just visible. The nearest monument was two huge slabs of black polished marble, each seven feet tall, containing hundreds of names of local soldiers lost in Vietnam. Further in, a ghostly platoon of statues, nearly twenty of them, in rain ponchos and helmets, marched eternally as a tribute to those who'd died in the Korean War. Alex stared at the frozen marchers. He too had served, and fallen, but he'd woken and come back, whether he liked it or not. The day would come when he stayed down, but unlike these men, he would be remembered by few.

Alex sensed the approach of the van before it glided into the end of the street. He watched as it pulled in a few blocks down from the cafe. Even though its windows were darkened, he knew the HAWC commander was inside. He also knew he hadn't come alone.

Alex eased back behind the plants. The van's front door opened and a solidly built older man stepped out onto the sidewalk. He rolled his sleeves down, placed his hands on his hips and turned slowly to scan the street from all angles. Colonel Jack 'Hammer' Hammerson. He put a hand over his eyes as though to shield them from the sun; his thumb was curled and Alex knew he held a scope. He turned slowly, stopping at the cafe building. Even though he doubted Hammerson would spot him, Alex backed further in behind a thick palm.

The van's side door slid back and the vehicle tilted sideways and down as one of the largest men Alex had ever seen – all shoulders and arms, and slightly older than himself – stepped down. Something about the way the man moved was odd, but Alex immediately knew him: First Lieutenant Sam Reid – Uncle Sam. The name came back to him easily.

He couldn't make out any unusual bulges or indentations on either man that might have indicated weaponry, but given what he knew of the HAWCs that didn't mean they weren't armed with something that could deliver unconsciousness or death instantaneously. Alex shook his head. *Now I'm being paranoid*, he thought. *If Hammerson wanted me dead, I wouldn't be breathing.* He sucked in a deep breath and stood. *Time to join the party.*

Hammerson stood at ease, his hands behind his back, as Alex approached, but Alex heard his soft aside to his companion: 'Heads-up.' Sam Reid moved to stand at Hammerson's shoulder. Alex could feel their apprehension, but no fear.

He stopped about six feet from them and looked from Jack Hammerson to the large HAWC behind him. 'Sam Reid.'

Immediately the large man's face broke into a grin, and he seemed about to step forward and shake Alex's hand.

'Stand fast, Reid.' Hammerson's eyes were like lasers.

Alex returned the unwavering gaze. 'You said you'd come alone.'

'I said I'd bring what I need. Sam's my left arm now … and besides, I couldn't have kept him away if I tried. You still have friends you know, Alex; people who want to see you, who believe in you … and want you to return to us.'

Hammerson kept his eyes on Alex's face as he spoke, no doubt searching for anything that might indicate instability. Alex conducted his own examination, reading the older warrior for signs of nerves, discomfort, a drip of perspiration on the forehead, a slight elevation in breathing, heart rate or body temperature – anything that might indicate deception.

'Not sure what you want or expect, Jack. You handed me over to the Israelis, remember. They tried to kill me.'

Hammerson's eyes were unwavering. 'I did, and they took a huge risk taking you in. But they panicked when you ran. Bottom line: they saved you when we couldn't. You were infected with a lethal necrotizing bacteria – I couldn't do anything for you here, so gave you into their care. You survived, intact. Everyone else that got infected wasn't so lucky.'

'Intact?' Alex shook his head.

'That's right.' Hammerson took a step forward. 'I know you lost a lot, and your memory's been fragmented. But I'm here to tell you that we're your friends. We can help you rebuild.'

'Adira said the US medical division wanted to cut me up –'

'Adira Senesh is gone,' Hammerson cut in. 'She caused some pain – to all of us. But she's home now, safe and sound. Forget her.'

'My own people wanted to pull me to pieces to see what makes me tick,' Alex finished. He still had nightmares about being tied down in a sterile white lab on cold stainless steel.

'I'll never let that happen, son. Circumstances have changed – one reason we're here today. I swear, you can trust us.'

'Alex looked up. 'And can you trust me?'

'I think so,' Hammerson said.

'That's why you wore body armor.'

Hammerson half-smiled as he tapped the plating under his shirt. 'Hope for the best, plan for the worst.'

The three men stood in silence, the seconds stretching.

Sam broke the quiet. 'It's good to see you again, boss.'

The big HAWC took a few steps forward and Alex looked down at his legs, his eyes narrowing slightly. The sound was almost imperceptible to normal hearing, but Alex had picked up the slight whine that accompanied the movement of turbo hydraulics.

'Did I do that?' he asked.

Sam shook his head. 'No. You saved my life. You sent what did this to me straight back to hell. But the mission went to shit, for both of us. I lost my legs, and you ... you lost a lot of your life.'

Alex nodded. 'I remember you ... in the jungle.'

'You're back,' Sam said. 'That's all that matters.'

'Not yet.' Alex slowly turned his head to scan the street, the buildings and other potential areas of concealment. Satisfied, he turned back to Hammerson. 'Well, you called me.'

'That I did,' Hammerson responded. 'Wanted to see how you were – in person. See if you've found what you were looking for.'

'You know the answer to that,' Alex said, and snorted softly. 'I've felt you on my shoulder the past few months now.'

Hammerson smiled back. 'Son, we were never *off* your shoulder. As I said, we were watching over you.' He took a step forward. 'Fact is, there's a lot of people out there who want to do you harm.'

'I can take care of myself. And no, I didn't find what I was looking for. When I got there, it had all changed. You know that.'

Hammerson took another step toward his protégé. 'Everything changes; it's what makes life interesting. We want you to come back to us. We think –'

'Makes life interesting?' Alex shook his head. 'I don't want interesting. I want normal. I want my life back the way it was. I want to have a wife, a family. I want to go home after a day's work, have a few beers with friends. I *want* normal.'

Hammerson shook his head slowly. 'We don't do normal. I know you know that, Alex.'

'Jack, I don't want this life anymore. I want to go home. I was nearly there.' Alex remembered Joshua waving goodbye to him. 'I was so close.' His eyes bored into Hammerson's. 'Do you know about Joshua?'

The older man seemed to relax. But Alex knew he was doing the complete opposite – he was making his body loose, ready.

'Yes,' Hammerson said.

Alex's jaw clenched. 'You knew. And you knew he was mine.'

'We suspected it. We assessed it was better to monitor the mother and child, stay away from them. Let them –'

'Let them what? Continue thinking I'm dead? Live a normal life without me? I should be there with them.'

Hammerson shook his head. 'You're not ready.'

He turned slightly side-on. Alex recognized the defense position. So much for trust. He rubbed his temple, feeling the ache again, deep inside.

'That's just it. I'll never be ready. You should have let me die after Chechnya.'

'I chose to stay away and make them safe,' Hammerson said. 'And I think you did too. I take risks – we both do, every single day of our lives – and sometimes it's my goddamn shitty job to decide what's an acceptable risk for someone else. When I authorized the Arcadian treatment for you, it was a risk. But the alternative was leaving you as a brain-dead bag of meat on a hospital bed. Is that what you would have preferred? You're alive and walking around – you got a good deal.'

'I'm a ghost – I don't exist! Alex Hunter, the real Alex Hunter, died on that damned operating table, and what's left is some sort of military killing machine. I can't even speak to my son. I've got nothing!'

Alex's head throbbed, and a small voice began to whisper its hate to him.

'Bullshit! Time to stop feeling sorry for yourself, soldier.' Hammerson yelled the words, chin jutting, jabbing his finger into Alex's face.

We'll all be better off if you're dead.

Alex ground his teeth. Did Hammerson just say that?

The experiment was a failure. Time to clean the books – wipe out you and your abomination offspring.

Alex shook his head. 'What did you say?'

Hammerson spoke again, but Alex couldn't hear his words. There was another voice, even louder in his head.

We don't need you any more ... we've got the kid. We can cut him up – see what makes him tick.

'Like hell you will!' Alex's hand shot out to grab Hammerson around the neck.

Sam moved at a fantastic speed for someone his size, took hold of Alex's forearm and yanked. Without releasing his hold on Hammerson, Alex grabbed Sam's shirtfront with the other hand. Sam was a big man, weighing in at around 250 pounds, with the MECH suit adding another eighty to that, but Alex slowly lifted him till his huge boots were clear of the ground.

'Put him down, Alex,' Hammerson wheezed through a constricted windpipe. 'You're fighting the wrong guys.'

Alex lifted Sam higher. His arm was beginning to vibrate, not so much from the strain but from the conflict going on in his head.

Remind them who you are. They'll only leave you and the boy alone if you teach them a lesson.

Alex's teeth were compressed, and his eyes blazed, as he fought against himself.

Sam remained calm, unresisting. He let go of Alex's forearm. 'We came here for you, Alex – as friends. Listen to me, Alex, hear my voice. You're safer with us. You want your life back … then you come back to us.'

'I don't need anyone any more,' Alex said, but he released both HAWCs and turned away. The voice in his head still raged, but he shut it out.

Hammerson coughed and rubbed his neck. 'So what now? You're just going to carry on drifting around and messing up muggers? There's more to life for you than that.'

Alex started to walk away and Hammerson raised his voice. 'You never spoke to Aimee, did you?'

Alex stopped but kept his back turned.

'Why not?' Hammerson asked. 'You tracked her down.'

'She doesn't need me,' Alex said. He heard Hammerson step toward him.

'You don't know that, son. She still calls me. One guess what we talk about.'

Alex turned, frowning. 'She thinks I'm dead, and she's better off that way.'

'Yeah? Maybe her head thinks so, but her heart tells her something different. Intuition, I guess. She always was pretty insightful. I'm betting she looks at that kid and sees you, every day.'

Alex shook his head. 'You were right; I'm not ready. Everything's messed up. Inside me is a tornado of chaos and violence. Not good for Aimee or the boy.'

'I can't make promises,' Hammerson said, 'but I know that you're out of options by yourself. With us, you still have some.' He put his hand on Alex's shoulder. 'What if I said we could give you back the stability you need? We can bring you back in undercover, and the medical division will work with you on your terms. Marshal's in charge there now.'

Alex felt like a door opened a crack and light shone through. 'Graham's gone?'

Hammerson nodded, but didn't expand on the subject. 'You have my word that we're here to help – fill in some of those blanks.'

Alex raised his head and gazed at the trees in Antelope Park. *Anything's better than the half-life I'm leading now*, he thought.

'There's something else,' Hammerson said. 'Uli Borshov's on our turf – could be fixing to pay you a visit.'

'Borshov.' The name conjured up an image of a giant of a man, freezing caves, and monstrous brutality. Alex remembered a gun barrel pointed at his face – the blast and then blackness. 'You want me to kill him?'

'No. If we can find him, we'll do that ourselves. He's snatched Captain Graham, which can't be a coincidence. If he's after you too, there's no telling who he'll try and get to. With Borshov, no one is safe ... *no one*.'

Alex's shoulders slumped. 'Aimee. Joshua.'

Hammerson nodded. 'We're watching them, but ...'

Alex stared into the distance, thinking. He knew he was being manipulated, but if there was a chance of curing the rages he suffered from, the price was negligible. He might even get to live a more normal life, and make it safer for those around him he cared about. He looked at Hammerson, and the older soldier's craggy face curved into a grin.

'Aimee and Joshua are safe. Don't worry about them. But we've all got some scores to settle with that big bastard, and we've got some leads. Let's grab a coffee and we can catch you up on a few things.'

'Borshov the beast.' After another few seconds, Alex returned the smile. 'Coffee sounds good. I know a place – I'm a regular.'

CHAPTER 7

Izmit, Turkey, sixty miles east of Istanbul

Arf-arf-arf-arf-arf-arf.

Zayda screwed up a weathered eye and tried to shut the sound of the dog's continued barking from her mind. It was hard enough trying to make sense of what was on the television when the reception made everything look like it was covered in radioactive snow. She looked across to Yarni, her husband, and then to the new antenna that was still a pile of metal poles, loops of wire and bags of screws stacked near the door.

Arf-arf-arf-arf-arf-arf – on and on the noise went, threatening to grind her brain to mush, and her fat husband just sat reading a paper, oblivious to the clamor. Zayda stared at him, hoping her volcanic gaze would set the newsprint on fire. But he continued to sit there, his head nodding slightly, blue cigarette smoke curling up beside his puffy, grizzled face.

Her lips moved in a curse, and she groaned to her feet and crossed to the window. Instead of throwing it open, she shouted at the glass: 'Shut up, cursed mongrel!' The window seemed to rattle with the ferocity of her words, but Yarni hadn't budged, and of course the barking didn't stop.

She turned back to the window. The sun was setting, and she could just make out the ancient clock tower in the city center. It was old, but just a speck in history compared to her home. She angled her vision so she could just glimpse the ruins of a Roman aqueduct touching one of the hills. Izmit, built on the fertile plain of the inland Sea of Marmara, had been one of the eastern-most capitals of the Roman Empire for more than half a century – but was old even back then. Now, the city was desperate to modernize, but in the hills, where Zayda and Yarni lived, life was still bucolic, insular, and resistant to anything more modern than television and the motor car.

Zayda pulled back from the window. She would have enjoyed the view if not for that fucking noisy dog! She spun around at her husband. 'That Boushkin – barking, barking … all the time with the barking.'

Yarni's cigarette went from one side of his mouth to the other and a slit opened in his lips. 'Must have seen a fox.'

Zayda stomped over to her husband and grabbed his arm. 'Well, get out there and shut him up. He's driving me crazy!'

Yarni jerked his arm away. 'Piss off, woman, it's cold out there.' He continued reading.

Zayda swatted her hand up through his paper. 'If you don't, I will.'

She waited a few seconds. The only movement was Yarni's eyes slowly taking in the print.

'Fine, then I will shut him up – permanently.'

She clomped to the door, snatching up the coal shovel on the way. She paused, daring him to stop her, but he lifted the paper higher so that only his gray hair was visible above its pages. Zayda pulled open the door.

Arf-arf-arf-arf-arf-arf. Out on the porch, the sound was even worse. There was just a faint glow on the horizon now, and the yellow luminescence from the windows only bathed the hard ground for little more than ten feet from the front steps. The dog was chained near the shed; she could see it was at the chain's full length and, oddly, facing toward the house, as if the fox, or whatever was upsetting him, had made its way inside.

'Boushkin, you stop!' she commanded.

The dog flattened its ears and whined, then continued barking.

Zayda made a guttural sound of annoyance that caused her breath to steam in the dark, cold air. She stepped down, gripping the shovel tighter. Either the dog, or the fox was about to get a headache to match her own.

*

Yarni curled his toes inside his socks. He drew on his cigarette but got nothing but cold, stale air. He thought about relighting it, but after examining its length decided instead to flick the butt into the fire.

He peered around their small cluttered room, and frowned. 'Zayda?'

How long had he been sitting there alone? Was his wife still outside? Stupid woman. The barking had stopped ages ago … or at least he thought it had. He shook his head. There was no way Zayda would really hit the dog. She might not like it, but it was the only thing keeping the foxes away from the chickens.

Yarni looked toward the curtains; it was dark and cold outside. *She's not that stupid*, he thought. He got slowly to his feet and stretched his back, then rolled down his sleeves. His forearms were massively muscled, attesting to a life of hard work. Dinner wouldn't cook itself – he'd see what was keeping her. He pulled his shirt down over a paunch that caused his belt to strain on its very last notch, and lumbered toward the door. He looked briefly at his jacket, but shrugged – he'd only be a few minutes.

He left the door ajar and stood on the porch, scanning the dark front yard. There was no sign of his wife.

'Zayda. *Zayda!*' He stepped down into the yard and called again. He stopped to listen. It was unusually silent – there should have at least been the hoot of an owl, or the rustle of creatures starting their night-time forage. Not to mention the dog.

He squinted at a shape beside the shed. It could be Boushkin, lying flat on his side, legs stiff like he was already frozen solid. *But it's not that cold*, he thought, and then, *The old witch really killed him.*

'Zayda, you can bury the dog,' he called out, walking toward the body. Maybe she'd gone to finish off the fox as well, or at least check on her chickens. As he kneeled he raised his head to yell again. 'And you can watch the chickens now – you get Boushkin's job.'

He put his hand on the dog. The body was cold and hard – even his fur was stiff spikes. His white eyes were wide, and his tongue protruded from his open mouth, stretched wide in terror or madness.

There was a small sound from behind him, *like weeping*, he thought. He half-turned. 'Stupid woman. I said, you can watch the –'

A figure moved in front of him, and he looked up. A feeling like a thousand razor blades welled up from his gut. He opened his mouth to scream, but nothing came. A small dot of pain in the center of his head grew to a stuffy inferno that pressed his eyes and ears from the inside. It was if something was blooming deep inside his brain.

His eyes began to cloud over, and he fell beside the dog. As he looked into Boushkin's cold, mute face, he seemed to say: *I tried to warn you.*

*

Guyve, Sakarya Province

The streets were narrow and empty. Many of the rooftops were newly tiled, or domed and rebuilt a hundred times over the centuries. The crowded architecture made Guyve look like a concrete scab on the green surrounding countryside. Smoke from fireplaces too numerous to count lifted from chimney tops, but struggled to rise more than a dozen feet in the still air before falling into the laneways to create a mist that reeked of pine wood, garlic, and roasting meat.

Gökhan and Maluk Demit walked home slowly, their backs sore and their boots muddy, after spending the last twelve hours pitching hay and mucking out barns on the town's outskirts. Both men were in their forties, had never married, and probably never would unless they sought a wife in one of the larger towns further up or down the main road.

Gökhan, the elder of the two, carried a parcel of goat meat. He reached out to slap his brother on the shoulder. 'This Sunday we'll go to Ulu Camii Mosque – the Great One.'

Maluk groaned. 'Again? I think you go to pay homage to the widows afterwards more than to worship inside on your knees.'

Gökhan laughed. 'I pray for love every time – is that such a bad thing? So far, all I have in return for my prayers is you.'

Maluk laughed. 'And my curse is worse – I ended up with you.'

Gökhan shoved his younger brother, and shifted the meat to his other arm. He jerked to a stop. 'Oh, oh, looks like we have a late traveler ... and sounds like he's sad. Do you hear that crying?'

Maluk followed his brother's gaze. 'What's that on his head?'

The figure was just coming out of the mist. As soon Maluk's eyes alighted on it, and he saw, really saw, he felt a fist clamp down deep in his skull.

Beside him, Gökhan grunted, doubled over and vomited. Instead of the wet splash of stomach juices and partially digested lunch, what actually hit the ground was more like drying cement.

Maluk's mouth opened in a silent scream and he dropped to his knees, clawing at his face. His skin started to crack and craze like a clay pot that had been left too long in the kiln.

*

The figure looked down at the two men, or what was left of them. One was doubled over, his fingers digging into the ancient cobblestones. The other's frozen hands clawed at a face that was now as solid as the ground beneath his knees.

The creature turned its head slowly. It didn't see the town of Guyve, just as it hadn't seen Izmit or any of the others it had passed through. Instead, it saw a land that had existed thousands of years ago, when the ancient towns were little more than huts, or caravan trails, and the humans were few. The small beings had worshiped it then, gladly offering up morsels that it had either consumed immediately, or stored for later use. But then it had been trapped and imprisoned.

It looked at the silvery orb overhead, hating its clarity and dryness. It longed for warmth, wetness, and an endless blue twilight. It ached for the tall cities of its homeland, with silver spires that touched the sky. Most of all, it felt the pain of separation from its own kind. The years of imprisonment, of solitude, had caused a loneliness and sadness that was fathomless. They had also given it a ravenous hunger that was all consuming.

It sensed the millions of living beings all around and felt overwhelmed. They had multiplied so quickly. Since its release, though, it was growing stronger; every small life absorbed gave it energy, nourishing it, making it more powerful than anything that had walked the land since the time of the saurian giants.

The moon's silvery light was strong enough to cast a weak shadow of the creature on the wall of the laneway. It saw itself and once again felt the irresistible urge to find its own kind. They still had work to do.

It drifted carelessly past the dried husks of the men. The small beings existed only to worship it, or feed it.

CHAPTER 8

Colonel Jack Hammerson watched Alex Hunter tossing and turning on the narrow bed. There were no adornments on the walls or surfaces in the billet he'd been assigned – no pictures, mementos, or personal items of any shape or form. Beside him on the floor was a duffel bag containing spare clothing and cash – the sum total of his possessions. Hammerson turned a dial, and the camera focused in on Alex's face. It was slick with perspiration. His lips moved, and the muscles in his jaw and cheeks bulged from time to time.

'That's some nightmare.'

Hammerson didn't turn to the voice. 'Been like that every night.'

Lieutenant Alan Marshal, formerly second-in-command of the Alpha Soldier Research Unit, raised his eyebrows as he looked at the readout. 'The EEG still looks like a cross between a migraine and epileptic seizure, but there's a change from when we first tested him a few years back. Something else within the primary rhythms. If I had to guess, I'd say there's another signature underlying his own – like two wave streams, one on top of the other.'

'You mean like a split personality?' Hammerson's forehead creased.

Marshal flipped a page. 'Don't know. But that encephalic thunderstorm raging in there sure is masking something weird.' He shook his head. 'The continual high alpha activity alone should be burning him up ... killing him.'

Hammerson turned slowly. 'Just like Captain Graham's experiments, huh?'

'Wasn't my call then, Jack, and it's not how I would have done things.' Marshal looked up from the feed and into Alex's room. 'I can't believe he's alive ... and here.'

'Well, he's here because I trusted you *would* do things differently ... so don't let me down. When Borshov snatched Graham, it gave me an opportunity. I can ease him back in, inform the brass he was on an undisclosed mission in deep cover. Meantime, we can work on his ... disabilities together. Try to manage the side effects of what you guys . . . what *we* did to him.'

Marshal held Hammerson's eyes for a moment, before looking back down at the initial blood results. 'But we didn't do this, Jack. The Arcadian treatment *couldn't* do this. This is beyond anything we tried in the program. There's something else inside him that was probably there to begin with – the thing that makes him so . . . different.'

'Can you isolate it?' Hammerson asked.

'Maybe, if I can find a place to start. Look here.' He pointed to the chart. 'Just two things off the top – the high proteolipid and phospholipid count across the entire cranial sphere. It shouldn't be there at his age, and it's leading to the myelin sheathing in his brain kickstarting again. Once you're over twenty, the myelin sheath around your axons and neurons weakens. However with Alex, his are actually rebuilding, reforming, and I think it's turbo-charging his ability to think.' Marshal slid his finger down the page, then looked up and grinned. 'But that's nothing compared to this – this is a doozy. The ends of his chromosomes have stopped fraying.'

'Once again, for the non-eggheads,' Hammerson said.

Marshal snorted. 'At the end of each strand of DNA there's something called a telomere – a biological capstone that stops the chromosomes deteriorating. Cells have an ability to divide many times before they start to deteriorate and shorten – that's how we age. But with Alex, his DNA strands don't fray anymore – in fact, the telomere tips look almost totally intact. This could be why he has such enormous potential for rapid cellular repair – his body rebuilds itself almost as fast as trauma or the elements tear it down. For all we know, Alex Hunter might live to be 200, or even longer. The only other cells like that, with no finite chronological barrier, are cancer cells.' Marshal blew air between his lips. 'If you asked a scientist, military man, or even a sports coach, to design the next generation of human being, you'd probably end up with Alex Hunter. The guy's a freak.'

'And we made him like that.' Hammerson sighed. 'Don't tell him about the potential longevity. He's struggling enough with one lifetime at the moment.' He turned to Marshal, his stare intense. 'Lieutenant, I want Arcadian back in operation. He's done more for his country than most, and if anyone deserves a second or third chance, it's him. With Graham gone, you're in charge. I'm taking a risk bringing you in on this, but he needs help. He'll tear himself, or us, apart unless we work out how to disengage those psychological cyclones. Can you do it?'

'I can try,' Marshal said.

'We need more than try,' Hammerson said evenly.

Marshal grimaced. 'Will he … remember me?'

'Do you mean will he remember how you guys tried to kill him? Or that you sent those biological robots up Black Mountain after him … and me?'

'Like I said, that wasn't me.'

Hammerson stared at the man on the bed again. 'Who knows? Probably. Maybe that's where his nightmares are coming from.' He gave the scientist a humorless smile. 'Don't worry about it – I'll deal with that. You just find a way to help him. Bottom line is, Alan, I need him back, now.'

*

Alex felt his neck tingle and tension run through his entire body as he followed Hammerson into the laboratory. The room was white-tiled, and at its center stood a single cot bed made of polished steel, with a half-inch metal railing running around its outside. Heavy-gauge wire attached to the railing ended in padded cuffs – one each on the lateral sides, and two at the far end. At the other end – the head end, Alex presumed – there was a single larger strap. All the cuff wires fed into digital monitors, currently inactive.

Marshal took a small step back as Alex turned toward him. His face was white, and his eyes unblinking. He nodded, trying to smile, but it looked more like a rictus. 'Captain Hunter … er … Alex. Hello … I wonder if you remember me? Alan Marshal?'

Alex looked from the cot to Hammerson. 'They're not chaining me to the bed again.'

Hammerson shrugged. 'Fine with me, but hear the lieutenant out. He's here to help you … really help. If anyone can give you some clear water on your condition, he can.'

Marshal stepped forward. 'I didn't approve of Captain Graham's methods. He cut corners, was impatient … reckless. Things got out of hand.' He swallowed. 'Jack's right: *I am* going to help. You just need to trust me.'

Alex snorted.

'I'll be here the whole time,' Hammerson said.

Marshal pointed to the bed. 'Sit down, please, and I'll tell you what I have planned.' He lifted a chart, took a page off the top and handed it to Alex. 'You can see for yourself.'

Alex read down the list of tests, then looked up and nodded. 'Go on.'

Marshal seemed to relax a little. 'We know that when you suffer an episode your strength peaks, and self-control is sometimes one of the first casualties. So I need to trigger that situation to see what effects it has on your brain, and on what areas of the brain.' He pointed to a cap with electrodes trailing from it. 'If you agree to me initiating an episode, I can see where your brain lights up and determine what's firing, over-firing, or misfiring. Once I understand the what and where, I can work on mitigating the effects with a management plan, or at least a palliative cure. How does that sound?'

Alex shrugged. 'Will I be out for the episode?'

'Yes.' Marshal picked up one of the cuffs. 'Hence the restraints. These are for your protection as well as mine. I expect your physical side will kick in while you're under, and you may get violent, which could disrupt the readings or damage the equipment, or us.' He placed a hand on the digital reader the cable fed into. 'These will give us some data on the correlation between strength and exertion.'

Hammerson placed a hand on Alex's shoulder. 'Like I said, I'll be right here. Any problems, I'll can the tests and drag you out pronto. Okay?'

Alex handed the test sheet back to Marshal. 'Let's do it.'

Marshal called in an orderly, a huge man, who strapped Alex to the cot without once meeting his eyes. 'No offense, sir,' he said as he attached multiple electrodes to Alex's head and chest.

'None taken,' Alex responded.

Marshal stood to the side, holding a small box. Another orderly stood at ease next to him, his face friendly but alert.

When Alex was secured, Marshal looked to Hammerson, who was already in the control room behind the glass wall.

'Comfortable?' Marshal asked Alex, before opening the box. Inside there were two enormous syringes. Alex raised his eyebrows.

Marshal pulled out the first syringe – finger-thick and filled with an amber fluid. 'This will put you into a full resting condition – more like being asleep and dreaming than unconscious.' He injected Alex's arm as he talked. 'It also contains neuropeptides, which will ease the problems you're having with some memory blank spots.'

He replaced the syringe in the box and lifted the second one, which was filled with a clear fluid. 'And this is my own cocktail. It's going to trick your system into thinking it's in a fight-or-flight situation. You'll be getting drowsy shortly, and just as well as this needs to go directly into your amygdala. It contains the neurotransmitter epinephrine plus the hormone cortisol in a glucose suspension. The catecholamine hormones will make your body think it's about to fight for its life.'

Marshal placed his gloved fingers on Alex's neck and turned his head away. He inserted the long needle into the base of the skull, pushing in deep. 'This is either going to be a good idea or a very bad one,' he said. 'Good luck.'

Alex rolled his head back and nodded. 'To both of us.'

*

Hammerson watched as Marshal bustled back into the room. He glanced at Alex and the military orderlies through the glass viewing panel, then flicked a switch to open communications between the two rooms.

'Clear the room,' he told the orderlies.

The two huge men quickly finished their tasks, and departed.

Marshal half-turned to Hammerson. 'We need to move quickly; his body will metabolize the drugs soon. A normal man would be under for eight to twelve hours. With Alex, if we get an hour I'll be happy. Got to start the mapping now.'

He pressed keys and switched on screens in a row of identical monitors, bringing them online. The first monitor displayed a real-time view of Alex's face; below it, pulse graphs showed his heart rate and other metabolic functions. The next screen showed a 3D image of his brain, detailing all the folds and creases. The next showed a skull-shaped matrix of flashes and luminous threads, like fireworks exploding along miniature electric highways.

'Walk me through it,' Hammerson said.

Marshal motioned to the screens. 'They're all showing part of Alex – his external physical self, his neuroarchitecture, and his brain's electrical pulse profile.' He fiddled with one of the screens, before continuing. 'When we combine them all, we see Alex's brain activity profile down the most minute detail.'

The final screen showed a ghostly image of Alex's face imposed over the cauliflower shape of the brain, and then within it the neural highways and synapses firing their impulses. Hammerson found it both eerie and fascinating.

Marshal keyed some more information, then motioned to the screens. 'What we're seeing right now is full resting normal. But when the epinephrine and cortisols kick in, we should see something very different.'

'That doesn't look normal now,' Hammerson said.

'That's because it's not.' Marshal sounded unconcerned. 'The normal brain has many sulcus folds and the cerebral cortex is highly wrinkled. Essentially this makes the brain more efficient as it increases its surface area and number of neurons – it's a brilliant design for packing so much into the confined space of the skull. When Alex first underwent the Arcadian treatment we immediately noticed that his brain grew significantly more sulcus folds. Bottom line: a bigger, more efficient brain in the same size skull.' He sighed. 'I could spend the rest of my life working on his brain alone – it's fantastic.'

Hammerson snorted. 'I doubt Alex'll give you many more chances. What are you looking for this time?'

Marshal straightened. 'Have you heard Alex mention "the Other One"?'

Hammerson nodded.

'He's referring to his own personal monster of the id; and that's who I'm looking for.' Marshal pointed a pen at Alex's cerebrum on the combined screen. 'I'll perform a structural analysis on the anatomy of the brain, looking first for formational deviations – such as tumors, hemorrhages, blood clots or lesions – and combine it with a functional analysis to locate and measure brain activity and diagnose any seizures or any degenerative diseases affecting it.' Marshal used a small ball set into the keypad to rotate the 3D image. 'This "Other One" that Alex has referred to – remember that secondary reading we found earlier on his EEG? There could be a link – two brainwave readings, in the same mind. It's worth us...'

There was a lightning-like flash on the screen that showed the electrical impulse map of Alex's brain.

'Boom,' Marshal said, and stood straighter. 'Here we go.'

The lieutenant's eyes remained fixed on the screen as Alex's brain started to move from dream state to high activity. He traced his pen along the pathways being lit by the pulses and explained to Hammerson what was happening.

'The largest part of the human brain is the cerebrum or cortex, associated with higher functions such as thought and action. The cerebral cortex is divided into four sections called lobes, with each lobe involved in separate functions. The frontal lobe's associated with reasoning, planning, movement, emotions, and problem solving. The parietal lobe controls orientation, recognition, and perception of stimuli. The occipital lobe at the back here manages visual processing.' He rotated the brain. 'And down under here is the temporal lobe, associated with perception and recognition of auditory stimuli, memory, and speech.

'Whoa.' Marshal shook his head as light flashes appeared in every quadrant of Alex's brain, jumping back and forth as if his entire brain was involved in whatever action sequence was playing out in his mind.

Suddenly, Alex gave a roar that sent Hammerson rushing to the blastproof window. Alex's teeth were clamped together and veins stood out like cords on his neck. The graph showing his brain waves was jumping wildly.

'Well, Doc, looks like you've got your episode,' Hammerson said.

Alex's eyes remained clamped shut, but he opened his mouth wide and emanated a sound of pure fury and pain. His arms came up, pulling on the steel cables, which gave a foot before they stopped the movement.

'They're holding,' Marshal said, and blew air through compressed lips. 'He just dragged the equivalent of a small car with each arm.'

'Let's hope they continue to hold,' Hammerson said. 'Wouldn't be a good idea to send anyone in there right about now.'

Marshal swallowed. 'They'll hold.' He turned back to the monitors and leaned in close. 'The electrical impulses in his brain are centralizing and moving deeper into the sub-neopallium.'

'The what?' Hammerson frowned.

'The neopallium is considered the most recently evolved brain structure in animals. It's unusual for it to be the most highly active area during a perceived high-aggression event.'

Marshal enlarged the image of Alex's brain, making the resolution near transparent so they could follow the impulses as they coalesced.

'What the hell?' Hammerson said, leaning in close. 'Where is it?'

'Where's what?'

'The thing that started all this – Borshov's damned bullet. It was lodged deep inside the man's head, remember, in an inoperable position?'

'Of course – the bullet fragment.' Marshal turned back to the monitor, his forehead creasing. He tapped at keyboards, and moved over different screens, changing angles and sharpening the resolution. 'It's gone. Nothing, no metallic traces at all. Absorbed maybe? It can happen.' He fiddled some more, then pointed to an area deep inside the neocortex. 'But there is something in there, driving the electrical activity. It's certainly biological, and quite dense.'

'Scar tissue?' Hammerson asked.

'Unlikely. If it was just a mass of solid tissue there wouldn't be any activity in the area.'

As they watched, the electrical impulse lightshow retreated to the small central area, and seemed to flare as the activity level increased. Hammerson looked through the glass window to Alex lying on the metal cot. His face was a savage mask. Never had Jack Hammerson seen such an expression on a human being.

He turned back to the scientist. 'Well, whatever that *activity* is, it doesn't look like it's benign. Can you isolate that area; find out what it is?'

'Already on it.' Marshal's fingers flew over a keyboard. 'It's some sort of dense biological core deep in the subcortical area. This mass, or synaptic bundle, is actually firing off its own electrical impulses. It's also secreting chemical substances that have molecular chains similar to natural steroids, but much more powerful.'

'Get a sample.' Hammerson was still watching Alex. 'Fast.'

Alex roared again, and pulled one of the cables to its maximum tension. His arm strained against it, the cable-stress reader registering a colossal force. At the same moment, the electrical activity deep in Alex's brain flared like an explosion. Alex surged again, his face filled with pure animalistic rage.

Hammerson's eyes narrowed. 'So, there you are – the Other One.'

The unnerving sound of screaming steel filled the room, and individual strands of the high-tensile cable started to pop.

Hammerson spoke over his shoulder. 'Too late for samples. The experiment is over.'

With a metallic tearing sound, Alex's arm was free. He gripped the metal railing around the bed and lifted. The steel bent upwards and broke with a sound like a gun shot. Alex continued to drag at it, the heavy steel bending like taffy.

Hammerson's voice rose. 'Wake him up, Lieutenant, or this is about to go real bad.'

Marshal's fingers danced over the keyboard. Inside the room, a slot opened in the steel bench behind Alex's head, and a needle shot out and into the side of his neck.

'Neuroleptic,' Marshal said. 'Should bring him down.'

Alex held the broken bar in his fist, but didn't pull on it any further. He exhaled, long and slow, and his face relaxed. Slowly, he lowered his arm.

Marshal wiped a sleeve over his face. 'I think it's over – look.' The 3D image of Alex's brain showed the impulse activity dissipating from the mystifying central core and moving back up into the neocortex. 'It was a good start. At least now we know where to look.'

Hammerson watched as one of the orderlies entered the room and undid Alex's remaining cuffs. The man's eyes were wide, his movements quick.

Alex sat up and rubbed his hands through his hair, now slick with perspiration. 'Thanks.'

The man nodded and exited.

Marshal pressed a button on the console. 'How do you feel?' he asked Alex.

Alex looked up. 'Okay ... hungover. How'd I do?'

'You did fine,' Hammerson responded. 'Get cleaned up and head over to the HAWCs' Nest. You can acclimatize there, and catch up with some old friends.'

Alex waved and nodded. Hammerson flicked off the communications.

Marshal was replaying some of the final minutes of the tests. 'My technical guess is he's got some sort of tumor growing there, but hopefully benign. The fact that this synaptic mass is firing off its own electrical impulses is intriguing – that alone is worth more study. But the chemicals that it's secreting ... now that's a mystery.' He looked at the spectrum readout. 'The computer can only guess too, as it's not working from an actual sample, but it's as baffled as we are. Substance unknown.' He swiveled in his seat to look at Hammerson. 'Just what did Alex have inside him when he came back from Chechnya all those years ago?'

Hammerson frowned and shook his head. 'Maybe some kind of contaminant. What's your non-technical guess?'

Marshal stared for a moment, then swung back to his screen. 'That the synaptic mass is all the hate, anger, and fury Alex Hunter's ever felt in his life. And it's all being super-compressed, stored, and then harnessed somehow to power up this dark side that he calls the Other One. It's part of him now, maybe with far worse effects than the bullet ever caused. And there may be nothing we can do about it.'

'Great, just great,' Hammerson said, and exhaled in a long sigh.

*

Alex stood before a huge hangar that was painted drab green on the outside, and had no windows or markings of any kind. Alex knew it was fortified and sound-proofed, but still he could hear activity inside – the clank of steel, weapons being worked on, muted voices. He pulled back the heavy steel door and stepped in and to the side, away from the backlight. He smiled as he breathed in sweat, gun oil, and exhaust fumes – this was the HAWCs' Nest, a warehouse-sized hangar that worked as a target range, weapons test site, gym, meeting room, and general hangout club for the specialized commandos. Membership was for life, and for a HAWC that could be brutally short.

Today, there were just two people inside. Sam Reid's huge form lay on a bench, holding above his chest a bar with enough weight that the reinforced steel bar bent like a banana. He lowered and lifted it a couple more times, and then placed it gently back on the rack. He sat up, took a deep breath, exhaled, and grinned at Alex. Following the weight session, his muscles looked ready to explode; his torso was ripped with veins, burn marks, and zippered scars. He got smoothly to his feet, the MECH suit's hydraulics lifting his 250-pound bulk as though he weighed nothing, and started to unwrap the leather gloves and straps from his hands and wrists.

Behind him, a woman had stopped cleaning a stripped-down machine gun to stare at Alex. She snorted, and wiped her hands on a rag. She had close-cropped white hair, a brutal scar that pulled her mouth into a sneer, and face that made her look like she'd been born angry. Her other cheek pulled up into an approximation of a smile – probably. Casey Franks.

'Welcome home, boss,' she said, followed by the hint of a salute.

Alex nodded in return. Franks was one of their best. She was tough, and very hard to hurt in the field, let alone kill. The memories came flooding back as he looked at her – the missions they'd shared. He had overseen her initial training. These were *his* people.

'The HAWCs' Nest – our fortress of solitude,' he said, and breathed deeply. 'I missed it.'

'You're back now. All that matters,' Franks said.

'You look loose,' Sam said, grinning. 'What's your secret?'

'Get shot in the face, travel to hell and back, and lose everything,' Alex replied.

Sam grunted. 'Yep, and we were along for the ride on a few of those trips to hell. And you haven't lost everything: we're still standing.'

'We're still standing,' Alex agreed, and took off his jacket. 'The Hammer said I need to acclimatize ... and I got nothing but time.'

Sam motioned to the weight bench. 'Take a seat. Being a civilian for a while can soften a man up. We might need to get you back in shape.'

Franks grinned. 'Better start him off light. Muscle strains are a bitch.'

Alex went to the bench. 'What have you got on?'

Sam walked around behind the bar. 'Two fifty each side. With the bar, around 520, give or take. Want me to take some off?'

Alex shook his head and sat down.

Franks clapped her hands and whooped. 'Ten bucks on the boss.' She made a fist, her grin pulling her scar up even further.

Alex paused. 'I'm not the boss. Just consulting for now.'

'Sure.' Sam laid his hands on the bar to spot him. 'Less talk, more action.'

Alex lay down and gripped the bar, feeling the pattern of the steel. He lifted it clear and then lowered it to his chest. He raised and lowered it three more times, his face calm, then placed it back on the rack. 'When do we get started?' He knew what Sam was doing – there would be lots more tests along the way.

'Let's try something here.' Sam called Franks to help him lift the bar off the rack, remove the discs and replace the rod with a power-lifting bar – tempered steel and twice as thick. He and Franks replaced the weights, adding even more. They stopped at 800 pounds. Sam grunted, satisfied. 'You know, back in '97, Big Jim Henderson bench-pressed 713 pounds. Record's never been broken. So, let's see what you got ... if you've still got it, that is.'

Alex gripped the bar with one hand and then the other. He lifted it free, lowered it to his chest and raised it again, and again. Sam stopped spotting him and instead leaned forward on the bar, adding his own weight – an extra 250, at least – bringing the total to more than 1000 pounds.

Alex stared straight ahead, not seeing the bar or Sam – and raised both without the slightest strain.

Franks clapped her hands again. 'Yeah. Our very own weapon of mass destruction. Stand back, children.'

Children. An image flashed into Alex's mind: a small boy holding a snake in his hand, squeezing until the flesh was crushed. He saw the boy waving to him as his mother carried him away . . . *his child, his child.* Alex lowered and raised the bar, again and again, machine-like, picking up speed.

The small boy was on a table now, strapped down, with wires attached to his head and body. People looked in at him through a toughened-glass window. Inside the room, a white-coated scientist was about to flick a switch – *his child, his child, his child* – Alex pushed his way to the blastproof window and drew back his fist . . .

Someone yelled into his ear, so loud it punctured his waking dream. 'Huh?' Alex blinked. He still on his back, holding the weighted bar up in the air. Sam was crouching beside him, his hand gripping Alex's forearm.

'Take it easy, boss. Put them down, slowly.'

Alex lowered the bar back onto its rack. He sat up and shook his head. 'Sorry, must have zoned out for a second there.'

'More like five minutes,' Sam said.

His face was creased with concern. Franks' wore a dead expression.

'It's nothing ... I'm working on it.' Alex rubbed his face, hard.

'I know you are.' Sam was still frowning. 'And that's good.'

'Later,' Franks said, and went back to her gun – but not before Alex had seen the suspicion in her eyes.

Sam pulled another bench over and sat down, looking deep into Alex's face. 'How're the demons? Because you looked like you wanted to kill someone just now.'

Alex shrugged. 'Under control, most of the time. But now and then ... I'm a Jonah, Sam. People die around me. Not sure this is a good idea, coming back in and all.'

Sam sat back. 'They die around me too – and sometimes I mean them to. That's why we're both here – with the only people who understand what it is we do, and maybe keep up with us.' He leaned in closer and punched Alex's knuckles with his own. 'Remember, we are you, and you are us ... always were, always will be.'

We are you, and you are us, Alex repeated in his mind. *I can live with that.* 'I'm okay,' he said aloud.

'Hope so,' Sam said. 'No room to zone out in the field.'

'I said it's under control.' Alex stared into Sam's face, and the big HAWC held his gaze for a few seconds.

Then he stood. 'Okay. If you're not worried, then I'm not worried. Let's take a walk around the base, get some air.'

Alex got to his feet. It felt good to be back, but that feeling of being pushed out of his own mind was happening more often. He hoped Marshal could give him some answers, fast.

CHAPTER 9

Polatli Military Base, 120 miles west of Ankara

Dawn was approaching slowly out of the east, for now little
more than a slight orange blush on the far horizon. The small
and ancient town of Polatli sat at the center of the Anatolian
plateau, a large grassy steppe that stretched away for miles, and
had a history stretching even farther. It was where Alexander
the Great had cut the Gordian knot, and the mythological
Phrygian King Midas was said to have been buried.

Corporal Mehmet Atalay rubbed his face with one hand
and breathed in the cool dry air. The military base on the
outskirts of the town was modest, with only around eighty
men and women. But what it lacked in numbers, it made
up for in sheer human toughness – these foot soldiers of the
Turkish army had a fearsome reputation. Atalay's soldiers
were known for never retreating, and never showing fear. He
was proud of every single one of them.

It was in this town, in 1922, that the bloody battle of
Sakarya was fought, and the Turkish army halted the advance
of the Greek war machine. In three weeks nearly 6000 troops

died, and nearly 20,000 were wounded. Atalay had another reason to feel pride – his own grandfather had given his life in that battle. To him, this land was sacred – it was in his flesh, blood, and bones.

There was another reason the base was important. It housed a long-wave low-frequency transmitter that was one of the biggest in the Middle East, even though it had been mostly forgotten in the time of satellite communications. Its powerful waves could reach all corners of the country; and because they traveled at ground level, they were not affected by the ionosphere static, which meant the transmitter would continue to operate even after a nuclear attack. Polatli was a vital communications safety net within a region that was rapidly scaling up on nuclear weapons.

Mehmet Atalay yelled orders at the top of his voice, smiling as he heard them echo away across the grassy plains. His troops were already up, and by now should be commencing tasks in preparation for the forthcoming exercises on the outer plains, to be undertaken in field kit, full pack, and rations. They would form up and march to the gates shortly, giving him an opportunity to assess them for untidy packs or injuries, or anything else that might present a problem … or simply displeased him. The day would be long and hard, and Atalay would do everything his soldiers did. He'd prefer to fall down dead before he showed them fatigue or pain.

The Polatli base was bordered by miles of nine-foot-high storm fencing, and had been for decades. The one nod to modernization was the introduction of tension break-sensors along the perimeter – not so much as a deterrent as early warning of a potential insurgent attack. The fanatics were everywhere these days. Three terrorists had been shot dead only a month ago, their suicide vests, grenade launchers, and thousands of rounds of ammunition all unused, praise be to God. Atalay had delighted in the encounter – it was what his soldiers needed to sharpen their skills, harden their hearts, and turn them into better warriors.

He let his eyes move over the dark plains – for some reason he felt uneasy. Something wasn't right, or he'd forgotten something. The feeling nagged at him. There was no moon, and sunrise was still some hours away. And there was an unusual mist blowing in from the north-west that smelled of . . . nothing – not the dry grasses of the steppes, nor the wild flowers. It didn't even have the moisture usual for mist.

He turned back to his troops, and gave them his customary glare – his eyes were so black they could have been pools of oil resting under twin overhangs of bushy brows. The soldiers began to form up, recognizing what their commanding officer wanted even before he ordered it. He was taking out a single platoon of sixty this time, leaving the rest behind. As he lifted a whistle to his lips to blow the short sharp blast indicating the formal fall-in, the sudden scream of sirens made him pause. A distant flashing red light immediately answered his unspoken question – a breach in the perimeter fence.

Atalay roared his instructions, and soldiers immediately ran in different directions to scan the surveillance equipment and break out large armaments. He then moved the platoon into three smaller squads, twenty apiece, and directed them toward the suspected breach.

He smiled flatly. If insurgents thought they could sneak onto the base and find the camp asleep, they were about to come face to face with sixty armed soldiers and one very pissed-off commander.

Atalay ordered a man to retrieve some flares, then headed out after his squads. He pulled his phone from his pocket – still the fastest means of communication in peacetime – and spoke to his administration center that acted as his command module. Nothing was on ground radar, they reported, and also nothing significant moving in the vicinity of the fence break.

Damn this mist, he thought angrily and roared again for the flares.

A soldier came running with a small case and a fat single-barreled gun. He stopped, broke open the stock, loaded a huge pellet into the pipe and snapped it shut, before handing the gun to his commanding officer.

Atalay nodded. 'Now, let us see what we will see.'

He pointed the gun upwards and pulled the trigger, then immediately handed it to the soldier to reload.

Explosive gases thumped the cigar-shaped silver pellet hundreds of feet into the air, where it exploded into a glaring red ball of light dangling on a small parachute. The flare floated to the ground, a miniature sun of heat and light that illuminated the terrain for hundreds of feet in every direction.

Atalay grabbed the loaded flare gun again, and fired off another round. This followed the first's trajectory, and a few seconds later added its light to the scene.

His men had fanned out in a line at the fence break. The flare had colored the mist a boiling red, and within it, just inside the fence, a figure was visible – tall, large, and wearing something on its head. It stood stock still, but also seemed to be in constant motion, like a film dubbed over itself with all versions playing at once. The storm-fencing wire behind it looked torn apart rather than cut.

'What in God's name ...?' Atalay lifted his phone to his ear. 'Onbaşi, what do you have on ground radar for our position ... approximately 500 feet to our direct east?'

There was the sound of confusion, then, 'I only have you, sir, and the squads. There is nothing else.'

Atalay swore. 'There is something here – I can see it with my own eyes. It tore a hole in our fence. It's too big to not show up on ground radar – check again.'

More silence, then, 'Nothing … no physical signature at all. Are you sure it's not a shadow, sir?'

Atalay swore even louder and hung up. He pointed to his closest squad leader. 'Bylak, see to the intruder.'

The soldier saluted, then waved his men forward. Atalay fired another flare as the squad approached the figure. It remained standing as still as a post, and as Bylak and his men circled it, Atalay could see that it was at least seven feet tall, and had either a strange helmet on its head, or …

The new flare descended. In its red light, Atalay saw Bylak stop just a dozen feet in front of the towering figure, raise his gun and yell instructions. There was no response for several seconds, then the huge head seemed to slowly lift and, though Atalay couldn't be sure due to the swirling mist, crane forward to stare into his man's face. Bylak dropped his gun and staggered back a step. He went down to his knees, raking at his eyes, then froze in place.

Atalay's eyes went wide. He dropped the flare gun and drew his own revolver, then roared a single instruction: 'Fire.'

Automatic gunfire shattered the dawn air, and muzzle flashes dotted the small hillside, as hundreds of rounds sped toward the figure. It seemed to writhe and shake at their impact, but didn't fall. The head swiveled slowly, seeming to take in the men on the hill. At each sweep, the sound of gunfire lessened.

When the huge head finally swung toward Mehmet Atalay, he had the fleeting impression of a ghastly white face streaked red by the flare, and slitted reptilian eyes that could only be hell-born. Images of snakes, fiery pits, roaring giants, and monstrous many-headed hounds crowded his brain, and it seemed to slow, like a clock winding down. A tiny dot of pain in his forehead grew and bloomed, and he saw the figure was gliding toward him. He wanted to fire his gun, or stab at it, or throw a punch, but his muscles refused to obey.

The thing went past him without a glance, and he realized he was as inconsequential to it as an insect that just happened to be in the way.

A veil of gray started to pull over his vision. He turned his head on a creaking neck to glance at his men. They were frozen in place on the hill, some with rifles still at their shoulders. A stone army, armed and ready for battle, for eternity.

*

Gülhane Military Hospital, Ankara

Doctor Layla Ayhan pushed the long curved needle in through the flesh of the young boy's tricep and lifted it out the other side of the vicious gash. She tugged and the skin came together like the mouth of a purse being pulled closed. She repeated the zippering stitch a few more times, felt the flesh around the wound, as if testing for ripeness, and then gave it a quick swab of alcohol. She stood back to survey her work.

'Looks good ... and you'll have a nice scar to frighten the girls.' She smiled and pulled off her gloves.

The boy bobbed his head and grinned back, trying to pull the skin on his arm around to see her work.

'*Ack.*' She batted his hand away from the wound.

The pager vibrated on her hip, making her jump. The electronic relic was only ever called by her mother and some select close friends. She lifted the small black box from her belt to read the brief message that scrolled across its miniature screen: *PRIORITY – BAYKAL – COMING IN AT LOADING BAY – 5 MINS.*

She raised an eyebrow as she tapped the box against her chin for a moment. *What are you bringing me that is so important and secretive you have to use the back door of my hospital, Kemel?*

She pushed some loose hair back behind her ear, turned to the boy and lifted him off the gurney. 'Out,' she said with a smile, and pushed him into the arms of his mother, who looked far less impressed by the wound than he was.

Layla quickly tidied her combined office and laboratory, sweeping coffee cups and food wrappers into a wastepaper basket. She went to an old wooden cupboard that doubled as a filing cabinet and pulled open the door, quickly checking her face in a small mirror on its inside. Satisfied, she shut the door, and was straightening her clothes when there was a knock on the door and it was immediately being pushed open.

Kemel Baykal stared at her for a second or two, his bushy moustache turned up at the corners with the hint of a smile, then gave a little bow. The large Special Forces commander was twice as fearsome as any man Layla knew, but in her presence he always seemed to revert to the stumbling school-boy. She liked that.

Baykal stepped to the side to allow two soldiers to push a covered gurney into the room. He dismissed them and turned to her, his face serious.

'A puzzle, Doctor … and an urgent one, I'm afraid.'

He flipped back the sheet, and the question forming on her lips was immediately cut off.

She approached slowly. 'Is this a joke?'

'Far from it,' Baykal responded softly.

She walked the length of the gurney, her hand hovering over the figure. She reached into her pocket to retrieve some rubber gloves, pulled them on, and touched the corpse. It was rock-hard.

'Impossible. This is not real.'

Baykal stared down at the figure. 'I agree it is impossible. And I wish it wasn't real. But this was one of my men, and I think there will be others.' He looked up, his eyes tormented. 'Layla, help us understand it.'

She pressed the man's cheek. Powder drifted down onto the gurney. She noticed some fragments had broken away, and went to her bench to gather a spare slide and a scalpel. She used the blade to scrape the debris onto the slide, and took it back to her bench where a large microscope stood waiting. She flicked on a light at its base and placed her eye over the lens.

'Where did this occur?' She adjusted the microscope's resolution, then lifted her head to look once again at the strange remains on the gurney. '*How* did it occur?'

Baykal was leaning against the wall, his arms folded, his face dark with concentration. He blinked at the sound of her voice.

'The Basilica Cistern – something happened to him in a newly discovered deep vault. Been sealed for centuries, we think.'

She peered into the microscope again, using the tip of one finger to fractionally move the slide to examine different aspects of the sample.

'Cell structures, blood vessels, muscle striation, bone – it's all there. If I hadn't seen this myself, I would never have believed it. Full ossification . . . amazing.' She stood up and turned to the SFC commander. 'When did this happen – I mean, over what period of time?'

Baykal used his shoulders to push off the wall. 'Just a few hours ago ... and it took only minutes.' He blinked, remembering. 'I saw it happen myself.'

She raised an eyebrow. 'Hours ago?' She leaned back from the scope. 'Impossible.' Layla moved quickly to the gurney, where she pulled back more of the sheet. The body lay among fragments of stone and mounds of gray dust. 'Simply amazing.' She picked up one of the fragments with her gloved hand and rolled it between thumb and forefinger.

Baykal sighed. 'It's impossible, I know. But trust me, I saw it. He must have become infected or contaminated by something.' His eyes widened. 'In the deepest pit, there was a huge bronze urn. It had just been opened. It was empty when we got there, but we had the feeling there had been something in it.'

Layla turned to him. 'You think something came out of it?'

Baykal shook his head. 'Came out, taken out, I don't know, nothing is making sense. But could there have been something contagious in there?'

Layla wiped a finger along the body's upper arm and lifted it to her face. 'It's degrading, becoming even more ossified to the point of losing its chemical cohesion – turning into powder. Soon it'll be gone.'

Baykal grunted. 'Perhaps to the same place where all the other bodies went. Well, is it? Contagious?'

She rubbed her thumb and finger together, and the smooth dust floated away. 'Contagious? I don't see how – there are no living cells anywhere in the matrix, neither internally nor externally. There is absolutely nothing living here – it's as sterile as can be. So, no – no vectors, no transferable fluids, no biological residues, nothing.' She looked down at the frozen face of the soldier. 'Whatever caused this, it switched on very quickly, and then just . . . switched off again.'

She pulled more of the sheet back. 'What is his clothing made from?'

Baykal frowned momentarily. 'Flame-retardant wool.'

She nodded. 'But not the belt – that's nylon mesh, right?'

He nodded.

She reached out to the stone hand. 'There's a ring on his finger.' The digit snapped off in her hand and she held it up. 'See, still gold. But everything else with a biological base, the flesh, bone, clothing, was . . . infected.' She pushed a strand of hair back off her face. 'That might not be the right word – *afflicted* might be better.'

'Afflicted, infected.' He shrugged. 'By what?'

Layla walked to a bookshelf, and reached up to select a couple of monstrous tomes that made her strain with the effort. Baykal rushed over to take them from her. She pointed to the table, and he set them down. She immediately began to flick through the first volume's thousands of pages. She slowed her search, and ran a finger down one of the columns.

'It is near impossible,' she said, 'and it's certainly rare. But something like this has been documented before – just never on this scale or acting with such aggressive rapidity.'

Baykal pointed to the gurney. 'This has happened before? When?'

She was reading down the page, her brow furrowed in concentration. 'Hmm, well, not exactly like this, but ... here ...' She waved him over, and started to read. 'Okay, here we go. There are actually several conditions that can cause flesh to solidify, or ossify, as it's termed.' She looked at the gurney. 'Nothing as complete as that ...'

Baykal leaned over her shoulder. 'Please, tell me everything. Anything might be helpful right now.'

She saw the worry on his face. It was one of his men lying there, and more were still missing. The odds were they had met the same fate.

'Well, there is a disease called scleroderma,' she said, 'which means "hard skin". It's characterized by a thickening of the epidermis. However, the real damage is done under the surface of the skin, where the immune system destroys the small blood vessels through the creation of excessive collagen. The patient ends up with thick and tight leathery skin that feels like it's burning. Supposed to be very painful.'

Baykal's mouth turned down. 'Yes, his face . . . it certainly looked painful. But isn't collagen the stuff they inject into Hollywood stars' lips?'

She laughed, but stopped quickly when she saw his question was genuine. 'No, not quite. Eventually the build-up of the leathery, fibrous connective tissue destroys the lungs, heart, gastrointestinal tract, kidneys, muscles, just about everything. Pretty horrible.'

Baykal motioned to the gurney, his voice a little louder. 'But this isn't just the skin becoming leathery – look at him.'

'I know, I know.' Layla quickly flipped through some more pages of the medical tome, running her finger down a dense column of information. 'This is more what I was thinking of. Fibrodysplasia ossificans progressiva.' She looked up at Baykal. 'Stone man syndrome. Maybe . . . possibly . . .'

Baykal leaned closer, trying to see over her shoulder. 'Right now, possibly will do. Tell me about it.'

'It's very, very rare, and was described as early as 2000 BC by the early Greeks, although there are cases documented all over the world. Basically, the body starts to over-produce calcium, which causes unnecessary changes to the skeletal structure, turning the skeleton into a series of bony plates.' She frowned as she read down the page. 'Hmm, and not only the skeleton – eventually all the organs succumb. You can cut away the affected tissue or bone, but it simply repairs itself – not with connective tissue, but with more bone.'

She pushed the book nearer so he could see.

Baykal read the text aloud. 'An American, Harry Raymond Eastlack, began to develop calcium build-up in his system at ten years of age. By the time he died, his body had completely ossified. He could just move his lips to speak, but everything else was as hard as stone.' He frowned. 'Yes, but ...'

'But the process usually takes several years,' Layla finished. 'You say this happened to your man in just a few hours?'

Baykal looked up at her slowly. 'No – while we watched – in minutes.' He sighed. 'He just stopped moving, then dried up – turned to rock and dust.'

Layla frowned and went back to the microscope. 'No, not dried up, of that I am sure. The cells are still hydrated. This body was not desiccated, it was just ...' she sighed. 'I don't know, it's as if its life force was extracted, leaving nothing living behind. I bet if I had an electron microscope I'd see that even the bacteria on his skin and in his gut is ossified as well.' She shrugged. 'I don't think I have many answers for you. Sorry.'

He smiled. 'Actually I've learned a lot. But I've also learned there is a lot more we don't know. More work to do.' He made a small bow. 'As always, you are amazing, Dr. Ayhan. Ah, I almost forget. Can you get this analyzed?' He pulled a small bottle from his pocket, and shook it before handing it to her.

'Sure.' She held it up, peering at it closely. 'Looks like old fish scales ... very old. The cisterns have carp – some quite large.' She looked back at the bottle. 'I might be wrong, and we won't know for sure until we get it analyzed.' She reached into a drawer to pull out a padded envelope, wrote an address on the outside, dropped the sample inside and sealed it. "I'll send this to a friend at the museum. He'll identify it. But it's your job to find out how it got there.' She placed a hand on his shoulder. 'You'll figure it out, Kemel. You always do.'

He reached up to place his hand over hers, just as his phone jangled in his pocket. He made a guttural sound in his throat and pointed at her chest. 'Don't go away.'

He put the phone to his ear and turned his back on her, lowering his voice. 'All of them?' He closed his eyes, and Layla could see his teeth grinding behind his cheeks. He disconnected, but remained staring out of the large window over the city rooftops.

'What is it?' Layla came up behind him.

'It has happened again.'

'Another stone man? In the Palace Cisterns?'

He shook his head, turning slowly. 'No, many miles away ... and this time an entire army base. All dead ... all turned to stone.'

She froze. 'What? But ...'

Baykal headed for the door. 'I'll be back – we still need to talk.'

Layla grabbed her coat. 'We'll talk on the way – I have to see this myself.'

CHAPTER 10

1st Senate Building, Moscow Kremlin Complex

President Vladimir Volkov read the single page of briefing notes. He could have spent an hour in a full briefing with his security chiefs, but he preferred the information summarized and delivered immediately – especially when it was of this nature. Though Russia had some of the most sophisticated electronic surveillance in the world, Volkov found that lowly paid people in all areas of office, in any city on the globe, were quite happy to sell out their country for the right price. Technology was expensive – people were cheap.

He dropped the page and looked up, his almost colorless eyes fixing on the general standing rod-straight before him. The man was staring straight ahead, but Volkov knew he was aware of the scrutiny. He saw the man's Adam's apple bob as he swallowed, and a small bead of perspiration ran down the side of his face.

Volkov laid his hands flat on the desk and spoke slowly. 'A Turkish Special Forces team disappears while engaging with a force or forces unknown. A platoon of eighty soldiers in

Polatli is totally wiped out, without a single enemy body being recovered – again, by a force or forces unknown. General Zhirinovsky, your thoughts?'

The man swallowed again. 'The Turks either have no idea what caused the deaths and disappearances, or they have succeeded in keeping it a secret.'

One of Volkov's hands curled into a fist. 'Is that so? I know of the Turkish Special Forces Komandos – pretty tough guys. And taking out a force of eighty standard military, some with battle experience – also, not easy. To do all that without leaving behind a single fallen soldier of your own forces? I'm not sure even we could achieve that sort of surgical precision.' He shook his head. 'No, that requires something special, something we have never seen before.' He grinned, his eyes unblinking. 'Perhaps, like a new weapon.'

Zhirinovsky finally looked at Volkov. 'You think a testing ground? Possible. We know the Chinese are trialing magnetic pulse devices, and the Americans have new microwave technology. Perhaps someone is experimenting with something else … in the field.'

Volkov nodded slowly. 'Yes, my friend, and I can smell it – something new and fantastic; powerful, unique, and unstoppable.' His pale gaze bored into the senior-ranking soldier. 'General, listen carefully. I don't care who has it now, but if it is a new weapon, I want to know more.'

Zhirinovsky saluted and stood to even more erect attention. 'Yes, my President. We will find it, and obtain it. We will not fail you.'

Volkov smiled, showing a row of small sharp teeth. 'I know you won't. I want a small force, one that will get in and out quickly and quietly, without a trace. I want someone who will not deviate from the mission, and will not be stopped.' His smile widened, showing even more teeth. 'Send Uli Borshov.'

*

The massive torpedo-shaped vessel breached the surface near the exact center of the Bering Sea. The *Yeltsin's* 13,000-ton displacement and 390-foot length made for an impressive sight as the giant metal fish exploded out of the freezing gray water to cut the surface at twenty knots, down from its full attack speed of thirty-five. There would be no turbulence or acoustic signal, as the pressurized fourth-generation nuclear reactor gave the single muscular shaft enormous but near silent power.

The Severodvinsk submarine was one of Russia's new attack-class submersibles, and one of the fastest in the world. Its multi-billion-ruble technologies and array of air, surface, and deep-water armaments made it a conflict-theater game-changer. But it also had other non-lethal uses – the submarine's advanced silencing technology made it ideal for close runs inside a country's territorial waters for surveillance, or covert pickups of special cargo … like Uli Borshov and his package.

The *Yeltsin* had been ordered to breach the surface once again when it was in international waters and well clear of the Alaskan bay where the assassin had boarded. The captain had cursed; even though they were near invisible, the American satellites could still pick up their vapor trails – changes to temperature and radiation given out as minuscule emissions. However, their guest was to receive an incoming call from Command; and refusal to obey orders would mean the captain's next ship would probably be a fishing trawler.

Alone in the conning tower, Borshov lit one of his stinking cigars and exhaled the smoke into the freezing, salty wind, waiting patiently for the call to arrive. The large man towered over and intimidated the crew, and he knew they were as glad as he was that he'd separated himself from them, even briefly.

Borshov was descended from the Bogatyrs, an ancient race of warriors from the Volga Region of central Russia. They were known for their great strength, ferocity and mercilessness in battle – traits that were in demand for the jobs he was called upon to do.

He stretched and stood upright. At six eight, around 300 pounds and as wide as a doorframe, Borshov didn't enjoy traveling in a submerged coffin. He would have made the entire journey back to Russia topside if given the choice, no matter how bitterly cold it was. He had felt suffocated and compressed within the steel confines of the submarine's metal walls. If ever he were captured, he would kill himself rather than be incarcerated in a small cage for the rest of his life. Borshov hated confined spaces – a little psychological tic he had picked up during a mission below the Antarctic ice, where he had spent days in caves under miles of rock, some so thin that each inch forward had to be fought for, slid under, or squeezed through.

Borshov pulled the draw cords on his hood, tightening it around his face to protect his nose and cheeks, and slitted his single good eye against the icy wind. He was tired and had been traveling for many days without sleep. There had been speeding vans, a relay of ultra-fast helicopters up the coast of Canada, and then out along the lonely cliffs up to Alaska's western coast. From there he and his package had been ferried out to the center of the deep, dark, cold Alaskan bay to be picked up by the *Yeltsin*.

As ordered, Borshov had captured Captain Robert Graham, the American military scientist, and now had him alive and secured in the hold. That should have been the end of his mission and involvement, but when the man was drugged he had babbled about his work with the Alpha Soldier Research Unit at Fort Detrick's Medical Command Installation. Borshov's curiosity was pricked, and had exploded when Graham mentioned the experimental Arcadian treatment. He knew that name, knew what it referred to.

He had questioned the man further. Graham was not a brave soldier, and Borshov had only needed to break a single finger before the man started to unload his secrets. It had turned out that he was the man responsible for rescuing Alex Hunter and literally bringing him back from the grave. It was his treatment that had made Hunter stronger and faster than before. Now Borshov understood the value of this man to his command. Perhaps he would one day benefit from this Arcadian treatment. And if he had that power, even for a day, he would crush the life from the HAWC who had cost him an eye and left him buried beneath miles of rock and ice in the Antarctic.

The call came through. The big man dragged on his cigar and listened – an entire Turkish Special Forces team had been decimated, followed by a regular army base – eighty soldiers. Borshov grunted; regular military he couldn't give a shit about, but he knew of the SFC – they were well trained. Not the best, not like the American HAWCs, but certainly hard to kill. Taking down a whole squad would have been difficult.

He puffed and nodded as he listened. A biological or chemical weapon was suspected. The few bodies that had been retrieved had been taken away for analysis, and details of the killer or killers had been suppressed. Borshov was intrigued. Turkey had been involved in several political skirmishes – their relationship with Israel was fraying due to a surge of Islamic political power in their own country; and there was trouble with Greece over ownership of the disputed Aegean Sea. In addition, there were ongoing tensions with China over its occupation of East Turkistan. But these battles were fought in closed-door meetings by old men in suits. They were not likely to generate a military response, or even an incisive covert attack. Someone or something else was in play.

Borshov blew more smoke, his mind plotting scenarios. Could it have been a weapon test? Possible; after all, Russia had been using Chechnya to field-test new weapons for decades. Borshov gripped the phone tighter, his knuckles becoming locked from the cold. He knew what was coming. If there was a formidable new weapon in existence, especially one so close to the motherland, Russia wanted it.

Borshov flicked the damp stub of his cigar into the thrashing water, and concentrated on the instructions issued by the dispassionate senior official. Captain Graham would be handed over to the Security Division, Borshov's role as minder over. He would be met on the water by a Mi-26 transport helicopter – a massive, long-range machine that could travel 1000 miles without refueling. He would be dropped in Poronaysk on the Russian east coast, for further travel by jet and then truck across the continent to Turkey. A team of his choice, fully equipped, would be waiting for him at the border. They must be in Istanbul within forty-eight hours.

'Retrieve or destroy the weapon.' The official's voice was mechanical, almost artificial.

Borshov grunted.

'Classification: *vse deystviya vlasti* – other priorities subsumed.'

Borshov grunted again.

'All actions authorized.' The line went dead.

All actions authorized. Borshov smiled. *Good.* He headed back down into the steel coffin to retrieve his things.

*

Borshov and his team crossed the Black Sea around two in the morning, coming ashore at Kumkoy. The weather was cool, but compared to where Borshov had just come from it was paradise. He had stripped down to a T-shirt, his huge arms bulging from the sleeves and covered in homemade tattoos that were gang badges earned in prison farms during his youth. Black grizzled hair bushed up at his collar from both his chest and back, and a protruding gut told more of an interest in power lifting than of overeating. He stretched his back and inhaled the Turkish air.

A covered truck met them, and Borshov stood aside and allowed his team to climb into the rear. As he took his own seat, he looked them over. Each of the six men he had selected were brutal-looking, icy-eyed, and gave up little in conversation, even to each other. They were his hand-picked Spetsnaz: the most efficient marksmen, electronics experts, explosives, unarmed combat specialists, and lethal assassins in the whole of Russia. If not for Borshov, these men would be roaming the underworld as muscle for crime gangs, or jailed for their psychopathic tendencies.

Borshov was larger and more formidable than any of them. A boxer in a former life, and a criminal who developed a talent for killing, he'd come to the attention of the Russian Security apparatus. He had risen in the ranks of the Spetsnaz, and eventually been withdrawn from standard duty to undertake international off-the-book missions. Quite simply, Borshov got the job done – if sometimes messily.

The truck eased to a halt to avoid the loud hiss of its pneumatic brakes. Each man jumped down into central Istanbul's pre-dawn light, holding a duffel bag of equipment. More would be waiting for them at the apartment – everything they could possibly need for sleeping rough or carrying out an armed assault on a fortified building.

Borshov retreated into the shadows as a delivery van whizzed past. It was still a few hours before the city's population would rise, and the more invisible they were, the more efficient and potentially less bloody their mission would be. He already knew they were only a few blocks back from the

Basilica's deep cisterns. The streets were modern and paved, and decades-old multistory apartment blocks dominated the landscape. The new entrance to the cisterns was an unassuming flat-roofed building; it could easily be missed except for the police cordon and floodlights. Borshov knew there were dozens of other less well-known entrances, all less heavily fortified. He'd also been informed that a low-ranking police officer who had been operating one of the surveillance cameras would speak to them ... at a price.

At the safe house, Borshov and his team went straight to work, setting up satellite technology and computer equipment. His first task was to question their informant, and he called up the man's image, address, and background data.

'This man, he is here,' he briefed two of his men, pointing to a split screen image that showed a young smiling face, street map and number. 'Bring him to me.'

The agents looked at the data, then spun and disappeared into the darkness.

The big Russian looked at his watch – just a few more things to prepare before his guest arrived. He hummed as he went about his tasks. Well-placed informants, especially those in police or security bodies, were highly regarded for their access to sensitive, high-value data. They were paid handsomely, and sometimes remained on foreign payrolls for decades. However, they could also procrastinate, be expensive, and worse, be time wasters if they thought it might drive up their price during negotiations. Borshov didn't care about the money; it wasn't his. But time ... that was a commodity that was far more valuable to him.

Borshov had his orders – *all actions authorized*. There would be no wasting of time on this mission; he'd make that very clear upfront.

CHAPTER 11

Colonel Jack Hammerson made notes as he watched the VELA satellite images of Uli Borshov and his men jumping from the truck and entering a small apartment in Istanbul. Hammerson was familiar with the way the men moved, their kit, and the size of each individual – *a Spec Ops strike force*, he thought. *Could Graham be in there with them?* He pondered the question for a few moments, then dropped the pen and folded his arms. *Unlikely.*

'Well, something's going down', he said aloud to the empty office.

Hammerson knew that if Borshov had abducted an American scientist one day, and then turned up in goddamn Turkey within thirty hours, there had to be a connection. The guy had been under a rock for two years, and now he was all over the place.

He tapped his chin with one callused knuckle, thinking. *Where's Graham then? Offloaded somewhere?* If Borshov had stayed on US soil, he'd have made a run at Alex Hunter. Instead he'd been rerouted – which meant a higher priority had arisen. Hammerson reached across to a pile of string-tied folders on the corner of his desk, and sorted through them until he found the one he was looking for. An entire Turkish SFC squad had recently been reclassified as inactive – code for taken out. Seeing it had happened within their own borders, he hadn't given it too much attention. This time he read further, until he found the location … just a few blocks from where Borshov was dug in now. In this game, there was no such thing as coincidence.

He read the intel about the blackout cordon around the Basilica Cistern, and bodies being removed in contamination bags. He also read about the strange indecipherable script within the newly discovered caverns. The intel report was detailed, but Hammerson also had another information source – MUSE, the trillion-dollar Military Universal Search Engine that was a lot more technologically accurate and invasive.

He dropped the folder – he needed to take it down another layer. He reached for the phone and dialed through to Gerry Harris.

'Gerry, it's Jack. Good work on the Borshov images, but it invites a truckload more questions.'

'Yeah, I figured that,' Harris said. 'And still no sign of Captain Graham. We're keeping eyes on them 24/7.'

'There's something else. What the hell is that big bastard doing in Istanbul?' Hammerson stared at the image of Borshov in the darkened street. 'This is getting weird. See if there's anything else in the Askeri Komandos' or Special Forces Command's secure databases. Look at the interaction site in those chambers below the ground – I want to see it all.'

'When?'

'Now … I'll wait,' Hammerson said.

'Give me ten – I'll do it myself.'

Jack Hammerson could imagine multiple keyboards and screens being attacked furiously, and knew his wizard of a technical officer would be slipping under, around or punching straight through firewalls, data silos, and directory mazes to dive deep into databases on the other side of the world. He'd be using MUSE, probably the world's most powerful penetration technology.

While Hammerson waited, he turned to his large window overlooking the training grounds at the USSTRATCOM base, and let his mind sift through the facts. Borshov had been acting alone when he was in the States, but something was important enough for the Russian high command to rush him and a team to Istanbul. Hammerson's mind worked to connect dots – real or imaginary. *At least Alex and Aimee are safe from Borshov for the time being*, he thought.

Harris came back on the line. 'Jack, got something.'

'Go, Gerry.'

'Okay, managed to pull a few interesting things from the Turkish Special Forces' database. At the Basilica Cistern, the site where the operatives were taken down, they've recovered a backpack from the upper chambers, and now have a suspect in a robbery or act of terrorism. Unclear which they're trying to hang on him, but they want him, bad – name's Janus Caresche. I've also grabbed an informal autopsy report on one of the re-covered Spec Ops agents. And as icing on the cake, I've got images of the writing or symbols they found in the deeper tun-nels. You can read the notes yourself – some are in English – but the gist is that these catacombs seem newly discovered. Not even the Turks knew they existed until a few days ago.' Harris exhaled. 'And, Jack, they found something ... well, not sure what, but it's some pretty weird shit. Sending through to you now. Anything else, you know where to find me. Good luck.'

'Thanks, Gerry.'

Hammerson hung up, and almost immediately his com-puter pinged with an incoming message from the technical officer. He opened the files, spreading them on his screen. He found the name of the suspect and copied it into MUSE; it immediately returned both a public and private profile of the man. Hammerson sat back and folded his arms. The man that stared back at him was young, confident and good-looking, with slightly olive skin and a healthy jawline. His public bio had him as an antiquities dealer and archeological detective; his unofficial bio said black-market antiquities thief, and persona non grata in several European countries.

Hammerson flicked to the next file, the autopsy report on the SFC agent, and read what he could of the mixed English–Turkish notes. He dragged the images up onto the screen, and leaned forward. 'What the fuck?'

One image showed what looked like several broken statues; however, the details were too perfect, and close-ups of the facial areas showed imperfections like scars and raised moles. There were even individual strands of hair. The more he looked at them, the more they seemed like a person made from something like plaster. As he stared, a thought started to form. He grabbed the image of the statue onto the screen and rotated it slightly. Then he moved Janus Caresche's image next to it, increasing the size so it matched the other image.

He sat back. 'You gotta be shitting me.'

The images matched, right down to the small mole on Caresche's lip.

'What the hell happened in there?'

He exhaled and reached forward to enlarge Caresche's face. There was pain etched into the frozen features, and even what could be a tear on one cheek.

'Poor bastard.' Hammerson clicked his teeth. 'I don't think they're going to find you at home, are they, Mr. Caresche?' He folded his arms. 'What did you discover down there?'

Hammerson continued to stare at the image. He knew down in their own R&D labs they were working on pulse weapons to pulverize bones, or microwave devices that could cook internal organs hard but leave the outer skin intact. But this ... this defied belief.

He quickly read through the attached data. The man had been super-calcified – turned to stone – source, initiator, method, promotion, all unknown. The next few pictures were a montage of the strange writing newly scratched into the cavern walls. It was indecipherable to him, but a mystery to the Turkish experts as well. Notes beside the images offered suggestions: *Zoroastrian, Sumerian, proto-Greek … nonsense?*

Hammerson steepled his fingers, and spoke to the screen. 'So, Mr. Caresche opened up a new level in the Basilica Cistern catacombs and found something that turned him and an entire Special Ops team to rock. Then vanished.'

He read the last few lines of the local police notes: *It is on the move. Atsubay Kemel Baykal has assumed control and is commanding the search. Police are now under SFC sequestration orders.*

Good, Hammerson thought. He knew Baykal. *And now Borshov is in the mix.*

He drummed his fingers on the desk, letting his mind work. New weapon? But why test it in such an obscure place? He drummed some more. Unless it was biological or chemical and needed an enclosed environment for testing. Aum Shinrikyo had used the Tokyo subway for its sarin gas attack. Maybe Caresche was after the tourists as test subjects and the SFC team just got in the way.

His fingers stopped and he frowned. Something was bugging him. He looked back at the notes. That was it … the police notes, the way they'd phrased those last lines: they'd written 'it' was on the move, not him or her or them.

Hammerson sat forward again. 'And you want *it*, don't you, Borshov? You son of a bitch.'

He exhaled angrily. *Look out, Kemel – shark in your pond.*

He looked back at the picture of the calcified body and narrowed his eyes. 'What did you find down there, Mr. Caresche?'

*

Hammerson waited for the call to be routed through several different filters and code scramblers before Turkish Commander Kemel Baykal finally picked it up. He smiled as he heard the familiar deep voice's heavily accented English.

'Colonel Jack – I thought you were dead years ago. Perhaps you are, and this is a call from hell.'

Hammerson laughed. 'Hell would send me straight back. Besides, only the good die young, you know that, Kemel.'

A snort. 'Perhaps that is why I too am still here.' There was a pause. 'So, long time without speaking, and then you call me out of the air. What is it that brings us to your attention, Colonel Jack?'

Hammerson gripped the phone and glanced at the frozen images of the corpses on his computer screen. 'You have a problem, Kemel … a bigger one than you realize. We know about the deaths of your soldiers, and the inscription in the cisterns. And we know a Russian Spetsnaz squad has moved into your neighborhood. There's a gathering storm, and it's forming up around you, my friend.'

There was a grunt on the line. 'I cannot discuss this.' Then a sigh. 'Spetsnaz … here? I won't ask how you know all this, but the investigation is ongoing. We have good leads, and we are sure we will make an arrest soon.'

'Janus Caresche? Forget it; he's dead. They're all dead.'

'No formal identification of the bodies has been –'

'No. Look at the faces, Kemel.' Hammerson knew the soldier on the other end of the line needed facts, not more theories. 'Kemel, your chief suspect is standing right there, and he's a block of stone.'

There was silence for a moment, and Hammerson heard Baykal's bulk shifting in a leather chair. The words, when they came, were slow, as though fatigue had attached lead weights to every syllable.

'This is a lot worse than you think, my friend. My superiors think there may be foreign forces involved in the … attacks. Now would not be a good time for me to be running to the Americans. The West is always a suspect. Leave it alone for now, my friend. I think we must deal with this on our own.'

The call disconnected.

'Ah, shit!' Hammerson hung up, and stared again at the images. 'We'll see.'

*

'Sir.'

Hammerson turned to the hulking man standing at attention in the doorway and waved him in. 'At ease.'

Sam Reid joined him in front of the computer screen. Hammerson hoped that one day the military's regeneration work would give Sam back his own mobility. But for now, he could do anything he could before … with the additional bonus of being able to run at fifty miles per hour and kick a hole in a metal door.

'MECH framework okay?' Hammerson asked.

'I forget it's there most times.' Sam grinned. 'Unless I try and jump for something and end up ten feet in the air.'

Hammerson nodded. 'Good, because we got work to do.'

'Still no sign of Graham?' Sam asked.

'Not yet, but Borshov has just turned up with a bunch of heavy-hitters in Istanbul. His time of arrival, and the place, coincides with a local Spec Ops team mysteriously being taken out. Might be a new weapon – and might be Uli Borshov has dropped in to acquire it.' Hammerson sat back. 'We need to know what's going on – firsthand.'

Sam pressed his large knuckles down on the desk and frowned. 'Borshov the beast is in Turkey?'

Hammerson pulled up the VELA images of the Russian assassin in the Istanbul street. Even though it was dark, the bearded face and his size was unmistakable. Hammerson smiled without humor. 'Like I said: we got work to do.'

Sam nodded. 'Oh yeah, count me in.'

'Knew you'd say that.' Hammerson pulled up another screen. 'Now take a look at this.'

Hammerson flicked through the range of images that Captain Gerry Harris had just sent through to him.

Sam read quickly. 'Zoroastrian, Sumerian, proto-Greek ... they're all long-dead languages, or languages that have evolved into something linguistically different. I can read a few of the words, and some of it certainly looks like Greek, but I don't recognize all of it ... maybe it *is* nonsense.'

Hammerson sat back with crossed arms. 'Maybe, but I don't think so. The Turks are stumped. You know, if we can decipher some of this, we've got something to offer the Turkish Special Forces ... something to trade.' He looked at the big HAWC. 'So who do we know who could possibly read this, hmm? Who's helped us in the past, and I'm sure would be just dying to come and give us a hand again?'

Sam smiled. 'Why, young Professor Matthew Kearns.'

Hammerson pointed a finger at him, gun-like. 'Bingo. So let's get him in here.'

CHAPTER 12

The front door opened and the Turkish policeman was led in, looking confident and brash. Borshov hung back in the shadows of the darkened room and examined him: young, handsome, shiny wedding ring – perhaps he had been passed over for an expected promotion, or had a new wife who liked gifts that were a little beyond his policeman's wage. A little extra spending money might be welcome.

Borshov moved out of the shadows, and the young man stepped back, his face immediately losing its grin.

The giant Russian stuck out one enormous hand. 'English?'

The man nodded warily, ignoring the Russian's hand. 'English … a little.' He held his finger and thumb about an inch apart.

Borshov nodded. 'Good. We must hurry. Please sit and make comfortable.' He motioned to one of two heavy wooden chairs his men were bringing into the room. 'Tea, coffee?' he asked the policeman and raised his eyebrows.

'Yes; coffee.' The man sat down with legs splayed, confidence returning to his young athletic frame. He grinned. 'This … ah …' He sniffed as he searched for the right words. 'This secret information is gold for you, yes?'

Borshov shrugged, then laughed darkly. He held up a thick wad of Turkish notes. 'Gold for us, and maybe gold for you, *da*?'

The policeman allowed his turned-down lips to express his disappointment at the sum of money. 'I could lose my job or go to jail if anyone finds out I tell you this. I think is very high value … maybe to others as well.'

Borshov smiled, dragged the other chair closer to the man and sat down facing him. One of Borshov's agents brought a single mug of steaming coffee and held it out.

Borshov raised his eyebrows. 'Hot?'

The agent nodded once.

'Good.' Borshov threw the boiling liquid into the young policeman's face, eliciting a howl of surprise and pain.

Immediately a Spetsnaz agent grabbed his shoulders and held him in the chair. The policeman's hands were over his face, and his skin had turned an angry red. His screams turned to sobs. 'My eyes.'

Borshov nodded and his men grabbed the man's hands away from his face and held them flat against the chair's wooden armrests. In a few savage motions, they drove large nails into each hand, pinning them flat.

Borshov threw the empty cup to the side of the room and sat forward, gripping the man's knees. 'So, I think you might lose more than your job today, *da*?'

The man moaned and tried to hunch over, but Borshov's men now held him securely in place again, as did the thick nails spiking his hands.

The big Russian patted one of the man's knees. 'Okay, no more playtime. We understand each other good now, okay?'

The policeman sobbed again, but nodded.

'Good. Now, you tell me everything about the attack on your police, and the weapon that was used.'

Within fifteen minutes Borshov had what he needed. He knew that the man the Turks believed responsible for the attack was also killed – some sort of petrification disorder. Whether it was caused by a radiation, biological, or chemical weapon was still unknown. He stood in the front doorway, watching the dark street. Muffled screams still emanated from inside, but he knew anything else that dribbled from the man's mouth would be less reliable and more a result of the madness caused by pain. He puffed on a cigar, and blew a plume of smoke out into the dark. The man responsible, Janus Caresche, an antiquities thief, had gone down there looking for something.

Borshov grunted. 'Found more than you bargained for, *da?*' His laugh sounded like two metal plates grating against each other.

He dropped the cigar and ground it out. He would contact his command, and find out more about this man and what he was looking for deep down in a 2000-year-old drain.

*

Matt Kearns tried to concentrate, but he couldn't help staring at Sam. His head turned from the hulking HAWC to the computer screen, back to Sam, and then back to the screen, as if he couldn't quite make his mind up what to do next.

He cleared his throat. 'You look ... well.'

Jack Hammerson smirked. Sam just nodded.

'You're standing ... by yourself,' Matt went on. 'And I heard you ...'

Sam half-smiled. 'The wonders of science, Professor.' He motioned to the screen. 'We got work to do.'

'O-kay.' Matt swiveled back to the computer and the images. 'And this was recently found written, um, scratched into a wall in a newly discovered chamber beneath the Basilica Cisterns of ancient Constantinople?' Matt rubbed his temples as he frowned at the computer screen. 'You know, this new antechamber could be 2000 years old ... or even older.'

Hammerson remained silent, watching the languages professor examine the data. He knew the young man hadn't wanted to come, but he'd personally pulled the guy out of a pretty sticky situation in the Appalachians last fall. Kearns owed him. Normally, Hammerson kept those kinds of debts on ice, but he needed the man's expertise, and he needed it now.

The professor pushed his long hair back from his face and shook his head as he read the Turkish notes. 'Nope, nope, nope – not Zoroastrian. It doesn't have this tight curling form, and its glyphs are more like Egyptian.' He half-turned to Hammerson. 'Way too sophisticated for Sumerian either. Who wrote these notes – some grad student?' He shrugged. 'However, I can see a lot of similarities to proto-Greek ... Still, there's too much circular imprinting of the letters that doesn't exist in that early alphabet.' He sat back. 'As for it being nonsense, I can tell you right now, that's wrong. It's a language, all right.'

Jack Hammerson walked around the desk to stand directly in front of Matt. 'If it's a language, you can decipher it, read it, right?'

Matt shrugged. 'Maybe.' He looked back at the screen. 'I'm not surprised they thought it might be an early form of Greek ... I think they were close. Look, this is right out there, and just my own view ... but I believe it could be Eteocretan, or perhaps even an authentic representation of Minoan, and if it is –'

Sam scoffed. 'Minoan? Theseus and the Minotaur Minoan?'

Matt turned. 'Got a better suggestion?'

Sam held up his hands. 'Not yet.'

'Well, let me know. And everyone knows those pumped-up Hollywood stories, but that was only one of their legends. They had mermaids, Cyclopses, Gorgons, dozens of light-and-darkness-dwelling entities – Crete is riddled with limestone caves that were inhabited for tens of thousands of years. In fact, the first real humans left traces there as far back as 130,000 years ago ... that's Paleolithic. On other continents, Neanderthals were still cracking heads with bone clubs.' Matt sat back and folded his arms. 'It was a strange thing. The Minoan civilization, one of the mightiest in the world, simply collapsed, and no one really knows why.' He indicated some of the strange markings. 'Whoever wrote this into the wall was a scholar of antiquities or a specialist in paleolinguistics – and I mean a real specialist. No one has spoken this language for about 5000 years, and only a handful of people in the world would even know what it is.' He glared at Sam. 'With even fewer being able to read it.'

Sam slapped him on the shoulder, making Matt wince. 'And I'm betting you're one of them?'

Matt rubbed his shoulder. 'Ouch ... Yes, but not well, and mainly by fluke. My first languages professor was captivated by Minoan art and culture, and taught me how to appreciate it, first, and understand it, second.'

Hammerson looked hard at Sam. 'It's okay, Matt – we appreciate and value your opinion. Where's your professor now?'

'Dead, I'm afraid.' Matt sat back. 'You could try Professor Gerhard Reinhalt in Germany, Doctor Francis Lin Bao in China, whereabouts unknown, or maybe the great Margaret Watchorn in England. She's pushing ninety, but she's recognized as the pre-eminent Minoan expert living today.' He tilted his head. 'She's also the undisputed expert in their theological mythologies.'

Hammerson grunted and shook his head. 'No, we're happy to have you assisting us.' He began to pace. 'So, the million-dollar question – what does it say?'

Matt turned back to the screen, and adjusted the contrast and magnification. 'Unfortunately, it's what we call Linear-A form – classed as near unreadable. Basically, all we can do is take the later Linear-B form and use the Greek Euboean-derived alphabet as a guide. Not perfect, and far from exact.' He sucked in a deep breath, and after a few moments shook his head. 'Not a lot that makes sense, but from what I can make out it says: *Fear is risen again, children of Zeus, slayers of ...*' He turned. '*Children of Zeus* – that's us by the way. According to ancient Greek mythology, we mortals were created by Zeus when he gave us the Earth as our home.' He turned back to the writing. '... *shall be forever locked in stone ... Magera will consume ...* Hmm, Magera, that rings a bell. Obviously ancient Greek, but can't place its significance.'

Hammerson stopped pacing. 'That's it?'

'Pretty much,' Matt said. 'The rest is either undecipherable or obscured. Some of the words could be slightly wrong, but that's the gist of it.'

Hammerson grunted. 'Not a lot to go on.' He paced some more. 'Another question for you. Janus Caresche – heard of him? Could he understand it? Write it?'

Matt scoffed. 'Janus the Anus ... sure I've heard of him. He's a liar, a thief, and an asshole. The guy's responsible for the theft of dozens of high-value artifacts all around the world. He's rumored to have removed an entire wall of Egyptian crypt art. He's got a bounty on his head, and he's –'

Hammerson held up one hand. 'Okay, we get it, he wasn't a great guy ... but was he capable of writing it?'

Matt shook his head. 'Absolutely not, no way. Understand it? Still no way. Could someone like Caresche recognize it? Maybe ... that's his job. He could have copied it from another source, I guess, but why would he?'

Hammerson shrugged; he didn't have any answers.

'I'd love to send some of this to Margaret Watchorn,' Matt started, but Hammerson shook his head. 'Okay, well then ... next option is I need to see more. If you can get me more shots, maybe different angles, I might be able to be a little more conclusive.' He looked at the writing again. 'Interesting thought ... it could be a warning. But if so, why write it in a language that hasn't existed for thousands of years? That's what's so weird; whoever wrote this went to a lot of trouble to make sure it only a few people could ever read it.' He looked up, his face excited. 'Or they assumed more people could understand it ... Fascinating, and intriguing. I'd love to see more.'

Hammerson was pacing again. He still didn't have enough information ... yet.

He heard Matt snort, then the professor said softly, 'I'll tell you one thing. If Caresche was down there, he wasn't there as a tourist – he was after something. I wonder if he found it.'

Hammerson turned, frowning. 'You think he went there for something specific – an artifact?'

Matt nodded. 'Like I said before, that's his job. He went down into those catacombs with a brief. That's how he works. I think he was filling an order for someone; you just need to find out who that was.'

Hammerson looked at Sam, and the big man smiled in return. 'Yeah, we can do that.'

'Make it happen, Lieutenant,' the HAWC commander said, then turned back to see Matt leaning in close to the screen, his forehead creased. 'What is it – you got something else?'

Matt leaned back a few inches. 'Maybe ... something weird. Check this out.' He enlarged one of the characters that had been gouged into the wall. Hammerson and Sam crowded in close. 'You see that? Just at the edge of the letter stroke?'

Hammerson shook his head.

Sam pushed Matt along and took over the keypad. 'Let me do this.' He opened a box around the character, and the computer immediately zoomed in and digitally cleaned up the image.

Jack Hammerson leaned forward and squinted. There looked to be a few quarter-sized chips or flakes stuck into one of the grooves in the stone. 'What is that ... a fingernail?'

Matt shook his head. 'That's what I thought, at first. Call me crazy, but I think a hand of sorts made these marks.'

'Jesus, what sort of hand could make those gouges ... in solid stone?' Sam said, tidying up the resolution even more. The objects came into sharper focus.

Hammerson frowned at him. 'You're showing me how you do that before you get outta here, Reid.' He stared at the image. 'Could be nails. But I think you'd lose more than just a few of them if you raked your hand down a solid wall.'

'You're right; so I don't think they're nails at all,' Matt said softly. 'I think they're scales. See the uniform size? But thick, like armor plating.'

Sam grunted. 'Makes sense; there's carp in the cisterns. Maybe they –'

'Nope. That's not a fish scale. I still remember my senior biology classes. C'mon, think, Sam.' Matt nudged the big HAWC. 'Fish have scales embedded into their dermis, deep but thinner; they also have slime glands. These babies are more rounded, thicker, and there are growth marks. I bet if we got a better look at one of those, we'd find it was pure reptilian keratin. Reptile scales actually grow like hair.'

'What sort of reptile?' Sam frowned, and folded his huge arms across his chest.

Matt snorted, and swung around in his chair. 'Well, I'm not talking alligators in the sewers. I'm betting this is a reptile that knows Minoan, and, according to where these scales are located, stands about seven feet tall.'

Hammerson clapped his hands together. 'Good work, Matt. Good information. I agree with what you said before – it is fascinating and intriguing. Hang around for a day or so, and we might have something even more interesting for you.' He pointed to Sam. 'Lieutenant, find me Caresche's paymaster.'

*

City of Uşak, interior Aegean region, Turkey

The Uşak rug bazaar was one of the largest in the country, with buyers coming from neighboring provinces to select the best, which they would sell internationally at greatly inflated prices. Before dawn, hundreds of sellers crossed the Lydian Cilandiras Bridge over the Banaz Stream, to compete for space in the bazaar and for the buyers' attention. It was still dark, but soon the sun would rise, and the cacophony of hawkers' voices, haggling traders, and playing children would turn the park-like grassland into a riotous circus of sound and color.

Halim watched his mother and grandmother unroll a pair of enormous rugs, their best. Pressure was on all of them to sell their wares early and then be off home. There was death about, a grotesque illness sweeping the countryside. The whispers hinted that the army had collected the bodies of the afflicted, and whole families, whole towns had been wiped out. The newspapers had urged people to stay indoors. A *djinn*, his grandmother had whispered knowingly. Other old women had picked up the word, and made the sign of the evil eye over their faces, so the devil would not see them this day.

Halim's mother held his shoulders tight and stared into his face as she laid down the law to him: he was to stay close to her or his grandmother. Halim hummed and drew on the ground with a stick, watching his mother smooth the rug's edges, and then work with a fine pick to adjust any thread that dared to lift its head above its brothers. He knew why she paid the rug such fussy attention – it took many months to weave, dye, and then dry, but a single sale could deliver enough money to keep the family comfortable for the next half-year.

Bored, Halim said he was going to have to pee, and headed off to the tree line. Once out of sight, he changed course and instead made for the bridge. His mother would scold him if she knew, and his father would more than likely thrash him for disobeying her. But this time of year, snakes, frogs, salamanders, and all sorts of wonderful creatures came out to bask in the day's warmth. If he could catch one, it would keep him amused for the entire day.

He leaned over the side of the bridge, and waved at his dark reflection. He had the stream to himself, save for several large dragonflies, about a thousand chirruping crickets, and a few small birds warbling in the trees hanging over the water. There was a chill on the back of his neck – cold, but not unpleasant. Halim had collected a handful of stones, and now he dropped them one at a time into the cool swirling water, causing a few minnows to dart out of the reed banks to investigate, before vanishing in flashes of silver and green. He hummed tunelessly in the pre-dawn. He knew if they didn't make a sale early, they would be there all day and long into the warm evening, before grandfather came with the truck to carry the three of them back home for a late supper. Until then, it was dry flatbread with pickle jam – luckily, he liked pickle jam.

As he watched the water, chin on his hand, the air misted and became cooler – like smoke lazily drifting across the stream surface to dull its sparkle. He looked skyward, expecting to see clouds pulling across the sky – which would be a tragedy for his mother, and all the rug sellers. Three hundred and sixty-four days a year they prayed for rain, but on the day the rugs were unfurled in all their brilliant dyed glory, they prayed for it to be dry. Today there were no clouds, just the same thin mist drifting in from the east. He squinted; it seemed thickest down the road, as if his grandfather's truck was backing up, blowing exhaust fumes. But there was no truck, no noise, and even the birds and crickets had grown quiet.

Halim angled his head, his face creasing as he concentrated. In the center of the rolling mist, something was taking form, rising up, solidifying, a dark center appearing as if the cloud was denser at its core. The shape was tall, moving toward him, but gliding rather than walking. He grimaced, rooted to the spot. Something about the dark mass instilled dread in the pit of his stomach.

'Hello?' His voice was weak, betraying his nervousness. *Speak like a man*, his father would have said. Halim regretted wandering away from his mother and grandmother. He had the urge to turn and flee, and not stop until he was hugging his mother. But he couldn't move.

The mist began to clear, and just as the form became a figure, something warned him to look away. He spun, crushed his eyes shut, and placed his hands over his face. He leaned far out over the bridge, holding his breath while he waited. He could feel it now, freezing cold on his back, every hair on his body standing erect, his skin prickly with goose bumps. There was no sound; it was like he had stuffed cotton in his ears, the air muffled and silent around him.

He couldn't take it any longer and opened his eyes, looking down into the stream. He saw himself in the water, and looming up behind him, something so monstrous, so horrible and terrifying, that he immediately voided his bladder into his trousers. He felt bile in his throat and an explosion of pain behind his eyes. The warmth down his legs unlocked his stricken throat and he found his voice, screaming so long and loud he thought he would never stop.

He did, when consciousness left him.

When he awoke, his head hurt, and there was a needle-like pain behind both eyes. His senses slowly returned – he felt the sun hot on his face; he heard the stream slipping by underneath the bridge, crickets singing, dragonflies zooming about, their iridescent wings and green eyes like tiny jewels.

Halim had never owned a wristwatch, but the sun was well above the horizon – hours must have passed. His mother would skin him alive. He got to his feet, staggered a few steps, then began to run, back along the path, through the trees and into the bazaar. But instead of the swirling dust, riot of color, and noise of hundreds of people haggling, fighting or laughing, there was nothing. A silence so total, he had to rub his ear to make sure he hadn't been struck deaf.

'Mama? Nana?'

People everywhere, but all so still. Some were lying down, others were kneeling or sitting, many with hands thrown up trying to shield their faces. Halim saw that all were a ghastly white, even their eyes were the bleached blankness of dry sand.

He found the small square of ground marked out by the beautiful reds and blues of the rug dyes his family preferred. Mama was there, sitting crosslegged, one arm out, the other hand over her face. Nana was kneeling, tiny as always, her hand in front of her face, warding off the evil eye. It hadn't worked.

'Mama?' He touched her – she was as hard as stone.

He nudged his grandmother, and she toppled over, her body remaining in its pose, stiff and unbending.

Halim crouched next to his mother and edged in under her outstretched arm. 'I'm sorry, Mama. I fell asleep. I'm sorry, I'm sorry.'

His head ached terribly as he leaned against her, feeling the hardness under her clothes. The familiar feel and smell of her, of her warmth, perfume, and love, was gone. A tear rolled from his cheek, to splash onto her leg. It dried quickly on the stone.

*

'One survivor.' Kemel Baykal leaned forward on his knuckles, hearing them crack against the wooden desktop. 'One fucking survivor, and over 2000 dead.' He spat the word distastefully. 'Turned into stone, who knows how, by something we can't see and can't find.'

'The Land Forces have been mobilized,' began the soldier who had brought the report.

'No.' Baykal shook his head. 'No, have them stand down. We could just be sending thousands more to the same fate. Find it, tell me what or who it is, and what weapon it's using. Then we can send forces to engage it.' The big commander walked to a window and stared out at the Special Forces training grounds. 'We must know our enemy first.'

He returned to his desk and picked up the cup of coffee sitting there. 'How many helicopters have we in the air?'

'Eighty-two, sir. Also seventeen spotter planes, but as yet they have found nothing.'

Baykal took a sip of the thick, dark liquid. 'Three hundred thousand square miles of country, and we have under 100 sets of eyes in the air looking for it.' He turned back to the window. 'It covered 170 miles in a single day. We thought they, *it*, was on foot, but it's moving too fast.' He laughed mirthlessly. 'That is, unless we now have two of these ... things wandering our countryside. And the attacks are getting larger.' His jaw clenched, the words hissing out between his teeth. 'What is it?'

The soldier stayed mute.

Baykal bared his teeth. 'What is it? What is killing us?' He threw his cup across the room, and it shattered on the wall. An explosion of dark coffee ran slowly to the carpet. He rubbed his forehead with one large hand, then, as if remembering he wasn't alone, looked up. 'Dismissed.' He turned away, then spun back. 'Wait. I want Doctor Layla Ayhan to attend to the survivor. Tell her I'll join her when the boy is able to speak. I need answers, quickly … any answers.'

The soldier closed the door as he exited. Kemel Baykal sat down heavily at his desk, his fingers drumming its surface for many minutes.

CHAPTER 13

'James Caresche, Janus Caresche, Janus Carew, Janus Caruthers … the list goes on,' Sam Reid said. 'This guy is, *was*, unreal – he had multiple aliases, and properties all across Europe, Asia, and even in Australia. He was worth millions, and all of it secreted away via shell corporations in tax havens from Switzerland to the Caymans.'

Sam zoomed in one after the other on images from the satellite feed of Caresche's properties, which were projected onto the giant screen on Jack Hammerson's office wall.

Hammerson pointed to several open doors, showing glimpses of scattered items inside. 'Looks like most have been turned over. I'm thinking the Turks are running down their leads pretty quickly.'

Sam switched to view communications cables from the Turkish Ministry of Finance. 'Well, well, looks like they haven't managed to pry open his private banking information yet. They're applying to the BIS in Switzerland for an overriding emergency authority based on a national threat. So far the Swiss are dragging their heels.' Sam laughed softly. 'Ah, bless those Swiss.'

'Excellent. Which accounts are they after?' Hammerson rubbed his hands together.

'Got a list, sir – long- and short-term investments. We'll need a bit more firepower to crack them open.'

Sam moved aside, and Hammerson sat down and commenced typing long strings of characters into MUSE. He placed his hand on the screen for its whorls, indentations, and scars to be recognized by the system's security. The screen went blank for a few seconds before welcoming him into the most powerful and intuitive search engine in the world.

'Okay, now, let's have a look at any recent deposits into Mr. Caresche's accounts, then track them back to their source.'

In twenty minutes, Hammerson had traced multiple enormous cash and securities deposits to shell organizations originating in the Seychelles, then transferred from Guernsey, one of the Channel Islands off the coast of England, all the way back to Italy, to a small company called Jupiter Import-Export, rolled up into a massive conglomerate owned by local billionaire Gianfranco Ruffino Monti.

Sam whistled as MUSE organized the data on the screen. 'Shipping, warehousing, construction, movie production. Wow, this is serious money. And Monti's rumored to hold one of the largest private collections of Asian and Middle Eastern art and antiquities in the world. Hmm, and what do you know? Italy's FBI equivalent has a permanent watch on the guy for drugs and arms smuggling. Seems if there's money in it, then Mr. Monti is also into it.' Sam straightened. 'This is our guy – right profile, and could probably buy and sell whatever was in that vault a thousand times over.'

Hammerson pulled up the surveillance information from the local police and Interpol files, and came up with a primary residence – a castle on the northern shore of Lake Como in Italy.

Sam looked impressed. 'Fit for a king ... and with his own private security.'

Hammerson grunted. 'Private army more like it. I recognize some of those Italian security names – they're soldiers of fortune and ex-paratroopers.' He sat back and folded his arms. 'Well, Mr. Monti has something we need. I think we should pay him a visit, find out if he can assist us.' Hammerson reached for the phone. 'And time for the prodigal son to earn his pay.'

He dialed. The call was answered immediately.

'Alex, we have a project. Time to get you some new HAWC kit,' Hammerson said. 'You're officially out of retirement, Arcadian.' He disconnected and turned to Sam. 'Pick him up, collect the team, and get in there – today.'

Sam got to his feet with a small whine of electronics. 'You got it.'

'One more thing – put Alex in harm's way. I want him to remember what he was good at.'

*

USSTRATCOM *Research and Development – Weapons Division*

'Colonel Hammerson has provided the authorization, but I didn't catch the name,' said the scientist, Walter Gray, who was accompanying Alex down the long white corridor several levels below the USSTRATCOM base.

Alex ignored the man, his mind on the work he'd been doing with Alan Marshal in the Alpha Soldier Research Unit. His memory, so long like a moth-eaten rug, was now almost fully intact. The neural pathways were still there; seemed they just needed a little chemical kickstart. But the more doors Alex opened in his mind, the more he became aware of the presence lurking there. He referred to it as the Other One, and

Marshal now did the same. The young scientist had told him that they would eventually be able to eradicate the psychological shadow, but for now they would manage it. Alex just hoped the Other One didn't turn out to be stronger than he was, and eradicate him first.

Gray's voice rose as he talked faster, nervously, pointing to different sealed doors as they passed: laser technology, biologicals, handguns, rifles, combat body armor, sensory enhancement. Alex nodded, but stayed silent. He knew all these weapons intimately; it was his team – former team – that had trialed them in the field. He had already opted for active camouflage – micro-panels capable of altering their appearance, color and reflective properties, enabling the soldiers wearing it to blend into their surroundings. It was something he'd used before and knew it was invaluable for an incursion that required stealth.

Alex decided it was time to stop Gray talking. 'Give me two HK CTs with variant triggers and a nitride finish. Throw in some frequency shifters while you're at it ... and leave off the over-rails – I won't need a scope.'

Gray smiled, raising his eyebrows. 'Good choices ... and will you –'

'Long and short Ka-Bar, tanto edge,' Alex said. 'Also, the usual HAWC field kit.'

'Excellent.'

Alex found he remembered the powerful weapons with absolute clarity. The Heckler & Koch USP45CT pistol, his favorite, was a smooth matte-black sidearm made of a molded polymer with recoil reduction and a hostile-environment nitride finish. The variant trigger made it lightning quick, and the upgraded frequency shifting didn't so much muffle the sound as shift it beyond the range of human hearing. The knives – the Ka-Bar with its distinctive chisel-shaped head and black laser-honed blade – were scalpel-sharp, and thick enough to be both lethal weapon and field tool. He'd used them many times, on all sorts of materials – flesh and armor.

Alex became aware that Gray was talking again. He blinked and listened as the man pointed to the sensory-enhancement section.

'For night-time incursions we have some new pupil-lenses that will –'

'No, thanks, I have my own,' Alex said.

Gray snorted. 'Well, I doubt very much they'll be as good as –'

'No.'

Alex kept walking until he came abreast of the next room – combat body armor. He turned and raised his eyebrows.

Gray caught up. 'Ahh, you've come at the right time. We've just completed testing on some new plating that is literally out of this world. One of Colonel Hammerson's former operatives brought in a biological sample of some creature's carapace – toughest thing we've ever seen – sea creature we think. We analyzed its chemical and amino acid components and then simply grew it ourselves. It's light, harder than the toughest metals – about nine-point-five on the Mohs scale – and surprisingly easy to work with. We can grow it into any shape we need in a matter of hours.'

Gray pushed a stud, and the door slid back into the wall. The dark room lit up the moment the pair entered as sensors picked up their movement. The small space turned out to be about as small as a warehouse, complete with a single-lane firing range. At its end was a target dummy kitted out in mottled gray body armor, which looked heavily scarred from repeated direct hits.

Alex exhaled, eyes narrowing. The last time he had seen that mottled armor plating in place it was during a little jaunt to an Iranian nuclear facility, when some naive scientists opened up a black hole that allowed a chitinous-shelled nightmare to come through. The scientists all ended up dead – mostly as food for the creature.

Gray handed Alex a sample of the armor – it was light and tough, like a combination of ceramic and compressed chalk. Alex tried to break or bend it, but couldn't. The piece he had retrieved all those years ago had been a shell fragment blown from a living creature. However, the piece he held was square, polished, and round-edged. The white coats had been busy.

Gray took it from him and held it up. 'We can grow it to mold to any body size or shape. We can even build it directly into the active camouflage suit – you won't even know it's there ... until you get shot at point-blank range, and are able to get straight back onto your feet.'

Alex nodded. 'What can it stop?'

'All small arms – even a .357. Most rifles, unless they have armor-piercing or uranium-tipped projectiles.'

'Good. Make it happen,' Alex said.

Gray grabbed him by the arm. 'We can do it right now ... step up on here.'

'Here' was a small circular platform, with a console nearby. Alex did as requested, and Gray stood behind the console, his eyes moving from Alex to the controls.

'More toward the middle, please, sir ... that's it. On the mission, will you be engaging in hand-to-hand combat?'

Alex smiled. 'More than likely.'

'Then you'll need glove, elbow and knee plating. Open your hands and spread the fingers so I can get a clear reading.'

Alex did as requested, and a curtain of light fell around him. It closed on him, analyzing, measuring, designing a template of his exact shape. In another minute the light disappeared.

'That's it?' Alex asked.

'All done; you can step down. The growth medium and presses will do the rest. It'll be built into your camo suit in a few hours. The active camouflage technology will be woven around the biological plating so you still have the stealth capabilities,' he grinned, 'but now with enough lightweight armor to stop an M16 at close range. How's that sound?'

'That sounds real good.' Alex stepped down from the podium and looked up at the ceiling above.

'There's 120 laser-based micro-sensors up there,' Gray told him. 'They can measure your body shape to a nanoscopic scale. Don't be putting on weight any time soon now, will you?' He chuckled, and directed Alex back toward the door.

As they passed another alcove, Alex stopped and his face broke into a broad grin. 'Holy shit ... what the hell is that?'

The suit in the corner looked like a gunmetal-hued skeleton that had been hollowed out and mounted like a hunting trophy. Small power packs at the small of the back, neck, and chest blinked with tiny iridescent green lights.

Gray scurried over, rubbing his hands together. 'Like it?'

'A lot.' Alex ran his eyes over the formidable-looking suit. 'Tell me about it.'

'Not fully tested yet, but this,' Gray motioned to the suit like a game-show host, 'is the full-body Military Exoskeleton Combat Harness – MECH suit, the next-generation heavy-combat armor. This is just the base model; we have ... accessories.'

Like a kid delighted at showing off his favorite baseball card collection, Gray moved quickly to the wall and pressed several small studs, causing various doors to slide back. More suits were revealed, some with built-in helmets, others with weapons built into the forearms, shoulders, and chest. Some of the frameworks were just legs, and others were upper-body sections that fit over the arms and shoulders.

Alex was impressed. 'Operational?'

Gray bobbed his head. 'Sort of. We have one of the HAWCs trialing a half unit, but that's more for mobility.

No one's taken the full kit out yet – still a few things to iron out. With all its electronic and hydraulic-assisted technology, the suit weighs about 200 pounds – too much for your average soldier, especially as you need more than a degree of finesse to move this monster around. Maybe next gen.'

Alex nodded, still staring at the armor-plated technology. 'Nice.'

Gray laughed. 'Come back in a few years, when we've managed to solve the weight-to-support capability ratios.'

He led Alex back out into the corridor, and stopped at the emitted-light weaponry vault. He raised his eyebrows. 'Lasers? Great for stealth incursions – no noise, can move from pulse to beam, and put a hole through a skull at half a mile.' He grinned and jiggled his raised brows.

Alex considered it, then shook his head. 'Not this time. Leave that to the other guys. I'll be getting in close, real close.'

Gray sighed and motioned to the elevator at the end of the corridor. He pressed his thumb to a dark pad, which ringed it with red. Immediately, the hiss of machinery moving could be heard behind the huge brushed-steel plate.

He turned to Alex, staring up at him and frowning slightly. 'I could swear I've seen you before.'

Alex simply stared back, his gray-blue eyes never wavering.

After a while Gray shrugged and turned away. 'But if Colonel Hammerson says you're the new guy, maybe I've been doing this job too long and you're all starting to look the same to me. I'll get your kit sent up to the colonel's office. Pleasure doing business with you, ah …?'

Alex stepped into the elevator and pressed the button to close the doors, cutting off Gray's question. Alone in the steel box, he held up his hands and looked at them – rock solid. He hoped he was doing the right thing. People would be relying on him, and him on them – the change would take some getting used to. There would be no more lone wolf now that Hammerson had intervened.

Of the memories Alex had regained, the good ones were fleeting. Most involved brutality on an unimaginable scale; and in the sea of blood, there were the faces of those who had fallen beside him – good men and women who had died under his command. They stayed with him now, and haunted him.

He made fists, heard the knuckles pop. He remembered something Franklin D Roosevelt had said: *Men are not prisoners of fate, but only prisoners of their own minds.* For Alex, his own mind was his biggest fear.

CHAPTER 14

Aviano Air Base, Italy

Sam and Alex waited to climb into the chopper – they were the last. The huge propeller was already spinning overhead, invisible and almost soundless, its blue-edge rotor blades ending in a distinctive gull-wing double-sweep shape to reduce the noise. There was a downdraft, but little more. The entire stealth craft was coated in the new carbon-nano paint, designed by NASA for its space missions and the "blackest" material known. It absorbed ninety-nine percent of any light in various spectrums that struck its surface. The military had gotten interested when it was discovered the paint also absorbed radar waves, thereby making anything coated in it invisible.

Already inside the chopper, bathed in the red gloom of the blackout lighting, were three large men, fairly new to the HAWCs, and a single woman – Casey Franks. They were in two-by-two teams, coded Red and Blue. Even though Sam was taking lead on the mission, all of them turned toward Alex when he stepped inside. They stood as he passed, not saying a word but nodding to acknowledge his authority. It seemed the rumor mill had gotten ahead of them. Sam had no doubt all the HAWCs knew who the special advisor was accompanying them that night. He noted that Franks was the only one to watch Alex with the hint of suspicion on her face. He wondered what was going on there.

The chopper sped low and silently over the Italian countryside. They had little more than an hour to their destination, after flying nonstop from the United States to Aviano, one of the last American air bases in Italy. Now the stealth chopper was taking them the 120 miles to Gianfranco Monti's compound on the shore of Lake Como.

Hammerson had charged Sam with assessing Alex during the mission. He noted Alex flexing his hands beneath the plated gloves, making iron-hard fists. Those hands had been broken many times, Sam knew, but they healed quickly, too quickly for a normal man. Alex's body could produce coagulants and collagen deposition, form new tissue and calcium deposits, in minutes, not days, which meant any wounds closed over almost immediately. But sometimes the scars remained. Just like the damage to his mind.

Alex reached up and touched a small indentation over his left eye, before running his hand up through his dark cropped hair. Sam knew there was a small star-shaped scar there – an intended kill shot delivered by Borshov, the giant Russian assassin who had obliterated Alex's HAWC team in Chechnya. It was a debt Alex had wanted to square for far too long.

The pilot's voice came through on his comm set. 'Cloudbank coming up – we'll have moon-shade in ten minutes. Mission up.'

'Mission up in ten,' Sam relayed to his team.

The chopper slowed in the air, and a single small light came on overhead in the rear cabin. The HAWCs pulled their full-face masks down. The black lenses covering their eyes looked a little like rounded swimming goggles, but were high-technology lens that could be moved up and down the thermal, telescopic or infrared ranges. Only Alex's mask had no lenses; science had already given him everything he needed within his own body. The HAWCs' suits were compressed to their bodies, and dappled between black and gunmetal gray, taking on the colors and characteristics of their surroundings. The material was woven through with Kevlar fiber, and had integrated biological combat plating over the chest, shoulders and other vulnerable areas.

'Let's get it on,' said Casey Franks. She made fists and growled, pumping herself up.

Sam held a small electronic tablet that showed a real-time VELA satellite feed of Monti's property. He knew Jack Hammerson would be watching the same feed back home.

VELA was able to see through stone and steel, delivering the building's secrets up to the incoming HAWCs. Multiple thermal images flared in and around the property – either two-by-two patrols, or guardian positions close to the walls, on terraces, and on rooftops. Inside, there were more, patrolling the hallways. In an upper room was a single figure, seated and alone – Monti.

Sam grunted, and pressed the stud in his ear to contact Hammerson back at base. 'Multiple shields, all armed. Primary target in upper bedroom in eastern wing. Confirm green light on mission.'

Hammerson's voice came back immediately. 'Mission is green light – you are good to go.'

'Mission is green, people,' Sam said.

He thought of Jack Hammerson seated in his dark office, the large wall-screen the only illumination. He would seem emotionless as he watched the mission unfold, but Sam knew the older warrior would be churning inside as his team went out. Once he gave the green light, things were out of his hands.

Sam checked his watch; once they hit the dirt, they had thirty minutes to get in, punch a hole through to Monti, and be gone before anyone outside of the compound even knew they were there. Bottom line was, they needed unimpeded time to question Monti and retrieve whatever information he had on what Caresche had been searching for deep in those Istanbul catacombs. Time was not a negotiable commodity.

The plan was for Alex to take the guards out of action first – non-lethal means if possible. But as the private security force were ex elite soldiers, they'd hardly drop their weapons when requested. They were on allied soil, but Sam had to hope, for their sake, the paid soldiers would choose life over gold. Because if it came to a fight to the death, it would be theirs.

Sam put a large hand on Alex's shoulder. 'Okay?'

'I'm good.' Alex spoke without turning.

Sam saw that his eyes shone silver in the dark, like some sort of nocturnal animal. He just hoped the animal inside him stayed sleeping.

'Just remember, we need Monti, not a massacre,' he said.

Alex smiled and nudged Sam's ribs. 'Don't worry about me.'

Sam grinned. 'I'm not worried about you – I'm worried for anyone in front of you.'

Sam pulled his own visor down. A second light went on – two minutes. He saw Alex began flexing his hands again, then he sucked in a huge breath and quickly checked his equipment, expert hands running automatically over weaponry, communications and extraneous kit, all packed down tight over his body.

Sam leaned in close, showing him the tablet. 'You're up first – you'll go in the front, take out any wandering sentinels on the perimeter.' He pointed to the small screen. 'There are three teams two-by-two patrolling, and one larger unit of six stationed on the front landing. Soft takedowns if possible. Red and Blue will position themselves at the west and east walls. I'm going to drop onto the roof, where I'll immediately deploy a white-noise net to fry their comms. That'll be the signal for you to make some noise – draw interest from inside the house.'

Alex stared at the small screen, his eyes moving over the figures, the building, the geography. He nodded once; Sam knew he would have missed nothing.

'With no comms, Monti's men will need line of sight – they'll come to you.' Sam switched off the screen and slid it away, then gave Alex a grim smile. 'We're going to need to punch it. Once the fireworks start, we'll have less than a minute to get to Monti before he tries to seal himself inside his secure panic room. We do not have the time to dig him out.'

The final light came on, and the cabin light changed from amber to hellish red again.

Sam lifted his voice: 'Game time.'

'HUA!' The HAWCs punched knuckles and rolled their shoulders, then formed up. *HUA* stood for Heard, Understood and Acknowledged. Nothing else needed to be said.

Sam nudged Alex again. 'How do you feel, Arcadian?'

The chopper door whined open, the ground close and shooting past at a seeming impossible speed.

Alex turned, smiling, his fists balled. 'Dangerous.' He dived out.

Sam shook his head. 'Dangerous, but in control, I hope.'

Casey Franks muscled up to the door. 'Me next.'

Sam sighed. 'What a surprise.'

*

Alex hit the ground, rolled, and came up running, fast. He was a black blur as he moved among the overhanging trees, his suit immediately taking on the hues and shades of the huge willows and ivy-covered oaks. He stayed in tight at the edge of tree line, already hearing the tread of the first patrol. As expected, the two men were professionals, no flashlights and walking softly and carefully in the dark. Without night vision, they would have been near invisible. Alex saw them as clearly as if they were in an open field.

He felt the adrenaline surge into his system, and increased his pace as he came up on the men. By the time they knew he was there, they lay unconscious at his feet. He kneeled, checking them over; not out of any concern for their wellbeing, more as a lightning-quick assessment of their weapons and capabilities.

He grunted. As he had assumed, both had night vision and also infrared scopes on top of their Beretta SCP 70/90 assault carbines. The skeletal black guns had the barrel adaptor attached so they could launch rifle grenades – not good news if the HAWCS were caught in the open.

In seconds he had lashed their hands behind their backs, then to their ankles, and was sprinting away, homing in on the next patrol on the opposite tree line. He skirted some ornamental shrubs, still staying low, then burst forth to cover the last hundred feet of open ground like an express train. He dived the last ten when one of the men suddenly turned, perhaps sensing movement or seeing a flash of red on his scope. The Beretta was coming up just as Alex struck, so hard it sounded like tree branches snapping as the men's bones and flesh were crushed by the impact.

Shit – no deaths if possible, he recalled. He crouched over the fallen men, noting that one's head had been turned completely around on a now very loose neck. He closed his eyes for a few seconds, trying to feel remorse. Were humans that fragile? *Only they are.*

He checked his watch and saw that he was on schedule. However, the easy part was over. Now he needed to disable the remaining six men at the front of the villa.

When the lights of the compound showed through the trees, Alex got down on his belly and crawled. Pausing at the tree line, he saw ahead a few hundred feet of manicured grass, an open walkway, and a huge stone verandah that could probably fit hundreds of well-heeled guests at a Monti party. Unfortunately, the massive open space afforded the guards at the front of the house an unimpeded view of anyone approaching. For Alex, it meant a direct assault was impossible – unless he wanted six professionals shooting at him with scoped Berettas.

He crawled closer, burrowing into the cool earth to dampen his thermal silhouette. Finally he came to a seven-foot marble statue of a discus thrower. He took cover behind it, and looked at the verandah and the men patrolling it from end to end. There were two permanently stationed at each side of the door – vigilant, armed, and professional-looking. Monti had chosen his security force well.

No matter how fast he was, Alex knew it would be impossible to get to the building without being shot. But maybe something else could manage it. He looked up at the statue and then back to the guards, calculating. He smiled; Sam wanted some noise ...

He checked his watch, counting down the seconds until Sam and the Red and Blue teams were in place. His body was humming with energy, and he felt good, alive; he had a purpose again. He wasn't the disembodied spirit wandering from town to town, waiting for random acts of violence to be rained down on him so he could exercise his fury. He flexed his hands in their gloves. *What would I have become,* he wondered, *if Hammerson hadn't brought me in?* He already knew the answer. He would have eventually turned into the Other One that struggled within him – the pure violence and hate that he only ever just managed to keep caged. He would have ended up a rabid dog that needed to be put down – just another monster in the darkness. He crushed his eyes shut for a moment, saying a small prayer, finishing with a request to bring a little luck to Alan Marshal's work in the lab.

The communication pellet pinged twice in his ear – the signal that Sam had cast the white-noise net. Now all non-HAWC communications would be useless – and they were ready to go.

Alex peered around the statue base at the men on the verandah, then looked up again at the discus thrower. He eased himself to his feet.

*

The 200-pound marble arm holding the enormous disc landed at one end of the balcony, and exploded like a bomb, obliterating a good six feet of expensive flagstones and carved balustrade, and raining dust and debris down on the guards.

The men flattened themselves to the ground in the confusion, but it was only a second or two before their experience and professionalism kicked in. Several rolled and crouched with weapons up and pointing to the impact site; the two guards at the door got down on one knee, guns pointed in opposite directions, ready for any threat. However, by the time the dust cloud cleared and one of them sighted the figure speeding across the lawn, Alex was already two-thirds of the way there. In one hand he held his HK pistol, which he fired with precision into the shoulders of the two men either side of the doorway. Bullets zipped toward him in return.

The other men had scattered so he reholstered the weapon, and concentrated on speed … and his next throw. In his other hand he had a chunk of statue the size of a melon, which he launched at one of the shooters. It flew faster than any eyes could follow, struck the six-foot guard in the gut, and punched him backward over the side of the verandah.

More bullets flew past him or thwacked into the soft ground as Alex zigzagged the last few dozen feet, leaping up the steps to crash into another of the guards. He was among them now, their advantage of distance gone. Bullets still flew, but their fear of hitting each other slowed their firing, and their reaction times were inconsequential compared to his own. He ducked and weaved, disappearing from in front of one to appear beside another, landing blows, or sliding low to smash a fist into a knee, then another into an exposed temple. Another guard went down.

The last two proved the most difficult. They had chosen their combat positions wisely and it became obvious they knew how to work in tandem. One finally came in close to engage, but it was only a feint. As he pulled back, the other caught Alex's neck with his gun butt.

Flashes of light and pain exploded in Alex's head, momentarily stunning him. He dropped and turned, blocking another of the steel-weighted punches. Behind him, a gun went off, and the bullet kicked him flat to the ground. The suit armor held, but excruciating pain flared and he knew there would be cracked ribs in his back.

The two men were big and fearless, and using everything they had. Alex rolled and came up fast, his resolve to pull his punches slipping away. Another two shots – Alex moved out of the way in a blur, and one whizzed past his cheek. The second caught him dead center in the chest. He absorbed it, his teeth clenched and eyes furious.

He flew at the gunman and punched him, an uppercut delivered with enough ferocity to lift the man off his feet and throw him back into the huge wooden doors. Alex knew it was unlikely he would ever rise. He stared at the body. *No deaths if possible.* It took a microsecond for the thought to enter his mind ... and be answered. *Kill or be killed.* Alex knew the voice. It was the Other One, straining against his bonds.

The thought was a distraction – enough to allow a blade, gleaming blue in the moonlight, to flash into his back. Such was the force of the delivery and the sharpness of the weapon, it managed to find its way between two of the armor plates and into his shoulder. The flash of pain was like an electric shock, kicking open a door in his mind, ripping him in two, letting the Other One free.

Alex felt as if he had been thrown outside of his mind and body. He felt powerless as another Alex spun at the man to grab the hand holding the blade – the Italian Special Ops Titan, seven inches of carbon fiber wrapped around an inner core of titanium, and one of the deadliest knives in the world. The guard pushed down hard, using both hands to try to force the blade back into his opponent's face. Alex held on, turning the blade, and easing it up under the man's chin. The man's expression moved from determination to exertion and then fear as the blade touched his skin.

Time seemed to freeze as the other Alex and the guard locked eyes. In both stares there was recognition of impending death, but for only one of them. Alex gave the weapon another push, continuing until only the hilt stopped it going any further. The man's body danced and juddered momentarily as the nerves short-circuited.

The other Alex reached up to tear the mask from his head. If he could have seen himself, his expression would have appeared emotionless – the guard's life was nothing to him. With one hand, he held the body up off the ground, impaled on the blade, then pulled it close and looked into the slack face.

He lifted his own head toward the roofline, anger pulling his features into a mask of fury. 'You wanted some noise?' He dragged the body down the steps to the front of the huge building, and held it up with one arm, shaking it. 'This is all you've got?'

His lips pulled back in a snarl and his eyes were round with fury, shining silver in the darkness. He threw his head back and roared up to the windows, no words, just a primal sound of anger and challenge.

Figures appeared in windows, and gave their answer quickly – heavy-caliber machine-gun fire raked toward him, blowing fist-sized clods of earth into the air.

Alex grabbed the body in both hands, lifted it, and threw it toward the gunner, forcing him to take shelter behind the window frame. By the time the gunfire resumed, Alex had vanished, but not back to the tree line. He threw himself against the heavy door, exploding it inwards. He was in.

Gunfire sounded from inside several areas of the huge building – the HAWC Red and Blue teams had joined the party.

*

Jack Hammerson grimaced as he watched the action at Monti's villa unfold. He would send the recording down to Alan Marshal – the man had his work cut out for him. Hammerson could pinpoint almost to the second when Alex Hunter had changed. The knife coming down into his shoulder – deep but not lethal. The Arcadian should have shaken it off, and he did, physically. But from that moment, he seemed to stop being himself. The new Alex was faster, stronger, more savage and totally without mercy. He had brutalized the guard, even after he was dead, parading the body; and then seemed to call for his own death – standing arms wide in the open, spotlit and tormenting the guards.

Hammerson exhaled long and slow. *Did I send him out too soon?*

He watched Alex explode through the front door, a blur of fury. 'Pull it back, son,' he whispered. A phrase came to mind from a book he'd read many decades before: *You must suffer me to go my own dark way.* The book was *The Strange Case of Dr. Jekyll and Mr. Hyde* – a tale about a man's struggle between his good self and the monster that also lived within him.

CHAPTER 15

After setting off the white-noise net, Sam pulled a four-foot loop of beaded wire from over his shoulder and placed it on the roof. He turned his back on it, and pressed a stud on a small box. The ring detonated, primarily downwards, cutting a near perfect hole through concrete, wood, and plaster. He turned, and immediately jumped through it.

The big HAWC landed hard, his near 500-pound electronic and hydraulic-assisted frame sinking an inch into the parquetry floor. Switching his lenses to thermal, he searched quickly in the swirling cloud of dust and darkness – he knew he only had seconds before his quarry made his way to a fortified space. As if in direct response to his thought, a wall slid back at one end of the room, revealing a door with a dull metallic sheen, and so thick it wouldn't have been out of place in a bank vault.

A coughing, spitting sound from behind a huge couch sent Sam rushing over to heave the large piece of furniture out of the way. He lifted the crawling man to his feet, dragged him to a chair, and slammed him down hard. He grabbed his jaw, looking into his face to assess his identity.

'Don't kill me.' Monti flinched away, crushing his eyes shut. It was a logical reaction to being confronted by a towering stranger dressed in black with bulb-like goggles, who had just dropped down through a hole in your roof.

Ready for a chat then, Sam thought. The big HAWC slapped the man hard. He needed Monti talking … and fast. There was no time for negotiation or pleasantries. Today, lives depended on speed … and brutality.

He grabbed Monti's jaw again, and got so close his face nearly touched the Italian's. 'Live or die?'

Monti babbled and tried to reach up to Sam's hand on his jaw.

Sam slapped him again, even harder. 'Live or die?' he screamed.

Monti looked like he'd been physically beaten. He began to weep, and pointed with one shaking finger. 'There's money in my safe.'

Another slap, this time so hard Monti was almost knocked from the chair and his eyes rolled in his head for a moment.

Sam grabbed his face again and pulled him close. 'Fuck your money. Live or die, you get to choose. Last chance.'

He reached into a pocket and pulled out a photograph; it showed a tanned and handsome Janus Caresche. He held it up in front of the trembling man's face. 'What was he after in the Basilica Cistern?'

'Huh …' Monti squinted at the picture. 'I … I don't know.'

Sam exploded, lifting the man and throwing him into the wall. Monti lay still for a moment, then scuttled toward an ornate desk. He reached for something underneath it, then spun with a small silver pistol in his hand. He fired point-blank, hitting Sam in the chest. Sam was rocked back a half-step, and snorted. The biological plating wasn't even dented.

Monti turned to crawl toward the panic room, but Sam lifted one large boot and stomped down on his gun wrist, breaking the bones. Gianfranco Monti screamed, holding his arm, the hand flopping loosely at the end of the crushed radius and ulna.

Sam gritted his teeth; he hated this part. But men and women were dying out there, while this creep had been happily sipping champagne.

'What was in the Basilica Cistern in Istanbul?' he roared. He flipped the desk over and dragged Monti back to the seat.

The Italian shook his head, weeping. 'I don't know ... no one knows.'

There was a commotion outside the locked door, and a few zipping shots from an automatic weapon. Sam saw Monti lean forward, an atom of hope in his eyes. Perhaps his men had come at last to deal with this monstrous brute.

The door crashed inwards, and Monti slumped as four HAWCs appeared. They nodded to Sam, then stationed themselves outside the room.

Monti's face paled at what came in next. The Arcadian moved smoothly, seeming to absorb the light and air around him. He was like a large predator, eyes silver, his suit dappled with camouflage, almost invisible amid the floating plaster dust and flickering light. The only areas of the suit that stayed in focus were splattered red with blood.

'No.' Monti held up a hand, but seemed unable to tear his eyes away.

Sam nodded to Alex, but the other man wasn't watching him. His stare was fixed on the small Italian, so intense it could have been a pair of machine lasers set to burn holes right through him.

'Time's up; my turn.' Alex's voice was without pity.

Sam drew back a fist that was as big as Monti's head. 'Last chance, asshole, or I turn you over to *him*.'

Monti reached into his pocket, and pulled out a silver key. He pointed toward the vault room with a shaking hand. 'The locked cabinet, bottom drawer – Constantine's Sauromatian Codex.'

*

'Hold.' Sam held up a hand, stopping the HAWCs on the ornate oaken staircase. They froze, weapons up, sighting at different quadrants through their scopes.

Sam listened closely to the incoming coded message from Hammerson. 'New team – ten gatecrashers coming in from your east using Spec Ops stealth pattern four. Look like they know what they're doing. Could be Spetsnaz.'

'Roger that,' Sam said. 'Engage?'

There was silence for a second, before Hammerson's voice came back low and slow. 'If Russian, send 'em to hell. Payback for Graham. Put your masks on them and leave the bodies exposed. Let Volkov explain that to the Italians.'

'Acknowledged.' Sam turned to his Red and Blue teams. 'We got ten incoming in an S4 double wedge from the east. We are authorized to use all force. Trident formation – no mess, people.'

The HAWCs reloaded, then flew down the steps toward the front doors. Red and Blue would take the sides, while Alex and Sam would get between the two five-man teams.

Sam's comm unit pinged again. 'Hold,' he said, repeating the order that had just blasted into his ear.

'Be advised, new team are carrying HKMP5 submachine guns, and I can see an L96 sniper rifle. They're SAS – send 'em home, and then wrap things up.' Hammerson spoke matter-of-factly, all urgency gone.

Sam knew Hammerson was drilling down with VELA – he'd be able to tell the color of their eyes if they were visible. He grunted. 'Acknowledged.'

Hammerson's voice lowered. 'Be advised, Mission Leader, that Prodigal Son may not be in control.'

'Fuck it,' Sam whispered.

'Send him to negotiate – a little friend-from-foe test,' Hammerson ordered, and signed off.

'Acknowledged, out.' Sam looked at his teams. 'At ease, people, we got friendlies.' His eyes stayed on Alex a while longer. The man looked calm, in control. 'You're up,' Sam told him. He cradled his weapon, and motioned with a small bow to the front door. 'Go and consult with our British friends ... and be nice.'

*

Alex pushed his rifle up over his shoulder, and walked through the remains of the huge door he had obliterated only minutes before. Alone, he stepped out onto the front landing. The response was immediate: a flash grenade went off right at his feet.

The powerful percussion wave was accompanied by blinding light and momentary heat. Anything within twenty feet would be temporarily blinded. Anything closer would be blown backward and receive debilitating flash burns. Six of the SAS team came in low and fast, expecting to occupy the front landing, and neutralize any targets with any fight still in them. What they got was something very different.

When the smoke cleared, Alex was still standing, legs planted wide, a black-clad colossus. His body had immediately adjusted to the change in pressures, rebalancing him and keeping him rooted to the spot. His suit smoked in places, but the biological plating had absorbed the force of the small blast. His arms hung loosely by his side, relaxed. He looked at the six soldiers. 'Cupboard's bare; stand down.'

The men approaching froze, weapons up and trained on him. All wore black and green assault suits, with night black paint stripes on their faces. Several wore a Cyclops night scope over one eye.

'Fucking Yanks, great.' A man stood from where Alex knew the other four British Special Ops team had concealed themselves. He pointed at Alex with a gloved hand, the trigger finger exposed. 'Like shit we'll stand down. You're even further out of your jurisdiction than we are. We're here to do a job. Stand the fuck down yourself.'

Alex shook his head. 'There's nothing left. Go home, boys.'

The Red and Blue team HAWCs appeared from the east and west side of the building, guns loose but ready. Sam stood in the doorway, arms folded over his cradled weapon. Alex could see that the SAS men still concealed had their guns shouldered and their eyes to scopes, moving back and forth between the HAWCs. They were far from at ease.

He took several steps forward, coming to the edge of the verandah, and looked down at the seven SAS standing on the front lawn. 'Search if you want, but clear a path. We're leaving.'

'Bullshit.' This from a huge soldier standing out to the left side of the first speaker. 'You guys have cleaned us out – you better learn to share, and quick.'

The SAS ringed the steps, clearly ready to oppose any move the HAWCs made to vacate. Their guns were pointed down, but fingers were on the triggers.

Behind Alex, Sam's comm unit pinged, and he heard the big man say softly, 'Incoming – Polizia di Stato. Ten minutes.'

Alex looked back at the first speaker with the fingerless glove – obviously the SAS group leader. 'You heard. Italian police coming in – things are about to get messy. Next time, get here earlier.'

The bigger SAS man stepped to within a dozen feet of Alex, barring his path. 'Messy for you maybe. We got you outnumbered nearly two to one. Show us what you retrieved and we all go home happy. Okay, sunshine?' He grinned, his long teeth overly white in his black-painted face. 'I'd hate to have to take it off you now.'

The smile dropped as the big man rolled his enormous shoulders. Alex took a last look along the line of SAS soldiers, assessing distance and readiness. He held his arms wide and yelled, 'Attention!' The word had the desired effect – the seven standing turned toward him, and the three sniper scopes followed. He'd drawn their focus, and then he moved – fast.

One minute he was on the verandah, and then he just … wasn't. He struck the huge British soldier first, up under the chin, causing the long white teeth to clack together like castanets. He didn't stop to see if the man was unconscious, he didn't need to. He continued on to the leader of the group, grabbing him around the throat and dragging him quickly to the tree line and away from his forces. His men tried to follow him with their guns, but Alex used him as a shield. The tough warrior struggled against Alex, but Alex's grip was like iron cable.

Alex whispered into his ear: 'We're all on the side of the angels here. I'm sure you'll negotiate a better outcome through other channels. Don't push us – not here, not today.'

He quickly disarmed the man, released him, and let his weapons fall to the ground. The British soldier was up in a flash, hands bunched into hard fists, but Alex had already turned away.

'Hey.' The SAS man took a step and then paused. 'No one's that bloody fast.'

Alex kept walking, and the other Brits moved their aim between him and the HAWCs on the verandah. The HAWCs came down the steps to join Alex, stepping over the SAS giant still out cold on the grass.

The SAS leader rubbed his neck as he angrily picked up his weapons. He waved his men down, and they stepped aside.

Alex turned to him and gave a small salute. 'Next time.'

The man walked toward Alex, looking him up and down. 'Well, well, what do you fucking know – the freak is real. The fucking Arcadian.' He gave Alex a small salute that ended with him pointing at Alex's chest. 'Next time it is then, sunshine.'

He turned to his men and pointed to the big downed soldier. 'All right, lads, get that arsehole up on his feet, and let's bunk it. Party's over.'

Alex waved the HAWCs on, and they started to jog, picking up speed on the way to their concealed chopper.

*

The SAS leader watched them go, then barked an order. 'Jimmy, Bolter, get up there and see what state they left Monti in. If he's breathing, he's coming with us. Bag him if you have to.'

CHAPTER 16

Alex leaned against the wall, brooding. Hammerson had debriefed him, making him watch the VELA playback from the mission. He'd seen himself hurling the dead body like it was a sack of trash. The HAWC commander hadn't raised his voice, thumped the table or even cursed. But Alex knew he was furious. Hammerson's personal judgement had been called into question by the harshest judge of all – himself. That Alex had been able to pull it together later in the mission was his only saving grace. Marshal had been in the room, and had supported Alex. 'Small setbacks are to be expected,' he'd said. He was sure that while they were working on eradicating the rages, they would be able to help Alex manage them, perhaps even make them work for him.

Control it before it controls me – that's the plan, thought Alex now.

He, Sam, and Matt Kearns were in Hammerson's office, trying to understand what it was they'd actually liberated from Gianfranco Monti. Alex felt Matt Kearns staring at him. The last time Matt had seen him was on the peak of Black Mountain in the Appalachians. Alex bet the guy still had nightmares about giant beasts ... and probably about

Alex too. Initially Matt's expression had suggested he'd seen a ghost. Now he just looked disorientated.

Alex nodded to the languages professor, who shook his head as though to clear his mind. He looked back down at the ancient paper in front of him, and ran his fingertips over its surface.

'Papyrus – not great quality – working man's paper.' He leaned down to sniff the paper, then pulled back to scrutinize it with a magnifying glass to one eye. 'Aluminum salts in the fibers; also egg and tree gum used to starch out the edges … definitely not fake.'

'Old, huh?' Hammerson said, circling the young paleolinguist as he hunched over the illuminated desk.

Matt nodded. 'Oh yeah, it's old all right. Hey, did you know this type of paper was probably sold in bulk to the Romans, and all along the ancient Mediterranean? Egypt exported tons of it.' He looked up. 'Around 2000 years ago.'

Hammerson nodded, not looking impressed. 'So, old. What else you got?'

Matt turned back to the parchment. 'It was written by a soldier in the year 334 AD. It's a record of sorts.'

'And?'

'And . . . weird.' Matt shook his head as he scanned the faded Latin text.

Hammerson gritted his teeth. 'Jee-zuz, man, don't make me pull this out of you. Weird, how? Give me something, Professor.'

'Okay, okay … have you heard of the Roman emperor Constantine?'

Hammerson snorted. 'Flavius Valerius Aurelius Constantinus Augustus – the warrior Caesar. Of course; we studied his tactics. He was a great man. Go on.' He half-turned toward the two huge men who were standing back, listening. 'Alex, Sam, get over here. I want your eyes on this.'

'The warrior Caesar – yeah, that's certainly true.' Matt tilted his head. 'As well as being the first Roman emperor to convert to Christianity, he also defeated the emperors Maxentius and Licinius during civil wars when he was little more than a youth. Then he fought and beat the Franks, the Alamanni, and the Visigoths, retook the parts of Dacia that had been lost during the previous century, and also had time to build a new imperial residence at Byzantium, which he named New Rome. The people loved him so much they re-named it Constantinople in his honor.'

'Constantinople, now Istanbul,' Alex said.

'That's right. Formally renamed in 1923 by the Turks. So, what we seem to have recovered from Gianfranco Monti is a record of one of Constantine's campaigns by someone who was involved.' Matt bobbed his head side to side. 'Hmm, maybe a bit less formal than a record; more like a soldier writing about his adventures for his loved ones back home. The guy was a centurion – in charge of hundreds of foot soldiers. The Roman army was unbelievably organized, and –' He stopped at a flat stare from Hammerson. 'But you know all that.' He cleared his throat. 'About 1800 years ago, give or take, the world was a wild and dangerous place. Russia was still largely unknown to the Romans. It was populated by clans of wild bearded giants, and tribes with filed teeth or body decorations made by scarifying or searing the skin.'

Sam snorted. 'Sounds like the New York subway.'

Alex grinned.

Hammerson's glare shut them both down. 'Continue, Professor.'

'Anyway, in southern Russia there used to be a kingdom called Sarmatia, or Sauromatia in ancient Roman, in the land of Scythia.'

Hammerson folded his arms, his jaw jutting. 'Will you get on with it, son?'

Matt nodded. 'Look, the thing about the Sauromatian was that no one really knew where they came from. They were a race out of time and place.'

Hammerson exhaled loudly, and Alex and Sam grinned.

'Okay, got it.' Matt cracked his knuckles, cleared his throat again, sipped some water, and began to read the parchment's text aloud.

A time of my service for the great Emperor Constantine during the Sauromatian campaign, by Aleianus Drusus Cornelius Cassianus, Centurion of the 5th Cohort.

We stood obediently, pretending the pummeling rain caused us no discomfort, but it was hard and cold, and bounced back up from the sodden earth to coat us in mud to the thighs. The rain is never-ending in this accursed place. I miss the sun, and the fields of Rome, and most of all, Aemilia my darling, I miss you. I will come home, I promise you.

In this place I feel there is no love and the Gods jest with us. It is said that no man can defeat the army of Rome under Constantine, yet we fight something far stranger than mere men, and it tests our nerve as well as our metal.

This very day, I saw the first of these beings up close. The bound warrior was dragged before our Emperor and let fall at his feet. Even though the great man stood upon reed matting, some mud splashed upwards, and we held our breath. But he ignored it, his eyes moving over our foe, looking over its armor, its decorations, its physical form. Like all the warriors we have fought in this campaign, this too was a woman, dressed for war, with battle-armor plating that was like the scales of a snake.

Constantine drew his sword, and ran it down the breastplate, and then back up, lifting some of the shingles. We saw that they were sliced segments of horses' hooves, sewn together in an interlocking fashion.

'Strong and light,' our Emperor said. We nodded, and he added, 'But no match for Roman steel.'

He laughed, and so did we. It filled us with pride.

He used his sword again to examine the armaments in more detail. The helmet and gauntlets were of leather, but carved with a design of intertwining snakes. On the front of the skullcap helmet, an etching of a vile snake covered the woman's face.

Constantine curled his lip in distaste. 'Sauromatian,' he muttered.

It was the ancient Greek name for the race of peoples we had come to make war on: the followers of the Snake Goddess.

'Remove her gag,' he ordered.

Matt lightly turned the page. 'I've heard of this race of people, the Sauromatian,' he said. 'The women were bloodthirsty as hell – they fought to the death. It's believed they were the source for the stories of the giant female Amazonian warriors. This is amazing stuff.'

He turned back to the ancient parchment and continued.

The cloth binding her lower face was ripped away, and the creature immediately convulsed and tried to fling herself at Constantine's legs. He stepped back quickly, pointing his sword, as the woman's blackened teeth, coated in a sticky resin, clacked shut just inches from his foreleg. One bite, and the black poison rotted the flesh.

Constantine did not recoil at the sight of her monstrous teeth filed to wicked points, even though they were more like the jaws of a wild animal than of a human. One of our men stomped a large mud-covered foot onto her chest, pinning her writhing form to the ground. She spat and convulsed before lying still, but her eyes were filled with venom. These people did not fear us, or even death at our hands.

Constantine commenced to turn away, but, like us, saw her body shake again, a little at first, and then more, until she erupted with laughter.

'*Arknoah unsor Magera. Urganoha enhoka, Magera!*' *she snarled, her burning eyes never leaving our Emperor.*

Her words were harsh, like the growl of a low beast, and the sound revolted us. She laughed again, but there was only scorn in the expression, and something else … A mocking tone of victory. Even now, I remember her scarred and ugly visage twisted in perverted triumph.

Constantine was unmoved and waved the miserable creature away. She was dragged backward, her horrible laughter ringing loudly over the falling rain, until it was abruptly cut off by a soldier's blade … at last.

The great man called to me, as I am one of his advisors, and spoke soft to me. 'Did you hear her words?'

I told him I had, and asked if it was the thing he sought.

He nodded once, then looked beyond me to the walled city. 'It is the Magera. The legend is real.'

Matt looked up again. 'That name: Magera – exactly like the script carved into the wall of the chamber. I've been doing some research, and for the life of me I can't find any reference to it. It's driving me nuts as it rings a bell – I'm certain I've heard it before.'

'Make a note and move on. I want to hear the rest,' Hammerson said.

Matt nodded. 'Picks up again with Aleianus seeing a rider approach.'

A centurion rider skidded his horse to a halt in the greasy soil and jumped down. On seeing the Emperor, he threw himself to the wet ground, prostrating himself. It was young Varinius, son of Nonus, whom we had met at the theater one score years ago. He is a fine young man now.

Constantine looked down at him, sheathing his sword. 'Speak.'

Varinius sucked in a huge lungful of air, and spat some mud. 'We have reached the inner temple, sire.'

Constantine did not speak; he just looked again to the city. From our position on the hillside, it was possible to see inside the high wooden palisades that surrounded a collection of several hundred squat wood and stone buildings, which grew larger as they approached the city's center. It had taken our men only days to breach the walls, but twice that time again to reach its middle. Instead of a palace, we found a temple, larger and richer than all other buildings in the compound. It seemed their god was their royalty.

The battle was hard; fanatics always fight to the death. We had done our best to ensure the Sauromatian got their wish. Now, at last, we had reached their heart.

Constantine stood for many minutes staring through the rain at the smoldering city. He held out his hand, and immediately a dry cloth was placed there for him to wipe his face.

I know a little of what our Emperor seeks in this hellhole, from the few details he has shared with me. A Greek legend, older than Rome itself, has drawn him here to this god-forsaken place filled with endless rain and worthless tribes of fanged pagan warriors. This kingdom of Sauromatia in the land of Scythia has stood for untold ages, secretive and savage. Its people are said to be the keepers of a weapon that has made them invincible to the surrounding hordes.

Our Emperor's best scholars have spent many years unraveling the secrets of the first Greeks, and his men have purchased, stolen or unearthed fragments of their myths from their mountains, and islands, and from the lands of the ancient bull dancers. All spoke of something of great religious significance here; maybe even proof of the Gods themselves. Our great Emperor's determination is as strong and unyielding as the iron of his sword, and I know that whether what lies within the Sauromatian temple is a sacred relic, a weapon, or even just a vase with the writing of the angels upon it, he intends to possess it.

Varinius looked up. 'We have not yet entered, sire, but …' He paused to suck in more air.

Constantine looked hard at the man, perhaps really seeing him for the first time. There was a gash on his neck that was still bloody and dirty with soot, a piece of his ear was missing, and there were many marks to his armor – the injuries of a soldier who leads by example; a fighter. Constantine smiled and motioned for the young man to get to his feet. He called for water, and handed his cloth to the soldier to clean his face.

'Their warriors still fight?' he asked.

'No, sire; this time there are men, priests, but …' His lips worked for a few seconds without forming words. We waited, with just the sound of the drumming rain falling in gray sheets all around us. At last he went on. 'They are all blind. I mean blinded … their eyes have been removed. And their heads … tattooed.'

Constantine motioned the young soldier to drink. He stood close for a few seconds, studying his face. After a time, he said softly, 'Blinded, all of them?'

Varinius nodded jerkily. 'The priests have formed a line in front of the temple, but will not enter it themselves, even for their own protection. It seems they fear their god more than they fear our steel.'

One of Constantine's generals, Titus, laughed. 'Woman and blind priests; is it any wonder they have fallen so easily before us.'

Our Emperor rounded on Titus, his voice fierce. 'But stood undefeated for more centuries than you can count.'

The general, a huge bear of a man, went down on one knee.

Constantine turned back to the city and spoke as if to the large stone temple at its core, rather than to us, his assembled heads of war. 'Those who behold the Gorgos will be forever imprisoned in stone.'

His eyes were slightly glazed, as if seeing something far re-moved from the rain and mud around us. I recognized the name from an ancient legend in the work of the philosopher Pliny the Elder, of creatures far too horrible to be real.

He turned to the kneeling general. 'Dear faithful Titus, if their city was truly protected only by women and priests, it could never have stood for so long. There must be something else.' He turned to us all. 'A hidden weapon perhaps?'

We remained silent, Titus still pale from the rebuke.

Constantine returned his attention to Varinius. 'Could it be that the priests' gaze was … unworthy? They were blinded as punishment for looking upon their ruler or deity? Or perhaps the simple act of "seeing" means something far worse.' He looked into the young man's face. 'Was there anything else? Be clear and be quick.'

Varinius stood straighter, and nodded. 'The translators said the blind men only spoke one thing, over and over: "She must not be freed."' His brow creased. 'They think that is what the priests said. Their tongue is … difficult.'

'Yes.' The Emperor nodded and walked a few paces from us, then spun quickly. 'Ready my horse. I wish to see for myself.'

We immediately flew into furious activity. The Caesar does not travel anywhere at whim. Our Emperor's private guard readied themselves and his mount, and the great man ordered Varinius back onto his horse.

'Let us see what the Sauromatian priests are trying to keep from us.' He added in an aside for my ears only, 'Or are they trying to protect us from it?'

Matt held up his hands, wincing. 'That's the end – well, the end of what we have here. Where's the rest?'

Sam shook his head. 'That's all Monti had.'

Matt exhaled. 'Probably destroyed, then – after all, it's lucky this page is in such condition given it was written almost 1800 years ago.' He sat back. 'Well, that's it then:

whatever Constantine found, they brought back and then sealed it away in the deep catacombs under the Basilica. It was probably Constantine's personal vault back then.'

'Why?' Sam was looking over Matt's shoulder at the parchment.

'Why what? Why was it converted into a cistern?'

'No; why would they bury it?'

Matt shrugged. 'Perhaps it was something so valuable they wanted to –'

'Valuable from a military perspective, more like,' Alex cut in. 'You said the Sauromatian were savages with filed teeth and armor made essentially from bone. At that time in the region there were the Cimmerians, the Goths, the Slavs, the Tartars – all powerful warlike tribes with hundreds of fighters. Yet the Sauromatian resisted them all for nearly 800 years.'

Matt nodded. 'Yes, I see.'

'Go on,' Hammerson said.

'Maybe this thing was sealed away because it was too dangerous,' Alex said. 'Constantine realized he had a tiger by the tail, and couldn't deal with it. Maybe he'd discovered the world's first weapon of mass destruction, and found it too horrible to use … or even understand. Maybe he tried to destroy it and couldn't, so the best he could do was seal it up and hide it away.'

The three men looked at Alex in silence.

Then Hammerson grunted. 'This is getting real interesting.'

'But what could it be?' Sam folded his massive arms. 'An object, device, a manuscript maybe, something biological? What exactly?'

Matt shook his head. 'Doesn't say. Hey, I know, I bet it's on page two. Go back and ask Monti.'

Sam's face darkened. 'Maybe you'd like to come with us next time.'

'Ease up, big guy,' Alex said. He turned to Matt. 'If we knew there was more to the codex, you can damn well bet we'd have asked Monti for it.' He turned back to Sam. 'And I'm sure he'd have happily given it up.'

Sam half-smiled.

'One thing's for sure,' Alex continued, 'whatever it was, it must have been something the Sauromatian thought was mystical, magical. And Constantine had a healthy respect for it.'

'*Any sufficiently advanced technology is indistinguishable from magic*,' Sam said slowly. 'Arthur C. Clarke wrote that over fifty years ago.'

'Magic … technology …' Matt stood up. 'You think the Sauromatians had some kind of technology that enabled them to remain the premier force in ancient Russia for over half a millennium?'

Alex shrugged. 'It's possible. Constantine was a warrior general, he'd have been used to assessing risks.'

'So he buried the weapon, leaving it for the future to sort out?' Sam asked.

Alex grunted. 'Maybe he tried to destroy it and couldn't. Maybe he buried it hoping it would never be found.'

'What could a race of savages have that would instill that sort of fear in a Caesar?' Matt mused. 'A weapon, a god, a disease, a book of spells, a relic …?' He shrugged. 'All we really know is that there was something down there in that hidden chamber, sealed in the bronze urn, and now it's not there anymore. It's been taken, or it … walked away.'

'Walked away – that doesn't make me feel real good,' Sam said. 'And if that isn't enough of a problem, now Borshov's tracking it.'

'And now Borshov's tracking it,' Hammerson repeated slowly. He walked over to the world map that covered one of the walls in his office. There were thousands of dots indicating locations of US bases – red for those known to the general public, black for covert. He gazed at them and shook his head slowly. 'If it *is* a weapon, and if it's still operational, you can count on the Russians trying to use it if they get hold of it.' He turned, his face unreadable. 'There's a lot of tension between our countries at the moment. Not a great time for one side to be heavily tipping the scales.'

'And tipping them away from us,' Sam said.

Hammerson nodded. 'Still a domestic problem at the moment, though. Unless we get invited, we can only goddamn watch and wait.'

'And if Russia gets hold of this thing and makes it a global problem?' Alex asked.

Hammerson's face turned to granite. 'Then it'll be too damn late.'

'Can we see the coordinates of attacks so far?' Alex said.

Matt sat forward, his hands hovering over the keyboard. 'How do I ...?'

'Move it.' Hammerson pushed him sideways and started typing.

A map appeared onscreen, showing a series of red dots starting at the Basilica Cistern in Istanbul and ending at Uşak. The number of victims at each location increased progressively, as did the distance between events.

'It's taking more victims and getting stronger, moving faster,' Alex said.

'Could it be a natural phenomenon, or some sort of toxic cloud?' Sam asked. 'It's certainly obscuring satellite imagery.'

Alex shook his head. 'Unlikely. Seems to be following a specific path – like it knows where it's going.'

'Looks like it's heading for the coast,' Sam said, moving a few steps toward the screen. 'Why can't the Turkish military see this?'

'They probably can,' Hammerson said, 'but I think they're doing exactly what I would do – get everyone out of the way, and watch and wait. I'd be pretty damned cautious about sending anyone else in until I knew what we were dealing with. Might just be throwing them into the meat grinder.'

'I think Sam was right ... about the coast, I mean.'

The three soldiers turned to look at Matt.

He indicated the keyboard. 'May I?'

Hammerson slid his chair back. 'The bridge is yours, Professor.'

Matt joined the dots of the affected areas with a line. 'We might need to look at it with fresh eyes ... or better yet, very old eyes. 'About the time of the Minoans, there were several significant trading routes running through this region, and small villages sprang up beside them – a bit like settlements appearing beside rivers. This line could be one of the old Phrygian routes.' He concentrated on typing, and brought up a much simpler map that showed just a few colored lines, and ancient cities such as Ur, Babylon, Susa, and Khalab, now long turned to dust beneath the desert sands. Matt adjusted its size and then laid it over the top of the modern map.

Sam snorted. 'Holy shit.'

There was no doubt. One of the trading routes ran from Istanbul, through Izmit, Guyve, Polatli, Uşak, and continued on to the coast.

Matt pointed to the line. 'The Middle East was the cradle of civilization. In some of these towns, human habitation has been traced back as far as 26,000 years.'

Hammerson frowned. 'It seems to be veering off the route in places, then coming back.'

'For the people,' Alex said. 'It's veering off to areas of large population.'

Hammerson's frown deepened. 'It's goddamn seeking them out. It *wants* to kill.'

'Based on this projection, it'll pass close to Salihli and Sardes on its way to Izmir,' Matt said. 'Sardes was the capital city of Lydia about 2500 years ago, until it was captured by the Persian Empire. After that, it –'

'Izmir.' Hammerson cut Matt off, and turned to Alex and Sam. Both men nodded.

'Yes, that's right,' Matt said. 'The route ends at Izmir. Makes sense, as it was one of the oldest settlements in the Mediterranean basin. There are several graves there dating from about 3000 BC – that's contemporary with the first city of Troy.'

Hammerson folded his arms, his face like stone. 'Based on speed to date, it should be there within three days.'

'Yeah, looks like it.' Matt said, then looked from Hammerson to Alex and Sam, catching their expressions. 'Huh? What is it?'

'We got a base there,' Hammerson said.

'In Turkey? You mean a NATO base?'

'Sort of. The official story is Turkey took over control of the NATO bases in 2004. But the unofficial story is they want to be part of the UN Security Council, and so we're allowed to keep a few bits and pieces there. So do the Brits and Germans – just one big happy family.' Hammerson smiled flatly.

Matt leaned back in his chair. 'What are a few bits and pieces?'

'Forty-two airplanes, twelve heavy choppers, Roland and Hawk mobile missile systems, and about 300 personnel. That's just at Izmir.'

Matt nodded. 'Now I see why it's important.'

Hammerson came around the desk and grabbed his bomber jacket. 'Damn right it's important. And if that's where this thing is going, then we're involved, whether the Turks like it or not. Time to light a fuse.' He pulled on the jacket, its material straining at his shoulders. 'Sam, get me some eyes on what's going on down there. If VELA's still blind from up top, shoot down some pipes.'

CHAPTER 17

Miles above the Earth a satellite bay door opened, displaying dozens of arm-thick matte-black spikes. Eight pipes vented gas and propelled themselves silently away from the large spindly craft. Their destination was set: the Middle East, Turkey, targeting the ancient trading route between Uşak and Izmir.

There were no ignition plumes, no heat signatures or metallic flashes, to give any sort of object profile to the numerous public and military scanning devices that watched the heavens every minute of the day. More gas vented from the pipes' side jets, each second-long burst causing minuscule adjustments to their direction in the upper atmosphere, but translating to hundreds of miles difference in where they would land.

The pipes briefly flamed as they entered the mesosphere. Once through, their outer casings broke away, leaving a dull brown spike to travel the final few dozen miles to the Earth's surface. The spikes readjusted their supersonic descent one last time, selecting landing spots that avoided dwellings, water, rocky outcrops, and any other micro-obstructions. Clear vision was critical.

All the spikes struck the ground along the old trade route, many miles apart, and buried themselves halfway into the soil. Unless someone was standing right in front of them, they simply looked like metal fence spikes that had been abandoned to the elements. Immediately, their small cameras flickered to life.

Hammerson now had his eyes on the ground.

*

In his office, a headset over his iron-gray crew cut, Hammerson paced as he waited to be put through to five-star General Marcus Chilton. Hammerson had known 'Chili' Chilton for many years; the two men weren't close enough to be called friends, but each respected the other's competence and ability to get the job done when others couldn't. Many times, Chilton had used Hammerson and his team to intervene in various places in the world, usually brutally, when diplomacy had failed. In turn, Hammerson knew that if something was important enough, he could by-pass the chain of command and go to the general direct … like now.

Hammerson stopped pacing as the call went through.

'Jack, been hearing your name a lot lately.' Chilton's voice was basement deep.

Hammerson was immediately wary. As the senior officer running a team of ultra-elite Special Forces soldiers, maintaining a zero profile was near mandatory.

'Only good things, I hope, Marcus. How've you been?'

'Good. Just doing my best to avoid war, as always. Getting harder every day.'

'Volatile times, Marcus. But we both know there'll always be war, that's why we're in business,' Hammerson responded matter-of-factly.

Chilton grunted. 'Volatile times indeed. And the more powerful we get, the more we should fear war. It's my burden to fear it on behalf of over 300 million Americans.'

'Glad that's your job and not mine. We *should* fear war, but I'm just a soldier who does his best to make sure the other guy fears it more.'

Hammerson knew he would never be a general; essentially, a military political animal. His problem was he'd never be able to turn the other cheek.

Chilton gave a deep soft laugh. 'And that's why hardheads get to do the hard jobs. I heard you boys kicked some ass in Italy recently.'

Hammerson's jaw clenched; he didn't like the fact that the mission had come onto Chilton's radar. 'Only enough to establish our credentials. We did our job and everyone went home in one piece – no mess.'

'Not everyone. Gianfranco Monti was taken. The Italians are not happy. They knew he was a crook, but he was their crook,' Chilton said.

'The fucking Brits.' Hammerson pressed his knuckles down on the desk. He heard the general shift in his chair.

'And that brings us to why we're talking now ... Istanbul.'

Hammerson waited.

'Still no ideas what's behind these strange events?' Chilton asked.

'None. Chemical, biological, elemental force – we still have no idea, and neither do the Turks. And now they're getting into the thousands dead.' Hammerson remembered the images of the petrified bodies and grimaced.

'I'm aware of the casualties, that's for the Turkish to deal with.' The general's voice became lower. 'There's talk it could it be a new weapon.'

Hammerson began pacing again. 'Unknown, Marcus. Could be. Whatever it is, it's on a collision course with Izmir.'

'Yes, Izmir, that's different. Can't let that chaos happen, can we, Jack?'

'No, sir, we cannot. We need to be over there.' Hammerson stopped pacing, and stared out the window.

'And you should be there,' Chilton said. 'But Turkey isn't Italy, and it's a damn volatile place to kick down doors un-invited. We don't have many people in our corner in the Middle East these days. Turkey's one of them, and we'd prefer to keep it that way. We need a gold pass, Jack. In case things get ... messy.'

Hammerson exhaled. 'I'm working on it. But events are moving faster than my persuasion skills right now.'

'Try again. Don't give your contact a reason to ask for your help, give him a reason to demand it. If it's a weapon, secure it. Anything else, destroy it.'

'That's the plan, sir. One more thing: we now know the Russians are there.'

Hammerson allowed himself a small smile. The silence told him he knew something the general didn't.

'Already?' Chilton exhaled. 'Goddamit, that complicates things. I'll make a few calls, see if we can push that invitation to the top of the queue. Have you got a team together?'

'Yes, sir, the best. We're just waiting on the green light.'

'Good, then I have something extra for you. Something you're not going to like. Took a call from an old military friend of mine from over the water – Sir David Barrington.'

Hammerson groaned. 'Chief of Defense, British Armed Forces.'

'That's him. Seems they've been watching events in Turkey as well. Not surprising given they've got nearly eighty men and women in Izmir. They want to go in, but don't have the contacts we do ... or the ones I've said we do. Jack, I'm hold-ing them back for now. There's absolutely no value in having two separate teams falling over each other.'

Hammerson now knew how the general had managed to be so informed. 'I'll keep them in the loop.'

'You want to be leading this. Either we send a couple of operatives along with their team, or a few of theirs tag along with ours. Make the right call, Jack.'

'Jesus Christ, Marcus. With all due respect –'

Chilton cut him off. 'They've deciphered the inscriptions. They know you're using Professor Kearns. He's good, but they think he's made mistakes. They've got Margaret Watchorn – she can read Minoan like you and I read the Sunday papers. It's in our interest to join forces. It's going to happen with or without you.'

Hammerson exhaled, knowing he'd be sidelined if he pushed any harder. 'Okay, what have they got?'

'You'll find out soon enough; they're already on their way. They're sending us three specialists – two of them SAS. Play nice, Jack.'

Hammerson tilted his head back, shutting his eyes. 'Always.'

'Keep me informed, and be ready.'

Chilton ended the call. Hammerson pulled the headset off his head. *Could be worse*, he thought. *At least the SAS can handle themselves.*

*

'His name is Halim.' Doctor Layla Ayhan flipped a page in the boy's medical chart and handed it to Kemel Baykal. She grimaced. 'He has significant encephelon cell degeneration.'

Baykal read quickly and handed back the chart. 'Brain damage.' His voice was flat.

'Yes. He's moving in and out of a catatonic state, and it's getting worse. The cell destruction is still ongoing. Whatever happened to him is still happening.'

'Did he speak at all?' Baykal looked down at the tiny figure on the bed. Halim's eyes were open, but his face was blank. He held one curled hand up to the side of his head. 'He is the only person to have experienced this thing and survived.'

'He won't survive,' Layla said quickly. 'But yes, he did speak.' She read through her notes and shook her head. 'He said he saw the face of a djinn, an evil spirit. He said it was as tall as a house, and it floated by him.'

'Floated?' Baykal exhaled. 'Why didn't he succumb immediately, like the rest? Can you tell me anything more?'

'What is happening to him, and what happened to all those people, is a mystery,' Layla said. 'Maybe the boy had some sort of temporary immunity. He said it didn't eat him because he didn't look at it.'

Baykal groaned. 'Anything else?'

She shook her head.

'Not much to work with.' Baykal looked at his watch and went to turn away. Her soft voice stopped him.

'Kemel . . . the samples, the flakes you discovered. My colleagues at the university are mystified by their origin. Ankara's top herpetologist says it is probably a reptile scale, but the keratin pattern isn't recognizable in anything living today, or in any fossil record. It doesn't make evolutionary sense, he said.' She shook her head and stepped in close to the large Special Forces commander. 'Kemel, I want you to hand this case over to someone else. Do not pursue this horror. Please, for me.'

He reached up to touch her face with the back of his hand. 'Layla, I must pursue it, *because* of you. If everyone ran from horror, then horror would be everywhere.' He looked back at the small figure, at the curled hand beside his face. He frowned. 'In his hand . . . he's holding something.'

Layla's face fell as she too gazed at the boy. 'Yes; the petrified finger of his mother.'

'Over 2000 dead – women, children, old, young. This thing has a massive appetite.' Baykal's face hardened. 'Perhaps it is time we met it with something a little more formidable.'

'Then I'm definitely not letting you go.' She smiled, taking his hand. 'Not alone anyway.' Baykal shook his head, but she gripped his hand harder. 'I am an excellent field doctor, and the only one who knows what to expect from this thing. I can, and will, help.'

He smiled at last, pulling her closer. 'Modern women – so forceful. Where will it all end?'

*

Hammerson's phone buzzed again. 'What is it, Margie?' he asked.

'Turkey on the secure line.'

'Jesus. I'll take it.'

The line opened out to a scrubbed and scrambled international band, and he heard the heavy breathing of a man under pressure.

'Kemel?'

'Jack, it ends here – we are going in.'

Baykal's voice was heavy with resignation. Hammerson didn't like it.

'One word – don't. There's too much we don't know.'

'*You* don't know? What *do* you know?' Baykal's voice rose a fraction.

'We know this thing is actively seeking out populations to decimate. We know you can't look at it, physically or electronically. We know you're in an evolving and dangerous situation. *You're not ready.*'

Hammerson stared out the window, all his focus on the call. He gripped the phone, and waited. There was only dead air.

'Commander, please, wait one day,' he said. 'We're working as fast as we can. We've got a team –'

'There has been enough waiting,' Baykal cut in, 'and it has resulted in too many dead. The time now is for action.'

'Listen to me,' Hammerson barked.

'Not this time, Jack. If I am right, it is over. If I am not …' He gave a small mirthless laugh, 'I'm sure you will be watching. Learn from my mistakes, my friend.'

The line went dead. Hammerson ground his teeth, gripping the phone hard.

'Stupid, stupid man.' He slammed the phone down, swore, then snorted softly. 'Exactly what I would have done.'

*

Uli Borshov sat hunched over a small table, listening intently to the Russian translation of the intercepted Turkish Special Forces' communications. Behind him, a roll of thick plastic was pushed against a wall; a boot and a bloody foot, minus four toes, were just visible at one end, evidence of the completion of their successful interview with the police informant.

While Borshov listened, he looked at a small computer screen displaying the pictures his men had taken of the deep chamber below the Basilica Cistern. They had entered last night, killing several guards, and searched the site, photographed the writing, the bronze burial urn, and the stone fragments littering the floor, all within four minutes. Then they'd exited like smoke. The strange writing had been sent back to Russia, where it had been identified as Minoan. A linguistics expert had been found via one of their agents in Germany, and Professor Gerhard Reinhalt had translated the script at great expense. He had been told he would be held on a retainer for his services, whether he liked it or not, and warned that if he spoke to anyone about his work, he would be beheaded. Reinhart had been contracted for life ... however long that turned out to be. They had tracked down the dead artifact thief, Janus Caresche, but before they could move to intercept the man's paymaster, the Americans had intervened. They had moved quickly; Borshov knew he needed to move quicker – now more than ever.

He replayed the images from the new Persona satellite, a massive 14,000-pound bird with optical subsystems based on the Korsch-type telescope. Its reach and clarity was matched only by the Americans' VELA series. Borshov had been jolted by the sight of the man standing on the front verandah of the Italian villa. A flash grenade had gone off at his feet, but he'd remained upright, as solid as rock, untroubled by the heat and percussion.

'So, all old friends back in the field again,' Borshov said aloud. 'Maybe I will pay you a visit when this mission over.'

Borshov was about to replay the images again, when a fresh piece of information came from his headquarters. He clicked his fingers to get the attention of one of his men. 'Get the truck ready,' he ordered.

He waved over another of the tall, fearsome-looking Spetsnaz soldiers. The man motioned with his chin to the screen. 'We have a fix on the target?'

Borshov snapped the screen shut and stood. 'Yes. Not sure where exactly, but we have a direction. We need to get closer. Put ourselves in front of it.' He waved a hand around the room. 'Burn everything. We move in five minutes.'

CHAPTER 18

Bill Watkins, a USSTRATCOM technician, watched the multiple monitors displaying Manisa Province, specifically around the outskirts of the small town of Kula. Four of the pipes had landed along a route bordered by volcanic outcrops that looked like gnarled and burned tree trunks, hence the name for the area of the burning lands. One of the pipes had hit solid rock and failed to embed, but the other three were active. The technician slowly rotated the small lens in each, watching up and down the old trade route. He checked the local time and frowned; it was early evening after a cloudless day, yet a fog had started to blow down the rock and dirt roadway.

'Heads-up, got a fog bank coming in over spike 1. I'm gonna go to thermal,' Watkins said over his shoulder to his colleague, who was chewing a drinking straw and watching another spread of pipes further down the trade route.

The straw-chewer shook his head. 'Doubt it. That area has about five percent moisture in the air. More likely it's a truck exhaust. Seen some of the things they drive? I think they burn hay.'

Watkins snorted. 'Maybe, but it's getting thicker ... Hang on, I think there's something inside it.'

He increased the camera's magnification and fiddled with the resolution.

'So, was I right?' his colleague asked. 'Was it a truck?'

'No ... I think it's ...' Watkins shrieked as pain exploded between his eyes. He projectile-vomited a cement-like substance onto his control panel, then fell back out of his chair, clawing at his eyes. 'Jesus, help me!'

The other technician kneeled beside him. No one saw the surveillance screens white out one after the other as the dark shape passed by.

*

Hammerson looked at the figure on the bed; his head was bandaged, he had a drip in each arm, and tubes ran from his throat and nose. He'd been placed in an induced coma to allow the gross swelling of his brain to subside.

Hammerson turned to Major Gerry Harris who was standing silently next to him. 'So, the effects can be telegraphed via electronic media, though they're diluted. That means we can record it, but if we look at it with the naked eye it'll fuck up our internal organs and go blind. That about sum it up?'

'Yep. Strangest thing we've ever seen. Impossible really.'

'Impossible.' Hammerson gritted his teeth. 'Give me something. A theory for Chrissakes.'

Harris shrugged. 'Okay, try this. Basically, light rays first enter the eye through a transparent layer called the cornea, which translates them into electrical signals and sends them to the back of the brain. It's the brain that really does the seeing – the eye is just the window; the brain is the workshop.' He exhaled. 'Some sort of ray, biological vector or chemical substance is coming in through that window and destroying the workshop. Then, given enough time, the entire body.' Harris rubbed his chin. 'You know, I've heard of some sophisticated cyber viruses that can induce epileptic fits or render you unconscious. But this is way beyond anything I've experienced.'

Hammerson grunted. 'So we got nothing.'

Harris' mouth turned down as he looked at the figure surrounded by hissing and beeping equipment. 'Watkins is alive, just. Seems the camera feed, or the distance, or something we just don't know about, diluted the full effects. But yes, seems we still need to work out a way to view it safely.'

'I need to know what we're dealing with. Can the image be cleaned up?'

'Well, if it can be partially filtered, then we just need to work out what defrays the effect and then amplify it. Unfortunately we won't know how effective it is until someone tests it.' He looked up at Hammerson. 'Going to need some volunteers.'

Hammerson grimaced. 'Now there's a crappy job. Leave it with me. And call me the minute you've got something … anything.'

*

Five miles north-east of Salihli, Turkey

Commander Kemel Baykal's stomach roiled. He had organized his men in five twenty-man squads in the low hills surrounding the Izmir–Ankara highway. They were several hundred feet apart on each side of the shimmering roadway in one long killing zone, ready to face down whatever was coming. His men were the best of the best, and would fight to the death – Baykal too. But that wasn't what troubled him right now.

He cursed his own stupidity for allowing Layla Ayhan to accompany them. Though she'd had experience with the victims and her insights were better than anyone else's, this was no place for a civilian. He'd given in to her, allowing her damned persuasive powers to override his training and common sense. *Which head is doing the thinking for you these days?* he wondered as he turned to look at her.

Layla gave him a small salute from under a camouflage net. She had set up a small mobile laboratory and field hospital, and was ready to treat the sick and gather samples. He smiled at her – she was so beautiful. Her advice *would* be valuable.

He looked back toward the city of Salihli. It had been evacuated: 200,000 people dragged or pushed from their homes within a few hours in an emergency order. There were no lights in the windows, even though the sun was sinking now behind the city's buildings. Baykal lifted his powerful field glasses to look over the dark city before scanning the featureless tarmac of the highway. The broad road had been laid over an ancient caravan trail that pre-dated the Persian Empire. In the distance, the road curled out of the slopes of the Bozdag Mountain chain along the southern alluvial plains of the Gediz River. It was the pass between these huge folds in the flat landscape he focused on now.

'Still nothing on the satellite, Keysari?' he asked his captain, who was hunched over a small laptop.

The man shook his head. 'Nothing, sir. Unfortunately we do not have the resolution to pick up something smaller than a large truck.'

Baykal cursed softly. 'Go to flat radar.'

He wished he'd cajoled Jack Hammerson into letting him make use of the Americans' more powerful satellite feeds – their orbiting bird could see inside someone's ear if the they ordered it.

Baykal looked at his Special Forces soldiers camouflaged among the rocks. They were armed with RPGs with both fragmentation and thermobaric rounds, light and heavy machine guns, and just about anything else they could bring in for a rapid deployment scenario. The soldiers he had chosen were battle-hardened veterans with combat experience in the constant brutal skirmishes that took place along Turkey's border – tough, professional, and lethal.

As the sun dipped to become a golden line on the horizon, something began to take form in the distance. Baykal raised the glasses to his eyes again. What looked like a dust cloud with a dark nucleus was moving down beside the road.

'There,' he said.

'What is it?' Layla was kneeling up under the camouflage net.

Baykal waved her back. 'Stay down.'

Keysari's hands moved frantically over his keyboard. 'Just got something on radar horizon, sir. Twenty miles out and coming fast. Solid object ... slowing, slowing ... Doppler says it's down to five miles per hour now.' He looked up. 'Has it spotted us?'

Baykal narrowed his eyes. The Russian RPG-7s had an effective killing range of about 500 feet, but his men were skilled with the weapon and could hit a target at twice that range.

He stood, the glasses still to his eyes. 'Doesn't matter; it'll just be coming within range of the advance squad. Inform Kirmizi team I want a fragmentation barrage – on my count.'

Keysari spoke into the radio, relaying Baykal's instructions.

'Three, two, one ... fire.'

There was a thump of ignition and several three-foot darts raced away from the rocks, clouds of blue-gray smoke trailing behind them. Each almost immediately reached an initial speed of 300 feet per second, but by the time the explosive spears reached their target they were traveling at around 600 feet per second. The miniature missiles all struck the dark nucleus within the swirling mist cloud within the same second, their orange plumes lighting the highway momentarily. Then came the primary blast, which threw out rooster-tails of burning debris followed by a powerful super-sonic shock wave that scattered thousands of lethal fragments in all directions.

Baykal began to smile. 'Very good. Direct hits.'

He was lowering the glasses when Keysari said softly, 'I have contact – movement coming out of the cloud. Moving toward us at five miles per hour.'

'What?' Baykal's jaw clenched. 'Must be armored. Give me a thermo volley. Let's see how good its armor is against a thermobaric warhead and 1000 degrees of hell.'

Once again Keysari counted down, and half a dozen of the high-speed darts flew out from the rocks. In seconds they had crossed the several hundred feet to their target and detonated. This time the warheads contained an explosive that reacted with the surrounding air to generate an intense high-temperature explosion. The blast wave was significantly longer and more destructive than the conventional fragment-ation explosive. A plume thirty feet in diameter lit the land-scape. Baykal crushed his eyes shut against the intense white light and waited for the small motes of stars on his retinas to clear. When he opened them, he held his breath ... and then the eerie body of mist moved on.

'*Shikran!*' Baykal's curse rolled down the slope. 'That thing cannot be allowed to enter the town. Order the squads to advance laying down a field of fire – armor-piercing rounds. Create a wall of steel. I want that accursed thing in a hundred pieces.'

Kirmizi team scurried forward and then took cover, again and again, firing with unerring aim into the center of the mist on the dark highway. The ten Kommandos created an arc around the cloud and fired continuously into its center, until the sound of their gunfire became a continuous roar.

Baykal changed the light spectrum of his field glasses to dark enhancement and saw the green phosphorescent images of his men surrounding the mass on the highway. He switched again to thermal and his men flared red and the road turned orange, the residual heat from the day still leaking into the atmosphere. But the swirling mist with the dark form at its center was as cold and dead as a fish ... or reptile.

A breeze blew up from behind them and the cloud thinned momentarily. Kirmizi squad had continued their advance and were now within a hundred feet of their target as its dark center was revealed. Baykal, still using the thermal spectrum, was too far away to see clearly, but he saw his men's reactions. His lips drew back in a combination of disgust and horror as his Kirmizi team stopped firing and instead grabbed at their throats or eyes. As he watched, the warm red glow of their bodies changed to the cold blue of stone.

'*Ach*. The Prophet protect us.' He shook his head, gulping. 'They . . . they saw it, they saw it ... and then they turned to stone.' He spun to Keysari. 'Have the squads cover their eyes. They must not look at it. We will direct their fire. Switch to tracers so we can monitor the trajectory of the rounds. Quickly, quickly.'

The other teams were within striking distance of the cloud as Keysari sent the communication burst. For many, it was too late. The huge spectral figure left the swirling mist behind and glided toward them. They froze, turning to gray cold stone – new warrior statues in an ancient land.

At the rear, some soldiers fell back, having received Keysari's communication. They pulled strips of material from their uniform or their packs and wrapped it around their heads. Two men advanced, guns up. Baykal watched them through his thermal lens, and spoke quietly and clearly to Keysari, who relayed the information to the men.

'Advance – target directly ahead – fifty paces. Target moving – angle twenty degrees to left flank – target slowing.'

Keysari frowned as he listened in on the microphone attached to one of the two men. 'Commander Baykal, I can hear … I think … *it's weeping.*'

Baykal's jaw set hard for a moment. 'Good, we have hurt it. Proceed.'

Keysari concentrated. 'Five degree adjustment left. Target now twenty paces … ten paces … engage, engage.'

The men fired, their bullets causing flaring orange trails in Baykal's vision as they flew the few feet into the being before them. At first Baykal had thought the thing was some kind of chemical cloud or a biological weapon, but now he saw how wrong he was. The thing dwarfed his men – at least seven feet tall – and had what looked like an overly large head. The rounds entered its core, but didn't stop it, or even slow it.

Keysari's voice rose in panic as he blurted more instructions to the men. 'Closing to two feet, right in front of you, hurry, fire, fire.'

Baykal turned to him. 'Pull them back.'

It was too late. One man threw down his weapon and ripped the mask from his face. Immediately, he threw his hands up before his eyes and froze. The second man lifted a long dark blade from his belt and hacked back and forth; he must have felt the huge presence looming over him, Baykal thought. He watched in horror, and screamed again, 'Pull … them … back!'

The man with the blade was lifted high in the air as though he weighed nothing. A sudden jerk and he was ripped in two, his legs flung one way, his spurting torso the other.

The thing moved quickly now, grabbing another concealed man and tearing away the cloth that bound his eyes. He froze, and was thrown to the ground to shatter into a dozen fragments.

'It knows. It knows it must make them see it.' Keysari's voice was little more than a squeak as more men met the same fate.

As the thing drew closer to his position, Baykal dropped his glasses before he too caught a glimpse of the being's true form. Beside him, Keysari was gagging.

Baykal roared his final instruction. 'I said, pull ... them ... fucking ... back!'

Keysari slumped, turning his face to the sky. 'There's no one left to pull back. It's coming for us.'

Baykal looked over at Layla. Her eyes were wide. All he could do was mouth a single word – *sorry*. She nodded, and started to pack up her things.

'Quickly, send a communication to Colonel Jack Hammerson,' Baykal ordered Keysari. 'Tell him what has happened. Tell him they must not look at it. Anyone who has looked at it has died – turned to stone.' He turned away. 'It is his turn now.'

Keysari sent the communication, and then threw himself flat, sighting along his rifle and firing at will.

Baykal drew his sidearm and looked to Layla. 'You need to go.'

She came to him, ignoring the sounds of gunfire. Her face was wet with tears. She was trying to look brave, but Baykal could see her bottom lip trembled as she spoke. 'It's too late.'

Baykal nodded, and she reached up to hold his face in both her hands. 'I always wanted to give you this.' She kissed him hard on the mouth.

He folded her into his arms. *Give me one more day*, he wished.

He felt needle-like coldness on the back of his neck, and heard Keysari stop firing. He turned to see a grayness creeping along Keysari's body, and the mist rising up over the rocky ledge. In his arms, Layla said a single word – 'oh' – and then he felt her stiffen. He looked down to see her large beautiful eyes mist over, and her body become hard stone in his arms.

It was only then that Commander Kemel Baykal gave up. He turned to look.

*

Jack Hammerson sank down in his seat. On the large wall-screen was an unbelievable image of two figures, like a classical sculpture – a man shielding a woman from some kind of attack, his large arms embracing her, the woman's face just visible under one of his arms, both frozen in a lovers' embrace for eternity.

Hammerson rubbed his face, and then shook his head. His jaws clenched, building pressure, until his fist came down on the desk so hard several items flew to the floor. '*No, fucking dammit, no!*'

He pushed his chair back, got to his feet and paced with one large hand pressing his temples. He turned back to the screen and sighed. 'I'm sorry, Kemel.'

He pulled a handkerchief from his pocket and mopped at the spilled coffee. The phone buzzed on his desk – the secure line. He grabbed the phone up. 'Hammerson.'

'Jack.'

Hammerson straightened at the deep voice – General Marcus Chilton. 'Sir.'

'You're going in. Get your best team together.'

'You got our pass?'

'We'll have it within six hours, from General Necdet himself,' Chilton said.

Hammerson knew of Necdet; he was the commander of the entire Turkish armed forces.

'They still have no answers as to what's decimating their towns,' Chilton continued. 'But that little tidbit you gave me about the Russians being in their yard tipped the balance – they've had enough of Russian interference in the Middle East.'

Hammerson grunted. 'Good.'

'Jack, we can't let this thing get to Izmir. There's a lot at stake and a lot of people watching – I know you won't fuck this up. Iron fists in velvet gloves – you understand?'

'Got it, sir. Diplomacy is my middle name.'

Chilton snorted. 'Not in a million years. We know why you're called "the Hammer". Just make sure you hammer the right things.'

Hammerson smiled without humor. 'And the Brits?'

'They're on your team and on their way now.'

'I'll assess them, sir, and keep you informed.' Hammerson had no intention of using the Brits if they had nothing to offer him.

Chilton disconnected, and Hammerson turned back to the projected image of the petrified couple. 'Better late than never, my friend.'

CHAPTER 19

'One of the most valuable military weapons a soldier can possess is information,' Hammerson told the team gathered in his office. 'Entering a lethal theater of operation with poor quality, too little or wrong data is usually fatal in our game.'

His eyes moved to Alex, who nodded once.

'Turkey has closed its borders – nationwide quarantine, and media blackout,' the HAWC commander continued. 'The death toll is now in the thousands, and they still have no real understanding of what they're up against. At 0800 hours, Special Forces Commander Kemel Baykal led a team in a frontal engagement with ... whatever it is.'

'Magera,' Matt Kearns said softly.

'Magera.' It seemed to Alex that Hammerson was testing the name.

'You said they *led* a team in?' Sam stood at the back of the group, his huge arms folded.

'Yes.' Hammerson's gaze was flat. 'They were wiped out.'

'Commandos?' Sam asked.

Hammerson nodded. 'Eighty high-performance Turkish Special Forces.'

'Fuck me, this thing is a killing machine,' Casey Franks muttered.

Hammerson looked around at everyone in the room. 'We need to learn from their losses. We believe Magera is now making its way to Izmir, and that makes it our problem. And we damn well better come up with a plan, because we're not ready yet.'

'High-altitude drop of a large-scale incendiary device,' Franks said, and shrugged. 'A single non-nuclear MOAB will raise the ground temperature to over 4000 degrees – anything within 500 feet of the detonation point will be vaporized. We know Turkey has that weaponry in their arsenal. We gave it to 'em.'

Hammerson nodded. 'It's on the list. However, much as I like things done in a conclusive way, I can't see the Turkish parliament approving the dropping of the mother of all bombs on their own country.' He folded his arms. 'You need to brainstorm this – we've only got a few hours until go time and there's still too many pieces of the puzzle missing. We need to do better or we'll end up as just more piles of rock in the Turkish landscape.'

Hammerson dismissed the HAWCs and Kearns, but motioned to Alex to stay behind. He closed the door, and waited till the others were visible walking across the training ground to the HAWCs' Nest. Alex could see Franks nudge Matt Kearns hard in the ribs as she spoke. Matt winced and held his side, but nodded and smiled as he listened.

'We're going in, and you'll be leading the team. End of story,' Hammerson said, his eyes boring into Alex's.

Alex looked away. 'I don't know, Jack. You've seen the VELA footage of what happened in Italy. What if I ...' He stopped and shrugged.

'What if you explode? Put the mission at risk? Then maybe I'll have Sam shoot you.' Hammerson's expression turned serious. 'Look, Alex, we don't have time for more training wheels. We know Borshov is on the ground making mischief, and we have a couple of SAS coming in who need to be folded into a single team – ours. And there's something running wild over in Turkey, laying waste to entire villages and heading for our base. I believe you and you alone are the man to get us in front of all three obstacles quickly and effectively. Reid and I agree on this. My question is ... do *you* agree?'

Alex knew that if he said no, he'd be back walking the streets. No more sessions with Marshal, no more chance to get a normal life back, or ever see Aimee or Joshua again. Trepidation added weight to his shoulders, but it was fear for those around him, not himself. He paced over to the window and looked out. He wanted back in, but he needed to prove himself. That was what the HAWCs were for – with them, he would succeed or die. Right now, either outcome suited him.

He turned to Hammerson. 'I'm in.'

Hammerson reached out and shook his hand. 'Good man. We'll break it to the professor gently that he'll be doing a little fieldwork. Franks can set him up.'

*

Casey Franks had given Matt the smallest of the HAWC allover suits she could find. Her own suit was turned down, the sleeves tied around her waist, displaying an upper torso covered in tattoos and scars, and ripped with sinewy muscles.

'Stand up straight, pretty boy,' she said as she walked behind him, then pulled his long hair. 'You look more like a surfer than a soldier.'

Matt snorted; he liked Casey. They'd worked together before, on Black Mountain in the Appalachians, and had formed an easy-going relationship based on a shared sharp and sarcastic sense of humor. He knew the powerful woman was as ferocious as they came – he'd seen her in action. But within that muscled chest, he bet there was a kind heart. He'd just never tell her that.

'You might make a good HAWC one day, Professor.' She slapped his back hard, making him stumble forward.

'Yeah, right.'

Matt knew he was just an advisor, and didn't really want to be anything more. The HAWCs were a singularly aggressive group, intelligent, hard as iron, and capable of dealing with anything anywhere on the planet. He was just thankful they were on his side.

The other HAWCs milled around, some working out with various martial arts blocks or bags, others stripping down pistols, or modifying some piece of weaponry to their own personal preference. Alex and Sam stood over a map, deciding on the mission kit they would need.

Matt rolled his shoulders in the suit. It was made of a material he couldn't identify, supposedly able to offer some resistance to knife penetration. On his frame, it felt hot and restrictive. He contemplated doing what Sam had done – removing the arms of his suit. Matt felt one of his biceps beneath the material – it was athletically muscled, but would look like spaghetti next to Sam's bulging arms ... or even next to Casey's, for that matter. He decided to leave the suit intact.

Casey sauntered to the back of the HAWCs' Nest calling to a few of the other huge soldiers there either stripping weapons or working out.

Matt looked across to Alex Hunter. The man had saved his life on Black Mountain, and then vanished. Matt owed him for that. There was something different about Alex now, he thought. His appearance hadn't changed, but there seemed to be a kind of hollowness inside him; as though his exterior was a suit, like the armor plating he was wearing. Every now and then when he looked at you, you got the feeling there was someone other than Alex Hunter looking back.

Matt looked around at the team of lethal men and women in the hangar-like building. It was an exclusive club, and outsiders were rarely tolerated. *Am I ever the odd one out*, he thought. *What am I doing here?* He'd worked with these guys twice before, or rather he'd ended up being thrown in with them. And both times things had ended up bloody and brutal.

He was making his way over to Sam and Alex when the heavy steel door at one end of the large building was pulled back. Three people entered – two men, one woman; and one of the men was huge. Matt saw Alex stare at them for a half-second, then smile before turning back to the map.

'Our friends from Italy,' he said to Sam.

Sam didn't turn to look. 'The Brits ... already?'

'Yep, and the big one looks like he has an axe to grind.' Alex grinned at the big HAWC. 'He must remember us.'

'Who are they?' Matt asked. He found it hard to look at the men, whose unblinking gaze made him feel like a bug under a lens. However, the woman with them was strangely familiar. Matt tilted his head. 'I know you, don't I?'

She looked him up and down for a few seconds. 'No, you don't. But you must be Professor Matthew Kearns.'

'Yeah, yeah, that's right.' Matt gave her his best boyish grin and stepped forward with his hand out. 'How did you know?'

She didn't reciprocate his action. 'Because you're the only one in here who looks as though he couldn't fight his way out of a paper bag.'

Matt lowered his hand. 'Nice to meet you too, Ms. Charm School. By the way, at college I could bench-press 200 pounds.'

'Great; I'll let you know when I've got a sofa to move.' She moved past him, her hands on her hips. 'Which one of you is Alex Hunter?'

'I think we already know that, don't we, sunshine?' The huge newcomer glared at Alex, his brick-like jaw jutting. There was raw animosity there, Matt thought.

Alex turned to study the trio. Matt could see he was suppressing a grin.

Sam stepped up beside Alex. He was as tall as the giant doing the talking.

The woman glanced at him, then turned to the SAS man. 'Looks like they make them big here too, Jackson.'

Jackson snorted. 'You must be Sam Reid … big as life and,' he looked at Sam's legs, 'still on your fucking feet – if they are your own feet down there.'

Sam folded his arms across his chest. 'You're in our yard. You want to introduce yourself, or would you like me to show you the door?'

Casey Franks came and stood in front of the other two HAWCs. She'd pulled on gloves with plating over the knuckles, and banged one fist into a palm, then placed her fists on her hips. Her glare made it clear she was itching to get in on the action.

Alex put his hand on her shoulder and pulled her back a step, then he looked at the three newcomers. 'Ten seconds.'

The woman folded her arms, her lips compressed defiantly.

After nine seconds, Alex turned away. 'Sam, show them out.'

The smaller of the two men – smaller in that he only stood about six two, Matt noted – shook his head and stepped forward. 'That'll be the pleasantries over with.' He saluted casually and stuck out his hand. 'Sergeant Reece Thompson, Special Air Service Regiment.'

Alex turned back. 'Okay.' He gripped Thompson's hand.

Thompson nodded toward his colleagues. 'The big lug is Corporal Barclay Jackson, also SAS; and the dangerous one doing all the talking is Rebecca Watchorn.' He gave her a look that mixed humor with a warning. 'Advisor … and resident angry ant to boot.' He turned back to Alex. 'I was told we'd be expected.'

Matt snorted. 'Watchorn? Not related to Margaret Watchorn?'

'Margaret is my great-aunt,' Rebecca said, keeping her eyes on Alex. 'She told me to tell you that your Minoan is passable at best.'

Barclay Jackson's eyes continually moved between Alex and Sam. He was up on his toes.

Sam angled his head toward him. 'Something on your mind?'

Sam took a step forward, and so did Jackson. They were both cut from the same mold, Matt thought: big, fit men who were trained to be lethal killers.

'Yeah, there is,' Jackson said. 'You both deserve to have your arses kicked after that fucking stunt in Italy. But I reckon if I wipe the floor with you, the freak will jump me again.' He motioned to Alex with his chin.

'Kick my *arrr*-se?' Sam drew out the English pronunciation, then snorted. 'It's ass, you asshole. And *you* kick it? Not today, boy, and not ever.'

Alex laughed softly and nudged Sam. 'Freak? Looks like they do know me, after all. Bonding session over. Let's get down to it. What you got for us, Ms. Watchorn, gentlemen?'

'You first,' Rebecca said.

'Go home.' Alex turned to walk back to the map table.

'Wait.' Thompson let out an exasperated breath and looked at the woman. 'You want to lay it out? Or, I swear, you'll be on the next plane home.'

Rebecca's lips stayed compressed for a few seconds. Then, 'Fuck it,' she said. 'By now you know we're dealing with Magera?'

Alex nodded. 'We've heard the name, but as yet we don't know what it is exactly. Neither do the Turks.'

'Professor Kearns, we know you read the Minoan carved into the lower chambers. What did you make of it?' Rebecca tilted her head as she waited for Matt's reply.

He shrugged. 'It was strange – didn't make a lot of sense. *Fear is risen again, children of Zeus, slayers of ...*' He grimaced. 'Slayers of something, and then, *be forever locked in stone ... Magera will consume ...* That's all we could decipher. At least from the angles we had available to us.'

Rebecca nodded, as though only partially satisfied with his analysis. 'Okay then, let's lay out the facts ... and perhaps make some intuitive, but educated leaps.' She put her hands on her hips and began to pace.' I think Emperor Constantine captured something in Sarmatia –'

'Captured?' Alex repeated, frowning.

'Yes. And it cost him over a thousand dead soldiers. And what happened to them directly relates to what's happening now.'

She raised her eyebrows to Matt, who frowned and folded his arms.

'What? How do you know what happened? There's no record of it anywhere.'

Rebecca rolled her eyes. 'The world does not revolve around us in the West, much as we'd like to think so. Consider the Scythians or Sarmatians, Sauromatians or however you want to pronounce them – they were a warlike race that flourished for around 800 years, an enormous stretch of time in a barbaric and violent world. And their territory was huge, from Iran to southern Russia, and even into the Balkans.'

Matt nodded. 'I agree. They weren't particularly advanced, but I think they might have had superior weaponry ... or a weapon. Which was what Constantine retrieved.'

Rebecca came and stood in front of him. 'Or something ... alive. And without it, they were nothing. There are historical records of the Sauromatians rising to power in the fifth century BC, and then abruptly crumbling around 300 AD – the time of Constantine's campaign.'

'That's right – 334 AD to be exact,' Matt said.

She tilted her head. 'From the codex, right?'

He nodded. 'And your proof?'

'The bodies left behind. Russian archeologists first found a reference to the fallen warriors of stone on pottery shards in Iran; which led them to the statues themselves. At first they thought they were the work of some great Roman sculptor, so great was the detail. They made China's terracotta warriors look like Pottery Barn knockoffs. They performed an MRI on the artefacts – each soldier was perfect down to eyelashes, scars, and even internal organs. All made of stone. No one's ever been able to explain them. Then the Russians did what they always do when they find something that's beyond them – they hide it away until an answer presents itself. So now they're all packed up and stored away in the basement of the State Hermitage Museum in Saint Petersburg.' She shrugged. 'And forgotten.'

'How do you know this?' Alex asked.

'Margaret, my great-aunt, has been studying the Minoans all her life,' Rebecca said. 'The language, the people, the culture – it was as beautiful as it was mystical. But what intrigued her most was the evidence of them turning up in odd places – Japan, Italy, the Middle East, Russia. The Minoan culture, the mightiest on earth in its day, collapsed and disappeared, seemingly without reason. Some of the remnant Minoans must have scattered – fled, or perhaps they were led away.'

'To Sauramatia,' Matt said softly. 'How did your aunt find them?'

Rebecca smiled. 'She used her detective skills and contacts, and something else we modern types hardly ever use anymore – books!'

Alex grunted. 'I guess those statues were just an unexplained oddity ... until now.'

'Until something happened in the Basilica Cistern in Istanbul,' Rebecca confirmed. 'Where Emperor Constantine secreted or imprisoned Magera, or its remains. You see, I don't think Janus Caresche stole what he found in there. I think he somehow . . . freed it.'

Casey Franks scoffed. 'You reckon it was still alive after nearly 2000 years? That's bullshit, babe.' She tilted her head. 'What is it you do exactly, Ms. Watchorn?'

Rebecca met Casey's flat stare. 'I teach at Cambridge University – both evolutionary biology and anthropology, specializing in myths and pre-Christian religions. And yes, it's my belief that something came out of that urn, even after 2000 years, that's not like us, or like any other living thing on this planet.'

Casey gave a hard laugh. 'Some*thing* came out of the urn, by itself? Really? I thought we were looking for a weapon.'

Rebecca shrugged. 'It might be a weapon – in the wrong hands.'

'Oh, for fuck's sake.' Casey turned away.

'Let's hear her out,' Matt said, his own mind buzzing. 'After all, reptiles and some fish can hibernate for decades. Why not something unique hibernating for even longer?'

Rebecca smiled at Matt. 'Thank you. So, let's back up a moment and talk about some historical events. You're up, Professor: tell us what you know about Gorgons.'

'Gorgons? The three cursed sisters?' He looked at Alex, who nodded. 'Ah, okay.' He looked to the roof as he searched his memory. 'Okay, let's see. The most famous Gorgon was Medusa, but she also had two sisters, Stheno and Euryale. All three were the daughters of the Titans, giant beings of immense strength, who were eventually overpowered by Zeus. Originally, the Gorgons were priestesses to the goddess of wisdom, Athena. However, Poseidon, the god of the sea, lusted after the beautiful Medusa. She repelled him, but he raped her inside Athena's temple – a huge insult to the goddess.' He paced as he warmed to his subject. 'Athena blamed Medusa for Poseidon's act and for the defiling of her temple – some legends say that Athena was jealous of Medusa's beauty. Anyway, she turned Medusa and her sisters into horrifying beasts with scaly skin, needle-like teeth, and dozens of coiling snakes for hair. In a final act of revenge, Athena made sure no man could ever look upon Medusa again. Anyone who did would be instantly turned to stone.'

'Right, that's the legend,' Rebecca said. 'Now let's imagine for a moment that it's not a legend. Let's analyze it based on the new evidence, as if it's a historical account.'

Alex raised his eyebrows. 'Turned to stone.' He turned to Sam. 'Remember the reptile scale embedded in the wall of the deep chamber below the cistern? Fits, sort of.'

Sam nodded, picking up Matt's thread. 'According to the legends, Medusa was killed by Perseus, who was given gifts by the gods to do so – winged sandals, a helmet of invisibility, and Athena's own silver shield. Perseus avoided looking at Medusa directly by using the shield to see her reflection and so didn't get turned to stone. He cut off her head and gave it as a gift to Athena, who placed it in the center of the protective shield on her armored breastplate.'

Rebecca looked impressed. 'Very good, big guy. Brains and brawn.'

'The face of Medusa is still used today to ward off evil,' Matt added.

'Superstition,' Alex said.

Rebecca nodded. 'Sure, superstition, magic, myth – but if you take any myth back to its roots, you find the kernel of truth. There's always a genesis event, even if it changes and evolves over millennia, and I guarantee something like that created the myth of the Gorgons. We need to keep an open mind, and use current technology to work it out.'

'Well, yesterday's magic is tomorrow's science,' Matt said. 'The Gorgon faces in the Basilica Cistern – they were there to guard something. Or to warn against something.'

'That's a big help,' Casey scoffed. 'Could they have made it any more fucking obscure? Why didn't they just write in big Roman letters, *stay the fuck away?*'

'Well, obscure to us, but perhaps not to someone in 300 AD,' Matt said. 'Or maybe they wanted it to be obscure. Maybe Constantine didn't want anyone going looking for Magera, or finding it. Now we know why.'

Alex nodded. 'So, Medusa was beheaded, but what happened to the other sisters?'

Matt shrugged. 'They vanished from the formal mythological record. There are vague references to them being scattered to the four corners of the world. There are ancient tales of snake-headed women in Japan, India, the Middle East, Russia, dozens of countries; and there's certainly evidence of stone man syndrome down the millennia too. Just bits and pieces though.'

Rebecca pointed at Matt's chest. 'Think harder, Professor. We need to broaden our search. There might be clues we're failing to see. There's Aboriginal rock art in Australia showing images of snake-headed creatures dating back 40,000 years; but the earliest formally recorded information is in Crete. I still think that's the source.' She began pacing again. 'You know, there are deep caves all through Greece and Crete, some displaying evidence of structures dating back many thousands of years – some even pre-dating the Minoans. And there was evidence of habitation down there. As well as the usual artifacts, the archeologists found things that they simply termed Cretan troglodytic anomalies.'

There was silence in the large hangar as Rebecca looked around the group.

'Boo!' Casey Franks said, then burst into laughter as Matt jumped. 'Something living there? Yeah, people. That's why they used to call them cave men.'

'Not *just* people,' Rebecca said coldly.

'So what then?' Casey asked.

Rebecca didn't answer; she just raised her eyebrows at Matt.

He rubbed his chin. It sounded crazy, but he'd thought the Sasquatch was a myth until he'd come face to face with one on Black Mountain. 'If the Gorgons actually existed, surely they'd all be dead by now?'

'Or in hibernation,' Alex added, 'like whatever was in that bronze urn in Turkey.'

Rebecca nodded. 'Hibernation . . . waiting to be set free again.' She tilted her head at Alex. 'So, how about you guys let us in on what you have?'

Sam and Matt looked to Alex, who slowly shook his head. 'We don't know much more than you just told us. And the reason for that is, no one does. The Turkish military and science teams are in the dark on this. We still haven't had access to all their autopsy records, but obtaining them is a priority. When we know how the creature is killing, we can work out how to defend ourselves against it.'

Reece Thompson grunted. 'The Turks are the only ones on the ground, and so far their strategy seems to be to get out of its way.'

Alex nodded. 'Makes sense – observe, gather data, identify weaknesses. But we can't let them continue with that strategy. Bottom line is, it's heading for Izmir, and we're not going to let it get there. Added to that, the Russians are on the ground, and now in front of us.' He raised his eyebrows. 'Spetsnaz ... and worse.'

Thompson winced.

Rebecca threw her arms up. 'Great. So let me sum this up: we've got something called Magera that might or might not be a weapon, or might or might not be a Gorgon, turning people to stone, and it's unstoppable. However, we're sitting on our hands over here, but the Russians have some sort of super hit-squad already in there.'

Alex smiled. 'That's about it.'

Rebecca glared at him. 'Then we're stuffed.'

Casey Franks glared back. 'It's been beaten before, the prof said – some guy cut its head cut off. I'm happy to provide that level of surgery myself, even without an invisible helmet.' Her lips curled into a ruthless smile.

Matt grinned. 'That's a helmet of invisibility, not an invisible … Oh, forget it. Look, it might not be that straightforward. Yes, Medusa was beheaded, but the Gorgons had different powers and … tastes. Medusa turned you immediately to stone, but others liked to torture their victims first, then eat their flesh, and others only appeared during a full moon. We don't know what Magera does specifically.'

'We know we can't look at it directly, even electronically,' Alex said. 'One of our technicians suffered some sort of seizure just by seeing its image remotely. That happens in the field, we're all dead.' He began to turn away. 'We're not ready.'

Sam nodded. 'Agreed. We need more intel. Don't like the idea of dropping in and then fighting blind. Or even trying to fight a reflection and then finding out that strategy doesn't work with Magera.'

Casey Franks snapped to attention, staring straight ahead. 'Officer on the floor.'

Colonel Jack Hammerson strolled toward them, and all the HAWCs came to attention. Even the SAS soldiers, Thompson and Jackson, stood erect and saluted.

'At ease, people.' Hammerson walked in between them, hands clasped behind his back. 'All good here?'

'Sharing information, sir.' Alex had a slight smile on his lips.

Hammerson stopped in front of Sergeant Reece Thompson. 'Good, because it seems to me we've all got pieces of the same puzzle. At ease, soldier.'

Thompson dropped the salute. 'Sir, perhaps there are too many holes for it all to fit together just yet.'

Hammerson shook the SAS man's hand. 'Good to have you with us, even though it seems to have been a little forced.'

'We'll try and keep up, sir,' Thompson responded.

'You better do more than just try, soldier.' Hammerson half-smiled and turned to Jackson. He shook his hand, then stood in front of Rebecca.

'I was told we needed to join you so we could get this mission moving,' she said. 'Seems all the movement is around in circles. You guys know less than we do.'

'Pleased to meet you too, Ms. Watchorn.' Hammerson smiled flatly, and walked a few paces away from the group so he could take them all in. But Matt saw his eyes were on Rebecca as he spoke. 'So why don't you help us poor dumb Yanks out and tell us exactly what we're dealing with?'

Rebecca shook her head. 'No one knows. At least, no one living today.' Her eyes held a hint of mischief. 'But I bet a centurion of the fifth cohort knew.'

'The codex – the second half.' Matt shook his head. 'We don't have it.'

'I know you don't ... because we do.'

CHAPTER 20

Within fifteen minutes, they were all gathered in Hammerson's office, and the second page of the codex was projected onto the large wall-screen. Matt and Rebecca hunched over the parchment itself, a large magnifying glass between them.

Matt nudged her. 'You can't read it, can you?'

Rebecca pursed her lips, then smiled. 'Just a word here and there. Margaret's not well. We could have spent days finding another translator, or …' She shrugged.

'Or do the right thing and bring it to us.' Matt smiled back. 'But how the hell did you get it? Not from Monti?'

Hammerson looked from Thompson to Sam from underneath lowered brows. 'That's what I'd like to know.'

Sam shook his head. 'Monti had nothing else. Believe me, if he did, he would have given it up.'

The SAS soldier grinned. 'Yeah see, that's what happens when you blunder in and crap all over everything. You can miss the important stuff.'

Sam's jaw jutted and Thompson snorted. He held up a hand to Sam's glare. 'Ease up big fella; you were right, he gave you everything he had. But what he didn't tell you was where he got the codex page, and what else he left behind. Mr. Gianfranco Ruffino Monti happily informed us that he'd obtained the first page on the Greek black market, and...'

'And it seems the price for the second sheet was exorbitant, but he didn't think he needed it anyway.' Rebecca folded her arms and paced towards Thompson. 'He felt he had enough information to confirm there was a high-value artifact to re-cover in Istanbul, and sent Caresche on his mission.' She turned and nodded for her colleague to continue.

'That's about it.' Thompson half smiled at the interruption. 'Monti just needed to be persuaded to tell us who the seller was.'

Sam folded tree trunk like arms. 'And let me guess; you guys went over there and splashed all that Euro funny money around. Nice to have deep pockets.'

Thompson smiled grimly. 'No money changed hands.'

Rebecca placed a hand on Thompson's shoulder. 'The ser-geant can be very persuasive.' She raised an eyebrow. 'And he wouldn't take no for an answer.'

Casey Franks winked. 'Yep, we know how that works.'

Hammerson folded his arms and turned to Matt and Rebecca, who had resumed her seat. 'Good. Now let's hear again from our centurion friend. He's been waiting nearly 2000 years to tell us something important.'

'Sure. Just need to make sure it all checks out okay.' Matt used forceps to drag the first page of the codex across and align it with the second – the fibers lined up perfectly. He hunched over the parchment again with the magnifying glass. 'Looks good – the papyrus has the right amount of aluminum salts in the fibers. Also the edges line up to form a single long roll. In my opinion, it's the real deal.' He cleared his throat. 'Okay, here we go . . . it picks up with the blinded priests ...'

Constantine dismounted, and his Praetorian Guard formed up either side of him. I fell in behind, along with Titus and Varinius.

Sauramatia had been subdued, but there was one strong-hold not yet fully under our control: the citadel in the center of the walled city. It was built of mud-brick, strong, and ancient. Several priests lay dead at its entrance. Others were kneeling, their empty eye sockets turned toward us, as though seeing without their orbs. They were of strange appearance: their heads were shaven, and their skulls heavily tattooed with raised markings that gave the appearance of blue ropes constantly coiling across their heads. These men were fanatics, and some had gone so far as to nail themselves to the stout wooden door to the temple.

Andronicus, a centurion charged with taking the city, stood bloody and weary, but his eyes still burned with the fury of war. 'No one has yet entered, my Emperor.'

Caesar placed a hand on his filthy shoulder. Such was this great man, never fearing the grime of battle. He looked into Andronicus' face. 'The priests – have they spoken?'

'Yes, sire. They say they will die before standing aside.'

Constantine looked over the wretched beings. 'Not this day. Free those men nailed there.' He then motioned to the translators. 'Tell them we are the mightiest power in the world and we will enter their temple. Tell them Sauramatia has fallen, and they are alone. We will care for them now; all will be treated with respect.'

The three translators conferred, as if deciding on the right words. One of them spoke to the priests; the tongue was harsh and grating, spitting words like sharp chips of stone.

Many of the priests began to wail; others simply fell forward and rubbed their faces into the dirt. But there was one, taller than the rest, who stood at the very center of the massive door, his chin up, his black eye sockets trained on Constantine. His own words poured forth, and the translators listened and responded, seeming to rebuke him.

'Speak!' Constantine's word cut the air and made the translators cringe. 'Tell me what he says – all of it.'

The three men looked pained. At last one swallowed and then spoke. 'His name is Hemlagh, the chief priest. He says they do not fear you, or us, or death. He says your power is nothing but a blink of the eye, and Caesar is a flea compared to their mistress. They fear you not, but they do fear for mankind if she is freed.'

'She?' Constantine looked from his translators to the priest. 'Magera?'

Hemlagh's lips became thin, and then he nodded.

Constantine looked up at the sky. Crows wheeled above us, cawing impatiently, waiting to feed on the mounds of dead throughout the city.

Our Emperor exhaled. 'Tell them they are free. Tell them to stand aside and no one will be hurt. Magera is now the property of Rome.'

The tall priest responded in the lingua latīna.

Matt looked up at Hammerson, gauging his understanding.

'Latin, I get it.' The HAWC commander waved him on.

'Your property? No. Your curse,' Hemlagh said. 'If you have gods and fear them, you know what becomes of mortals who defy them. Enter if you wish, Caesar, but do so knowing that man is a bug before the Gorgos.'

Constantine pointed at the door and its single long bolt as thick as a man's leg. 'Open it.'

One of his generals, Titus, stepped in front of him. 'My Emperor, let me enter first.'

Constantine looked as if he were about to object, but he glanced back to me, and I nodded. It would not be brave but foolish for our Emperor to enter an unknown place.

The great bolt was drawn back, and Titus covered his lower face as a draft of humid air escaped. Those nearby also covered their faces, such was the stench.

Hemlagh sucked in the air, his hollowed face rapturous. 'The scent of a God.'

Titus coughed. 'The scent of death.' He drew his sword, and crouched down to see past the thick walls of stone bordering the doorframe. He called over his shoulder for a flame. A burning torch was handed to him, and he glanced back once, before ducking under the heavy lintel.

We waited several long minutes for him to reappear. Just as our patience was stretching, there came a coughing sound from the doorway. A figure stepped out: Titus, but not the Titus who had entered only minutes before. His face and entire being were pale, not with illness or fear, but something worse. He staggered painfully toward us, staring, but not seeming to see. His mouth opened, but no words came. Instead, he uttered a gurgling sound followed by a rush of liquid stone.

I was first to him, placing an arm around his shoulders. To my shame, I recoiled, for I did not touch flesh and blood, but skin as hard and cold as a column of stone.

While we watched, his paleness became absolute, and even his dark eyes frosted over to a milky whiteness. Now down on all fours, he raised his face to our Emperor one last time, his face twisted in hellish agony. And then he froze.

We did too, in horrified silence, as mute as Titus, now turned to stone. Our eyes lifted to the door of the citadel, and we waited, expecting some monster to emerge.

Bit by bit, the world crept back – a tiny whisper of wind rustling a standard banner, a crow calling high overhead, the snorting of a horse.

Constantine breathed out the first words. 'Those who behold the Gorgos will be forever imprisoned in stone.'

A new sound began – small at first, but rising. The tall priest, Hemlagh, was laughing, but there was no humor in it.

He spoke again in our tongue. 'She will lay waste to all of you.'

Titus' body was wrapped in a rug and removed. Constantine ordered that no one was to speak of him to the men. Next he had his Praetorian Guard line up before the door. Each soldier was half a head taller than any normal man, his iron-hard body encased in gleaming armor. All stared into the dark doorway, waiting for the word.

Constantine stood before the priest and placed his hand on the man's shoulders. He looked deep into the dark eye sockets. 'She comes with us, or she burns.'

Hemlagh shook his head. 'You cannot kill her. You cannot take her. She needs us. She has promised to take us all to heaven in her golden chariot.'

Constantine narrowed his eyes. 'Where she goes, you go. You may continue to serve her.'

Hemlagh remained silent, and Constantine leaned in closer. 'I did not come here to kill her. Tell us how to ... save her.'

Hemlagh's head turned to the open doorway. 'Kill her? She and her kind have walked this world since before we men rose from the dust. She will be here long after we and all our kind are food for the worms.' He turned back to Constantine. 'But without the warriors to serve us, we can cannot serve her. We must go with you.'

Constantine nodded. 'Good man. Now tell us how the mighty Magera can be controlled.'

'With words, not swords. You must ... sing to her.'

Matt sat back. 'This is it.'

Hammerson's forehead creased. 'Huh? Sing to her? What the hell does that mean?'

Matt found his place, and continued reading.

Hemlagh began to sing in a language that was like nothing any of us had ever heard. It was not beautiful, nor lyrical, more like the sibilant hissing of a serpent. Still singing, the tall priest entered the citadel, and bade Constantine to follow.

Against my advice, he entered the dark doorway, and I, along with his guards, rushed to follow.

The only light inside the large domed room came from the sputtering torch dropped by Titus. In the gloom, I could make out a large throne upon which a lone figure sat. It was tall, taller than the biggest man in our entire army. I have faced death a dozen times on this campaign alone, but in the presence of this thing I felt my knees weaken and an illness boil in my belly.

Thankfully, it seemed to sleep, and I pulled all my courage together and stepped closer. What at first I took to be a crown was a mass of thick sightless worms, each with a mouth of its own, continually opening and closing as if tasting the air – no, tasting us. The face was scaled, and though it had features, they were not at all like our own. There were two eyes, closed thankfully, and a double slit for a nose, which flapped open as breath rushed in and out. The mouth, slightly open, was a circle of gristle, like a single lip, and inside rows of needle-like teeth were just visible.

Even our mighty Caesar was sickened by the sight. I half-turned to him, not wishing to look away entirely lest the creature spring to life in that moment. I whispered my words. 'Kill this foul thing now.'

Hemlagh had continued to sing softly, but on hearing my words, he stopped and turned his sightless face toward me. 'Kill Magera? You could not. The Gorgos cannot be cut, or burned, or drowned. She lifts herself from the ashes, reassembles herself from the blade, and rises again, more powerful and vengeful than ever. She is truly a god.'

Caesar's features were drawn in disgust. 'Maybe it is a god to some. And perhaps it knows of other gods.'

Magera shifted, and Hemlagh began to sing again.

Caesar turned away. 'If the thing wakes, its gaze will kill us.' He spoke to his guard. 'Bind it ... cover its head.'

And so Magera became Emperor Constantine's possession, burden, and curse. The priests sang to it constantly, taking turns to keep the creature in a stupor.

The long journey home took many months, and we lost many men – not by sword, or ambush, or misadventure, but by a sickness that affected us all, and seemed to suck the life from us. Some woke with a rash, that eventually opened and ran with black blood. Others shrank down to their bones, no matter how much they ate; and others went mad, biting at their fellow soldiers. It was as if Magera drew our souls from our bodies.

When Constantine asked where the being had come from, Hemlagh pointed skyward. 'Caelestis,' he said, then, 'Creta. She came from Caelestis to live in the Caverns of Zeusa.'

Matt sat back and rubbed his hands through his hair. 'Caelestis – heaven. And they lost 5000 men on their march home.'

Rebecca frowned. 'Sounds like some sort of virus or transmitted disease.'

'Or something from Magera,' Alex said. 'Something it radiates.'

Matt ran his eyes down the rest of the scroll. 'That's pretty much it. A bit more about the arduous trip home, and then it ends.'

Hammerson exhaled. 'Let's see what we've got. Constantine captured this … Magera nearly 2000 years ago. He brings it back to Constantinople, now Istanbul, and hides it deep under the Basilica Cistern. Janus Caresche somehow wakes it up, sets it free, and now it's stalking the Turkish landscape and turning anything in its path into stone.' Hammerson placed one hand on his forehead. 'I feel nuts just saying that out loud. I can't take that to the brass.'

Matt shook his head. 'Amazing; the legend of the Gorgon … not a legend at all. They're freakin' real.' He rubbed his face. 'The song must have hypnotized it – you know, the same way you can hypnotize snakes. I've seen it.'

'But we don't know the words or the tune,' Sam said, folding his massive arms.

Alex paced toward the screen. 'No, but we do have a place to start. Creta is Crete, right?' He turned to Matt. 'Okay, Brains, where are the Caverns of Zeusa?'

Matt snorted. 'That's an easy one.' He pulled up a map on the wall-screen and started to drill down toward Greece. 'The Caves of Zeus are part of a large system excavated in Crete in 1886 on the Lasithi Plateau. Today we refer to them as the Psychro Caves. There are signs of human visitation there dating back tens of thousands of years.'

'And they're deep,' Rebecca added. 'Mostly explored, but there are collapsed passages that are now closed off to the public. A lot of relics were taken from the caves in the late 1800s – there might be some clues there.'

'Collapsed passageways?' Alex repeated. 'Maybe there's evidence of this thing still down there somewhere ... buried. Who knows how old Magera was . . . is? If it had already been alive for a long time when Constantine came across it, it must operate on a different chronological plane to us.'

Matt nodded. 'Remember the words scratched into the wall? They were Minoan. And the Minoans were established as a great race at least 5000 years ago.' He looked around at the others, excited. 'You know, it all actually fits. The first people in Crete were Neolithic, then came the Minoans who worshiped cave deities. Maybe the priest in the codex was singing in Minoan – I mean, it was a dead language even by the time of Constantine.'

'I can't believe I'm saying this,' Sam said slowly, 'but maybe it truly is an immortal.'

Matt got to his feet and started pacing. 'Okay, stay with me here . . . but how about a wild theory? When Hemlagh was asked where Magera came from, he pointed skyward and said, "*Caelestis*".' Sam groaned, but Matt waved him to silence. 'Did he mean heaven, Olympus? Maybe. Certainly fits with Greek mythology. But … but what if he meant something more than that? What if he meant somewhere higher, much higher, like the stars?'

Sam covered his face with his hands and shook his head. He spoke from between his fingers. 'Yeah, maybe it's a Klingon.'

Rebecca rolled her eyes at Matt. 'Don't you dare go there, Professor.'

Alex held up his hand. 'All theories are worthwhile right now. Go on, Matt.'

Matt smiled, and shrugged. 'There's no such thing as immortality … on Earth.'

Hammerson folded his arms. 'I'm not convinced. Sure, the priest pointing skyward is interesting, but not even mildly conclusive. Even I know that to the ancient Greeks Olympus *was* up in the stars.'

'But Hemlagh wasn't a Greek,' Matt said. 'And there's more that points toward something other than a Greek legend. The gods of the Minoans were mostly women – they had goddesses for fertility, the harvest, animals, the city, the household, and one we should be most interested in, the underworld.' Matt looked around the group. 'A serpent goddess.'

Rebecca tilted her head back and scoffed. 'Interesting, Professor, but not science. I can tell you right now that most mythological-based religions – the Greeks, Romans, Cretans, Egyptians, Vikings – involved an *axis mundi*, a heavenly cosmic center. No one stepped out of a flying saucer.'

Alex switched off the wall-screen. 'Well, I think we've got all we're going to get from the codex. I'm not convinced this thing is from anywhere other than right here, on Earth.'

He looked at Matt. 'I do, however, think it could be some sort of creature not seen for thousands of years – perhaps it's just come out of hibernation, or was reanimated somehow. Sounds strange, but we've dealt with plenty of strange stuff before.'

Hammerson nodded, smiling grimly.

'Everything points to this Magera thing being the genesis for the Gorgon myth,' Alex continued. 'Not sure how that helps us, if at all, but at least it's given us somewhere to start. Now it's time to fill in the blanks and find some way to take it out.'

Matt stepped forward, about to speak, then stopped.

'Well, go on … spit it out, son,' Hammerson said.

Matt cleared his throat. 'It's just . . . before we try and kill it, we need to consider that this thing, or being, or whatever it is, has to have intelligence. I'm convinced we could communicate with it first; maybe even instead of killing it.'

Hammerson glared. 'Really? So far, anyone who's got close enough to say "how you doing" gets turned to goddamn stone. Last I checked, communication was a two-way street. So far, Magera's only form of communication is death.'

Sam smiled without humor. 'Maybe after sleeping for nearly 2000 years, it just woke up in a bad mood.'

Matt rolled his eyes. 'Just promise me one thing. If we can work out the words, or song, or whatever the priests used to subdue it, you'll give us a chance to try it?'

Alex's voice was unyielding. 'No.'

Matt turned to Hammerson. 'Colonel, not every problem has a military solution. Just … keep it in mind.'

Hammerson was silent for a few seconds, then nodded. 'Gentlemen, never hurts to have more options than we need. But just so we're all clear: the primary option is termination.'

Alex and Sam nodded, and Matt half-bowed. 'That'll do. Thank you.'

'One more thing, Professor Kearns.' Hammerson's eyes were unblinking. 'In my experience, every problem *does* have a military solution.' He went to the phone on his desk, and began punching in numbers. 'I'll get your rides fueled up. Professor Kearns and Ms. Watchorn, you'll be going to Crete to look for clues among the recovered artifacts, and also to scope out the Psychro Caves. Thompson, you're going with them. Hunter, you'll take Reid, Franks, and our other guest into Turkey, to stand in front of Magera. Put your team together, and be on the pad and ready to go in an hour.' He paused and looked at Alex. 'Don't forget that you'll probably have Borshov at your back. Dismissed.'

At the mention of the Russian's name, Matt saw Alex's face change, as if suddenly there was someone else looking out through his eyes. Matt recognized the look: up in Canada once, he'd seen two huge wolves face off over a deer carcass. Before they tore each other to shreds, there was a look that passed between them – unblinking, focused, and without fear. Then the two massive bodies had hurled themselves together in a brutal fight to the death.

These guys are a different species all right, he thought. He was glad he was going to Crete.

CHAPTER 21

Alex and Sam led Corporal Barclay Jackson, Casey Franks, and HAWCs Ben Rogers and Steve 'DK' Dankirk, to the secure elevator that would take them down to the R&D facility several stories below the USSTRATCOM base. Even though the elevator could operationally accommodate ten, it would be filled by the bulk of these six.

'Form up,' Alex ordered, and they came to attention. Alex walked along the line, looking each soldier in the face. He stopped in front of Casey Franks – he knew and trusted her, and had been in the field with her before. She'd leap into a furnace if he asked her to. At five nine, she was half a head smaller than most HAWCs but he knew that under her suit she was all gristle, corded muscle, and tattoos. And she could fight like the devil itself.

Alex nodded to her. 'Franks.'

'Sir.' Her eyes slid briefly to meet his. There might have been a small smile too, but it was quickly replaced by a hint of suspicion. It was hard to tell with the scar on her cheek pulling her face up on one side.

He moved on to Rogers and Dankirk – two blocky midwesterners, both Sam's choice. Alex had read their charts –

both had good histories in the Rangers and SEALS. They had the right experience and excelled out in the field.

'Rogers, Dankirk. You know where we're going?' Alex asked.

'Hell and back, sir,' they responded in unison.

It was the standard HAWC response. Basically it didn't matter which hellhole or meat grinder they were dropped into; they'd enter, win, and then vanish like smoke. *Leave with a smile and a shoeshine*, as Hammerson always said.

Alex nodded, and moved on to Barclay Jackson. The SAS man stood a couple inches taller than him. He had scars on his cheek that ran down underneath his chin – evidence of a brutal life.

'Jackson, I don't know you yet, or what you can do,' Alex said. 'The moment we step on that plane, we cease to exist on paper – we're effectively dead. But if you fuck up in the field, then you might get us all dead, real dead. I'm not going to let that happen. Understand?'

The man's eyes never wavered. 'I'll keep up.'

'Damn right you will.'

Once again, the technician, Walter Gray, met them as they exited the elevator.

He rubbed his hands together when he saw Sam. 'Lieutenant Reid, good to see you again.' He smiled briefly at the others, and then looked at Alex, who nodded, then continued down the sterile white tunnel. The others fell in behind him.

Gray walked fast to keep up. 'Er, Lieutenant Reid ... Sam, how's the combat harness?'

Sam didn't slow, but looked down. 'Good. Fair bit of weight, but manageable.'

Gray was walking in a crouch, peering at Sam's lower half. He reached out to touch Sam's leg, but Sam batted his hand away, then grabbed the man's shoulder. 'Easy there, Doc, I already had my physical.'

Barclay Jackson grinned. 'I think he was hoping to do a quick prostate check. You're not a young man any more, Reid.'

Sam glared at Jackson. 'You and me are gonna have at it before long.'

'Don't mind him,' Franks said, jerking a thumb at Jackson. 'Him and me don't have to worry about getting ours checked – I hear it's really only a problem if you have balls.'

Jackson threw his head back and laughed. 'I'll show you mine if you show me yours, Franks.'

She snorted. 'You're not my type – too girly.'

Walter Gray cleared his throat. 'Very good everyone.' He turned to Sam again. 'I have the new power packs if you're interested. Might lighten your load a bit.'

'What you got?'

'You're using the standard Mark V, right?' Gray asked.

Sam nodded.

'Thought so – gives 5000 watts of power for ninety-six hours, or twenty-four in a maximum activity burst. But they're heavy cells. With the Mark VI, we're using degraded plutonium sheeting – it's smaller, lighter, and will last a month, even at high activity.'

Sam nodded, impressed. 'Any radiation or heat signature?'

Gray smiled. 'No more than normal background trace.'

Sam grunted. 'Sign me up.'

The HAWCs went from room to room, stocking up on the gear they needed – knives, explosives, and handguns. They selected some wireless assault projectiles, or WASPS: mini over-the-horizon missiles with enough smarts built into the tiny launcher that you could pick a target several miles away, and then let it go and do its job. The blast radius and impact was equivalent to a fragmentation grenade – a small delivery package with a big punch.

In the close-quarters room, Gray looked over his glasses at Alex. 'Cartridges for your HKs – I'm assuming 9mm parabellums?'

Alex shrugged. 'Sure. They get the job done.'

'Sure do ... for standard kit. But I want you to see something else.'

Gray pushed a stud and a door slid back into the wall to reveal a long narrow corridor with a target dummy at one end. On one wall hung a row of guns and other weapons, many of which Alex had never seen before. The HAWCs and Jackson crowded around, and Gray looked delighted with the sudden interest and attention. He took a pistol from the wall, selected some ammunition from a red box, and loaded a single bullet, also red-coated, into the chamber. He handed the pistol to Alex, then nodded to the dummy.

In one smooth motion Alex spun and fired, hitting the dummy in the center of its chest. Almost immediately a red spot appeared between the pectorals and bloomed outwards. Even from a hundred feet away Alex could feel the heat, and as he watched, the dummy melted from the inside out. Jets of halon gas whooshed down on the mess, suppressing but not fully dousing the flames.

'*Bam!*' Franks clapped. 'I like it.'

Alex sniffed the barrel, then handed the gun back to Gray. 'Thermite?'

Gray nodded. 'Aluminum oxide thermite packed into a standard shell. Safe and stable until the projectile's impact friction delivers enough heat to start the exothermic reaction. Burns at 4000 degrees, wet or dry.' He grinned. 'Makes for some great fun in the dark, and sure to get your adversary's attention.'

Alex couldn't help smiling at the scientist's boyish enthusiasm for the deadly ammunition. 'Pack a box ... for each of us.'

'Yeah!' Casey Franks high-fived Ben Rogers.

Next stop was the combat body armor room.

'It's like Christmas, isn't it?' Gray chortled, rubbing his hands together.

Alex grinned. 'Okay, Santa. The biological body armor – I want it for the entire team, and we need it processed now.'

Gray nodded. 'We can do that. I can get the design programs started immediately, as soon as we've got the morphology measurements.' He motioned the team into the room. 'Lady and gentlemen.'

Alex hung back, and stopped Gray following them in. 'The laser prototype.'

Gray nodded. 'Yes, yes, the KBELT – klystron beam emitted-light technology. We've perfected the miniaturization, and added a pistol to the range. You have experience with them?'

Alex nodded, remembering the rifle he'd used on the Dark Rising mission in Iran. No stock, held like a sawn-off pump action, with a square casing over the trigger. There were two settings for the laser – high and low energy pulse. High energy cut a pencil-sized hole through anything; low energy gave about the same result as a hundred pounds of TNT delivered in a single, focused, explosive punch.

'Did you overcome the short battery life?' he asked.

Gray nodded, and took a step closer to Alex, his voice dropping. 'It's still highly classified. Only one man below the rank of general knows about it – Colonel Jack Hammerson. And now you.' He looked up into Alex's face, studying his features. His eyebrows came together. 'You sure we've never met?'

'Yes.' Alex put his hand on Gray's shoulder. 'Now show me the KBELT pistol.'

*

Hammerson stood with his two teams on the runway. Alex, Sam, and their unit would leave first; with Reece Thompson, Matt Kearns, and Rebecca Watchorn boarding the second aircraft to Crete. The HAWCs' suits, with the inbuilt synthetic biological armor plating, made them look like dark segmented insects.

Their rides, Lockheed SR-71 Blackbirds, were supposed to have been retired around 1996; however, the long-range reconnaissance aircraft were far too valuable to mothball, and were still in use for special payloads – Spec-Op teams that needed to be somewhere, fast. Each looked like a missile with its short wings and two huge muscular thrusters in close to the night-dark body painted with radar-reflecting paint. With a J58-P4 engine that could produce a static thrust of 32,000 pounds, the Blackbirds could cruise at Mach 3.2 – fast and near invisible. And if they *were* detected, at high altitude they could outrun a surface-to-air missile. Both planes had no insignia, and their pilots were also off the books. Once they crossed out of US airspace, they stopped existing.

Hammerson knew too well the burden this anonymity placed on the HAWCs, and on him. Too many young men and women lay in shallow unmarked graves around the world – Alex Hunter's father being one of them. Hammerson gazed at Alex. The young man's gray-blue eyes were clear; no hint of anything other than eagerness, intelligence, and explosive energy. He hoped the thing lurking somewhere within his mind remained chained behind whatever barrier Alex had created for it. If not … Hammerson didn't want to think about the Other One taking control of his protégé in the field.

He looked around the group – no tension; just eagerness to get underway. *Time for the talk*, he thought.

'The impossible jobs are ours,' he said, and looked hard at his two senior soldiers. 'Win or lose, no one knows but us – this is our lot. We are the HAWCs, the first line, the strongest line, and the last line. When we go in, others stand aside, or they die. Clear?'

'HUA,' the HAWCs said in unison, their eyes blazing.

Hammerson placed his hands on his hips. 'Commander Kemel Baykal of the Turkish SF Kommandos went down to this thing. One hundred Special Forces soldiers, all lost. They threw everything at their target, but Magera went through them like they weren't there. General Chilton has authorized a small HAWC unit intervention.' He stepped in closer to the two big men. 'So, goddamn intervene. I want to know what this thing really is. We know line of sight is high risk, and even viewing it remotely can be hazardous. We're working on some tech to get around those limitations, but for now, use caution. As a minimum we want to know if it has a physical form. If it does, we can destroy it. And watch your backs – Borshov is on the ground there somewhere.'

He stood back and saluted. 'HAWCs, it's our turn now – make it count. Good luck and God speed.'

Alex saluted, then turned to his team. 'Load 'em up, people.'

The HAWCs and the SAS man piled into the first Blackbird. Alex was last, and he turned and nodded to Hammerson before following his team onto the plane.

Hammerson's face was grim. *Magera, Borshov, and the Arcadian all in the same place at the same time*, he thought. *Hell on earth.*

*

Turgutlu, twenty-four miles west of Izmir NATO Base

Uli Borshov and his six Spetsnaz left the truck several miles outside the town. It was still dark, with dawn several hours away. The communication intercepts had informed him of the fate of the Turkish Special Forces team, and he had to guess the Americans were here by now, or on their way. Whoever or whatever was wielding the weapon that had been decimating the Turkish population must be taken, alive or dead. The value of such power to Russia was incalculable.

Borshov knew he had a head start on the Americans, and he would use it to prepare a little surprise party. Obtaining the weapon was his priority order, but to him it was secondary to his personal objective. If he got to tear Alex Hunter's head from his body, then he would be happy. He had fought HAWCS before and obliterated them. And he had killed Alex Hunter ... or so he'd thought. This time, he would make sure. This time he would take a trophy; cut the head clean from his body, or slice his beating heart from his chest. *No coming back from the dead this time,* he thought grimly.

From his position overlooking the city, he saw that at its center the buildings were fairly modern, but on the outskirts the dwellings were more modest – single- and double-story homes, some looking well over a hundred years old, with smoke curling from their chimneys. It was if the further away from the center of Turgutlu you went, the farther back in time you traveled.

Borshov split his team into three units, with himself as a fourth. They would find dwellings to hide out in, and wait – for either the mysterious weapon to arrive or the HAWCs. He circled his finger in the air and the groups split and jogged toward the houses. If there were occupants, they would be subdued or killed.

CHAPTER 22

The Lockheed Blackbird dropped to just a few thousand feet above the ground, and its bay doors whined open. The hypersonic craft was virtually soundless at high altitude, but lower down its engine sounded like the scream of an oncoming train. It dropped again and slowed even further, and three large drum-like objects were ejected, falling several hundred feet before their large chutes opened. Dawn was still a couple hours off, and the dark night-chutes and matte-black canisters were invisible as they fell to the ground. The plane roared away, climbing rapidly. In a few moments it was nothing but a dark speck on a dark horizon. The canisters burst apart on impact with the ground, and the HAWCs walked free, like they'd just stepped out of an elevator.

Alex turned in a slow circle, scanning the dark countryside. Satisfied, he turned back to his team. 'Weapons check.'

Guns, grenades, knives, lasers were slid out, pulled back, ratcheted, and sighted one after the other in smooth, almost mechanical fashion. It was all over in sixty seconds, and the four men and single woman came to attention. All were clothed in the active camouflaged biological armor, and their outlines dappled between full black and silver stripes as shafts of moonlight ran across them. Sam and Corporal Barclay Jackson were at the center, half a head taller than anyone else. Lieutenants Casey Franks, Ben Rogers, and Steve Dankirk looked like three tethered wolves waiting to be let off the leash.

Alex pointed in the direction of the small town. 'We take up a defensive position on the urban perimeter. Plant some pipes and try and get an idea of what we're dealing with be-fore we get in its face.'

'If it has one,' Sam responded.

Alex nodded. 'We know it has a physical form. Commander Baykal said that any soldier who got close to it got torn to pieces. We should be safe from a distance, but we don't know what that distance is yet.' He looked along their faces. 'Basically, we don't have workable intel – so we get that first. Questions?'

'We didn't come here just to take pictures,' Jackson said. 'Will we engage?'

'When I say so. And that's *sir*.'

Jackson raised his voice. 'Listen, *sir*, we've got a base full of men and women just down the road. If we get a shot, we should take it.'

Alex looked Jackson full in the face. 'Are we going to have an authority problem, Jackson? Because I got a real fast solu-tion for that.'

Words seemed to form in Barclay Jackson's mouth, but as he met Alex's eyes, his lips clamped shut and he looked away. He shook his head and mumbled.

Alex stepped forward. 'What was that, soldier?'

'No, sir.'

Alex glared at him a moment longer, before turning to gaze along the dark strip of highway leading into the city. He closed his eyes, breathing in and out slowly, and allowing his consciousness to reach out. He could feel … something. He grunted and turned away, then paused. He turned back to the city, his eyes narrowing.

'Something up, boss?' Sam asked.

Alex continued to stare in the direction of the first row of buildings for several more seconds. 'Maybe. We stay alert; we stay alive. I get the feeling we might have a reception committee waiting for us.'

'Borshov?' Sam put a scope to his eye.

Alex shrugged. 'Someone down there is watching us.'

Alex kept Sam at his shoulder as they jogged toward the line of buildings. He could hear the faint whine of the MECH suit's hydraulics.

The big HAWC turned to run backward for a few moments, holding out a small silver device, before spinning back. 'Got something coming in fast behind us – larger signature than a person, but reader can't decide if it's a single biological mass or a million of 'em. Gotta be our primary target.'

Alex nodded. 'I know, I can feel it. It's like a cold breeze on my neck. We'll take cover and read the data from the pipes we laid down.'

Alex turned to address his team, then felt his senses jolt. 'Hit the dirt!' he roared as he dived to the ground, dragging Sam with him.

Alex had sensed the bullets before they arrived. Sniper or high-velocity rifles used rounds that were shaped for speed and traveled at over 3000 feet per second. The farther they traveled, the more friction slowed them down, but by the time they reached the HAWC team they were still moving at a subsonic velocity. Alex had tried to warn his team, but they could never hope to move as fast as he did.

The first bullet took Franks in the chest, blowing her backward to lie sprawled in the dirt. More bullets thwacked into the ground and exploded off rocks.

Sam rolled and lifted his rifle, sighting at the first row of buildings. He quickly reached into a pouch for a longer scope, which he slotted onto the weapon rail. He resighted and said softly, 'Guess that answers the reception committee question.'

Alex rolled onto his back. 'HAWCs, sound off.'

One after the other his team shouted their call numbers. Franks' groaning voice was last.

'Franks, you okay?'

'Yeah. No holes, boss. But reckon I got one doozy of a hickey on my left tit.'

Alex grinned; the biological armor plating had done its job.

He rolled back into position. 'You got 'em, Sam?'

Sam continued to scan along the dark houses. 'Not until they fire again. I can take a guess, but I don't want to total a house full of civs if I'm wrong.'

Alex looked over his shoulder. 'Well, we can't let them keep us pinned down out here – we got a storm coming in behind us. Armor's holding up, but a single headshot and we're dead.' He concentrated on the dark shapes of the buildings in the distance. 'Got a window open, first house to the left of the small lane.'

Sam looked through the scope. 'I see it, but it's black as a coalminer's ass in there.'

'Put a round in and see what happens.'

Sam fired. The bullet hit the window frame, blowing woodchips into the air. The response was immediate – a volley of high-velocity bullets smacking into the earth around them.

Alex pulled his KBELT and held it in a two-hand grip. He flicked it to narrow beam, and fired a two-second burst. The stream of super-compressed plasma-charged particles struck the wood and passed through, and probably continued through a number of internal walls. Anything biological wouldn't stand a chance.

'That'll give them something to think about,' he said.

Sam lifted slightly and scanned the rows of houses until another few rounds smacked into the rock near his face. He snapped his head back down. 'Jesus, they're good.'

'Not that good – they missed.' Alex grinned. 'But got to be Borshov's Spetsnaz.' He popped his head up for just a second. 'They must be using bafflers. There's no muzzle flash, and I can't pinpoint the source by sound alone. I think we'll –' He felt a strange tingling at the back of his neck, and quickly rolled. 'Oh, Christ.'

Sam hunkered down. 'I hate it when you do that.'

Alex could see it now – in the distance, what looked to be mist coming fast down the highway. Not rolling in along the entire plain, but concentrated along the roadway. It slowed about five miles out. He could pick out a dark mass at its amorphous center, a nucleus at the core of a dreadful atom. He closed his eyes and concentrated . . . there was something else . . . a sound. Weeping.

He rolled back toward Sam. 'We're about to be the meat in a sandwich.'

Alex looked up at the sky – a small blush of light on the horizon signaled sunrise within the hour. He peeked again over the rocks they were hunkered behind – there was still no sign of where the snipers were hiding. He knew he needed to buy some time.

'We can't stay pinned down while this thing washes over the top of us. I'm going down the highway to try and slow it down. I can't look at it, so you need to guide me in – use the scanners.'

Alex peeked over the rocks again, then touched a button over his ear, sending his instructions to all team members. 'Primary target is coming down fast on our six. I'm going to buy us some time. Stay low while I draw fire, but keep moving forward. Do not, I repeat, *do not* turn around to look at me. If things get too hot, zero sniper positions are to remain viable. No exceptions.'

Alex looked at Sam, who nodded. He knew what Alex was asking: they'd need to obliterate most of the houses closest to them, confirmed enemy targets or not. Innocent people were about to die.

'Ready?' Alex said.

Sam raised an eyebrow. 'Are you?'

Alex smiled grimly, and exploded up from the ground. He'd sprinted half a mile back down the road before the snipers even got a bead on him. He dived and came up hard behind a large rock. Bullets flew past, but he was safe.

He glanced briefly at the mist ahead, now moving again, then instantly looked away. *Don't look at it, don't look at it,* he told himself. It was just a few miles away now, and closing fast. He heard the sound, the weeping, clearly now. It sounded almost human.

'What the hell are you?' he whispered.

He sensed it slowing even more, and knew it was aware of him. He looked over the line of rocks at the HAWCs. All except for Sam were belly-crawling below the sniper fire toward the line of buildings. The air was slate-gray now as dawn rapidly approached. Soon the sun would lift over the horizon and be at their backs – giving them an edge, and bad news for the snipers.

He drew the KBELT and took a deep breath. *Remember the force, Luke.* He grinned and closed his eyes, concentrating on pushing out his senses to determine where the thing was. He lifted the pistol and fired. The thin beam of pulses streamed across the desert roadway, traveling the single mile to its target at the speed of light. Even over the short distance the pencil-thin pulse opened to more than an inch, and entered the center of the swirling mass. Nothing happened. He could sense it still coming at him.

'Shit.' He put a finger to his comm unit. 'Sam, confirm hit on target.'

'Dead center, boss, and no pass-through. Fully absorbed with no discernible effect.'

Alex moved the pistol calibration up to pulse. 'Okay, let's see it swallow about a hundred pounds of TNT.'

He lifted the gun, allowed his arm to move a fraction to find the target, and fired twice. The twin pulses, like balls of lightning and as large as softballs, moved at a blinding speed. Once again they entered the mass, and this time there was a reaction. The mist boiled, and heat and a crackling of energy bounced back at Alex. He lifted an arm to cover his face, and felt the body armor scorch.

His comm unit pinged in his ear. 'Direct hits by two, but it's still coming.' Sam's voice had an edge to it. 'Boss, you better get back here, or you're about to meet an ancient god face to face – and it ain't the friendly type.'

Alex dropped his arm as the heat died away. 'I heard that. Coming back. Out.'

The creature was nearly on him now – a mere few hundred yards down the highway, but approaching slowly, almost with caution.

What did Baykal miss? Think. Burning, shooting, stabbing, lasers – it seemed the thing was immune to physical trauma. It couldn't be made of the same physical matter as they were.

Alex grimaced as the weeping became louder in his ears. *Think, dammit.*

He remembered Matt Kearns suggesting they try talking to it, or singing to it like the priest had. His mind sorted through the information Matt had given them, about the Gorgon legend, the codex, the few words written on the cavern wall in a long-dead language.

'Boss, get the hell out … *now!*' Sam's voice was barely audible above the creature's wail of pain and suffering.

Alex grunted as his eyes began to open. It was if they weren't under his control any more. He strained to stare at the ground, using every ounce of strength and willpower not to look up. The rocks before him were starting to cast a shadow as the sun rose. The mist enveloped him, hiding him from the snipers, but now he was facing another danger. Magera was on him.

He sucked in a breath, and slowly got to his feet. It hurt to look down now; every ounce of his being was being pulled from him. He felt the creature tugging at his face, trying to drag his vision upward. In the center of his brain, something just as ferocious fought tooth and nail against the force in front of him.

He held his hand up, and immediately felt a sensation of cold creep up his arm. Perspiration ran freely down his face as he pushed back – his own mind now pulling at Magera. Sensations washed over him, starting small like a tiny flicker of blue light, then exploding into images of darkness, water, a landscape dripping with mosses and lichens. In the blue twilight he saw cities with silver spires that touched the sky. Beings with heads writhing with monstrous ropey polyps escorted thousands upon thousands of smaller creatures, moving them like cattle along a silver highway. Above them in the sky, a dim orb that could have been a sun or moon was draped with a blue veil that gave the scene a subaqueous feel.

Alex's jaws clenched from the pain he was picking up from the creature. There was an overwhelming feeling of illness, sadness, and something else, like a longing for home. But there was also madness there – an insane rage – and it was building. Alex grunted as he struggled with it, as he probed deeper.

The thing seemed to become aware of what he was doing and immediately ejected him from its consciousness. The cold in his arm turned warm, rapidly getting hotter, building to an unbearable intensity that scalded his skin. Alex felt the blisters forming beneath his armor-plated glove.

'*Stop!*' he roared.

Amazingly, the heat snapped off and was replaced by the sensation of confusion.

Alex was suddenly enveloped in pain. He knew he was losing; he couldn't look down any more, he couldn't resist. It had won. He brought his face up.

As the thing came into focus, the golden glare of the rising sun blasted down the highway. The boiling mist dissipated, and the being itself, Magera, seemed to collapse into dust, or particles, flowing like water into the soil at his feet.

'What the ...' Alex watched it bleed away, and with it went the sobbing sound. A lingering sensation of anger and confusion remained, like a spirit hovering over the dark road, but then it too dissipated in the sunshine.

'Boss ... what just happened?' Sam asked.

Alex looked around. There was no physical trace of Magera, but he could still feel the thing close by. 'I ... I don't know. It just fell apart.'

'Did we get it?' Sam's voice was hopeful.

Alex shook his head. 'I don't think –'

The bullet took him between the shoulderblades, on the vertebra, punching him forward to the roadway. It hurt – physically and mentally. Once the mist had gone he was exposed – an amateur's mistake.

'Idiot,' he told himself, and rolled until he was behind cover. The armor had stopped the penetration of the round, and the vertebra was already knitting back into place due to his accelerated metabolism. He looked up, and another bullet whizzed past, slicing his cheek. 'Fucking Borshov.' He touched his comm unit. 'Sam, we're wasting time. We got to clean out that hornets' nest once and for all. Release some WASPS.'

'With pleasure, boss.'

Alex watched as Sam reached into his kit and pulled free a small box. He set some switches inside, before placing it on the ground beside him. Immediately a flurry of small machines lifted out and swirled over his head for a few seconds, before spreading out and heading toward the line of houses. Sam watched their progress on a small screen.

'Eyes in, boss.'

The miniaturized explosives split up as they approached the houses, then swirled in and out, through open windows, chimneys, and under doors, the vid-feeds on their twin rotator wings letting Sam see inside the buildings.

After a few minutes he shook his head. 'I know they're in there, but they must have gone to ground or be wearing some sort of deflective armor.'

'Time's up,' Alex said. 'We'll do it the old-fashioned way. Put some pulses into the front row of houses. I want Franks, Jackson, and DK to go in on left flank. I'll take the right. You and Rogers lay down suppressing fire. Pulses on three, two, one, go ...'

Balls of superheated plasma shot into the buildings and exploded inside. There were no fires as the heat of the charges literally seared everything in their path.

'Go, go, go!'

Alex shot out first, his speed making him an impossible target. He passed the other HAWCs as they were still getting to their feet. Franks, Jackson, and DK went in on the left flank, zigzagging fast while Sam and Rogers let fly a hail of bullets into the houses.

Alex went through a door in an explosion of wood. He rolled and came up fast, searching for a target. The three HAWCs on the left flank did the same, charging through doors or diving through windows, glass shattering and splinters flying.

Gunfire rang out. The fight had commenced.

CHAPTER 23

Casey Franks dived in through a window and rolled to her feet. Though the sun was rising, inside the house it was still near total dark. Before she could orientate herself, the gunshot, shatteringly loud in the small space, blew her across the room to land behind a ratty old sofa. Franks lay flat, her hearing temporarily useless, the ringing in her ears a continuous scream. She pressed her cheek to the floor, feeling the footfalls as the agent approached.

At the sofa, he leaped, confident, possibly expecting a fallen HAWC with a hole the size of his fist through their chest. Instead, he found empty floor. He spun, gun up, but still took the armor-plated fist directly on his jaw. Franks got in close and delivered another flat-handed strike up under his chin.

The Spetsnaz was big and fast, and clad all in black with Cyclops night-vision goggles over his face. He adjusted quickly to the attack, never making a sound, using his long leg to sweep around and take Franks off her feet. She went down on her back, feeling the bones grate where she was already bruised from the bullet strike. The pain was agonizing, but, like her foe, she didn't make a sound, and instead used the floor to bounce straight back to her feet.

She came up fast, but the agent had vanished. So too had the screaming in her ears – just in time for her to hear the tiny sound of a knife coming from its sheath. She could guess what sort – a Kizlyar, preferred by Spetsnaz and ex-KGB for wet work. There would be no gleam from its blackened blade.

Franks stayed low, and threw herself sideways and under the swinging fist that held the blade backward, trailing it to bring its razor edge across anything the fist struck. She counterpunched twice into her opponent's iron-hard torso, then blocked the blade again. This time she felt it work at her armored forearm.

She drew her own knife – the tanto-edged Ka-Bar; shorter and stouter, and laser sharpened enough to perform surgery. She grinned in the dark; in close-quarters combat, guns just got in the way.

The blades came together, clanging as if they were dueling in a long-gone age. The Spetsnaz managed to nick her body twice, but the armored suit easily deflected the steel each time. She feinted with her left arm, then swung down with the small blade in her right, looking for the side of his neck – the bunched trapezium muscle would be tough, but it was a gateway to nerve bundles that, if severed, would render his entire side useless.

Her knife never found its mark. Instead the Spetsnaz caught her wrist and head-butted her, the Cyclops goggles pounding into the bridge of her nose. Franks was trained to deal with pain, but nothing could stop the automatic physical reflex as her vision swam for a split second. She was propelled backward, her head hitting the ground, and found herself lying against an ancient wooden table and chairs.

Her blade was gone and he was on her now, coming at her with the wickedly sharp blade raised. There was no time to draw another weapon, and his skills seemed a match for hers. There was one last option: incidental proximity weaponing – use whatever the hell you can find.

She grabbed a chair by one leg and rolled, bringing it around fast and hard into the Spetsnaz's ribs. He angled one arm down and partially blocked the impact, but by then Franks was up on her feet and bringing the chair around in an arc to smash down on the top of his skull. This time it was his turn to go down.

On his knees, he drew his arm back, the blade held lightly between his thumb and fingers as he prepared to loose the dark spike at her. But time was on her side now, and a hundred options for disarming, disabling, or dispensing death went through her trained mind. She chose death.

She pulled her gun, its magazine loaded with red-coated thermobaric bullets, and fired at near point-blank range into his chest. The reaction was immediate – the Spetsnaz shuddered, his eyes wide, his mouth open. Steam poured from his throat as the exothermic reaction raised the temperature of his body to 4000 degrees. His torso glowed redly, giving off thick greasy smoke, before falling open. He dropped in a heap, the remaining mass hissing and bubbling.

'Damn fucking right,' Franks said. She wiped the blood and perspiration from her face and holstered her gun. She touched the button at her ear. 'Clear. One bad guy down. Moving to next building.'

*

The houses were small and close together, and DK could hear the sounds of smashing furniture, breaking glass, or the thump of fists and boots against human flesh. He eased open the door and snaked into the room. It was dark, just outlines showing, and his senses immediately moved into hyper-alert mode.

He crawled to a corner, came to his feet, and then froze, listening and allowing his peripheral vision to search out trigger shapes. In the outer area of the eye, the retina had more cone cells that were better at seeing in the dark, and all HAWCs were trained to use their peripheral vision to scan for body- or weapon-shaped targets, or even a hint of movement. He stayed that way for several minutes, barely breathing. He'd already seen the two bodies on the floor – an old man and woman. By the angle of their heads, their necks were broken. He brought in his other senses. There was no sound, but there was something – a smell – like bad breath and cheap vodka.

DK held his rifle loose but ready in his hands. He lifted it and looked along the scope, using the light enhancer to search the darker areas of the room that his peripheral vision couldn't penetrate. He slowly rotated, seeing nothing but phosphorescent green shapes. He switched the scope to thermal, and rotated again. The green shapes turned to various shades of blue and green. The bodies were pink, some residual warmth still evident in their core.

Gotta get moving, he thought and turned another few degrees. A flaring red giant stepped from behind the door. He'd been on DK the whole time. The giant grabbed the barrel of his gun, and wrenched it from his hands. DK was six foot and weighed 220 pounds, but his attacker outweighed him by at least another eighty pounds. *Ogre*, he thought as the man lifted him.

Muscle memory overrode shock and the HAWC struck out with his fists, the sharp edges of his elbows, and his feet. He connected, but even with the armor plating on his gloves, the figure absorbed the blows as if they were nothing. Then he countered, the pile-driver blows coming fast and accurately.

DK managed to use the force of the punches to throw himself backward. He landed on the floor, his face wet with blood, rolled, and came up smoothly already gripping a Ka-Bar blade. The big man followed, and a black spike appeared in his own massive fist. The big man slashed back and forth, feinting and lunging. DK parried some, but as he jumped back he felt a trickle of warm blood run from under his arm. Unbelievably, the giant had managed to get his spike in between the suit's biological plating.

The rulebook said to get in close when fighting a bigger adversary and neutralize his longer reach, then use his own body weight against him. However, DK didn't trust this maxim with the grizzly bear in front of him. The man was huge, but in no way lumbering or slow, and he seemed as expertly trained as the HAWC. Getting in close would probably only allow the beast to get a grip on him. DK needed space, he needed to even the odds, and he needed a single second to draw a gun. Hand-to-hand against this opponent would be a one-way street to death.

The bearded giant came at him again, feinting to the left and then coming back at him not with the blade but with the back of his fist. DK saw stars as the blow connected with his cheekbone. He went down, and before he could spring back to his feet, the slim black blade pounded down into the meat of his palm, pinning his hand to the wooden floor.

DK grunted from the pain. Before he could ward him off, the bearded giant was kneeling on his chest, swinging sledgehammer-like blows across his face – a left, then a right, sweeping back and forth, over and over, until blood and broken teeth filled his mouth. His head swam, and reality dropped away. The brutality seemed to be happening to someone else, and he was in a pit, watching it, then falling into the bottomless dark.

*

Borshov saw that the HAWC was losing consciousness, but he continued to rain blows down on the unprotected face.

It was hard to stop – the sensation of hot brutality was one of his few joys. He just wished it was Alex Hunter's face he was pounding.

The HAWC's muscles relaxed, and he lay still, a wet ragged breathing coming from his smashed nose and bloody mouth. Borshov grabbed a tablecloth and used it to roughly wipe the young man's face and then his own hands. He drew a small box from his belt, and pulled from it a long black needle, close to eight inches long and attached to the box by wires. He carefully inserted the spike into the HAWC's nostril, wiggled it once or twice and pushed again. There was a small feeling of resistance as it penetrated the upper nasal cavity, then traveled smoothly up into the brain. Clear cranial fluid momentarily flushed onto the HAWC's upper lip. Borshov ignored it as he continued to probe, slowly now. He needed to plant the spike in a specific area of the brain, between the hippocampus and the amygdala, associated with memory and emotion.

Borshov watched the small box he had set on the ground – the tiny light remained red. Eighty years ago, scientists had found that some brain functions could be reprogrammed through physical manipulation – the process was called a lobotomy. In Russia, they had taken it a step further, using the technique to make interrogation so much easier. The small light flashed green and Borshov let go of the probe. The HAWC's eyes fluttered as if he was in REM sleep. His brain's electrical impulses began to involuntarily fire.

Borshov leaned forward, his lips close to the man's ear. 'What do they call you?'

'DK, Lieutenant Steve Dankirk,' he responded dreamily.

Borshov smiled. 'DK, you are safe now. It is me, Alex Hunter. What is your operational status?'

'Boss?' DK frowned.

'Yes, I am Arcadian.'

'Did we get 'em?'

'Yes, all of them.' Borshov smirked. 'We need to move. What are our next steps?'

'You know, boss.'

Borshov exhaled impatiently, ignoring the temptation to pound the man's face some more. 'I know, but you are hurt, and I need to check if you are still … optimal.'

'Can't feel my legs … can't feel anything.'

'You're good … safe now. Now answer the question. That's an order, soldier.'

'We need to protect the NATO base at Izmir. And then hope that egghead Kearns finds something in Crete we can use to put Magera to sleep.' DK coughed blood onto his chin.

'Magera?' Borshov frowned. 'They go to Crete?'

'Yeah, to some cave. He and the English wom–'

The window behind Borshov exploded inward as a figure came through it like a missile, then readjusted its trajectory to hurtle toward the big Russian. Even though Borshov outweighed his new assailant by at least fifty pounds, he was thrown backward like he was a child. He was quickly on his feet, however, standing like a colossus in the center of the room. He drew another of his thin black blades, but didn't get a chance to lift it. He suddenly found himself in the air, lifted above the newcomer's head, then slammed down to the ground, splintering a chair as he landed. He cursed and rolled away, coming up with a heavy chair leg in his hands. In the dark he could just make out that the newcomer was kneeling over the fallen HAWC. Borshov knew him now.

'So, Arcadian. You were dead. I killed you. Then you came back, and you were stronger, faster.' His eyes narrowed. 'What did they do to you to make you so strong, huh? To make you this … Arcadian man?' He backed up, holding his hands up momentarily, before dropping one to feel behind his back. 'One day we will peel you open and find out.'

Alex Hunter turned toward him, his eyes shining silver, and slowly got to his feet, his fists balled. 'You're the dead man here.'

'Perhaps ... but not today.'

Borshov tossed the incendiary grenade at Hunter's feet, knowing he couldn't get to him and save his soldier at the same time. The Russian spun and dived through the smashed window, taking most of the frame with him. He rolled and was immediately up and running.

The explosion blew the roof off the small building. Superheated gas and flames gushed out of the door, every window, and every vent and crack in the walls.

CHAPTER 24

Sam sprinted into the burning house, scrabbling through rubble and lifting burning beams to search for his comrades. He found DK first. The man was a shredded mess, eyes open, the spike still embedded in his nasal cavity.

'Aw, fuck no.' Sam called over his shoulder, 'Jackson, get him out.'

The SAS soldier appeared behind Sam and kneeled next to the body. 'Goodbye, brother,' he said, then shut DK's eyes, lifted his ragged remains, and carried him out.

Sam continued his search. He lifted the burning couch to find another body, smoke curling up from it. Alex was intact – the armored suit had held him together, mostly – but the unprotected areas had paid the biggest price. His face was a mess – burned and ripped where debris or shrapnel had torn the flesh. On his forehead, a dime-sized piece of bone showed through, and a finger-thick splinter of wood was embedded in his cheek. Sam could also see that one arm was hanging wrong, and there were probably more bones fractured.

'Shit.' Sam splashed water on Alex's smoldering skin, then gripped the large splinter in his cheek and drew it out. He pressed his hand to the wound; as he'd expected, it coagulated quickly.

Alex groaned as Sam helped him up. He opened his eyes. 'Grenade?'

'Yep, incendiary, and I'm betting you just ate the lot of it.'

Sam held the canteen to Alex's lips. He pushed it away. 'DK?'

'Gone.' Sam kept his hand on Alex's back, feeling the strange heat the man generated. He knew that Alex's metabolism burned hotter than normal; more so, when fury took him – then he became like a furnace.

Alex nodded, and held his head, groaning again. 'Borshov got away?'

'For now.' Sam took his hand away. 'We took down four Spetsnaz, but two of them and Borshov are gone. You need medical –'

'No, just wrap me up, and let's get the hell out of here. This party's gonna attract attention and we need to be ghosts.' He grabbed Sam's arm, and hauled himself slowly to his feet. 'Besides, I doubt it was me that frightened Magera away. We don't want to be here when night falls.'

Franks and Jackson appeared at Sam's shoulder. The big SAS man took a look at Alex's face and whistled. 'Nasty. There goes the modeling gig.'

Alex turned to Jackson, smoke or steam still lifting from his battered shoulders. As he stared at the SAS man, the missing patch of skin on his forehead seemed to sizzle for a second, then the ragged flesh at its edges crept across the wound.

'Holy fuck, did you see that?' Jackson's mouth hung open as he turned to Franks.

She just smiled, ignoring him.

'No, we didn't,' Sam said.

He plastered some HAWC field patches over Alex's wounds, then wrapped his head and face in bandages, leaving just his eyes and mouth clear. The arm break was clean across the ulna and radius. Sam splinted it, and wrapped it as well.

'But his head just started to …' Jackson's eyes were wide. 'He was still fucking burning.'

'Leave it, soldier,' Sam said, and put his arm under Alex's shoulder.

Alex gritted his teeth and sucked in a deep breath. 'Let's move.'

Jackson snorted and shook his head. 'You *are* a freak. And now you look like a fucking mummy.'

Alex turned his bloodshot gaze on the big man. 'And you look like a pack mule – so you get to carry DK until we find a place to bury him.'

'More like a jackass,' Franks said. Then she turned to Alex, her face grim. 'We're winning.'

Alex nodded. 'We always do. Now, let's go. We need to call this in – Borshov engaged, we're one down, and Magera has disappeared. And I get the feeling not for good.'

*

The HAWCs jogged into morning sunshine. The temperature was already close to ninety degrees and rising steadily, but was still bearable because of the near total lack of humidity. However, Jackson, carrying DK's body, was struggling.

About fifteen miles from Izmir, Alex called a halt. He pointed to a patch of ground. 'I want that man at least three feet down, and the area above raked so smooth not even Sherlock Holmes could find him.'

'Aw, fuck.'

Alex rounded on Jackson and brought his face in close. 'I am not in a good mood, soldier.'

Jackson nodded quickly. 'I get it … boss.'

Alex turned away, and looked down at his splinted arm, flexing his fingers. He unwrapped the bandage, made a fist, then grunted. 'Sam, with me. The rest of you, take some rest.' He glared at Jackson. 'Not you. Start digging.'

Jackson's jaw clenched in anger, but he kept his lips clamped shut.

Alex and Sam walked a few dozen paces away, and sat on some exposed boulders.

Sam swigged from his canteen. 'Borshov used a cranial probe on DK.'

Alex nodded. 'Don't know how much time he had, but we proceed on the assumption that Borshov knows what we're doing and where we're going next.' He drank from his own canteen. 'That big bastard killed DK, and I let him get away.'

Sam blew air, dismissing the statement. 'He dropped a grenade on you. You won this round – you lived; he ran. You'll get him next time.'

Alex stared out into the desert. 'Next time.' He sucked in a breath. 'Now to give the Hammer the good news.'

He clipped an enhancer over the communication pill already in his ear. It immediately uplinked him to the satellite, signal jumping to confuse anyone trying to intercept the data sent and received.

The colonel was waiting. 'Go, Arcadian.'

'We encountered Magera five miles outside of Turgutlu. Also Borshov. We … lost DK,' Alex said slowly. 'We took down four, but Borshov and two others got away.'

'He lost four, you lost one – that tell you anything?' Hammerson's voice had an edge. 'This is the business we're in. Now tell me about Magera.'

'It was weird,' Alex said. 'I was right in front of it, then the sun came up and it just vanished.'

'You confronted it and it vanished?'

'No. I get the feeling I had nothing to do with it. I think the sun struck it and it disassembled, turned to powder or something. But it was still there, not dead, just … I don't know … waiting.' Alex's brow furrowed as he remembered. 'Have any of the attacks been during daylight hours?'

He heard Hammerson moving at his desk, and imagined him pulling data up onto his screen. He snorted softly. 'No.'

'Then maybe this thing doesn't like light. We might be able to use that.'

'Good. I'll get onto R&D, and also see if Kearns or Ms. Watchorn know anything about intolerance to sunlight from the legends.'

'Okay.' Alex's face was itching under the bandages. 'There's something else. Borshov probed DK before he died. Give Thompson a heads-up in case they get company.'

'You got it.' Hammerson paused for a second or two. 'You okay, son?'

Alex reached up to scratch his face, before violently ripping the bandages away. He tossed the bloody shreds onto the sand. 'I'll be better after I tear Borshov's head off.'

'Works for me,' Hammerson said evenly. 'Listen, just one thing – before you grind him into the dirt, ask him about Captain Graham. And make him answer. Graham's a son of a bitch, but he's our son of a bitch and I want him back.'

Alex remembered how Graham, head of the military's medical division, had sent three automatons after him, wanting to reel Alex in so he could cut him up and see how the Arcadian treatment was a success with him, but a failure with others.

'Do *I* want him back?' he wondered aloud.

'No one messes with our people,' Hammerson responded. 'I'll deal with Graham.'

Alex shrugged. 'Okay. We're heading into Izmir. Let me know if Kearns finds anything we can use. Over.'

'Over and out.'

*

'Lasithi Plateau,' Matt said as he looked out of the plane window at the mountains rising up around them and forming a massive horseshoe shape around the valley of Selakano. They were thickly forested with pines. 'Home of the Caves of Zeus – where we hope the pieces of the puzzle come together.'

Rebecca grinned. 'I've got a good feeling about this place. There might be some clues in the relics taken from the caves during the first excavations. Some were found in areas that are inaccessible today, though.' She looked across to Thompson. 'We might need to make them accessible.'

'And that's where I come in,' Thompson said evenly.

Matt nodded, continuing to look down at the landscape. 'There was once an underground river in the caves, but it was sealed off. At the very lowest level, several hundred feet down, there are still pools, some quite deep in places – and that's where the relics were located.'

'Cave diving and potential demolition work in a site of national and cultural significance.' Thompson grinned. 'And I thought you guys were supposed to be the nice ones.' He snorted softly and glanced out of the window. 'We're rising again – more mountains coming up.'

Matt pointed to a plateau. 'Where we're going has been described as the Machu Picchu of the Minoan civilization. That plateau area was the last stronghold of the race – a final sanctuary. After the fall of Knossos, the Minoans' political and cultural center, a fragment of the Minoan race survived there for another 400 years.'

'Then they simply vanished,' Rebecca added, 'and no one really knows why or how. This place is home to a myriad of myths and legends – the caves where Zeus was born, where Perseus fought with the Medusa, where Theseus battled the Minotaur ... We need to consider how all these things interrelate and overlap.'

'The Minotaur – the bull-headed beast? What's that got to do with Magera?' Thompson asked.

'Maybe nothing,' Matt said. 'But as a kid did you ever play that game where you sit in a circle and someone writes a phrase down on a piece of paper? The first kid reads it and whispers the phrase into the next kid's ear, then the next kid whispers it into the following kid's ear and so on and so on. At the end, you compare the final phrase with what was written, and guess what? It's different. Maybe only a word or two, but it's a perfect example of how things can alter over time. Now, imagine a myth or legend being told and re-told for hundreds or thousands of years. It can end up vastly different from the original telling, or several versions might develop, depending on the district or subculture. The tale of the Minotaur is like that. Something terrible might have lived in those caves once, but what exactly?'

'You think it might have been the Magera?' the SAS man asked.

Matt shrugged. 'There are no signs that Knossos was ever a military site – for example, it didn't have fortifications or places to store weapons – but it was the local center of power of its time. In Greek mythology, King Minos lived in a palace at Knossos, and had a labyrinth built to hold his son, the Minotaur. But other variations of the story say the labyrinth existed before the kingdom – that the palace was built over an existing system of caves, with something already living in their dark depths. Another variation has the early Minoans finding something down there, and then controlling it. Who knows – perhaps it was their secret weapon.'

Thompson shook his head. 'Still don't get how the bull Minotaur has anything to do with the Gorgons.'

'The Greek myth says that Theseus, a prince from Athens, was forced to fight a terrible creature called the Minotaur,' Rebecca said. 'But, as Matt mentioned, there are other variations of the story, recovered from pottery shards and wall tiles, that are markedly different. They don't refer to a bull-headed beast at all; a Knossos tablet written partly in Mycenaean Greek refers to the creature in the caves as the "Mistress of the Labyrinth". People who were sent down into the caves became "frozen with fear" when they saw what lived there.'

Thompson exhaled and sat back. 'A lot of theories – bloody old theories.'

Matt grinned, and opened his computer. 'Better to have a lot than none.' He scrolled through some images and turned his screen to show them. 'And I'm still going to be including this one until it's proven wrong. What does this look like?'

Rebecca groaned when she saw the screen. Thompson frowned.

'Well, what does it remind you of?' Matt asked with raised eyebrows.

The ancient image showed two tall figures surrounded by smaller bipeds. One figure's head was a mass of coiling tendrils; the other's was encased in a familiar round shape with a sort of open visor over the face.

Thompson snorted. 'You have got to be kidding me. A freakin' space helmet?'

Rebecca put her hands over her face. 'Oh, for god's sake.'

Matt nodded. "Remember the priest in the codex referred to *Caelestis*, and then pointed skyward?' He snapped his computer closed. 'Weird stuff – and I don't know how it helps yet. But in the absence of evidence, all information is useful.'

Thompson sighed. 'Sounds like you've got too much information, too many theories.'

'Perish the thought,' Matt said, and grinned. 'We scientists expect historical anomalies. But given what we're seeing in Turkey, they suddenly mean a helluva lot more.'

Thompson looked from Matt to Rebecca. 'There are masses of caves in Crete, right? How do we know we've got the right ones?'

'Good question,' Rebecca said. 'A lot of the caves were blasted open in the 1920s, but heavy rains caused silt to pour into them and many of the networks were destroyed or closed. Remember the story of the Minotaur – it lived in a labyrinth. The geology here is primarily carbonate – you combine that with heavy rainfall and you get significant tunnel systems. Maybe it all used to be a single massive network down there, but it's been blocked over time and become a series of individual caves. So they might all be the right cave – we just need to find the right way in.'

'So, what are we looking for?' Thompson said. 'First off, I mean.'

'First we need to go to Heraklion on the coast. It's the capital of the island, and where most of the artifacts from the caves ended up. It's also where we'll need to beg, borrow or steal any supplies we might need. Hammerson can't help us any more – the ground, sea, and air borders are closed.'

Thompson nodded. 'Sounds like a plan.' He jerked forward, and put a hand to his ear, concentrating, then turned to Matt. 'Hammerson wants to talk to you.'

Matt fumbled in his pocket, extracted a small flesh-colored pellet and jammed it into his ear.

'Go, Jack.'

'Professor Kearns, Matt, events are moving quickly, but we have news that I thought you needed to hear.' The older soldier paused, and Matt concentrated as he continued. 'Alex Hunter has engaged with Magera, or whatever the thing is out there. Just like during Baykal's interaction, it seems impervious to any physical assault, but there was something new. Alex said that when the sun came up, and touched the creature, it just seemed to melt away, or fall apart. Could have been the light, or warmth, he wasn't sure. But here's the thing, we checked, all the previous attacks occurred at night or underground.' He exhaled. 'Does that mean anything to you?'

'The sunlight.' Matt tried to remember any reference to a Gorgon being affected like this. '*Hmm*, I don't think it was the warmth,' he said at last.

'Me either,' Hammerson said. 'Matt, Alex also said that even though the thing seemed to vanish, he could still sense it – might mean it's there, and you just don't know it ... waiting for the dark.'

'Okay.' Matt sat back frowning. 'Anything else?'

'That's it,' Hammerson said. 'But be advised that Alex and his team are heading to you now. Until he arrives, be on guard ... and stay in contact, you hear?'

'Great, Jack, you got it.' Matt disconnected, and sat staring into the cabin.

'Well?' Rebecca said. 'What is it?'

'Interesting,' Matt murmured, his mind working furiously as he tried to assemble all the facts.

Thompson leaned forward. 'Give it up, buddy.'

'Alex and the team are en route to meet us now,' Matt said. 'They just encountered Magera outside of Turgutlu, but according to Alex, the sun came up and it just seemed to melt away, or rather disassemble. But ...' He frowned. 'He thought it was still there somehow, he could sense its presence.'

'Well, that sounds like crap – what the hell does it mean?' Thompson said.

Matt shook his head. 'If Alex said he still sensed it, then it was definitely there.'

Rebecca frowned. 'Melted away, or sort of disassembled? Like it deliberately vanished?'

Matt shrugged. 'Don't know. But I can't see the heat of the sun causing it. The Turkish used thermobarics on Magera – 1000 degrees – and it walked right through them.' He continued to stare at the cabin wall. 'Maybe the light, the sun's rays, or the energy ...' He sighed. 'Or something we don't know about yet.'

'The sunlight,' Rebecca said, musing. 'You know, that kind of makes sense. When Perseus killed Medusa, he had to enter her subterranean lair. Perhaps it needs the dark to survive.'

'No, not survive ... I don't think the sun killed it. But maybe the sun's rays ... change it.' He looked at her. 'And you're right, the Gorgons lived underground. Maybe we can use it.'

CHAPTER 25

NATO Base, Izmir, Turkey

Alex and his team were waved through the checkpoint and escorted directly to the command center. Mid-level brass from
several nations sat around a long table as Alex and Sam
pushed through the doors. The rest of the HAWCs sprawled
in chairs in the corridor, more than happy to let Alex and Sam
do the political work.

Alex looked along the table – four men sitting, and one
large, bearded older man, his face grim, standing with his
hands clasped behind his back. He was first to speak.

'Alex Hunter.' It wasn't a question.

Alex recognized the rank and came to attention. 'General.'

'General Aykut Bozlak Erdamir. At ease, Captain.'

Alex stood at ease with his big second-in-command behind
him. The general pointed to some chairs, and the two HAWCs sat.

'I understand you had the same success as we did at stopping Magera,' Erdamir said. 'And now it has disappeared.'

Alex nodded. 'The sun came up, and it vanished. But it's
not gone – I could still sense it.'

'Sense it?' One of the soldiers in a blue uniform, his accent clipped British, frowned with disbelief. 'Can you sense it now?'

Alex looked at the man, his own gaze flat and indifferent. The British officer reminded him of his own Captain Robert Graham, both from the physical appearance and also the way he carried the same sense of self-importance.

'No.' Alex turned away; he didn't feel the need to explain.

The general placed a hand on the British man's shoulder. 'Major Mallory Butler, British Armed Forces.' He indicated the men along the table. 'Colonel Frank Harper, US Armed Forces; Major Thierry Galloen, French Armed Forces; and Colonel Abdullah Yilmaz, Turkish Defense Forces.' Erdamir folded his arms and glared down at the British major. 'And we all need to hear anything new that may assist us against this strange and formidable force that is fast approaching.'

'Or already here,' Alex said. 'It was at the edge of the town when the sun's rays struck it. I'm not sure it was destroyed or even hurt. Perhaps it changes its state during the day – maybe becomes more ... benign, or goes into some sort of suspended animation.' He shrugged. 'I'm guessing. We know so little, because if you get close to it, you die.'

Erdamir clasped his hands behind his back and paced around the table. 'Then we have four hours before the sun goes down. And then it may return ... less benign.'

Mallory Butler tapped on the table. 'It's still basically following the old caravan trail along the Ankara Highway. Outside of Ulucak there's three miles of empty space. We can set up a wall of fire that a roach couldn't get through.'

Erdamir pursed his lips, making his moustache jut. 'Major, this thing went through hundreds of rounds of armor-piercing ammunition, fragmentation grenades, thermobaric RPGs, and also physically ripped our men in half. I lost nearly all my best SFCs and their commander – a good man and one of my best.'

His voice trembled with suppressed rage. 'Short of a nuke, what do you suggest?'

Butler looked down at his hands. 'There are around 1000 personnel at this base. But there are over 4 million people in Izmir, and you estimate we have four hours. We can't evacuate them all by sundown. And we can't sit on our thumbs and hope it passes us by.'

'Maybe we don't have a choice.' Erdamir sat down heavily.

Frank Harper leaned forward. 'Hunter, is there anything you can remember that might give us an edge? Anything at all?'

'Maybe the general is right,' Alex said. 'Maybe we don't have a choice. It's going to go through whatever we put in front of it, so ... don't put anything in front of it. My guess is, it's heading somewhere.'

His mind whirled as he remembered the feeling of torment within the creature. But there was something else, like it had a purpose, or a plan.

Harper rubbed his chin. 'Go on.'

'We don't need to evacuate the entire city,' Alex said slowly. 'Just leave a corridor.'

The general stood again and leaned forward onto the table, resting on his knuckles on the dark wood. 'The weeping ... you heard it?'

Alex nodded. 'It seems to be more focused. Originally it was seeking out populations to feed on, but now it seems to be in a hurry. It's only engaging when *it*'s engaged.'

'Well, if it's not coming here, where is it going?' Butler asked.

Sam spoke for the first time. 'It's going to Crete.'

'Good.' The British major sat back and exhaled. 'Very good.'

Harper got to his feet. 'Like hell it is. That's where the goddamn Seventh Fleet is right now. Gentlemen, I've got some calls to make.' He saluted, and pushed out of the room.

Alex rubbed his chin and turned to Sam. 'Makes sense. It's trying to get home.'

Sam nodded. 'We better get word to the colonel and Professor Kearns.'

'And we need to get over there, fast.' Alex got to his feet.

Erdamir walked over and placed a large hand on Alex's shoulder. 'We'll impose a curfew from sundown, and evacuate a route to the waterfront. Good news is, once it leaves Turkey, it's not our problem any more. Bad news is, the problem hasn't gone away. It now belongs to the world.'

*

Borshov hunched over a small table in a house in the hills overlooking Izmir. The sea in the distance was an electric blue, and the city's ancient minarets and Greek Orthodox churches rose above a plain of terracotta roofs and modern office blocks. The NATO base was tucked behind some hills to the south, and the gray steel of a ship's bow could just be seen easing around the headland.

Borshov spoke into a cell phone that was dwarfed by his large hand. 'We saw what this thing did to the Americans – it is unstoppable.'

He frowned as he listened, then shook his head. 'I don't know what it is, but I do know that the Americans have sent some scientists to Crete. They believe there is a way to either control or communicate with it. Maybe they find out in Crete, *da*?'

He looked out over the miles of houses, and grunted. 'No, there is no more we can do here. We will go to Crete, and stay ahead of the HAWCs.'

He listened for another second or two, and his broad face broke into a grin. 'Good. I knew this Graham would be helpful – both with the Arcadian treatment and access codes to their weapon archives. Send the package to Crete. I will collect it there. Now we will see who is the strongest.'

Borshov hung up, got to his feet, and stepped over the bodies of the house's owners. 'We move fast. A boat will meet us at main wharf in Alacati.'

He and his two remaining Spetsnaz jogged toward the sea.

*

Walter Gray whistled as he used a small and powerful mobile crane to load the crate onto a pallet. He pushed his clipboard under his arm and lifted the lid of the crate. Inside, carefully insulated, lay the top half of a metallic skeleton – gleaming steel armor plating, pistons, and wires. He checked the power pack, ticked off the items included, then sealed the crate back up.

He signed the release form under the twin signatures of General Marcus Chilton and Colonel Jack Hammerson – an urgent priority order.

'Someone's in a hurry,' he said, then started whistling again as he wheeled the pallet into the silver elevator. Destination: Crete.

*

Mustafa Kamalak spat tobacco from his lip. His small wooden cottage was so close to the sea, he could hear the ripples as the waves washed the pebbled shore. He was a fisherman, the same as his father, and his father's father before that. He hoped one day his sons might also be fishermen. But he had his doubts, given they were more interested in listening to music on those little boxes they had permanently plugged into their ears than spending six mornings a week hauling nets.

He sucked in a deep breath. He envied his boys their worlds of sound this night. Izmir hadn't been so quiet after sundown since the end of the Greco–Turkish war in 1923. All the buildings along the central roadway to the coast had been evacuated. Those who remained in their homes were huddled inside, lights out. Mustafa kept his small radio playing, its volume down low, as he listened to the news updates. Something was crossing the country, devastating towns – a poisonous cloud of gas, a deadly germ, a devil, a *djinn*. No one knew, but everyone whispered. The army quarantined whole areas after it had passed through, and no one from within the affected zones was ever heard of again.

The voices on the radio speculated, using scientific terms Mustafa had no hope of understanding. But one thing was clear – they all sounded scared, which made him feel sick in his guts. His lips moved in prayer. He'd heard the old women talking about God punishing them all for turning their backs on the traditional ways, for embracing a modernity that was repellent to the pious. 'It is *our* fault,' they wailed.

The voices on the radio rose in pitch – the monster was now in the streets of Izmir.

Mustafa turned the radio down so low it was little more than the breathy whine of a mosquito. Then he heard it – another sound beginning to manifest. He turned toward the boarded window, and through its slats saw a tall shadow pass by. There was sound too – weeping, moaning, a jeremiad of despair.

The sound was so pitiful, Mustafa also began to weep. 'May God save you,' he whispered.

The shadow paused, and Mustafa felt his heartbeat in his throat. *Move on, please move on*, he prayed, crushing his eyes shut and holding his hands over his ears.

CHAPTER 26

'I think I got it, Jack.'

Gerry Harris fed the images through to Hammerson's office. Hammerson's screen flickered and then he saw the dark mass moving along the Izmir street. It was like a fog bank with a solid center. He noted its size in relation to objects it passed – it was big, over seven feet tall, and broad.

'Still not clear, Gerry. Can you give me any more clarity?'

'Sorry, Jack, that's as good as it gets. The computers dismantle the original images, then reproduce them as a simulated best guess, building them up pixel by pixel. Takes a helluva lot of processing power to make it real time. You're seeing it without really seeing it. Also, the thing is literally giving off that gas that surrounds it.' There was a pause. 'Let me try something.'

The screen darkened, then flared, as Harris swapped between infrared and thermal. In thermal view, there was nothing but a cold outline.

'Giving off very little heat,' he said.

Hammerson grunted. 'Like a reptile.'

He narrowed his eyes as the images changed again. Harris moved to light enhancement, shadow management, and then contrast adjustment without any improvement. He went back to the original image. 'Nope; that's it, I'm afraid.'

'Okay, Gerry, good work. At least we can see the bitch now. I want this program sent down to Walter Gray in R&D. We need to fit it into something mobile for the field team so they don't have to fight blind.'

*

The creature stopped at the tip of the peninsula of a fishing village called Çeşme, which had been there since before the time of the Trojans. A cloud swirled around the dark figure, but its central core never wavered as it stood at the water's edge. Around it, plants wilted, moths fell from the air, and small lizards shuddered, froze, and then turned milky white.

In its mind it saw a land that had ceased to exist many millennia before. Gone were the songs of the priests, the race of bull-jumpers, the souls of a hundred other races down the centuries. They were all gone, washed away by wind and rain and sand a hundred thousand times over. Its loneliness was like a disease eating it up inside. It longed to be among its own kind, or back in its home so far away. Chronological time meant nothing to a creature that measured its life in many thousands of years, but emotions could last an eternity.

The dominant beings here had barely advanced. It had seen inside their minds – they were still primal, aggressive and weak. But there had been one in the desert that was different; that was unique, and alone, like it was. The brief meld with this mind – or two minds, one rational, the other primitive – had made it long for its own kind again. Sadness almost doubled it over, and then the pain racked it again – pain and hunger. It needed more energy, needed to consume more of the smaller beings. Its job here was not done; its people also needed to be fed. It must return.

It sensed the rays of the sun before the yellow orb appeared at the horizon. It would rest soon. Like the small beings that lived here, it was made of billions of living cells. But unlike them, each cell was an individual entity, which cooperated and worked together with the others. The sunlight broke the cohesive bonds between its cells, allowing them to flow free.

The dawn's light bathed it, and almost immediately it seemed to fragment and then collapse, its elements drifting away, like dust ... or a swarm.

*

At sun-up, the curfew ended and the residents of Izmir emerged. Delivery vans started their rounds, cars, trucks, and bikes clogged the roads, and boats were rigged and the crews threw off lines and headed out in pursuit of the day's catch. In another hour, no one would remember what the fuss was about.

Mustafa Kamalak edged open his front door, and peeked out. The radio had said the threat was gone. The dark sense of foreboding Mustafa had felt the night before was just a memory. It was as though a storm had blown up, but passed over without doing any damage. He stepped fully outside and sucked in the morning air. He grinned, and turned to shout for his two sons.

In no time, he was gripping the boat's wooden wheel, one eye closed against the stinging smoke from the thick cigarette of reeking tobacco in his mouth. His face showed a thousand lines, each one carved by wind, weather, and adversity. Fishing was hard, and even harder now that the large-net boats trawled the open waters. Today, he would go far out, past the islands of Mikonos and Ios. If the big Greek boats wanted to scoop up all the fish from his home waters, then he would travel to theirs.

Kamalak grinned and shook his head. His two sons were below deck, playing music so loud it hurt his ears. Though he scolded them daily, they were his pride and joy. Their laziness, girl-chasing and bad language reminded him of himself when he was a boy, and made him love them all the more.

He peered through the greasy window to look up at the sky. A few heavy clouds, dark and thick – maybe rain later. He caught sight of the mast, and frowned. There was a large mass clumped on the pole about ten feet up, like a swarm of bees. He cursed; he'd heard that bee swarms, and even wasp colonies, could take up residence in boats for years. People had been stung to death.

He tied a rope over the wheel to keep it steady, and left the cabin, walking with the wide-legged gait of all men moving about on a small boat at sea. He approached the mast, keeping his eyes fixed on the dark clump, then bent to lift a boat hook that was lashed to the rail. The mass wasn't moving like bees; it looked solid, but jelly-like. It was certainly something strange.

He spat his cigarette over the side and concentrated. He couldn't hear buzzing, but there was definitely a sound – soft, like … sobbing. A knot of foreboding balled in his gut.

He lifted the boat hook and got on his toes, drew his arm back. It was hard to concentrate on the mass as it seemed to move and shift, staying where it was but never remaining still. He grunted as he plunged the brass hook into its center. The tip sank in easily, as if the strange blob was something glutinous. He went to draw the boat hook out, but it stuck. The pole vibrated in his hands, and he gripped it harder, bracing himself to give it a good yank.

The sky darkened as a huge cloud covered the sun. Almost immediately the mass flowed down the pole like a torrent of sparkling ants. Before Mustafa could take his hands away, his arms were covered to the elbows. The mass surrounded him, light like dust, but prickling as it seemed to work its way into his very pores.

His hands were now welded to the pole. As the stinging substance grew up over his face, he saw it flowing toward the hold – toward his boys.

*

A seagull squawked its outrage as Mustafa Kamalak's boat crashed into the shore west of Heraklion and just a few miles short of Panormos. The coastline was rugged, and even though the sea was calm the vessel struck hard, partly beaching itself. The sharp rocks and the motion of the waves, even though they were small, would soon ensure the old wooden boat was broken down completely.

The bird kept a beady eye on the craft, always on the lookout for a meal. The mast with its strange growth floated for a while, before wedging itself among the oyster-covered rocks. The tide would soon expose it. Of Kamalak and his sons there was no trace; no sign that anyone had been on board. The life jackets and buoyant rings were some of the first items to wash ashore, all unused.

Above the hiss of the waves and the creak of timbers there was another noise – sobbing. Unsettled by the strange sound, the seagull took off, circling the boat once and then leaving it far behind. Some instinct told it to be far away when the sun went down in just a few hours' time.

CHAPTER 27

Matt, Rebecca, and Reece Thompson sat on a bench outside the car hire company's office in Heraklion, waiting for their vehicle to be brought around.

Rebecca groaned and massaged an ankle. 'My feet and legs are killing me.'

'Pilot got us as close as he could without being spotted,' Thompson said. 'We're not exactly clearing customs, are we? It was only a couple of miles – c'mon, toughen up.'

Rebecca blew a raspberry at him and continued to rub.

'Got it.' Matt had his computer open on his lap. He turned it around to show them the screen.

Thompson winced. 'Good Christ, it's fucking huge. How are we able to see it when it nearly killed that technician?'

'Major Gerry Harris, Hammerson's go-to guy for technology, put an application together for us,' Matt said. 'And in answer to your question, we're not seeing it, the computer is. The program washes down the images, deconstructs them, then rebuilds them pixel by pixel, as a mirror image of the real thing.' Matt moved the volume bar up its scale. 'One more thing – listen.'

Both Thompson and Rebecca concentrated.

'That's sobbing,' Rebecca said. 'Turn it up.' Matt upped the volume to maximum, and Rebecca leaned in a little more. After a second or two she nodded. 'Now that is weird.'

'Is it in pain?' Thompson asked, then shrugged. 'Could be its language for all we know. Or even how the big bastard shows enjoyment.'

'Language?' Matt raised an eyebrow. He swiveled the computer on his lap and started to type furiously.

Thompson looked at his watch, and folded his arms. 'What I don't get is why it's turning people to stone. Is that how it gets its jollies?'

'We don't know yet if it's even aware it's doing that to us,' Rebecca said.

Thompson snorted. 'That's not what Hunter's report says. He reckoned it was well aware of him.'

'Energy,' Matt said without lifting his eyes from his screen.

Rebecca nodded. 'Not a bad theory. After all, there are many organisms that absorb energy – plants, algae, bacteria. They convert light energy, normally from the sun, into chemical energy that's later released to fuel their activities. The energy's held inside certain organelles, or in bacteria it's embedded in the plasma membrane. It's quite a normal process in nature.' She looked up at the sky. 'Right here, on our Earth, the first photosynthetic organisms probably evolved. But what about something very different from us ... or from anything that we know, something that evolved differently?'

'We feed by ingesting sugars and proteins and converting them into energy,' Matt said. 'Our guts have evolved a specialized digestion process to allow it. But that doesn't mean there aren't other ways to obtain energy.'

Thompson grimaced. 'You think the turning to stone thing might be how Magera feeds? Fuck me, that's disgusting.'

Matt shrugged. 'Who knows, ingesting flesh like we do might seem pretty sickening to this thing. But yeah, that's how it could be getting its energy. Check this out.'

He pressed a key, and discordant musical notes played.

'Well, that's annoying,' Thompson said.

Matt smiled. 'That's Magera – I ran it through Musify. It's an app that turns anything into a song.'

Rebecca grinned. 'The priest's song.'

'I doubt it, but I'll play around with it a bit more. See if I get anything interesting.' Matt closed his computer. 'Heads-up.'

A dented black Land Rover squealed to a halt in front of them in a cloud of black exhaust.

'Wow.' Thompson got to his feet.

Rebecca groaned and Matt guffawed.

The driver handed the keys to Thompson, who opened the door for Rebecca. 'Beats walking – just.'

*

Jack Hammerson watched Walter Gray as he circled the silver skeleton, looking it up and down with his expert eye. This version of the MECH suit was more an exoskeleton, as its armor plating, ribs, and hydraulic pistons fitted close, and needle-like electrodes pierced the wearer's skin, giving the combat armor immediate response activity. It was a mechanized way to turn a soldier into a super soldier.

Gray had designed and built the MECH suit himself, and Hammerson knew he loved his work. The scientist hit some buttons on a keypad he was holding, and the suit's arm lifted and its hand opened. He drew a foot-long steel baton from his pocket and placed it within the skeletal fingers. The hand closed around the baton. Gray typed some more and the hand squeezed the toughened steel like it was dough.

'That's my bad boy,' Gray said, and typed again. 'Now please let it go.'

The hand remained closed. He tried some different instructions, with no result. He tried again, and again, and eventually the hand opened and the crushed bar fell to the ground.

'Shit, shit, shit.' Gray scowled at the immobile suit. 'You're supposed to hand it to me.'

'Good work anyway, Gray,' said Hammerson. 'Can't wait to get it into the field.

'I've been wanting to talk to you about the field test, Colonel,' Gray said. 'How did –'

Jack Hammerson waved him to silence. 'Walter, I need Gerry Harris' software uploaded into full-face shielding units for my field team. And I need them fast – all on a jet in an hour.'

Gray half-saluted. 'Yes, sir, I can do that. And about the field test – there's still a few bugs we're working on, but I've been waiting to get your feedback. Any problems so far?'

Hammerson had no idea what he was talking about. 'Say that again?'

'The MECH suit – are you having any problems in the field?'

Hammerson felt his temples throb as alarm bells went off in his head. 'Walter, be absolutely clear now. What the hell are you talking about?'

Gray looked puzzled. 'You wanted to field-test the suit. So we dispatched one.'

Hammerson grabbed the man's shoulder. 'I am *not* field-testing any goddamn suit.' He couldn't help yelling the words.

'But ... but *you are*.' Confusion creased Gray's forehead. 'You and General Chilton recently requested a field test on the MECH's upper-body system. It's already been delivered.'

Hammerson lowered his head, closed his eyes, and ground his teeth. He drew in a breath and opened his eyes, his calm restored. 'Walter, please tell me where that combat armor was delivered?'

'To the airfield this morning.'

'And then where?' Hammerson kept his smile warm.

'Crete. I have both your and General Chilton's digital signatures on the order.'

Fucking Crete. Hammerson closed his eyes again and nodded, working to calm his breathing. Security was only ever as good as the weakest link. He exhaled slowly, knowing they'd been compromised. There were only two countries in the world that could have achieved this sort of penetration – Russia and China. China was expert at industrial espionage, but Russia had the stronger motive ... and they had Borshov.

'Is everything okay?'

Hammerson barely heard Gray's words as his mind worked furiously. *Borshov in the field in Crete, with a MECH suit. He'd be like a psychopathic tank.* Hammerson had total confidence in the Arcadian and his team, but they were only flesh and blood, and Borshov would be wrapped in steel. And he still had a couple Spetsnaz. Plus, Matt Kearns and Rebecca Watchorn were running around over there too, and Magera was potentially in the vicinity. The odds were rapidly shifting away from the HAWCs.

'I need another Alex Hunter,' he whispered.

'What's that, sir?'

Hammerson spun around to Gray. 'Lieutenant Sam Reid is already using a lower-half MECH suit. I want an upper-body unit sent to him immediately.'

Gray shook his head. 'But the entire suit will be extremely heavy. We've mitigated some of the weight ratios with the technology's own power-assist, but if it were to lose power for any reason, no normal man would be able to move in it. Sam Reid's a big man, but –'

'I understand the risk,' Hammerson said. 'Upload Gerry's software into the suit as well, and prepare the package for immediate delivery. We've got to drop it in before Greece closes its borders.'

Gray opened his mouth.

'*That's an order!*' Hammerson barked.

Gray flew into action, and Hammerson headed for the elevator. He needed to let Alex and his HAWCs know that Borshov had just scaled up his offensive capabilities – all courtesy of their own weapons lab.

*

Alex tossed the rolled-up parachute to Sam, who squeezed it into a tiny ball and buried it, dropping a flat stone over the top. Alex edged down into the ditch and dragged a coffin-sized crate out of the scrub, then used his fingers to pry the nailed lid open. Inside was what looked like half a metal skeleton with a molded helmet.

'Compliments of the Hammer,' Alex said, and dug deeper. In smaller compartments there were additional helmets, each named and undoubtedly tailored to size. Alex lifted his head and looked over the countryside. 'Sam, take over.'

He walked a few paces, stopped, and looked back along the shoreline. A sensation of foreboding reached up the back of his neck. He concentrated, staring for miles along the rocky coast, then slowly scanning the scrub of olive trees, and the roadway in both directions. There was nothing in sight, but Alex knew there soon would be. The same desolation and loneliness he'd felt out in the Turkish desert had returned. He recognized the emotions because they mirrored his own, but magnified a thousand-fold.

Alex stood frozen as his mind turned inward. He saw Aimee holding the boy, Joshua. The kid turning in her arms to smile and wave at him – the pair of them getting smaller and smaller as they walked into the distance.

'Boss.' Sam tossed him a helmet and Alex spun to catch it.

Sam handed out the rest of the kit. 'Franks, Rogers.' He smiled. 'Even a gift for my big English friend.' He tossed Jackson a helmet.

'My lucky day,' Jackson said, turning the full-face gear over in his hands.

'It'll never go over that big ugly melon,' Sam said with a grin, and Jackson gave him the finger.

Alex examined the helmet, then walked back over to look inside the crate. All that was left was the skeleton, labeled for Sam. Hammerson had told Alex why he'd sent it – 'to even the playing field' he'd said.

'Uncle, you get first prize,' Alex said. 'The rest is all yours.'

Sam grunted as he tried to lift out the suit, even though he was a huge man and one of the strongest HAWCs ever. The machine-tooled super-alloy frame weighed in at over 200 pounds.

'Need a hand?' Alex asked.

'I got this, boss,' Sam wheezed, his face beet-red. 'Damn, it's stuck.'

'Probably lashed down. Turn around, I'll put it on you.'

Sam turned, and Alex pulled one side of the crate away. The suit looked like a large backpack, with a network of rods, pipes, and tubes running over and around the shoulders and chest, giving it the look of metallic footballer's body armor.

Alex picked it up, barely straining. 'Guess it's gonna work in tandem with the technology you're already wearing.'

Sam nodded. 'That's the plan.'

He took off his shirt to reveal huge bull-like muscles bunched beneath scarred and tattooed flesh. He planted his legs and braced himself as Alex placed the suit over his shoulders, then worked his arms into the metal framework sleeves, and his fingers into the metallic gloves. He attached it to the lower suit and powered it up. The skeletal framework gripped and tightened along his torso and arms.

Sam rolled his shoulders. 'Still experimental. I guess I'm its first real field test.' He looked over his shoulder at Alex. 'If it explodes, make sure you pass on my less than positive feedback to Walter Gray.'

'You got it,' Alex said. 'But I'll give him one star for at least making it look cool.'

Sam snorted, and began to insert the electrode needles into the muscle fibers along his lower spine and arms. They'd tap into the nerves, making the assisting mechanics part of his body's nervous system and immediately responsive.

Once the suit was fully in place, it was self-supporting, using its own biometric-assisted power used to sustain the weight of the super-alloy frame. It was still heavy though – Sam could barely move. He looked like a cross between an old-style gladiator and an android.

He sucked in a deep breath. 'Boss, you'll have to give me a hand with this last bit.'

He motioned to a small plate dangling at his neck, with eight one-inch pins sticking out from what look like a micro-processor chip the size of a matchbook.

'Into the skull at the base of the medulla oblongata?' Alex said.

'You got it.'

Alex raised his eyebrows. 'Need something to bite down on?'

'Borshov's throat?' Sam guffawed and then shook his head, staring straight forward. 'Do it.'

Alex didn't hesitate, knowing the big man wouldn't even blink as he pushed the pins into the skin at the base of his skull. There was a second of resistance and then Sam exhaled.

'That's got it.' He grinned and nodded. 'Ha, light as a feather now.'

He lifted his arms, now wrapped in a bodywork of armor plating and tubes. The movement was smooth and fast. He turned his hands over, then made fists.

'Looking good,' Alex said, walking around him.

Casey Franks grinned. 'Man, do I want one of those.'

Alex bent, picked up a fist-sized rock and tossed it to Sam, who spun and caught it with lightning-quick reflexes. He held the rock up and, with a faint whine of electronics, closed his fist tight. The rock pulverized.

Sam winked. 'Look out, Arcadian, you got competition.'

'About time, big guy.' Alex looked at his watch. 'Let's move. We need to get to Heraklion ASAP, and that's about a hundred miles.'

Sam put his biological suit top back on over the MECH framework. The material stretched to fit, but looked lumpy in places.

Jackson held up the helmet he'd been given. 'What do we do with these? They're fucking blacked out.'

Alex placed his over his head – it covered everything except his mouth. The visor slid down, and he pressed a button to darken it, turning it into a solid mass. He held his hand up in front of it, and saw an outline appear, then his entire hand, but a little less detailed than the real thing. Gerry Harris' software was using microprocessors to capture, analyze, and digitally rework the image, then instantly deliver a reproduction.

Alex switched off the screen and pushed the visor up. 'This, my friends, is how we see without actually looking. Thank god for nerds. Now we got something we can use to go toe to toe with Magera.'

'Yeah, if we want to get torn in half,' Jackson said. 'The Turkish guys said it made mincemeat out of anyone who got close to it.'

Sam rolled his shoulders. 'But they weren't HAWCs.'

'Got that right, Uncle.' Franks bumped knuckles with Rogers, her scarred face pulled up in a half-grin.

Alex checked a small GPS, and then pointed. 'All right, let's see what our scientists have been up to. Double time.'

They started to jog toward the Lasithi Plateau and the Caves of Psychro.

*

Matt, Rebecca, and Reece Thompson sat in a small outside café overlooking a sparkling expanse of water that shimmered with a thousand diamond reflections. Matt watched Thompson's eyes narrow as he read down a page of notes.

The SAS soldier shook his head. 'The scuba equipment's easy – we can get that anywhere; same for night-diving rigs. But the demolition charges are harder. Hunter and his HAWCs won't have the explosives we need – they'll be carrying anti-personnel, and we need dynamite, or better still, C-4. For that we have three options – buy it legitimately, buy it on the black market, or steal it.'

'We start buying explosives and we'll raise some eyebrows. Got to get them on the quiet,' Matt said. He sipped from a tiny cup and winced. 'This coffee'd strip paint it's so freakin' strong.' He pushed another small sweet cake into his mouth. 'That's better – the baklava are great.'

Rebecca scoffed. 'Grow a pair, Kearns. This is real-man territory, home to Jason, Achilles, and Hercules.'

Matt rolled his eyes and turned back to Thompson. 'We'll probably need to steal the explosives. Don't know where we'd buy them anyway.'

'I do,' Thompson said. 'I've worked out here before. You just have to decide whether you want to deal with the devil.'

'The devil? Not terrorists,' Rebecca said quickly.

'Agreed,' said Matt, and looked at the SAS man. 'How and who?'

Thompson shrugged. 'Well, I could steal it from a construction site, but that'd be hit and miss. Better if we find someone to help us navigate the black market – means we can tailor our order.'

'Okay; how long will it take?' Matt asked.

'Quantities, quality, and delivery time all depend on how much you're willing to pay.'

Rebecca snorted. 'Supply and demand – gotta love the capitalist system.'

Thompson stood up. 'Give me a minute.' He walked away from the table, phone to his ear. He only seemed to speak a few words before he returned and sat down. 'And now we wait.'

'For what?' Rebecca asked.

'For a call telling me we have a meeting. Until then … we wait.' He grinned at Matt. 'Get your credit card ready.'

Rebecca sighed, sat back and tilted her head toward the sun. 'There are worse things, I suppose.' She slid the empty plate back to Matt. 'Order some more cakes seeing you're about to be so liberal with the taxpayers' money.'

Matt looked at his watch. 'Just a few more – we've got work we can do while we wait. The museum opens in thirty minutes. We can check out what they recovered from those deep caves a few hundred years ago. Hopefully it'll give us an idea which level we need to enter first.'

A small bee had landed on the empty cake plate, perhaps attracted by the syrupy sugar streaking its surface. Rebecca leaned forward, examining it closely.

'You know, if a hive is destroyed, by fire, or predators, and a few bees return home to find it that way, then they've been known to commit suicide.' She sat back, her eyes on the busy insect. 'They just stop moving and die. Basically, they can't exist by themselves … or don't want to. The hive group is the body and the bees are like cells really.'

She narrowed her eyes. 'An individual, just like a cell.'

In the granite forecourt of the museum was a huge list of its rooms, galleries, and collections. While Matt and Rebecca worked out where they needed to go, Thompson stood surrounded by a group of Greek women who'd obviously taken a shine to his physique.

The SAS man's face became serious and he turned away, placing a hand over one ear. 'Go ahead, Jackson.' He grunted several times. 'Got it – keep me informed of progress. Out.'

'What is it?' Matt asked.

'The HAWCs are here. We can also expect a nationwide martial law order any time soon, which is going to make it difficult to move around if you're not a local.' His expression became wry. 'Only upside to any of this is Magera seems to have finally got the Turks and Greeks working together.'

Matt nodded. 'A catastrophe will do that. Let's just hope we'll be finished and gone by morning. When will the HAWCs get to us?'

'Tonight.'

'Good,' Rebecca said. 'No offense, Reece, but I'll feel a lot better when we've got a few more good guys with us.'

Thompson winked. 'Hey, none taken – so will I. Now, are we going to get some work done?'

As they walked away, Thompson turned to the group of Greek women and waved. They waved back, and he grinned and managed to inflate his chest another half inch, much to their obvious delight.

'You know, I could live here,' he said.

'Come on, Adonis,' Rebecca said, and led them inside.

Beautiful frescos decorated the walls, showing cavorting dolphins, women with long curling hair and red lips pouring wine, alabaster lions and tigers leaping and snarling, and everywhere the glimmer of gold, from tiny deformed coins through to impressive crowns.

Rebecca pointed to a sign for the Minoan hall and picked up speed. In the center of the hall stood a life-sized granite bull. It was degraded now by the passage of thousands of years, but once it would have been hard to distinguish it from the real thing.

Descending a set of stairs they came upon a massive hangar-like space, with an entire section set aside for artifacts recovered from the caves of Crete.

'There are over 3000 known caves here, and less than a quarter have been fully explored,' Rebecca said. 'Many cultures, not just Minoan, believed the caves were home to gods, demons, and other creatures and subdeities.'

'Over here.' Matt waved them over to the sculpture gallery, where statues, some tiny like dolls, some larger than life, were arranged by period. Many were marble, granite, or dark basalt, but there were a few of calcium carbonate.

Rebecca pointed out one in particular, a little less than five feet tall, wrapped in a small kilt-like skirt with a bare torso. The leg was broken off, and at the center of the break was something unmistakable to the trio: a shard of bone.

Reece Thompson bent lower. 'You gotta be shitting me. It's as if the sculptor had actually seen battlefield injuries.'

Rebecca read from the brass plate at the statue's base. 'As we thought: recovered from the Psychro Caves … in the Cave of Zeus. It says *Minoan youth* – look at his face.'

The features were contorted with terror, frozen for all time.

'And this …' Matt pointed to a stone tablet depicting several kneeling figures. It was heavily eroded, but all had the Minoan long curl of hair down beside their ears, and the fluted dress with wrapped tunic. They were praying before a huge figure, their eyes bound with cloth. The faint scratches underneath the image could easily have been mistaken for chisel marks, but to Matt and Rebecca they were another clue.

'Minoan writing.' Matt turned to Rebecca. 'I'll do my best, but Margaret would be helpful right about now.' He leaned in close. '*The goddess of night and darkness* ... something, something ... *will always protect us. Let Hades hide her palace* ... the symbols for 200 ... *kalamos beneath our feet.*' Matt frowned. 'A kalamos was a very ancient unit of measure. Equivalent to about ten feet. I think it might be telling us the depth of where the goddess was living.'

'Two thousand feet,' Rebecca said thoughtfully. 'There are no caves that deep here – the Psychro Cave's only about 400 feet deep. Even the pool soundings that were taken are less than that.'

'No caves that we know of,' Matt said. 'You said yourself that rockfalls and flooding could have sealed off some areas.'

'That cave dive's looking more likely all the time,' Thompson said quietly.

Matt shook his head. 'I hate caves. I'll be on the surface, eating baklava and keeping a lookout.'

Rebecca put her arm around his. 'No way – we need your Minoan expertise. Anything else written there?'

Matt grimaced and leaned in toward the glass. 'Yeah, there's more. It says something like: *Beware* or *be in fear of the Guardians.*' He groaned. 'Great.'

'I only know of one guardian of the underworld,' Rebecca said. 'Cerberus.'

'The big angry dog? Nice. This is turning out to be a real holiday adventure, isn't it?' Thompson said and grinned.

'These mythological tales are usually allegorical,' Rebecca said. 'They're designed to teach us about the dangers of greed, lust, violence, and the like.'

'And a big dog does that how?' Thompson asked.

Matt shrugged. 'I wish it was only a big dog. Cerberus was actually the offspring of a half-woman, half-serpent. You see?

The serpent crops up in ancient Greek and Minoan mythology time and time again.'

Rebecca nodded. 'Cerberus was commonly represented in Greek mythology as having either two or three heads, each with an appetite for live meat. His sole job was to guard the gates to the underworld – hell.'

Thompson shook his head. 'Jesus. Did these guys have any nice gods?'

Matt grinned. 'Sure, but fear always works best. Anyway, a guard is a good sign. After all, you don't guard something unless it's valuable, right? So, at least this narrows our search – seems to me the Psychro Cave is where we need to start. If it's been sealed off by rockfalls and a million gallons of water for several thousand years, it means whatever *was* down there is probably still down there.'

'Like a giant many-headed dog?' Thompson raised his eyebrows.

Rebecca laughed. 'After about 5000 years, anything that was alive or trapped down there will be bones.'

'Yeah, just like Magera.' Thompson's face became serious. He looked from Matt to Rebecca. 'So, now what?'

'Now … we wait for your devil to meet with us,' Matt said.

Thompson nodded. 'We wait.'

CHAPTER 28

Uli Borshov stepped out into the road, raised a hand and waved the battered truck to a stop.

The driver leaned out of the window, puffing on a cigarette. 'Blackbird?'

Borshov nodded, grinning.

The truck driver looked him up and down for a moment, then shrugged, pushed open the door and stepped down. He flicked his smoke to the dirt, walked to the back of the truck, dropped the backboard, and stood back.

He pointed to a large crate. 'Is heavy. I hurt my back.'

Borshov clicked his fingers and his Spetsnaz came out from the scrub. The driver became wary and stuck his hands in his pockets, seeming to feel around for something. Borshov's men hauled the crate out, then one went to stand by the truck's open door. The driver's eyes flicked to the man, then back to Borshov.

He licked his lips. 'My job finish now. Pay me 500 USA dollars and I go home.'

Borshov held up a one large finger. 'First we check contents okay. Maybe you damage.' He grinned again.

The driver shook his head. 'Only damage is to my back.'

The Spetsnaz prized open the lid. Borshov bent to look inside, examining the half exoskeleton. Satisfied everything was there, he took off his shirt and began to drag it out of the crate. He grunted from the weight, but managed to lift it free and hoist it onto his back, his hugely muscled legs planted wide like a pair of hair-covered columns. He switched the suit on, and it clamped onto his body, the smaller electrodes penetrating the dark curling hair covering his torso and then his flesh. He winced, and then cursed, feeling the small plate dangling behind his neck. He knew there was one more painful step to go.

He motioned to his Spetsnaz. 'Grigor, there is small plate with needles. Push it into the base of my skull.'

Grigor briefly examined the long needle-like electrodes, then roughly jammed them into Borshov's flesh.

Borshov gritted his teeth and made a hissing noise. Grigor grinned.

The truck driver grimaced, and edged toward his open door. The Spetsnaz standing there blocked him.

Borshov exhaled, and began swinging his arms, faster and increasingly fluidly as the MECH suit bonded with his body and nervous system. He threw fake punches, his speed increasing even more. He flicked one huge armor-plated fist into the truck's steel side; it impacted with a clang, leaving a huge dent.

'Good,' he said.

The truck driver stared at the ding in his vehicle. 'Okay, all works. Pay me and I go.' His brow was wet with perspiration.

'How much you say?' Borshov asked.

'Five hundred dollars … USA.'

Borshov nodded. He stepped toward the man, moving lightly even though he carried an extra few hundred pounds of hydraulics and armor plating. When he was within three feet of the driver, one of his arms shot out and grabbed the man's arm, dragging him closer.

The driver ripped a long machete blade from the leg of his trousers and swung it at Borshov, but the big Russian caught the hand and ripped the weapon free. The man frantically pummeled at Borshov's arm, but all he did was split his own knuckles on the metal frame.

The driver was a big man, weighing in excess of 220 pounds, but Borshov lifted him over his head and then smoothly brought his hands together. The driver screamed, and there was a sickening crunch as his body was folded in half.

Borshov threw the corpse into the dry scrub. His men laughed, and one clapped.

Borshov looked at his hands. 'Good. Very good.' He looked at his men, grinning. 'I just saved us 500 dollars ... and we also have a truck.'

One of the Spetsnaz touched a stud at his ear, listening. 'The local Ikoyennia have some information about Kearns, the American professor, to sell.'

Borshov nodded, looking at his hands again. 'Sell? Maybe I will save us some more money instead.' He flexed the armor-plated fingers. 'Now we will see what happens to you in *these* hands, Arcadian.'

*

'We're on.' Reece Thompson disconnected the call and set the phone down on the café table.

'You got the meeting?' Matt said. 'Excellent.'

'Sure, and they can fill our order,' Thompson said. 'They'll want to know why we want it though.'

'But we're not telling them, right?' Rebecca said.

'It's not negotiable,' Matt added, his expression deadpan.

Thompson shrugged. 'Then we might have to get it ourselves. But we're dealing with the Ikoyennia, the local mafia. Now they know about our request, they'll make sure we don't get it from anyone else if we cancel. Bottom line is, if they think we're planning a robbery, they know the heat will also come down on them. So, they'll want a cut.' He smiled. 'A juicy one.'

'Can we steal the dynamite?' Rebecca asked.

'From the Ikoyennia?' Thompson snorted. 'Then we'll end up in a war with an army of Greek and Cretan gangsters.'

Rebecca frowned. 'No, I mean from a mining company or the like.'

Thompson shook his head. 'Where do you think they're getting it? The difference is, they'll probably use someone on the inside – no alarms, no violence, no mess. No time-wasting.'

Matt exhaled and sat back. 'And if we tell them?'

Rebecca started to object, but Matt stopped her.

'Like I said, they'll want a cut of the action.' Thompson waved over a waiter and ordered a coffee.

Matt looked across the table at Rebecca. 'Do we care? Do we have the time to care?' He paused. 'If there are valuables down there, my professional self tells me to make sure they end up in a museum. But we need to look beyond that. What we seek has no value to the mafia, so as far as I'm concerned they're welcome to whatever else is down there.'

'Fine with me,' Thompson said.

Rebecca scowled. 'Anything and everything down there belongs to Crete.'

'Yeah, sure, except the stuff we might want to take,' Matt said. 'Look, we don't have time to make a moral stand. People are dying ... and more will die unless we can stop Magera. We get the C-4, they get a cut – like Reece says, no mess.' Matt raised his hand. 'In or out?'

Thompson nodded and raised his hand.

Rebecca scowled for a moment. 'Argh, okay.' Her hand went up briefly, then whipped down again.

Matt looked at Thompson. 'Let's make it happen.'

*

Matt, Rebecca, and Thompson sat in a room filled with polished antiques, and with beautiful artwork adorning every wall. Statues and other objects from various periods were displayed in cabinets around the walls, professionally uplit. Matt's eyes watered at the sight of so many stolen artifacts, all of which would have made any museum curator in the world drool. Behind the desk, a gray-haired but robust-looking older man poured tiny cups of coffee for them all. Carlo Vangelis was the head of the local Ikoyennia family; a businessman with fingers in too many pies to mention. He looked like a kindly uncle, Matt thought, until he fixed his green merciless gaze upon you.

Vangelis finished pouring and motioned for them each to take a cup. 'So, you want to blow something up?' he said, watching Matt over the rim of his own cup.

Matt decided to be candid. 'Maybe. We need to get into the Psychro Caves. There might be something down there we need, and it might be buried. We'll probably need to blast the rock.'

'A lot of rock, I think.' Vangelis grinned, showing extremely white teeth. 'What is it?'

Matt didn't hesitate. 'Maybe some writing on a wall, maybe an old document – we don't know yet. We'll know it when we see it.'

'You want to blow up one of Crete's national treasures, and you don't really know if it will be worth the trouble? Not, I think, something I want to be part of.' He lifted his cup to his lips again.

'There could be Minoan treasure,' Rebecca blurted out.

Vangelis put his cup down slowly. 'And now I am listening.'

Matt talked briefly about what might be found in the lower caves, omitting any reference to the living Magera. He described the piles of gold, rivers of oil, and encrusted jewels given as tribute over the centuries – all of it, or none of it, could be hidden in the very depths of the Psychro Caves.

Vangelis sipped slowly, his eyes steady as he watched Matt for a full minute after he'd finished. His gaze slid to Rebecca, then to Thompson. 'So, two scientists and one SAS soldier on a secret treasure hunt, and prepared to vandalize one of the wonders of Crete. And you want to do this for some words written on something maybe 5000 years ago?' His eyebrows shot up. 'They must be important words.'

'They are, but only to us,' Matt said evenly. 'They're of historical importance. In fact, after we've examined them, you can keep them.'

Vangelis nodded slowly. 'I have been inside the Psychro Caves. They are deep, and at the bottom there is only a lake. Why do you think there is something other than more water down there?'

Matt felt he was being subjected to a human lie detector. 'It's a risk that there is only water. But our research leads us to believe the caves run deeper, into other caverns. We strongly believe it's worth investigating.'

'And that investigation cannot involve the government because there is something down there that you do not wish to share with them?' Vangelis asked evenly.

Matt nodded. 'Unfortunately, yes. But we seek only the words ... the knowledge. Anything else is yours.'

Vangelis bobbed his head from side to side. 'It seems like a simple and worthwhile investment. But if you are caught ...'

Matt nodded. 'Then we never met.'

Vangelis grunted, scrutinizing Matt for another few moments. 'Dynamite, semtex or C-4?'

'C-4,' Thompson said. 'Better-quality plasticizer, and better for shaping charges, especially in a liquid environment. We'll take three one-kilo packs, plus detonators.'

Vangelis smiled. 'Very good.'

He lifted a phone and spoke rapidly in Greek for a few seconds. Matt followed the conversation, not letting on that he understood every word. Vangelis looked at his watch and hung up. He clasped his hands together on the desk.

'When will you be entering the cave?'

'Tomorrow morning, before dawn,' Matt said. 'We need diving equipment – cave diving equipment. We planned to buy it but ...'

Vangelis shrugged. 'No problem. I assume you'll also need keys to the security gate over the cave? My men will meet you there with the dive equipment and C-4 at say ... 4 am?'

Thompson sat forward. 'No way.'

Matt grabbed his arm. 'The extra security will be fine. But they take orders from us once we're below ground.'

Vangelis' face was like stone. 'They take orders from me – above and below ground.' The silence stretched, and his features softened. 'But on the descent, you are ... team leader.' He opened his arms. 'You see, we all work together just fine.'

*

As the day faded, a small cloud began to form on the shoreline west of Heraklion, just a few miles shy of Panormos, lifting from the rocks, shattered beams, tattered cloth, and broken mast of a fishing boat. The mist solidified at its center, then snaked along the jagged coastline, staying in the shadows.

Like a dark tide, it surged along gulleys, around rocks, and beneath trees. Insects, rodents, and small lizards scurried from its path, the slower ones shuddering, turning white and becoming rigid.

The mist flowed up into the mountains, and toward the ancient caves.

CHAPTER 29

Evening lengthened into night as the HAWCs jogged to the Psychro Caves. Franks ran beside Rogers, with Jackson a dozen paces behind them, and Sam and Alex the same distance out in front. A HAWC was trained to run all day and all night and still be fresh enough to enter a hand-to-hand combat scenario on arrival in a conflict zone. But they were all feeling the heat. Though the biological armored suits were lightweight, and the sun had gone down, the ground still gave off residual warmth.

The pace was hard, and Rogers blew air and wiped his brow. 'Hot.'

'Sure is.' Franks looked across at him. 'Lookin' a little flushed there, Junior.'

Rogers grinned. 'I'm the same age as you.'

'Yeah, but I've been a HAWC for four years. You've been in for one. To me that makes you just one year old ... Junior.'

The group pushed on, keeping in formation. They still had miles to go. The plan had been to commandeer a vehicle, but seeing they needed to keep a near-invisible profile they had to skirt towns and stay off major roads. The back roads were overgrown, dusty, and about as inhabited as Mars.

Rogers lowered his voice. 'What do you think about this Magera thing? The boss said he heard it weeping.'

Franks snorted. 'I'll fucking make it weep all right.'

Rogers laughed. 'I bet you will. Hey, you know that professor said it might be a living god.'

'A god?' She scoffed. 'Let me tell you about the time I was in the Appalachians. I went up against something the Native Americans used to refer to as the god of the mountains.'

'Let me guess. You killed it,' Rogers said wearily.

Franks grinned. 'Nah, it threw me off a cliff.'

Rogers laughed. 'That still makes you the expert in my book.' His face became serious. 'This thing tore the Turkish Spec Ops guys in half – legs one way, guts and head the other.'

'I read the briefing too,' she said, her eyes bright. 'That's a good thing.'

'Huh?' Rogers frowned.

'If it can do that, it has physical form. If it has physical form, we can inflict damage ... and if we can damage it, we can fucking kill it.'

'Yeah.' He reached up a forearm to wipe his brow. 'How much further?'

Franks looked at a small box strapped to the inside of her wrist. 'Just eighteen to go.'

She saw that Sam and Alex in front were chatting as they ran at a speed that was almost a sprint for her shorter stride. As far as she was concerned *the boss* was back. She still thought that inside him there lurked something unspeakably violent, but she guessed there were demons running loose in all of them. He'd kept it together and under control in Italy, and he'd been ice cool ever since. But she doubted that cool would be maintained if he got in front of Uli Borshov. *Good,* she thought.

Franks smiled; she rated herself highly skilled in combat and warfare, even among the HAWCs. With the Arcadian back, and Sam in a full MECH suit, the super-soldiers bolstered their team. *Look out, world*, she thought.

Alex and Sam kicked up the pace another notch.

'They aren't even sweating,' Rogers said.

'Go and complain.' Franks winked and lifted her stride.

He snorted, and increased his pace. 'I'd rather die.'

*

Matt lay on the bed in the hotel room, arms behind his head, staring up at the ceiling. They'd given themselves a few hours off while they waited to meet up with Vangelis' men at the cave. The room was cool, the sheets clean and pressed, and fatigue dragged on his frame. But still he couldn't drift off. His mind kept whispering warnings, refusing to let him slip away.

Truth was, he was dreading going into the deep caves. The thought of swimming in inky water beneath mega-tons of rock made him want to throw up. His mind was dredging up memories of previous encounters with things from his worst nightmares – things that really existed. He'd accompanied a team of scientists and HAWCs to the Antarctic, where they'd gone down into the darkness beneath the ice. Of all the fifty on that mission, only three had returned: Matt, scientist Aimee Weir, and Alex Hunter. There were things down in that subterranean darkness that had torn at his sanity. He'd spent years working hard to push them into a secure part of his brain, imprisoned under a mental lock and key. He was rarely successful at keeping them there.

The doorbell buzzed, and he nearly leaped a foot into the air.

'Matt.' It was Reece Thompson. 'Downstairs in ten.'

Matt tried to calm his rapid heartbeat and swung his legs over the side of the bed. 'Got it, Reece.'

He stood, and rubbed his face hard. 'In and out in a few hours – no problem,' he told himself. 'No problem at all.'

Fifteen minutes later, he exited the elevator and crossed the empty foyer to see Thompson standing outside in the humid night air. There was an enormous moon rising.

Thompson nodded and Matt returned the gesture. 'Nice night for a swim.'

'Or to blow some shit up,' Thompson replied.

'Let's hope our friends get us the right explosives.' Matt raised his eyebrows. 'And they're the real thing.'

Thompson grunted. 'I'll know if they're real or not, don't worry.'

Rebecca pushed through the doors and stretched. Her eyes were slightly puffy. 'Couldn't manage a cat nap – overtired, or overexcited, I guess.'

'Tell me about it.' Matt half-smiled. 'Don't worry, this'll be fun.'

She looked at him like he'd just grown another head. 'Fun … for who?'

His smile fell away, and he couldn't meet her eyes. 'Well, if we find something that gives us a clue how to control Magera, and perhaps save lives, it'll be worth it. Agreed?'

Rebecca bobbed her head once, and turned away.

'Load 'em up, people,' Thompson said. 'It's about an hour's drive up to the plateau.'

The road soon gave way to a dirt track, and the Land Rover rocked and bounced along it, heading up the mountain. Vapor rose from the ground like ghosts between the pine trees.

The moonlight showed three big men standing beside a truck near the entrance to the main cave. The truck looked in worse condition than their Land Rover, Matt thought.

Thompson eased the Land Rover to a stop. 'Welcoming committee's already here.'

'The birthplace of Zeus,' Rebecca said, and stepped down.

Matt and Thompson followed, but Matt noticed the soldier kept the car door open between himself and Vangelis' men, and his hand hovered near his gun. He quickly ran his eyes over the dark rocks bordering the cave, and the stands of pines rising around them, before returning to the men. Only then did he step out fully.

He nodded toward the men's truck. 'Where's our equipment?'

Matt began to translate, but one of the men waved at him to stop. 'We understand. That is why we are chosen to be here, to … help you.' He smirked. 'I am Antonis Papariga – call me Tony.' He pointed to the large man on his left. 'Petro.' And then to the one at his right. 'Andronus.'

Tony walked to the truck and dropped the backboard to reveal wetsuits, air tanks, goggles and flippers, knives, numerous lights, hammers and spike bars like long crowbars, shovels, and even some spear guns. There was also a heavy metal box with a yellow warning symbol on the front.

Tony flipped it open. 'This was not easy to get so quickly.'

Thompson walked over and peered inside. Matt could see there were six packages the size of a large block of butter, twice as many as they'd requested, each wrapped in brown paper with Greek writing and more warning symbols. Thompson lifted a block, squeezed it slightly, and held it to his nose. He nodded, replaced it, and then lifted what looked like a capped silver pen.

He turned to Matt. 'All good.'

Tony grinned and held his arms wide. 'Mr. Vangelis hopes for a good return on his investment.' He unbuttoned the front of his shirt, opening it slightly to show a wetsuit underneath. 'Now, you pay for equipment. Ten thousand euros.'

There were urgent words from behind him, and Tony nodded, then turned back to Matt. 'For each of us.'

'What?' Matt spluttered.

Rebecca crossed her arms and rolled her eyes. 'Why don't we see what Mr. Vangelis says about this, hmm?' She held up a slim phone, and started to press numbers.

Tony's face went red, then he grinned and waved his hand. 'No, no, do not call. I was only having big joke with you. We are ready when you are, Professor.'

Matt nodded. While the men unloaded the truck, he whispered to Rebecca, 'You don't really have his number, do you?'

She raised an eyebrow. 'Nope ... but they don't know that.' She leaned closer to him. 'Should we wait for the HAWCs?'

Matt thought for a second or two, then shook his head. 'The search could take hours, and they might be still miles away.' He sucked in a deep breath. 'Let's make a start.'

*

Matt's heart was racing. The night air surrounding them was warm, humid, and pine-scented, but he felt a depressing cold radiating from the blackness of the Psychro Cave. He detected a faint movement of air, and with it a whiff of rocks and moss and dampness. He shivered even though he wore a rubberized wetsuit.

Like Rebecca and Thompson, he had a backpack over his shoulders containing excavation equipment, climbing gear, and extra flashlight batteries. Thompson got to carry the explosives. Matt looked at their three Greek minders. All wore wetsuits over their sizable frames, and two had shoulder holsters. Matt wondered what they'd do with the guns when it came time to enter the water.

He pointed to Tony's holster. 'You know, a gun goes off down there, we could all be buried alive.'

Tony shrugged. 'Then we hope we don't need them.' He nodded toward Thompson. 'I think these peashooters are not as loud as your friend's gun, huh?' He winked, but Thompson ignored him.

'They're dangerous,' Matt persisted.

'And the fucking explosives – are they for redecorating?' Tony said with a grin. He nodded toward the dark cave opening. 'Do we go in or what?'

Rebecca narrowed her eyes. 'I've got a bad feeling about these guys,' she whispered to Matt. 'Once we get down there and show them anything of value, we may not get out again.'

'Yeah, well.' Matt gave her a crooked smile. 'It's not really them I'm worried about. There are far worse things in caves than thugs with guns.'

Thompson gave them the go-ahead, and Matt sighed. He switched on his headlamp and aimed his big flashlight into the stygian darkness. Behind a heavy metal gate, concrete steps with a railing led down into the dark.

'Abandon hope all ye who enter here,' he whispered.

Rebecca finished the quote. 'Through me you pass into the city of woe. Through me you pass into eternal pain.'

Thompson groaned. 'Is that supposed to be motivational? Because it's not working.'

Matt smiled despite his fear. 'Dante's 700-year-old poem about Virgil's travels to Hell.'

Thompson rolled his eyes. 'Like I said, motivational.'

Tony went first, unlocking the gate and heading down the steps into the darkness. Fifty feet in, he stopped at a small metal box fixed to the wall with a large padlock at the bottom. He inserted another key, popping the padlock open, and lifted the lid of the box to expose rows of switches. One after the other he flipped them down. With a clanking sound and a hiss of sodium, lights began to shine overhead, behind stalagmites and stalactites, and from within smaller grottos, all illuminating a wonderland of different mineral colors.

Matt snorted. 'You can see why earlier inhabitants thought this was a magical place.'

'Brave little buggers, coming in here in the dark,' Thompson observed as he looked around.

'And nothing but ghosts for company,' Rebecca said.

As they descended, the temperature seemed to drop a degree every dozen feet. The colored lighting gave the caverns a mystical feel, and signs on the walkway indicated the names the natural structures had been given: Hades' Grotto, Zeus' Throne, Titan's Spear.

Matt pointed out a pathway worn into the stone along one of the walls. 'Probably where Minoan feet trod thousands of years ago.'

After twenty minutes they came to an enormous central pit, with a lake another hundred or so feet below. The water was so still it could have been glass. There was a hoicking noise and then Petro let loose a gobbet of spit that sailed downwards.

Matt shook his head and cursed.

The blob struck the surface and created ripples on a lake that had probably lain undisturbed for over a century. The big man grinned, and was dragging up another gobbet when Thompson came up behind him and nudged him hard in the back.

'Ach!' Petro pulled back from the edge, looking panicked. He glared at the Englishman.

'We've got to swim in there, you dumb bastard,' Thompson said, his eyes daring the Greek.

Tony snorted, and smacked Petro over the back of the head. 'Work first, play later.'

It took them another hour to reach the lowest level of the cave. At a nod from Thompson, Matt stepped over the guard rail and edged along a narrow slab of rock to the lake's edge. Lights had been placed just at its surface to illuminate the shallows. The water was so clear that, unless you concentrated, it was hard to see where it started and the air stopped. He looked up and saw an alcove across the pool, with a portion of wall and a few fragments of paving tiles still embedded in the ground. Marble covered a flat rock that would have been a magnificent polished surface thousands of years before.

'Hercules' Table,' Matt said. 'This is where Professor Myres found many of the artifacts back in 1896 – axe heads, darts, and knives.' Matt looked at Tony. 'There were also gem-encrusted daggers, a golden chariot, and beautifully carved ivory figurines – all priceless.'

Tony grinned and nodded.

Matt adjusted the angle of his headlamp, shining it into the darker recesses of the cave. 'The ancient Greeks, Minoans, and even the early Neolithic tribes, held festivals deep in these caves, usually heralding the change of the seasons, and when they wanted to bring fertility back to the earth. Gifts of gold, weaponry and, in many cases, virgins were thrown into cave pools and volcanoes. Dozens of skeletons of young woman were pulled from the silt of this pool alone.'

He pointed to the deeper center of the pool. 'One story has it that the cave god of Crete was a mother goddess who rested upon hills of gold and gave birth each season to a son who was made of stone.'

Tony lit a cigarette. 'Hills of gold, you say?'

'Put that out,' Rebecca said. 'There's a chance we could open a cave filled with methane. One spark and you'll kill us all.'

Tony dragged hard on the cigarette, unmoved. Rebecca sighed and went and added her torch beam to Matt's.

'This is a good place to start,' she said. 'This cave flooded in the early 1800s after some dynamiting on the surface – it collapsed some of the deeper caves, and also allowed rain water to pour in during ensuing rainy seasons. The artifacts that Professor Myres found were believed to have washed out from smaller caves. We need to find out which ones.'

'So, what are we looking for?' Thompson was moving his light over the surface of the lake.

'The earth leaves us clues,' Matt said. 'The rock formations down here grow incredibly slowly – about a third of an inch in ten years.' He shone his light on an enormous column reaching from floor to ceiling. 'That started off as a single drip of water loaded with calcium carbonate and other minerals. A stalactite forms on the ceiling, a stalagmite on the floor, and over hundreds of thousands of years they grow toward each other, touch and then combine. So we're looking for new growths or scars on the rock, above and below water. Anything indicating fresh action that began in the last few hundred years.' He turned to Thompson and pointed with his thumb at the lake. 'And that means pool time, I'm afraid.'

He stood with Thompson, looking down into the water. It looked about two feet deep, but the clarity was deceptive – it could have been ten. Tumbled boulders were visible below the surface, with occasional snaggle-tooth islands lifting calcium carbonate and mineral spires toward corresponding stalactites on the cavern roof above. As they watched, a small sprat-type creature wriggled from one shard of stone to another.

'There are things living in there,' Thompson said.

Matt nodded. 'Could be blind eels, blind fish, blind shrimp – you name it. Could be all kinds of things, but all blind.'

Thompson stepped into the water – up to his waist. Clouds of silt billowed around his ankles.

'Try not to disturb the layer of slime and silt on the bottom, if possible. The water will end up like soup.'

Thompson nodded and lifted his feet, floating in the water. 'It's warmer than I expected.'

'Really?' Matt frowned and placed his hand into the water. 'Hmm, might be thermal vents.' He straightened. 'Well, lucky you. Remember, you're looking for rockfalls, scraped stone, tunnels below the surface, anything like that.'

Thompson pulled the mask over his face, gave Matt a thumbs-up, then rolled over. The small tank he wore only carried about twenty minutes of breathing time, so he used his snorkel, and the sound of his breathing through the tube was loud in the echoing cavern.

Matt went to supervise their three Greek minders, who were looking for treasure, while Rebecca edged along the waterline, bending now and then to examine small imperfections in the melted-candle-like cave formations.

After thirty minutes or so, the Greeks gave up their search and leaned against a metal guard rail, smoking and laughing. Reece Thompson had swum away into the darker recesses of the cave, his headlamp creating a glowing circle around him in the immaculate water. Matt and Rebecca were exploring different corners of the cave.

Matt found a small grotto and poked his head inside, noticing a glint of something pressed into the far wall. He leaned in further and extended his arm, straining toward it. *Could it be?* He couldn't reach past some stalagmites that were like teeth in a bottom jaw, creating bars over the opening. He stared at them, trying to find an angle he could squeeze through.

Rebecca came and kneeled beside him. 'Got something?'

'Maybe … if I can work out how to get it.'

He eased in against one of the stone columns.

'Oh, please,' Rebecca said.

She grabbed the calcium carbonate pillars and tugged. One – as thick as an arm – broke off. Matt looked at her horrified.

She snorted. 'What? We came down here to blow a hole in these caves if need be, remember?'

He grimaced, knowing she was right. 'Thanks.'

He leaned in again, using his flashlight to extend his arm another foot to scrape at the object. It broke off and tumbled down the wall, rolling toward him. He grabbed it and turned it over, his excitement abating.

Rebecca crowded in close. 'What is it?'

He held it out. 'Pretty jewel for a pretty lady?'

It was a crystal pressed into some glittering pyrite, perfectly formed like the end of a large diamond.

She sighed. 'Nice, but no cigar.'

In another half-hour they had exhausted all the obvious caves, nooks, and crannies. Most had been well and truly turned over by archeologists over the centuries.

Matt rested on his haunches as he sipped from his canteen. 'We're not looking at this right.'

Rebecca glanced around. 'We should have expected that any new passages would be hidden. We could do with some stratigraphic sonars to penetrate the rock.'

'Yep.' He nodded slowly, staring toward the dark end of the cave where Thompson had disappeared. 'I'm guessing it's a bit late to ask Vangelis, so ... let's think laterally. Imagine we're here a few thousands years ago, the only technology we have is burning torches. We've scaled down here in the darkness, using ropes and clambering along slippery walls. This place would be as scary as hell – in fact, a lot of early cultures thought these passages *were* a path to hell.'

She nodded, following his train of thought. 'Go on.'

'We know there were probably other paths into the cave, which have since collapsed or been flooded. We also know the early inhabitants of the island were good fishermen and not afraid of water. If you wanted to keep something hidden, or stay hidden yourself, the best place would be somewhere that's difficult to get to ...' Matt shone his light toward Thompson, now a hundred feet away in the enormous lake. 'When Reece entered the pool, he stirred up mud, and I immediately told him not to do that to keep the water clear. What if the clues we need to find are below the mud?'

She shrugged. 'It's possible – it's the only thing left that makes sense.'

Matt waved their Greek minder over. 'Tony, we need to search under the mud. Anything that might indicate another cave.'

Tony didn't look keen. 'Like what? A door handle or something?' He frowned in confusion.

Matt shrugged. 'At this point, just anything that shouldn't be there naturally. We're still looking for fresh gouges, or tumbled rocks, but man-made.'

Tony grunted in understanding, and turned, whistling sharply. 'Petro, Andronus, in the water, now.'

A rapid-fire conversation in Greek took place for a few moments, with Tony raising his voice at his men. Eventually, with a lot of cursing and grumbling, the two Greeks pulled goggles down over their faces and sloshed into the water. There was no need to tell them not to worry about stirring up the mud. In a second, the water was like milky coffee.

Matt pointed to the lake, then half-bowed to Rebecca. 'After you.'

She pulled her goggles down, put the snorkel in her mouth, switched on her headlamp and fell forward into the water.

Matt stayed standing, watching them paddle off in different directions. The once pristine pond now resembled a hotel swimming pool in summer. He chose a different direction to others, waded into the water and swam out.

All he could hear now was the sound of his breathing. Silt swirled around him, and even though the shallows were only a few feet deep, he had to feel his way along the bottom by hand, stopping from time to time to bring his flashlight in close to examine a raised surface or indentation. As he went deeper, the water cleared and he saw stalagmites rising up from the depths, like terracotta warriors standing guard in a sunken city.

Matt felt a chill run up his spine. He hated caves, hated the dark, and especially hated black water. He had witnessed men and women die horribly in caves. One man had been eaten from the inside out by a tiny carnivorous worm. Matt felt his groin contract at the thought of something swimming inside his wetsuit and into an open part of his body. He reached up and tugged the neck of his wetsuit tighter at his throat. *Don't think about it, don't think about it*, he repeated over and over.

He trod water for a few seconds, pushed the snorkel away from his mouth, and lifted the scuba tank mouthpiece to his lips. He sucked the dry and metallic-tasting air into his lungs, then floated again, sighting down into the depths for a moment, before diving ten feet.

Deeper, the water felt even more ominous. His lights were the only illumination in a world of dark liquid. He could hear the faint splashing of his fellow searchers, but his breathing was louder, and there was a faint pounding in his ears caused by his racing heartbeat.

Matt allowed himself to drift lower into a depression in the lake floor. He paused to repressurize his ears, and found himself hanging weightless between a pair of stalagmites. The giant columns would have originally formed on the dry cave floor, but flooding had submerged them long ago. He swam toward a wall made of large boulders covered in mosses, with silt piled against one side. A school of tiny fish shot past him to disappear into cracks between the boulders. As he watched, he saw some strands of lichen bend as if in a breeze. *Promising*, he thought, and drifted lower.

He bent forward to sweep his hand over the silt, a layer about six inches thick. Immediately it clouded his vision. He brought his face closer, ignoring the sliminess of the particles, and ran his hand over the cave floor beneath the silt. It was smooth. It could be flowstone, or calcium carbonate that had run like melted wax over the eons – or it could be something more. He carefully pushed more of the sludge out of the way, wishing he had an industrial underwater vacuum cleaner that could have sucked up a ton of muck in minutes.

He brought his flashlight around. A glimpse of something white ... He waved his hand in the water, trying to create a current to drag the silt away from where he was working. In another few seconds, he saw it again – the flash of white.

Matt felt his heartbeat kick up a gear, and he waved furiously at the water now, clearing more silt away. He could see tiles, small mosaics all fitted together, each no more than an inch square. They formed a structure, a floor. Other colors started to show too ...

Matt turned, grabbed onto a column, and used his flippers to create a huge torrent that billowed the debris into huge clouds. His thighs burned, but he kept at it, eventually displaying a tiled section half a dozen feet wide – and long. He was wrong; it wasn't a floor, but a path, and many of the newly exposed tiles were still vivid, protected by the oxygen-poor silt at the bottom of the deep pool.

A face showed at the center of the path. It didn't belong to a dark-haired Minoan beauty, or a bull-jumping athlete with bronzed muscles and aquiline nose. Instead, it was something designed to strike fear, or perhaps awe, into whoever saw it: the screaming face of the Gorgon, with writhing hair and the red-slitted eyes of a snake.

Got you, Matt thought, as he let himself descend to the cave bottom.

He used his hands like a snowplow, following the edge of the path until it met the wall. A huge column rose from the floor, blocking his way, but he could see a light current moving around its sides. He guessed the wall had probably collapsed many years before the cave flooded, and the column had grown up over its entrance. He looked upward, following the column to where it breached the water's surface – about ten feet around. Doing a quick calculation, he estimated the column to be about 5000 years old, which made the time scale right.

Matt let go of the column and drifted to the surface, immediately bumping his head on stone. The roof here was low; it was no wonder this end of the cave hadn't been fully explored.

He dragged his mask from his face and spat out the mouthpiece. 'Rebecca! Found it!'

CHAPTER 30

Gerry Harris' team were watching footage of the entity forming up on Crete's coast. It became larger, coalescing and solidifying, before flowing away from the shoreline. The new software allowed them to see the figure at the center of the mist.

One of the technicians leaned back in his chair. 'Major Harris, it's beginning to pick up speed.'

'Direction?' Harris came and leaned on the man's desk.

The man watched for another moment. 'So far, heading south – seems to be making for the Psychro Caves, as expected. Speed, twenty miles per hour, but moving up and down the scale – sometimes stopping, sometimes moving at over fifty.'

Harris pushed away from the desk. 'I better let Hammerson know his team's about to have company.'

*

Alex waved his team into cover, and walked alone to the dark cave mouth. The iron gate swung open. He slowly turned to take in the surrounding ridges, rocky outcrops, and stands of trees. He signaled to Franks, and pointed to two trucks pulled in behind a stand of trees. The HAWC moved fast and low to the vehicles.

Alex waved the others in as he returned to the cave mouth, and stood staring into its depths. Franks rejoined the team and they formed up around Alex.

'We're not far behind,' Franks said. 'The Land Rover smells like Rebecca's deodorant. The flatbed has some diving and excavation equipment on the back, but nothing to indicate who drove it here. One thing's for sure: it wasn't Borshov. The guy stinks like a vodka-soaked grizzly.'

Sam motioned to the cave entrance. 'Boss, anything?'

Alex nodded. 'They're already down there – Matt, Rebecca, and Thompson. Also another group of men, large, but not Special Forces.'

He continued to stare into the cave, his eyes narrowing. He could sense hopelessness, fear, and a thousand captive souls swirling about in the stygian darkness. He thought about the last time he'd entered a cave, the horrors he'd seen, the people who'd died ...

'You okay?' Sam asked.

'Ghosts,' Alex said, 'thousands of them ... all trapped down there.'

Sam snorted, but his face changed when he saw Alex's expression. 'Seriously?'

Alex nodded. 'This is the place Magera came from.' He slapped the big HAWC on the shoulder, feeling the mechanical frame. 'But we don't believe in ghosts, right? So, let's join the party.'

He turned to Jackson, and jerked a thumb at the truck. 'Grab anything you think we might need.'

The SAS soldier and the HAWCs checked their weapons, and secured everything else in close to their bodies – rigging for tight quarters.

Alex pointed to a lip of stone over the entrance. 'Rogers, give me a peep.'

Rogers reached into a pocket for a silver dollar-sized black disc with a single lens at its center. He twisted it and stuck it to the stone. The motion-sensor lens would activate on movement and send images to Rogers' visor screen. They now had eyes on their front door.

'Stay tight. Fast and quiet. On me,' Alex said, and waved them forward into the darkness.

*

Colonel Jack Hammerson listened to Harris' report, thanked him, and hung up. His eyes narrowed as he thought through the options.

He grunted and walked to his own screen to replay the re-layed data feeds and view the GPS map. Current estimates gave Alex and the team about an hour before Magera arrived.

There was now a no-fly zone over all of the Mediterranean, and communications had become useless the moment the HAWCs went deep below ground. There was nothing Hammerson could do now except trust his team were up to the task.

'Storm coming your way fast, Arcadian. Good luck.'

*

Matt sat on the rocks close to the walkway railing, mask pushed up onto his forehead. Rebecca and Reece Thompson squatted beside him as he explained what he'd found. The three Greeks stood nearby, listening in.

'I don't think we can get to it to plant charges,' he said. 'We might need to blow the stalagmites and columns first.'

Thompson shook his head. 'Not a great idea to be setting off multiple charges in an area that's structurally compromised. This place has already collapsed once in the last few centuries.'

Rebecca nodded. 'It only flooded 200 years ago. The pool was little more than a pond in Minoan times. There was also reference to a current after heavy rain.'

'A current?' Matt's eyebrows shot up. 'Maybe a river ran through here once – now sealed off.'

Tony flicked a cigarette butt into the pool. It hissed once before going out. Matt compressed his lips as he watched it bob on the surface, releasing minute amounts of ash into the pristine water.

Tony shrugged. 'We blow it. That's what we came here for. What else we gonna do – go home with our fucking dicks in our hands?' He winked at Rebecca.

'I so want to marry a man like that one day,' she said under her breath to Matt, and pretended to gag.

Thompson looked out over the water. 'Risky.'

Matt nodded. 'I agree. We need to think about it.'

Tony snorted. 'Petro is good at demolition work – cars, buildings ... people.'

He saluted Petro, who returned the gesture with a small bow.

Thompson got to his feet. 'Fine. We'll wait outside while you bury yourselves alive.'

Tony laughed and held up his hands, palms up. 'Sorry, sorry ... I mean *you* blow it.' He grinned. 'Happy now, fucking Prince Charlie?'

Thompson squared his stance. 'Ain't gonna happen unless the professor says so. And if he says it's too dangerous, then we work another option.'

Matt saw that Andronus and Petro suddenly had guns hanging loosely in their hands. They didn't look directly at Thompson, but stood side-on. Matt knew what they were doing – presenting a small target just in case things went bad.

'What? The professor is a demolition expert now?' Tony sneered. 'I suggest *you* get down there and have a look, Mr. Soldier. You are here for one reason, to fucking blow things up. Why don't you stick with Plan A until it's been proved wrong?'

Thompson half-turned to Matt and said quietly, 'Get ready to jump. I can take one or two, but if they're quick they might get lucky.'

Matt knew what that meant. If they got lucky, it meant Matt, Rebecca, and Thompson would get *unlucky* and take a hit. Matt felt light-headed at how fast things were spinning out of control.

He got slowly to his feet and held up his hands, calming things down. He knew they didn't have time for a stand-off. 'Let's just everyone take a breath. Maybe Tony's right. I'm no demolition expert. So maybe we should have another look.'

Tony scoffed. 'Maybe we just forget about this partnership. You got your C-4, and you showed us where the entrance to the secret cave is. Deal's over. You are right – we will blow it ourselves, and you can go home.' He grinned at his comrades. 'Go home, go to hell – we don't care.'

'You're dead first.' Thompson's expression was dark as he stared at Tony, then he paused, as if listening, and began to smile.

Tony's gun barrel was suddenly pointing at Rebecca's chest. 'One gun against three – not good odds for you. Put down your weapon, or the girl is dead … *first.*'

Matt wondered why Thompson was smiling, then saw that several figures had appeared high on the steps behind the three Greeks, as silent as ghosts. One shape broke away, moving so fast it seemed to disappear momentarily then reappear right behind the three gunmen. Matt's spirits soared – there would be no stand-off, after all.

'Put your guns down,' Alex told the Greeks.

Petro spun and, either reflexively or through shock, brought his gun up. Alex's hand shot out, taking the weapon so quickly that Petro was left blinking at his empty hand. Andronus staggered back, his arms pin-wheeling, and fell over the railing into the water.

Tony cursed, went to aim, then thought better of it. Alex grabbed him, dragging him close so their faces were only a few inches apart.

The Greek slowly turned his head to Matt. 'Tell him we are friends, okay?'

'Friends?' Matt said. 'You were about to shoot us.'

Alex lifted Tony off his feet one-handed. He screamed, his voice bouncing around in the cave, his legs kicking uselessly in the air.

'It's okay, we'll need them,' Matt said.

Alex lowered him, his eyes burning into the Greek's. Tony looked away.

Alex pushed him out of the way and leaped over the rail to join Matt, Thompson, and Rebecca. 'Making friends with the locals, I see,' he said.

Sam and Barclay Jackson came down to stand behind Petro, while Franks pulled Andronus out of the water. The big newcomers dwarfed the Greeks.

Thompson saluted, and Alex returned the gesture, followed by a bump of the knuckles.

'Took your time,' Thompson said with a half-smile. 'Heard you ran into some nasty shit in Turkey.'

Alex nodded. 'Lost a good man. And now that nasty shit is on its way to Crete. We need to stop it, pronto.' He motioned to the water. 'Find anything?'

'Yes, but we've got a problem,' Matt said. 'I think we've found Magera's lair, but we can't get close enough to it. And we're worried too many underwater explosions will weaken the cave structure.' He looked up at the ceiling. 'We might be able to get away with one, but ...' He shrugged.

Alex squatted at the water's edge, peering into its depths. He dipped a hand in and ran it up the pool's edge. 'This used to be shallower. Is it filling?'

'It was probably ten feet lower 200 years ago,' Rebecca said. 'It's filled from rain seepage. Back in the early 1800s they used explosives to open up some areas and caused some fissuring. Rainwater seeps in now, but can't get out. Seems they also managed to block up the outflow areas.'

Alex stood. 'And where are they?'

'What?' Matt frowned.

'The outflow areas.' Alex looked up and down the cave.

Matt sucked in a breath, thinking. 'My guess ...' He looked around for a second or two, then pointed. 'Probably down there ... it's the side where the river comes out from under the ground on the lower slopes.'

Alex shrugged the equipment off his back, grabbed Matt's goggles off his head, and walked into the water. 'I'll take a look. Give me five minutes.'

Alex stroked hard to the end of the cave and then dived beneath the water. Matt turned to Rebecca, who raised her eyebrows. 'We have a new plan?'

He grinned. 'Maybe.'

In a few minutes, Alex surfaced and pushed his goggles up. He breast-stroked back to the pool's edge. 'I think we might have something. Big boulder against the wall – like a cork. If we can move it, we might be able to restart the flow – maybe even drain this bathtub.'

'Empty the pool? Is there any other ...' Matt stopped and grimaced at the thought of what they were about to do, what they *had to do*, to the Psychro Cave pool. He sighed. 'Okay, but how?'

'Well, if we can't use explosives,' Alex looked across at Sam, 'we use a forklift.' He stood up. 'Okay, Uncle, you and me are up. We got some rocks to move ... and I'm dying to see what that full MECH suit can do.'

Sam snorted and dropped his kit, then took off his shirt.

'Oh my god.' Matt's mouth fell open. Sam looked like something from either the future or a torture chamber. There were pipes, pistons and tubing covering his combat-hardened physique, with spots of blood showing where the needles had penetrated his nervous system.

Thompson handed Sam a breathing tank and some goggles, then looked him over. 'Bad ... pure bad.'

Sam grinned. 'Time to see if it's waterproof.'

*

Alex watched as Sam walked into the water, sinking lower and lower. There was no way he was going to float while carrying several hundred pounds of technology.

Alex swam toward the dark area of the lake where Matt had found the mosaic. He peered down into the pristine water and saw the tumbled boulders, some the size of cars, some as small as loaves of bread. All were coated in slime and fine mineral sand that sparkled in his headlamp.

He heard Sam coming up behind him and swiveled to see the amazing sight of his big lieutenant walking along the bottom of the lake, as if taking a Sunday stroll.

Sam saluted, and Alex dived down to join him. He ran his hands over one of the rocks, roughly about five feet long and four high, and easily many tons. Even though Alex had enormous strength, the boulder had been wedged in place for several centuries and the rocks around it had bonded together.

He pointed to the large rock and then to Sam, indicating he would take one end and Sam the other. The big man nodded and moved into place. They looked at each other, and Alex nodded ... one, two, three.

He strained, and felt the blood rush in a thumping torrent throughout his system. Above the pulse in his ears, he heard the whine of Sam's suit and his grunt as he used the MECH technology and his own muscles together. Despite their combined efforts, nothing happened. There wasn't enough room to get a good purchase on the huge stone.

Alex held up five fingers to Sam, then swam back to the surface. He quick-stroked to the edge of the pool and stood, waist-deep in the water. He pointed to the pile of equipment. 'Franks, toss me the spike.'

Franks lifted the inch-thick, six-foot metal rod with a single sharpened end. It looked like a brutal javelin. She hefted it to her shoulder, nodding appreciatively. 'Heads-up.'

She threw it like a spear, and Alex caught it out of the air, instantly feeling its weight. *Perfect*, he thought, and sank once more below the surface.

He smiled around his breathing tube as he saw Sam sitting casually on the huge rock ten feet down. Sam gave Alex the thumbs-up, and once again took his position on one side of the boulder. He dug his fingers deep into the crack between the boulders, and Alex lifted the spike and, with all his strength, stabbed down, wedging the sharpened end between the stones. He looked to Sam and counted down once more.

There was a grinding sound, and rock fragments swirled in the water, but even with their boosted power, the stone refused to budge.

Alex motioned Sam closer and together they worked on just one end. Alex withdrew the spike and jammed it back in at a different spot. This time it slid in deep between the stones. The sparkling mineral sand swirled, and sludge lifted from the bottom of the pool to mix with it around their legs. A basketball-sized rock tumbled down from higher up the wall.

Alex paused and looked to Sam; he nodded the countdown from three again, and together they gave an almighty heave. There was the whine of the metal bar bending, then a huge cracking sound as the rocks, joined for centuries, moved. The pair heaved even harder, and the massive rock slid forward, then rolled. Above it, smaller rocks started to tumble, but falling inward instead of down.

A dark hole was revealed, and what started as a gentle current flowing into it soon became a torrent. Alex guessed the water was racing toward another underground cavern, or would spout out of the mountain to become a river flowing down its sides.

He felt himself lifted and sucked toward the hole. One of Sam's hands shot out and grabbed him by the wrist. With the other, Sam had anchored himself to another large stone, the weight of the MECH suit allowing him to resist the powerful drag of the water. Alex felt like a flag in a strong wind as he held onto Sam, his legs inside the hole, the torrent rushing past him on its way to the valley, miles below.

It took twenty minutes before the pool had drained to waist level, and Alex could pull himself out of the mouth of the tunnel and crawl up onto the stones above the lake.

Sam joined him. They pushed their masks up, and bumped fists.

Sam nudged him. 'I figured you didn't really want to see where that water was going.'

Alex laughed softly and looked toward the hole. The rush of water was a monstrous growl, falling away into the dark. He recalled another mission, when he'd been trapped underwater in the dark, and his stomach lurched.

When he stood again, the water was only at his calves, and still draining into the hole. Sam used the spike to move more stones out of the way, allowing the pool to empty more quickly.

Matt and Rebecca were quick to join them, sloshing through what remained of the water.

Matt peered into the hole, then stood back. 'Well, I guess if they want to refill the pool, they only need to seal this back up. No real damage done.'

Rebecca chortled. 'Let's just be long gone before the guides get here in the morning.'

'Works for me,' Alex said. 'Now, Professor, show us what you found.'

CHAPTER 31

Carlo Vangelis blinked in the dark, and sat up. His huge bed was unruffled by his night's sleep – he never tossed and turned, was never troubled by tics, twitches or dreams. But he was a light sleeper, a habit developed during his early life on the streets of Crete. If you didn't want to die while sleeping rough or in a doss-house, you had to remain on guard. He looked around the room at the heavy antique furniture – a wardrobe, dressing table, desk, and the huge four-poster bed he slept in: French, 400 years old and weighing as much as a small car. He frowned, wondering what had woken him. Lingering underneath the familiar smell of sandalwood and expensive aftershave, he detected another odor. Unpleasant. He'd get the cleaners to have a look later in the day.

He glanced across at the clock – it was still too early to rise. He lay back down, and almost immediately a huge hand clamped over his mouth. The intruder had been behind him the entire time. He was pulled from the bed as if he weighed nothing, punched in the stomach, and thrown to the ground.

He lay there, the wind knocked out of him. *A rival gang?* he wondered. Where were his men?

He got on all fours, straining to drag in a breath. A hand grabbed his thick white hair and pulled him up, and up. A massive ogre was holding him like a marionette doll. The giant had one eye, a dark beard, and a face that spoke of a psychopathic attraction to pain. Vangelis knew that look – there would be no mercy from this man. He could only hope his men would hear his screams.

The voice was deep and Russian. 'Your guards are all gone. I cut their throats.'

Vangelis felt his stomach drop. His survival instincts took over. 'I have a safe with a lot of money in it.'

There was also a gun, hidden behind the cash.

The giant shook him by the hair, causing him to cry out.

'Keep your money, Little Mafia Man. I only want one thing – where did you take American professor?' A wicked-looking black blade appeared beside Vangelis' face. 'I only ask once.'

The knife tip dug into his cheek.

*

Matt led the others to the huge column rising from the floor of the cave to the ceiling twenty feet above. It, and its smaller siblings each side, formed a massive barrier across the mosaic path. He got down on his knees and used his hand to wipe away the remaining silt, exposing more of the tiles. The face appeared in all its horror – the screaming Gorgon with writhing hair and red snake eyes.

'Pretty, isn't she,' Franks said as she looked at the vicious face. 'Not even I'd go that.'

'Gorgon,' Matt said softly. 'The word means "dreadful" in ancient Greek.'

Alex stared, transfixed. He knew this was the thing he'd encountered in the desert, but if he had seen it, he'd now be nothing but a crumbling block of stone among the sand. At the time, he had felt the anger and loneliness of something that didn't fit in or even belong among us. Perhaps he knew a little of what that was like.

Rebecca stared. 'I still can't believe it's real.'

'Well, we're here to see what we can do to put it back to sleep,' Alex said. He examined the huge column, then looked up. He shook his head. 'If we knock this down, it could pull the whole roof down on top of us.' He backed up. 'Maybe if we knock out a few of the smaller ones, we might be able to squeeze though. It'll be a tight fit, but we can do it.'

Sam rubbed his head. 'Just how tight a fit?'

Alex looked at him, and grinned. 'Suck it in, big guy.'

It took only twenty minutes to dig out one of the small stalagmites, and chip away some of the central column to create a three-foot-wide hole. Matt and Rebecca were first through, followed by Casey Franks, then the two SAS soldiers.

Alex, Sam, Ben Rogers, and the three Greeks remained on the other side.

Tony saluted, still grinning, but nervously. 'No hard feelings.' He edged back to the guard rail.

Alex grabbed him and pushed him toward the hole. 'You're coming too. Your men can stay here on guard duty.' Alex glared at them. 'Got it?'

They refused to look at him, so he lifted Tony with one hand and shook him. 'Got it?' His voice boomed around the cave.

Both nodded vigorously.

Sam growled, 'Be here when we come back ... or else.'

They nodded again. Alex pushed Tony toward the hole and he clambered through, cursing softly.

Alex turned to Ben Rogers. 'We need the back door kept open. Don't want these two thinking they can try out some dopey ambush when we come back.' He looked back toward the surface, many hundred feet overhead, then added, lowering his voice, 'And keep an eye on the peep – we're still expecting company.'

Rogers smiled. 'I'll keep our friends out of trouble and watch the surface. Door will be open when you get back, boss. Good luck.'

Sam pulled his huge body and the MECH suit's steel framework through the hole, scraping away a lot more of the stone. Alex turned to give Rogers a thumbs-up, and followed Sam through.

*

At the cave entrance, Borshov's Spetsnaz took up positions either side of the gate, staying well back. Borshov crouched, a single lens to his eye.

'Camera, on top of cave,' he said.

One of his men lifted his AK-12 to his eye. The black assault rifle was a significantly enhanced Kalashnikov-series weapon, and in the agent's hands deadly accurate. The rifle spat once and the small camera exploded into shards.

'Quick now,' Borshov ordered.

He knew the speed with which the device had been destroyed would make the operator think it had malfunctioned. But if he came to check, they needed to make first contact.

Borshov and his men sprinted into the cave, Borshov's feet pounding heavily under the extra weight of the MECH suit.

*

Matt was first to the wall, laying his hands against it. This section of the tunnel was roughly fifteen feet wide and just as long, stopping at the perfectly smooth wall of flowstone. It glistened, and when Matt held his light up to it, he could just make out more depth beyond the natural barrier – there was something behind it.

'Probably created long before the water filled the pool,' Rebecca said. 'It's a flowing shelf of limestone that's dripped down over the entrance and literally sealed it closed.' She walked backward, looking along its top and sides. 'Might be a foot thick – but that's not too bad as calcium carbonate is fairly soft.' She turned to Alex and raised her eyebrows. 'Can you dig through it?'

'Hey.' Casey Franks moved her boot sideways along the floor. 'More of those picture tiles on the ground here.'

The team crowded around her, shining their torches on the small tiled pathway. As they brushed aside the silt, more images were revealed – flames, huge urns filled with coins, other unidentifiable objects. Matt frowned, wishing he'd brought a camera. When he saw a huge beast the size of an ox, with three horned heads, holding the body of a man in one of its slavering jaws, he recognized it immediately.

'Cerberus,' he said.

Sam whistled. 'That is one damned mother of a dog.'

'Damned is right,' Matt said. 'Cerberus was the protector of Hades.'

He pushed away more of the silt, showing the creature's monstrous muscled body covered with what looked like scales, multiple legs, and a reptilian tail.

'Wasn't real, was it?' Franks asked, splashing water from her canteen over its head, clarifying the face and jaws.

'No, but neither is Magera, right?' Matt said slowly. He pointed. 'Look at the horns. What other horned beast do we know of that was supposed to live in a cave?'

'The Minotaur,' Sam said. 'This is gonna be fun.'

'If it ever did exist, it'll be dust now,' Jackson said.

Alex was examining the wall that blocked their path. 'Magera somehow reformed when it was released from its prison after eons, and survived thermobaric grenades and hundreds of armor-piercing rounds.' He half-turned. 'Franks, get me the spike we left outside.'

'On it.' Franks disappeared back through the hole.

Rebecca kneeled and laid her hand on one of the snarling faces. 'I've been thinking about what you said about Magera melting away in the sunlight,' she told Alex. 'This thing – it doesn't seem to be made the same way we are, out of trillions of cells, each with its own function and purpose.'

Franks returned and handed Alex the long spike. He nodded to her, but leaned on the spike, listening to the scientist.

Rebecca stood, wiping her hands on her thighs. 'New research has shown that some insects follow the same biological rules as individual creatures – which makes their colonies more like a super-organism. Ants, bees, termites, wasps – their controlled interactions are like cells working together in a single body.' She folded her arms, her eyes focused inward as she thought through what she was saying. 'So imagine this Magera thing is made up of cells, just like us, but each cell is more than just a self-functioning amino acid factory, and more like this super-organism entity. What if Magera's cells are capable of taking care of themselves individually, but work together as a whole when it suits?'

Alex shook his head. 'I got the impression of a single entity. And it was solid, powerful.'

Rebecca nodded. 'Maybe the single-entity shape is its usual formation. Each of our cells contains all the information needed to create another one of us, but Magera's cells might go a step further, in that they're a multi-celled organism acting as a collective.'

Sam exhaled loudly. 'So is it one creature, or an army of millions?'

Rebecca shrugged. 'I'm just guessing here. But we might know soon, if we can get through there.' She pointed to the wall.

Alex grunted. 'Right about now, everything helps, even good guesses.' He lifted the spike. 'Make room, people – time to see where Magera came from.'

He jammed the spike into the wall, once, twice, and then again, before punching through. Gas escaped through the hole, making everyone back away. Rebecca gagged.

'Don't breathe it in,' Matt said behind his hand. 'It was airtight.'

He put his entire arm across his face and backed up further, pulling the still-coughing Rebecca with him.

Alex held his breath and stepped in close, shining a light into the three-inch hole he had made.

'Clear,' he said, turning his head away and sucking in a deep breath. 'The stone must have flowed over it completely, like a wax seal on a bottle. Upside is, it'll be dry inside ... and anything in there should be preserved.'

'That's an upside?' Sam said and snorted.

Alex turned back and sniffed. 'It's stale, not toxic. Can't detect any explosive gases. But it smells ... strange.' He sniffed some more. 'Kind of ... primordial.'

Tony's nose wrinkled. 'Smells like a freakin' zoo.' He shone his flashlight into the small hole. 'Nobody home – that's a good thing.'

'Let's go take a look,' Alex said. He motioned Tony away, then jammed the spike into the hole again and again, working it in a circle to make it man-sized. He turned to Matt. 'After you.'

Matt lifted his flashlight to the hole. His hand shook slightly, making the beam wobble. Part of him, the curious, adventurous, and scientific part, wanted to dive through and hurtle like a bloodhound into the mysterious cave, seeking answers to age-old questions of myth, religion, and strange creatures. But the other part, the experienced part, wanted to flee back to the surface, back to the safety of sunlight and fresh air – that was the part that had been in caves before, and that was the part that had seen what can exist below the earth's fragile outer skin.

He sucked in a deep breath. *The farther backward you can look, the farther forward you can see – thanks Winston*, he thought, as he steadied himself.

Matt stepped through.

CHAPTER 32

HAWC lieutenant Ben Rogers stood with arms folded cradling his rifle. The smell of drying slime from the drained lake thickened the air; soon it would become so dominating that he knew it would overpower his sense of smell, making it useless. As a HAWC, he relied on every sense, every limb, every angle and sharp edge of his body in both defense and attack. Nothing was ever left idle – his life depended on it.

He turned to the two Greeks. Both were looking at him, but turned away sullenly when he caught them. They spoke softly to each other, obviously still pissed about getting a job that left them standing at the bottom of a stinking cave, and smoking, always smoking.

Rogers looked up at the steel walkways and steps leading back to the cave entrance. He guessed he must be about ten stories down. The lighting had been strategically placed to give a theatrical effect and highlight the more impressive structures. For tourists, the lighting would be an excellent feature. For a Special Forces soldier, it created too many shadows.

He walked a few paces into the center of the dry pool, between where the Greeks loitered and where Alex and the team had disappeared into the wall. He looked again at the two men – both seemed tough and capable, but they were amateurs. They'd be fine against other amateurs, but against professionals he doubted they'd last twenty seconds. He sucked in a deep breath and turned away again. There came a sound from high overhead and he froze. The Greeks didn't notice, continuing to laugh and talk loudly as if they were in a local bar.

'Shut up,' Rogers ordered, and backed up a step.

Both men looked from him to each other, and hiked their shoulders, comically mouthing, *What?*

Rogers held up a finger close to his lips.

The Greeks, sensing his unease, drew weapons. The sound came again, still high overhead, and then one of the lights went out. In quick succession the sound came again and again, and more lights winked out, the darkness marching down toward them.

Rogers put a finger to the small comms stud in his ear. 'Boss, we got company.'

He got nothing but a hiss of static – too much rock between them.

Gun up, he slowly moved one hand to his helmet, pulled down the visor, and switched on the image reproduction technology. As a HAWC, he had faced death dozens of times – and he was still standing. He liked to think he didn't know fear any more, but now, as he waited to see if Magera's image came up on his visor screen, something cold and dreadful crept up his spine.

He sucked in a breath, calming himself. The final lights went out. The Greeks started to whisper. One lit a cigarette, and kept the lighter on, holding up the flame. The other cursed, slapped at it, and turned on a flashlight instead.

Rogers' visor remained black. He willed the image to appear so he had a target.

He heard Andronus grunt and, out the corner of his eye, saw him disappear. He turned in time to see Petro's head explode in a mass of red and white bone fragments.

Rogers quickly pushed up the visor and brought down his night-vision scope – but it was too late.

*

Borshov put his foot on the HAWC's chest and ripped off his helmet. The man's eyes were open and his face was calm. Both his shoulders and legs had taken bullets – full incapacitation. The American's expression of resignation told Borshov he already knew he was finished.

The big Russian shook his head. 'Don't worry, I won't torture you.' He grinned. 'Only because I don't have time.' He grabbed the HAWC on each side of the head, his fingers digging into the flesh, and dragged him up so he could stare into his face. 'This is for my men in Turgutlu.'

Rogers smiled. 'You're already dead, asshole – you just don't know it.'

Borshov snorted. 'But not before you, I think.'

He pressed. There was a soft whine as the electronics and hydraulics of the MECH suit came into play. Rogers' teeth ground together and his eyes showed determination for a second or two, before they bulged with excruciating pain. Borshov pushed harder, the super-alloy pistons responding to his brain's commands immediately. There was a crack, then a wet crushing sound that echoed around the cave. Rogers' head collapsed in the big Russian's hands.

'Ha!' Borshov let go, and flicked his hands to remove blood and brain matter, then wiped his fingers on the American's armor suit. 'One by one, all little HAWCs fly back to hell.'

He motioned to his men. Like wraiths, the black-clad Spetsnaz moved lightly across the drained pool toward the newly opened cave – ghosts on their way down to Hades.

*

'This smells like crap,' Franks said.

She'd taken the lead, and Alex could see she was trying to breathe through her mouth.

'I smell oil,' he said. 'Perhaps some methane mixed in; we're certainly deep enough.'

He stopped to wait for Matt and Rebecca. They were still fifty paces back, studying the mosaic frescos that covered the walls of the cave. The tiles were perfectly preserved and vividly colored, and probably looked the same as they had over 5000 years ago. Matt and Rebecca were like children let loose in a toy store.

Sam caught up to Alex. 'Might be methane, might not. It's getting too hot for explosive gases.'

'Well, we'll know soon enough,' Alex said. 'Keep an eye on our Greek friend. We don't want him slipping away if anything unexpected happens.'

'You got it, boss.'

Alex whistled, and waved Matt and Rebecca forward. Matt waved back, and they both picked up their pace, but their eyes still darted around, trying to take in everything around them. Occasionally, Rebecca ran her hand along the walls, as if feeling the texture of the stone.

The mosaics were amazingly detailed, and painstakingly put together. Some of the chips were so tiny they were little more than grains, giving the characters a lifelike effect. In the fresco next to Alex, men and women, their hair in the long, thick curling Minoan style, kneeled in front of four huge beings, holding up urns, cloth, and jewelry. The figures were clothed, but not in the same style as the Minoans, and their hair was alive with movement. Behind them was a gigantic white ball – possibly a representation of the moon or sun, Alex thought.

Matt and Rebecca caught up, and turned their lights onto the image. Matt leaned in closer to examine the figures.

'There were three Gorgons of legend – Stheno, Euryale, and the most famous, Medusa. There have been stories of Gorgon-like creatures dating back thousands of years, though – from right here, on to Russia, Japan, and across Europe. Other than Medusa, who was killed by Perseus, all of them simply vanished from history.' He moved his light to a different angle. 'There was never any reference to a fourth Gorgon. Seems Magera is an anomaly – a myth within a myth.'

'A myth that's still alive,' Alex said.

Matt stepped back. 'We don't know that – or not alive as we know it, anyway.'

'We don't even know if it's the only one,' Alex said, and shook his head. 'I don't even want to think about that possibility.'

'There's so much about the Minoans that's a mystery,' Matt said. 'They were technological leaders of the world, so why did they disappear?' He looked again at the white sphere. 'And what's that? They supposedly lived down here, in the underworld – no astral bodies down here.'

'Maybe that's not what it is.' Rebecca fished in her pocket, and pulled out a small flashlight with a thick blue end. 'Let me try something. Turn off your lights, people.'

Matt looked at Alex, and shrugged. Everyone switched off their torches, plunging the cave into total darkness. Rebecca switched on her new flashlight – and the wall glowed blue.

'Wow – UV right?' Matt asked.

'Yep.' Rebecca moved the beam around: the entire area shone like a neon light.

'Is this a common effect?' Alex asked.

Rebecca shook her head, her face glowing blue in the reflected light. 'Not usually. Fluorescence in rocks occurs when there are a number of activators present – impurities within the mineral, crystal structural defects, organic impurities, or what I suspect: the result of significant gamma radiation.'

'Gamma?' Alex asked. 'Down here?'

She nodded. 'Occurs all around us, but at insignificant quantities. Of course there's much more outside the Earth's atmospheric shell. Natural sources of gamma rays on Earth include gamma decay from naturally occurring radioisotopes, radium and so on, and secondary radiation from atmospheric interactions with cosmic ray particles.' She turned to them. 'Or residue after a nuclear explosion, significant impact from space, or leakage from some sort of reactor.'

'Impact from space? Reactor?' Matt's eyebrows went up. 'So my space helmet theory wasn't so crazy, huh?'

She shrugged. 'Not necessarily. You've got to admit, it's weird.'

'So far everything down here is weird,' Matt said, and flicked his light back on. 'Well, I'm now moving my theory to the definite-maybe list.' He wiped his brow. 'Phew, it's gotta be over 100 degrees down here. We must be near some sort of volcanic activity.'

'Boss!' It was Franks. She was out of sight, several hundred feet ahead, scouting. 'Check this out.'

Alex turned to Matt and Rebecca. 'Stay close, no lagging behind now.'

He jogged to meet Franks, rounding the bend. '*Whoa!*' He eased back – the cave ended at a sheer drop-off. To their left, stairs were cut into the stone, leading down to the floor about 200 feet below. Franks stood out to the side, looking over the edge.

She pointed. 'Now we know where the heat's coming from.'

There were pools of black oil, some burning, obviously pure enough to ignite from the deeper volcanic vents from the heart of the earth. The roof of the cavern was way out of sight, probably the reason they hadn't been overwhelmed by the build-up of gases.

Sam appeared behind them, and Alex held him back. 'Not too close, big guy. Your weight could cause the edge to crumble.'

They all fanned out, staying back from the drop-off.

'Wow, and wow.' Matt shook his head, his mouth hanging open. 'You do know what this is, don't you?'

'Hades,' Rebecca said slowly.

He chuckled. 'Hey, thanks for spoiling my dramatic finish.' He stepped forward to peer over the edge. 'Could this be any more perfect? An underground space of fire, heat, and … a village.'

The single broad street of paved tiles, their rich red patina perfectly preserved, was lined with small flat-topped single-story houses, each about ten feet square. On the other side of the village, the ground fell away into an even deeper chasm of darkness. On the surface of the street, scattered in between the buildings, something glittered.

Alex concentrated his vision. 'Gold … gold coins.'

'Huh?' Tony reached for Franks' scope.

'Piss off,' she said, nudging him away, and he teetered near the edge for a moment.

Sam pointed across the pit. 'What the hell is that? Sure ain't Minoan.'

On the far side, embedded in the cliff wall, was an enormous ball-like structure. Steps led up to it, and a platform, or perhaps an altar, had been constructed at its edge.

'Just like in the mosaic,' Rebecca whispered.

Matt held his arms wide. 'And the stars shall fall and the gods will ride them to Earth.'

Rebecca's grin nearly split her face. 'I agree. Aristotle wrote that over 2300 years ago. He was said to have had insights into the future, and now I see why.' She started for the steps. 'We need to get over there to examine it.'

Alex pulled her back. 'Not yet. Looks like there might be some of Magera's handiwork down there.'

Behind the village was a forest of stalagmites, rising up in rows, and between them, in their hundreds, were magnificently detailed statues. Alex knew now that they were people. Everything down in the village – the figures, the walls of the houses, and the stalagmites – were covered in strange growths that looked like bulbous coral.

He looked at the steps, then tried a couple with his own weight. 'They seem solid, but watch your step,' he told Rebecca. 'The light is poor, and it'll make the shadows deceptive.' He waved his HAWCs over. 'Take us down, Franks. Greek, you're next, then you, Thompson, then me, Rebecca, Matt, and Jackson. You bring up the rear, Sam.'

Alex pushed his rifle up over his shoulder. 'Okay, let's ...' He froze, staring down into the village. Something had moved down there – fast.

He replayed the split-second glimpse of the thing over in his mind. He had an impression of a long body, multiple legs, and a coat that seemed to shimmer, not fur or hair, maybe some kind of bony plating.

The HAWCs and two SAS men shouldered their guns, training them around the interior of the cavern.

Jackson nudged Thompson. 'What the fuck's going on?'

Thompson shrugged. 'Hunter probably hears something we can't. So we pay attention.'

Jackson snorted. 'Freak.'

Sam edged closer to Alex, who still stood frozen, like he'd become part of the stone around them.

'What you got, boss?'

'Movement – end of the street – fast. I just caught it out of the corner of my eye.'

Silence hung as the seconds stretched. No one moved, or even seemed to breathe.

'My legs hurt,' Tony whispered, but it was loud enough to create an echo.

Alex shook his head. 'Nothing now.'

His senses still screamed at him – something was there, but what? *We'll know soon enough*, he thought.

'We're at alert level one, people.' He pointed to Casey Franks. 'Take us down to hell, Lieutenant.'

*

Borshov's two remaining Spetsnaz slid through the hole Alex had broken in the flowstone wall. They scouted the area, then quickly formed up as Borshov followed them.

The giant Russian stood with his head turned slightly, his one good eye moving quickly over the adorned walls and mosaic floor tiles. He didn't bother appreciating the aesthetics of the artisan's work, instead focusing on the footprints, their direction and probable speed.

One of his Spetsnaz kneeled to examine the tracks.

'How many?' Borshov asked quietly.

The man stood. 'Eight.' He pointed to some large, deep prints. 'One big, very big. Must be carrying something heavy.'

Borshov grunted. 'Like me.'

He circled his finger and the three moved silently down the tunnel.

CHAPTER 33

The stocky female HAWC started quickly down the steep steps. The rest followed, but their descent was slow. Sam took the longest; not from any lack of agility, but because his foot placement was critical given his size and the deadweight of the MECH suit. He found out very early that a misstep crumbled the ancient carved stonework from right underneath him.

At the bottom, Alex half-turned to Matt and Rebecca. 'Get in behind us.'

He pointed two fingers at Sam and Franks, then left and right. The two HAWCs spread out, keeping low, and took up positions in the paved street. Alex walked a dozen feet into the center of the street, his gun up.

Tony bent to scoop up coins, loading his pockets.

Matt picked up a few coins too, and turned them over to show Rebecca. 'Silver, gold, very old – not perfect – hand-cut.'

Rebecca took one from him. 'I've see these in museums, but never of this quality. They've probably lain here untouched for thousands of years.' She frowned at the various images on the coins: the Gorgon's terrifying face, a horned bull, a snarling dog. 'Looks like these were specially made – as offerings perhaps.'

Matt nodded. 'Tribute to the gods, or the Gorgons.'

Something swooped low over their heads, ruffling Matt's hair. 'Jesus Christ!' He dropped to the ground, pulling Rebecca with him.

Alex turned and fired in one motion. The thing dropped to the tiled street.

Casey Franks was first over it, nudging it with her toe. 'Looks like a giant freakin' bat.'

'Was this what you saw before?' Sam asked Alex.

He shook his head. 'I think the thing I saw was bigger ... much bigger.' He used the barrel of his gun to turn the creature's head toward him. 'But just as ugly.'

The thing did look like a bat, with a snub nose, long ribbed ears, and needle-sharp teeth. But instead of a bat's elongated forearms with membrane stretched underneath, it had proper legs. On top of its head were six eyes, making it look more like a spider than a mammal.

Rebecca dropped to her knees beside it, and pulled out a small knife to prod at the carcass. 'This thing has lived down here a long time – probably hundreds of thousands of years. It's undergone some kind of evolutionary deformation.'

She levered open its mouth, showing another row of sharp teeth inside the first.

Franks leaned closer. 'Look at those teeth – two sets. That thing bites you, you'd never get it off.'

'I'm not sure it's a bat,' Rebecca said. 'I think it might have been some sort of rodent once. Looking at the teeth, I'd say it's definitely a carnivore.'

'Carnivorous flying rats. Nice.' Franks snorted. 'What the hell does it eat down here?'

Rebecca stood and looked around, then pointed to one of the columns coated in the greenish sponge Alex had noticed earlier. 'Not sure, but those growths – plants or fungi – might be the basis for a food chain. There might be something in it that caused the deformity too.'

Alex turned slowly. There was near silence in the huge cavern, and also just beyond the red gloom of the fires there was nothing but darkness. But he was nearly overwhelmed, by the sensation of life, of scrutiny, and of danger.

Alex waved Sam, Franks, and the two SAS soldiers in close. 'Stay with our guests. I'm going to scout ahead – check out the sphere. Stay sharp.' He looked down at the dead creature. 'That thing leads me to believe there could be even larger predators down here.'

Alex turned to Matt. 'Find those words, or weapons, or whatever we need to stop Magera. I don't want to be down here any longer than we need to be.'

Matt waved without looking up, his focus back on the coins.

'Matt!'

Alex's voice caused Matt's head to jerk up fast. 'Huh, sorry … Oh, sure, we'll split up. I'll take the left side of the street.'

'I'll go with you, Prof,' Franks said, and winked at him.

Sam nodded to Rebecca. 'Looks like it's you and me, kid.' He turned to Reece Thompson. 'Give us some eyes on the street. See you in ten.'

Thompson nodded, and he and Jackson eased into the shadow of one of the buildings.

Sam turned to Tony. 'And you, stay where I can see you.'

⁂

Matt waited while Casey Franks peered into the gloom of the small house's interior. She'd pulled down her night vision after changing out of thermal scope, as the heat of the cavern floor exceeded 100 degrees, making everything in the environment a hellish red.

She nodded, lowering her weapon only slightly. 'Clear, but stay close, pretty boy.'

Matt stepped inside, and tilted his headlamp to look around the room. The terracotta color of the walls was still vivid, as were the frescos of boxing and running youths. On a stone table sat urns and platters, some still with food on them. When Matt touched the food, it collapsed into dust.

'I think that was an apple – about 5000 years ago.'

Franks snorted. 'I still can't get my head around the thought of people actually living down here. I mean, why the fuck would you?'

As she spoke, she kept moving, her eyes on every corner of the room.

'Not sure,' Matt said. 'Maybe they were priests, living out their lives in solitude, or in the service of their living god.'

He picked up a goblet, which immediately broke in half, the cup part falling to the floor with a clatter. Franks swung around and was down on one knee, the muzzle of her rifle pointed at Matt.

Her eyes blazed. 'Jesus Christ, Kearns – you trying to get yourself shot?'

Matt grimaced, hands up. 'Sorry, sorry.' He bent and picked up the broken goblet. 'This is lead, so probably didn't belong to a priest or official.' He looked at the wall below the table, and frowned. 'Something here.' When he got close, he could see rows of words scratched into the wall, hundreds of them, but only one and two words per line. 'Looks like names … so many of them.' He traced symbols next to the words. 'Also Aegean numbers – some in the tens, some in the hundreds. Was that the number of days they were down here? What else could they be counting?'

'You know who does that?' Franks said. 'Prisoners on death row – they carve their name and sentence in their cell. Bit of a *I was here* type thing.'

'Prisoners?' Matt stood, frowning. 'Maybe. But the names ... there are so many. Why would they be down here for so long? According to the numbers, this house was occupied for centuries, and by hundreds of people – men and women.'

'Then they just all up and left, huh?' Franks asked.

'They went somewhere.' Matt looked out one of the small windows. The gloom was just lit by the hellish red glow from the burning oil. *Dante's Inferno ever needs a location shoot, it's right here*, Matt thought. 'If you're going through Hell, keep going,' he whispered.

'Churchill.' Franks said over her shoulder. She turned briefly to wink. 'Yeah, we HAWCs have read a few books – at least about great military leaders.'

'Maybe they didn't leave. Maybe it was Magera and the Gorgons that left, and the people had no reason to be here any more.'

Franks grunted. 'Yeah, and maybe the freakin' Gorgons just ran out of food. You think about that?'

Matt exhaled slowly. 'Yeah, I did think about that. Let's get out of here. This place give me the creeps.'

They moved on to the next house. It was identical, as was the next one; again with evidence of many people over spans of years. Like they were halfway houses.

There was a larger building near the center of the row of houses. Once again, Franks was first in. After a few moments she whistled for Matt to follow.

She stood back, grinning. 'I'm no archeologist, but even I can see this was the garrison.' She gestured to the remains of sleeping bunks. 'Looks to have been about twenty of them stationed here.'

Matt nodded, his hands on his hips. 'You're right; I'll make a scientist of you yet.' He paced around the room. 'It's also an armory.'

A rack of spears lined a wall; shields too, with the face of the Gorgon in relief. There were a few swords, many little more than hilts now, but a few had been heavily greased, retaining their polish and edge.

Franks lifted one, and slashed it through the air. 'Nice balance, but heavy. Like a thick machete. Would have loved to see one of these babies in action.' She stuck it in her belt. 'I'm taking it.'

Matt frowned. 'I don't get it. Judging by what we've seen so far, and the number of houses overall, there can't have been more than a hundred people living here at any one time. Not exactly the sort of crowd you need twenty guards for.'

'Like I said, prisoners. Maybe these guys weren't just keeping the peace, they were keeping these poor saps down here.'

Matt sniffed the sulfurous air. 'You might be right. Not exactly a seaside resort, is it?'

Franks moved to the rear of the room, and used the barrel of her gun to lift the lid of a coffin-shaped box. The lid and sides collapsed outwards, spewing forth a cascade of gold coins.

'Holy shit. King Midas eat your heart out.'

Matt scooped some up. 'All brand new, uncirculated.'

'Why'd they need their own currency down here?' Franks asked. 'To buy what? Nothing makes sense.'

Matt shook his head. 'Nothing makes sense – *yet*. Come on, let's try the next house.'

*

Alex jogged to the end of the ancient street. Except for sounds of his team searching the houses, all was silent. To him, the village felt alive and dead at the same time. He expected to peek in a window and see a family sitting down and eating a meal. It reminded him of pictures he'd seen of Pompeii after it had been excavated and restored – the place had looked alive, vibrant, just … abandoned.

He'd seen more of the strange bat-like creatures swooping in and out of holes in the steep cave walls, and from time to time something that looked like a lizard scurrying away into the darkness. This wasn't a dead cave; it was a thriving habitat. And he knew what kinds of things could live in places like this. His senses were screaming warnings. He knew they weren't alone, hadn't been since they got here. They were being watched.

He came to an open space like a broad balcony, red-tiled, and ending at the chasm drop-off. Gold coins were scattered everywhere. He ignored them and peered down into the black canyon that stretched the entire length of the street behind the dwellings. It was hundreds of feet across, and about fifty deep. There were the remains of pillars fixed into the ground nearby, and he could see corresponding pillars on the opposite side. There had been some sort of bridge here once.

The sphere was on the other side of the chasm. He looked down into the blackness again, estimating, judging. His instincts told him the white orb held the answers to Magera.

His jaws clenched in disgust as his vision adjusted to the dark and he was able to pick out details at the bottom of the chasm: twisted limbs and shattered skulls. Most were stone – the results of meeting Magera, he guessed; but there were broken human bones down there too. It looked as if something had fed on the flesh, then splintered the bones to suck at the marrow. Alex thought again of the large shape he'd seen darting through the shadows.

He turned away from the canyon, and noticed a dark alcove near the balcony. He crossed to it and kneeled. There were the remains of about twenty people, judging by the cracked skulls strewn about, and the leather tunics, metal swords, and helmets – all broken and dented. Some of the swords were bent, as if they were tinfoil against whatever they'd struck. The alcove was a dead end, a trap.

A last stand, he thought. He picked up one of the larger leg bones and saw deep scratches in its surface. *And not against Magera. What the hell happened here?*

He dropped the bone and lifted one of the skulls. He calmed his breathing and closed his eyes, trying to draw out some image of the brutality that had taken place here.

'Alex.' He opened his eyes and turned. Matt was jogging toward him, waving. He stopped at the scattered bones and frowned. 'What the hell?'

Alex stood. 'Something ripped them to pieces ... before they could get turned to stone.' He nodded toward the chasm. 'There are more down there.'

'These aren't Minoans,' Matt said, lifting one of the swords. His eyes went wide. 'This is Roman. Constantine – he must have sent an expedition here to find out more about Magera.'

Alex nodded. 'Makes sense, but looks like they found more then they expected.'

'But what? Magera was long gone by then.' Matt crouched, using the sword to push at the remains. 'This is amazing. What would these men have made of this place? It would have been the stuff of legends to them. And they came down here with just these swords and some burning torches.' He went back into the open square and called to Rebecca.

Casey Franks came jogging up, scowling at Matt. 'Son of a bitch, Kearns.'

Alex gave her a hard look for letting her charge get away from her.

'Sorry, boss. He said he was going to take a leak.'

Jackson came up beside them, and leaned out over the edge of the chasm. 'That's fucking deep.'

Alex felt the skin on his neck prickle – that sensation of being watched again – no, *stalked*. He closed his eyes and pushed out his senses, trying to grasp whatever was out there. He felt a presence, but it was primitive, and hidden behind something harder than stone.

'We've got to get over there,' Matt said.

Alex opened his eyes and saw that Matt had walked closer to the chasm edge and was staring at the orb. As he watched, everything around him seemed to slow ... he felt his muscles automatically begin to bunch. Danger – lethal, and coming at them fast.

'Incoming!' he yelled.

He moved to grab Matt in the same instant that something struck the professor, lifted him off his feet, and swept him over the edge into the chasm. Another of the huge objects struck Jackson, and he grunted and disappeared into the darkness.

Franks fired several rounds after the attackers – whatever they were – but they were gone before she got a clear hit. They moved faster than anything Alex had ever seen, but a fleeting glimpse had given him an impression of a large, powerful beast with six legs and armor plating. He reacted immediately – his body exploding into action and diving into the canyon without a second thought.

He landed forty feet down on a flat boulder. He could just make out a shape bounding away into the dark, Jackson's body hanging loose and lifeless in the enormous jaws.

The other creature was dragging Matt along in its mouth. It was dark in the chasm, but Alex saw the thing as clearly as he knew it saw him. Matt beat uselessly on the monstrous snout, blood running down the side of his face and streaking his shirt. The beast obviously had one goal – finding somewhere quiet to consume its prey.

'Not today,' Alex said. He pulled the KBELT handgun, and fired a round.

The super-condensed pulse of light struck one side of the armored body and just bounced away. The beast turned to face Alex – seemed the laser burst had got its attention, at least. It placed Matt carefully behind it, and rested one clawed foot on his body, protecting its prey. It snarled, showing teeth longer than Alex's fingers.

Alex edged closer. The creature looked like a cross between an armadillo and a giant dog, and was easily the size of a bull. Huge claws on its six powerful legs gouged into the rock they gripped, but the most monstrous thing about it was its two heads, both constantly moving. One was large, while the other one was smaller and less formed; Alex thought it might be blind as there was little coordination in its movement. The larger head watched Alex, and gave a deep growl that ended in a reptilian hiss. Its tongue flickered out, purple and forked at the end.

'What the fuck are you?' Alex said, and fired again, this time at the larger head.

The thing lowered its brow and the armor plating came together like a shield, impenetrable to the condensed energy burst.

'Shit.' Alex holstered the gun. 'Okay, we do it the hard way.' He pulled his Ka-Bar blade, and leaped from one rock to the next, closing in on the thing.

The beast looked down at Matt, who groaned softly. It lowered its head and its tongue slid out to lick at the blood trickling from a wound on his forehead. It hissed again, then bunched itself to leap.

Alex did the same, and met it midair.

The creature was fast, but hampered by its large armor-plated body in an arena of boulders and broken rocks. Alex spun and brought an armor-plated fist down on the thing's forehead with all the force he could manage. There was a crack, and some of the armored scales chipped away. The creature shook its head and blinked in confusion.

Alex grinned without humor. 'Hurts, huh?'

He moved his blade from one hand to the other as more shadows materialized from the dark canyon. Two of the creatures approached, slinking like large cats over the tumbled rocks and human body parts, moving into an attack formation.

Like a true pack, the creatures encircled Alex, concentrating on their major threat. Sam and Franks rained laser pulses and bullets down on them from above, but they bounced off their armor plating.

'Jesus!' Alex ducked as a bullet ricocheted toward him. The fire from above immediately stopped.

One of the creatures leaped at him, but before it had covered the twenty feet between them, something huge crashed it to the ground. Sam rolled away from it, coming to his feet close to Alex.

'Mind if I join the party?' he said, grinning.

Alex returned the smile. 'About time. But watch it – they have a hide like iron.'

'So do I.' Sam rolled his shoulders, the MECH suit mimicking his movements.

He turned to deal with the beast that had gotten to its feet and was now circling him. For a large creature it flowed smoothly over the broken stones.

Alex turned to two others moving into an attack position in front of him. He grabbed a fist-sized chunk of stone and threw it at the closest. The ten-pound rock traveled fast and exploded against the beast's skull before it had time to evade it. It staggered momentarily.

'Yes, you can be hurt,' Alex said.

He grabbed another stone and threw it at the second beast, but his aim wasn't as good and the creature caught the missile in its jaws and pulverized it.

These things had cunning and intelligence, he realized. It had destroyed the rock deliberately, to display the power of its jaws. They needed to be careful – even with Sam's suit, and Alex's amazing strength and regenerative powers, these things could grind them to dust if they got the chance.

As if working to a signal, three beasts charged at Sam and Alex in unison. Sam met one of them head-on as it lunged, bracing his legs and trusting the combined weight of his body and suit to hold his ground. He grabbed each side of the larger head and hung on, using the hydraulics to try and crush its skull.

The other two came at Alex. He knew he couldn't beat them with strength alone, so he leaped a dozen feet into the air, leaving them snapping at his heels. He twisted in the air and landed lightly, bouncing away immediately to avoid another of the ferocious beasts. He leaped again while they formed themselves into another attacking formation, landing beside Matt and quickly feeling his neck for a pulse.

He was alive, and opened his eyes weakly at Alex's touch. 'Cerberus – it's real.'

'Matt, quickly – how do I fight them?' Alex asked, keeping his eyes on the approaching creatures.

Matt raised his head. 'Hercules blinded Cerberus. The eyes – it's the only area without scales.'

Alex pushed him back down. 'Play dead,' he told him, 'or you soon will be.'

He leaped away, yelling as he went to draw the beasts' attention away from Matt. They turned to follow him, but he knew he couldn't keep bouncing around like this. Eventually they'd either anticipate his landing point, or simply grow bored and return to Matt.

He landed and spun just in time to avoid one of the beasts crashing into him. Alex ran, jumping from rock to rock, until he came to the cavern wall. He could hear the creature speeding after him, a sound like rock pounding rock – it was obviously used to navigating the hard surfaces and fissures of its subterranean domain. Alex leaped at the wall, but as he struck it, he coiled his legs to bounce back hard, flying at the creature so fast, he was on it before it had a chance to react. He landed on its neck, and punched down with his blade, digging deep into an eye on the larger head.

The reptilian hiss became a roar that shook the air, and Alex was thrown free, his blade trailing a string of jellied optic fluid. The beast raked at its head, then searched again for its attacker. But Alex hadn't gone far. He was already leaping, knowing the creature's depth perception would be shot now one eye was gone.

He landed on its scaly shoulders, and stabbed his blade into its other eye. It reared up and fell over backward, writhing and screeching on the ground.

'No more humans for dinner tonight!' Alex told it.

He saw that Sam was struggling with another of the monsters. He had it by the neck, managing to hold it at bay so it couldn't get its jaws around him.

'The eyes, Sam,' Alex yelled. 'The only weak spot.'

Sam half-turned, his face red and streaming with sweat. He sucked in a huge breath, released the creature's neck, then brought his power-assisted fists together over each eye. Shards of the stone-like armor broke away, but the thing was hurt, not beaten. It raked a claw down Sam's body, ripping away the hyper-alloy tubing, plates and pins embedded in his flesh. Sam's movements slowed, hampered by the damage to the suit. He was a huge man, and fit, but he was fatigued and the suit was heavy. He rolled side-on, but the beast released him instead of attacking, and wheeled away.

Alex saw they were all now focusing their attention on an easier prey – the beast he'd blinded. One grasped it by the neck. The armor-plated skin was no match for the crushing power of the huge jaws, and with a noise like breaking plates the prey's neck collapsed. The huge beasts leaped away into the dark, the corpse of their fallen brother bouncing on the stones between them.

Alex fell to his knees, breathing hard. He looked at his hands resting on the dark rocks – the biological armor plating was shattered and ripped. He bet his body probably looked the same, and knew it couldn't sustain much more punishment. But he had a feeling their trials had only just begun.

He kneeled and wiped some blood and sweat from his eyes. *I did it*, he whispered. He had retained control – even under attack, his body and mind had continued to belong to him. He flicked away more blood, smiled, and got to his feet.

CHAPTER 34

Matt put his hand to his neck. It was hot and sticky. His mouth was dry and he knew he was losing a lot of blood. Sam and Alex appeared over him. They crouched down, pulled his collar back, and started to probe the wounds.

'Deep but clean,' Sam said.

'No way of knowing if the teeth carried infection or even venom,' Alex said. 'Going to have to give him a universal.'

Matt groaned as Alex helped him to sit up. 'Wait till I tell people I got attacked by Cerberus.'

Alex snorted. 'Sure, Prof.' He stuck a field patch over the wound. 'This has got steroids, antibiotics and painkillers all in one nice little cocktail. Should keep you together until we can get you home.'

He pulled the material back over the wound, and Sam slapped Matt's good shoulder. 'Good as new. And by the way, did we mention how the Hammer feels about people talking about what we do?' He grinned.

'Oh yeah, right.' Matt coughed as Alex pulled him to his feet. He rolled his shoulder, feeling the grating pain recede as the painkillers kicked in.

Sam made him sip some water from his canteen. 'You just lost the equivalent of a marathon runner's fluids in a few minutes,' the big HAWC said.

Matt looked properly around the chasm floor for the first time, and saw the carnage left behind by the Cerberus creatures over the years. There were bones and broken stone body parts in a thick layer on the ground, and coins too.

'There's thousands of them,' he said. 'And a fortune in gold and silver. They probably offered the coins in tribute to the Gorgons, not realizing Magera and her sisters didn't want them – they wanted the Minoans themselves. All the people that lived in those houses – they must have been brought down here by the priests.' He frowned. 'Was it just to feed to these creatures?'

Sam kicked at a long bone. 'Somehow the Gorgons escaped, or were forced out. If not, who knows how many more people would have ended up like this.'

'Well, our job's to ensure no one else ends up like this,' Alex said.

Casey Franks leaned over the edge of the chasm above, looking down at them. Beside her, Reece Thompson had a scope to his eye.

'What you wanna do, boss?' Franks called down.

Thompson yelled over the top of her. 'We need to find Barclay.'

Matt saw Alex's jaw set as he turned briefly in the direction the huge animal had taken the SAS man. Jackson's helmet was lying among the rocks, covered in blood. Alex retrieved it, and rubbed away some of the gore.

'He's dead,' he told Thompson.

'We don't know that, he could be –'

'Sergeant Thompson!' Alex's voice boomed around the chasm.

The SAS man fell silent, but glared at the HAWC.

Alex met his gaze. 'If he was alive ... I'd know it.'

The SAS man shook his head. '*Fuck, fuck, fuck.*' He shouldered his rifle and moved away from the edge.

'Hey,' Alex yelled. Thompson turned back, and Alex tossed the helmet up to him. 'Be prepared to use it.'

Thompson's jaw clenched as he stared at the helmet, then he lowered it and walked away.

Alex pointed to the large orb on the other side of the chasm. 'You wanted to check that out,' he said to Matt. 'You up to it?'

Matt looked up at the wall. The chasm seemed much deeper from down here than it had from up there. He nodded, not trusting his voice to mask his doubt.

Alex went over to Sam and looked over the damaged MECH suit. Some of the tubes were crushed and the wiring on one side hung loose – all impossible to repair in the caves.

'Not going to be easy getting you up there,' Alex said, 'but you can't stay down here. Our friendly pups might return.'

Sam blew air between his lips. 'They'll think twice before trying to make dog chow outta either of us again.'

Rebecca's head was just visible at the edge of the chasm. She looked like she was lying on her belly. 'Matt, you okay?' Her face was creased with concern.

Matt grinned, and waved. 'Sure; just a scratch. Pain and me are old friends now.' He pointed to the orb. 'Can you get across from up there?'

Rebecca kneeled up and turned to Casey Franks, who had a scope up to her eye. She said something to Rebecca, who dropped back onto her stomach again.

'We think we might be able to get across at the end of the street where it meets the wall,' she told Matt.

Alex nudged Sam. 'Our turn. I can give you a leg up ... if you need it.'

Sam's response was to snort derisively.

Alex rested a hand on Matt's shoulder. 'It's a tough climb, but there's plenty of handholds. How do you feel?'

Matt swung his arms, rolled his shoulders and nodded. 'I can do this.' He looked back up at the fifty feet of jagged rock and repeated it silently: *I can do this.*

Alex nodded. 'Good man. Okay, you go first. The field patch is numbing the pain, but when it wears off you're going to be in a world of hurt.'

'Well, that's something to look forward to,' Matt said, looking for a place to start.

*

Borshov and his two Spetsnaz lay on the high precipice above the ancient village, watching Hunter and one of his HAWCs scale out of the chasm. A second group at the far end of the enormous cavern were edging along a rock ledge. Their goal was obviously the strange-looking orb structure at the rear of the gigantic cave.

Borshov turned his attention to the cave floor, then the houses and the street. There were plenty of places for concealment … and for ambush.

He turned to his men. 'We'll go down into the town and take up attack positions there. Let them bring the Magera weapon to us.'

One of his Spetsnaz grabbed Borshov's forearm. 'No, we should stay here, up high. We can pick them off from here.'

Borshov placed one of his huge MECH-suited hands over his agent's hand and brought his fingers together, just enough to bruise the other man's bones. The man gritted his teeth, hissing as he sucked in the pain.

'I like your idea,' Borshov said. 'Thank you for the suggestion. But I don't get to fight Arcadian from up here.' He let the man's hand go. 'You ready to follow now?'

The Spetsnaz withdrew his hand and nodded.

They made their way down the stone steps, the two Spetsnaz men sometimes sliding on their bellies, and Borshov carefully moving his armored body like a crab on all fours.

*

It took Alex, Sam, and Matt twenty minutes to scale the chasm. Alex grabbed Matt's hand to haul him over the last few feet. The young professor rolled over to lie on his back for a few seconds, puffing hard. Sam was already on his feet, scanning the darker areas of the cave. Alex could see the rest of his team edging across a narrow path cut into the cliff face. He looked across the deep rent in the earth at the village. It was a surreal sight – still colorful and vibrant, but empty and without movement, save for the flames that danced on the surface of the dark pools of oil.

Sam joined Alex and Matt, who was looking pale and weak.

'Stay with us, Matt,' Alex said. 'We need you.'

'I'm fine; just a little light-headed.' Matt spoke through gritted teeth. 'By the way, if you ever have another opening for an ancient languages professor, don't call me.'

Alex smiled. 'I think you already mentioned that last time. And yet here you are again.' He peeled back Matt's collar; the wound was sticky-wet. 'Let me know if you need any help or painkillers.'

Matt waved him away. 'Let's just get through this. I miss the sunshine.'

'You and me both,' Sam said. 'Let's do this.'

The orb stood before them – huge, smooth, and almost luminous.

Matt paced in front of the enormous structure. 'Well, definitely not built by the Minoans.'

Alex stood back a few paces to take in the whole thing. 'I don't think it was built by anyone from around here – there's no door, not even any cracks or seals.'

'Must have punched in from above. Maybe the limestone grew over it.' Matt looked up at the cave ceiling hundreds of feet above. 'Can't see the roof – it's too dark. But I'm guessing this must have made one helluva hole.'

Alex stared upward with his enhanced vision. 'The roof is intact. And there are no impact fissures around the orb, which you'd expect if it landed here.'

Franks and the others joined them. Rebecca pointed her flashlight to join Alex's beam.

'There's a reason there's no hole in the ceiling,' she said, moving her light around the sides of the structure. 'I don't think this thing is being *buried*. It's emerging – look.' She pointed. 'The geology here isn't flowstone. The caves in these parts were formed by water running through limestone over millions of years.' She turned to face them, accidentally shining her light into Matt's eyes. 'I think this thing is actually being exposed by erosion, and has been here for a long time ... well before the time of the Minoans, or even the Paleolithic tribes.'

Alex motioned to the village across the chasm. 'And that?'

She nodded. 'Yeah, I've been wondering about that. Maybe the early Minoans, or some other earlier race, discovered the orb and somehow managed to open it.'

Matt spoke softly. 'And gods came out.'

Sam grunted. 'Hungry gods by the look of all the bones.'

Rebecca waved her light over the smooth surface again. 'Maybe the turning to stone is just an accident. Whatever came out of this orb is so different to us that we can't comprehend what it wants. For all we know, it had – *has* – no idea that it's hurting us.'

'Are you kidding?' Sam said. 'News flash: it's not *hurting* us ... it's freakin' killing us without mercy. Believe me, we'll give it the same treatment.'

'I agree with Sam,' Alex said. 'It's lethal, and we won't be taking any risks.' He looked at the orb's white surface. 'We need to open it. Ideas, people?'

'Just one.' Sam stepped up, raised the still functioning arm of his MECH suit and crashed it down on the orb's surface. Even though the blow had the force of a pile-driver, there was no dent or abrasion.

Matt smiled. 'Yeah, I'm betting the early humans used that approach. Good to see we've evolved from that.'

Sam scowled, and Matt winked in return.

Alex ran his gloved hand over the smooth surface, pushing out his senses, trying to get an impression of … anything. Nothing came back to him – no images, sounds or sensations at all. It was if the thing was a solid, inert mass.

'We could try blowing it,' Sam said to Alex, eyebrows raised.

Matt snorted his derision.

'We'll put that option on the shortlist,' Alex said, touching the surface again. 'Somehow the Minoans opened it. Think – what would they have had? What did they use?'

Rebecca shrugged. 'Did they open it? I mean, maybe the occupants sensed they were there and came out to meet them.'

Alex nodded. 'Either way, it must be able to be opened. We're running out of time.' He turned to Sam. 'Your option is moving up the list.'

Sam bowed and turned to grin at Matt.

Matt groaned. 'What did the Minoans do? They probably chipped at it, bashed it, maybe even tried to set it on fire. But its skin was impervious. So maybe they tried something less forceful.'

'They would have touched it,' Rebecca said. 'Before anything else, they would have laid their hands on it.'

'We did that,' Alex said.

Rebecca shook her head. 'No, we've laid our gloved hands on it. But there's been no flesh contact.'

Alex pulled off his glove and placed his palm against the smooth surface. He closed his eyes and concentrated. This time he felt something. It was like a swarm moving continuously in his head.

'I feel something. Like a hive.'

'Look.' Franks pointed to his hand.

A circle had appeared around it, glowing. The circle moved away from Alex's hand to the center of the orb, concentrated like a spot of light from a laser. The glowing dot widened, moving outward like a ripple on a pond. When it got to about ten feet across, it stopped and the center of the circle vanished, leaving a black hole.

Alex stepped back. 'Seems we're the key – it needed to feel flesh before it would open.'

Sam lifted his gun to his shoulder. 'Maybe it needed to know food was available to its crew.'

'You know what this is?' Matt said, turning to them. His tone was excited. 'This is why Magera's been moving across Turkey, making her way here. Whatever's inside, it's important enough for her to come out of hibernation after all those millennia of imprisonment.' He turned back to the orb. 'I think it's where she came from ... really came from.'

He stepped forward, but Alex yanked him back. 'Give us a few seconds first. Franks, Sam.'

Franks and Sam stepped forward, their guns ready. Alex moved toward the hole in the orb, then paused. He turned slowly, looking back over his shoulder at the ancient village.

'We okay here, boss?' Franks' gun was trained on the Minoan street. 'Your puppy dogs back?'

'No,' Alex said slowly, 'but something.' He turned back. 'Thompson, you're on watch.'

The SAS soldier nodded.

Alex stepped up to the black hole in the orb. 'Let's get this done, and then get the hell out of here.'

He felt Sam and Franks a pace back at each shoulder as he stepped through the hole. As soon as they entered the black interior, a dim illumination kicked in, as though motion sensors had detected their presence.

'Holy shit,' Sam whispered.

The interior wasn't a sphere at all; the three HAWCs were standing in a long tunnel. The lights continued to come on, all the way along the tunnel, until they stopped at a wall about a quarter of a mile in.

'Just how big is this thing?' Sam said. He took a few steps and more lights pinged on – smaller this time and on walls and panels. The big HAWC pulled out a small silver box and held it up, moving it over the interior.

'What've you got?' Alex hadn't moved any further along the tunnel.

Sam waited a second or two, then spoke without looking up. 'No detectable signs of life.' He looked up. 'Or *known* life, I should say.' He read the screen again. 'About 1500 feet before we hit that wall.' He frowned. 'Holy shit, there's more beyond the wall. I mean, it's not just a wall, it's probably a bulkhead.'

Alex finally stepped forward. 'Rebecca was right – this thing didn't crash and embed into the wall down here. It's been eroding out of it for millions of years.'

Franks was looking at a control panel. 'Yep, this baby definitely ain't from around here.'

'And then just powers up after all that time?' Sam said. 'There's no radiation trace, so what's the power source?'

'Bring the others in,' Alex said.

Sam walked to the entrance and waved in Matt, Rebecca, and Reece Thompson. Matt and Rebecca almost fell over each other clambering in, their eyes wide with wonder.

Thompson paused, taking it all in, then exhaled slowly. 'So, eons ago, humans knock on the door of this thing and the Gorgons walk out.'

'One didn't,' Alex said.

He'd moved further inside the enormous hangar-like room, and was now standing in front of a recessed section that held a ten-foot-high tube filled with a cloudy fluid and lit from within by a soft blue light. The figure suspended inside the milky liquid was enormous.

'Oh my god.' Matt's mouth hung open. 'Is that Magera? How did it get here before us?'

Rebecca peered at the tube. 'Bipedal, two arms, and just the one head, unlike those damned dogs. And what a head.' She moved to one side, trying to improve her view. 'You can see where the legend of the snake-hair came from – it looks like growths all over the cranium and neck, like rubbery extrusions … more representative of digits, I think. Maybe an extra set of fingers.' She shrugged. 'Or maybe sensory organs.'

'That is one ugly mother,' Franks said, blowing air through her teeth as she looked up at the thing's face.

Alex could see that its eyes were closed. The flattened face had no real nose, just two slits with a flap of skin either side that would probably operate like a valve. The mouth was a long slit with tough rubbery lips. Though it was hard to discern through the milky fluid, the Gorgon's skin seemed to have the pallor of wet clay.

'Holy crap – it's got scales,' Sam said, pointing to the small overlapping discs running from the neck to the torso, where they were larger, the size of poker chips. He stood back. 'Jesus Christ, tell me again how this thing is supposed to be a woman?'

There were no discernible genitalia; instead, below the creature's waist blood-red tendrils hung down to its knees. Alex placed a hand against the tank. He sensed a living presence – but not a single one; more like millions all operating in unison.

'I have no idea whether this is Magera or not,' he said, 'but this thing is alive. It's a cryo tank.' He took his hand away, flexing the fingers.

'We still haven't tried to speak to her yet,' Matt said. 'We should at least make the attempt.' He raised his eyebrows. 'I volunteer.'

Alex turned to look at him. 'Matt, these ... *things* have given us no indication at all that they can, or want to, communicate with us in any way. We don't even know if they're sentient. Maybe the real owners of this ship are dead, and these Magera things are just specimens they collected on their travels.'

Rebecca stepped in front of Alex. 'Colonel Hammerson said we could –'

'On a mission I make the calls,' Alex said, cutting her off. 'Sorry, Matt, Rebecca, we are not letting this thing out. No one's been able to overpower one of them so far. And I'd really like to have some sort of defense in place before the Magera out there joins our little party. So let's find whatever it was the priests used to subdue it.'

'Before we kill 'em all,' Casey Franks finished grimly.

CHAPTER 35

When he was sure they were all distracted by the huge white orb, Tony turned and slipped away. In a few minutes he was edging back across the narrow ledge, stopping several times to regain his balance. The weight of the gold secreted around his body surprised him – for such little objects, the coins were enormously heavy. Still, the gold value was one thing; the value of the coins themselves to collectors on the black market was incalculable.

Once off the ledge, he tore off his shirt to create a sack and transferred his booty into it. He threw the heavy weight over his shoulder, grunting, and glanced back. He was satisfied not to see anyone reappearing from inside the strange sphere, and even happier that nothing was crawling up out of the dark chasm toward him.

He knew there was another HAWC stationed with his own men in the Psychro Cave, but the three of them together should be able to subdue him. And if Petro or Andronus was lost in the skirmish, all the more gold for him.

He sucked in a deep breath, the sweat streaming down his body. He'd need all his energy for the climb back up the stone steps – hundreds of them. But he'd rather die than leave the gold behind. He stifled a giggle. He'd come back here with a private army – there wouldn't be a single coin or antiquity left when he was finished. He puffed and reached up an arm to wipe his streaming brow. In that split second, something struck the side of his head.

Tony went down hard, his makeshift sack spilling coins all around him. He looked up groggily. A man like a spider, all in black and with one glowing red eye, stood over him. Beside him, a one-eyed giant loomed.

The giant grinned through a bushy black beard, and pressed an enormous boot down on Tony's neck. 'How many inside circle door?'

*

The HAWCs spread out around the hangar-like space, while Matt and Rebecca explored the wonders surrounding them.

'There's a control panel here,' Rebecca called out.

She was already leaning over it when Alex turned toward her. 'For Chrissakes,' he muttered under his breath, feeling a small knot of frustration tighten inside him. He forced himself to exhale, recognizing that she was a scientist and being curious was her job. No matter it might get them all killed.

The control panel was set into a desk that seemed to grow up out of the floor. Rebecca touched one of the screens and it flared to life, showing lists of strange symbols.

'Wow; one side is Minoan, and the other...' He snorted. '... probably *their* language.' He turned; his eyes alight. 'You know what this is? It's a goddamn Rosetta Stone.'

'They were teaching themselves Minoan so they could communicate.' Rebecca said softly.

'Exactly.' Matt nodded. 'And the writing in the crypt below the Basilica Cisterns, was maybe the Gorgon attempting to communicate, assuming we'd understand it.' He turned to Alex. 'I told you we should try to...'

'Forget it.' Alex cut in.

Rebecca touched the screen again and the outline of a human being, arms and legs outstretched, appeared. She touched the figure and more lists of symbols scrolled up beside it.

'What the hell are you doing?' Alex said, pulling her arm away. 'Don't touch –'

'Wait; look!' she said, jerking her arm out of his hand. 'It's us. Or rather, information about us.' She touched the screen again, and it changed to show the human skeletal structure overlaid with the circulatory system. 'Like in a medical school.' She kept touching the screen and the magnification dived down lower, showing individual cells and then strands of DNA, with more lists of data. 'Very detailed information about our physiology.'

'They wanted to understand us,' Matt said. He tapped another screen, and a small circle opened on the desk beside them. A cylinder rose up out of the desktop; inside, suspended in clear fluid, floated a small brown hand and forearm.

Matt grimaced. 'Ah, shit.'

'That's one way to understand us,' Sam said, 'a piece at a time.'

'I'm guessing it's a tissue sample,' Rebecca said, peering at the foot-high tube.

'Like you said, it's exactly like what you'd find in a medical school,' Matt said. 'This isn't necessarily a bad thing. In fact, it's quite logical when you think about it.'

'Know your enemy?' Franks said.

Matt shook his head. 'Rubbish. You don't need to cut them up to know them.'

Alex backed up. 'You might if they were a different species.' An image of himself strapped down to a metal cot, and Captain Graham leaning over him with a scalpel jumped into his mind. *To understand a different species,* Alex thought darkly. He shook the images away, grabbed both scientists and pulled them away from the desk. Immediately, the screens went dark. He looked to Sam. 'We're done here, let's keep moving.'

Alex led the way down the long tunnel to the bulkhead, Matt and Rebecca following him, then Sam, followed by Franks and Thompson like a pair of guard dogs. They had their guns up, moving them back and forth, turning to spot on the far entrance they came through to cover their only exit. In another few minutes, they were standing before a huge smooth wall. Alex tried placing his bare hand against the surface. Just as before, his hand glowed momentarily before a circle formed around it. The glowing ring widened, then dissolved into an opening. Muted lighting flicked on inside.

Alex nodded to Sam to go through first.

'I don't believe this,' Sam said, his voice echoing as he stepped inside. 'This thing is bigger than an aircraft carrier.'

The others followed him through. Soft lights continued to come on in a peristaltic wave out and away from where they stood on a small walkway. There were a dozen levels above them, and at least that many below, in a circular design. Alex calculated it would take an hour or so to jog around the ship's circumference. Every ten feet or so along the wall was a small porthole window.

'Cargo hold?' Alex said. He walked to a window, needing to get up on his toes to peer in. 'What the hell?'

He dropped down and looked left and right, then placed his hand on the surface. The door dissolved away. Matt and Rebecca tried to crowd in at his sides, but he pushed them back. The cubicle looked like a storage room, and was filled with long silver tubes stacked one on top of the other. The top side of each had a clear panel, with another smaller panel showing a collection of blinking lights.

Alex wiped the surface of one tube and peered inside. 'Ah, Christ.'

He examined some of the other tubes, and found that each held a body. His mind jumped back to the vision he'd experienced when he'd confronted Magera in the Turkish desert. Fleeting impressions of darkness, water, a landscape dripping with moss and lichens, a city with tall silver spires that touched the sky. He'd seen beings like the one in the cryo tank, heads writhing with monstrous outgrowths, escorting thousands of smaller creatures toward the city. Their latest harvest, no doubt – transported there in a craft just like this one.

'What is it, boss?' Sam leaned in close, towering over Matt and Rebecca.

Alex grimaced as he straightened. 'I was right; it is a cargo hold.'

Matt wiped at the panel of another tube, clearing away the condensation. 'My god! I think they're alive.' He turned to the others, exhaling slowly. 'We've never known why the Minoan race, the most advanced culture of its time, disappeared. We guessed that successive wars, disease, or even earthquakes caused them to abandon their cities and scatter to the mountains. Looks like most of them ended up here instead.'

Alex pointed around the room. 'There are ten tubes in here. Judging by the number of rooms, there's got to be tens of thousands of them in this ship.'

'Stacked up like firewood.' Sam shook his head.

Alex looked at Matt. 'Still feel like to talking to these sons of bitches?'

Matt didn't reply – he seemed to be in a trance.

Rebecca peered in through the clear panel. 'Maybe the ship crashed here, and its owners couldn't complete their mission. Maybe we humans weren't evolved enough back then to help them repair their ship.' She shrugged. 'The thing is, thousands of years ago we woke them up, and they just continued going about their task. For all we know, they thought they were saving us. Keeping us safe in this … ark.'

'Ark?' Sam snorted and waved a huge arm toward the tanks. 'You don't collect this many of the same specimen. This isn't an ark, it's a fucking harvester.'

Alex nodded. 'A factory ship.' He narrowed his eyes. 'Like a modern whaling ship – hunt, capture, and process the prey aboard the vessel.' He nodded toward the cylinders. 'Are they alive or dead? We need to check.'

Sam grabbed one end of the cylinder and dragged it out of its harness. The movement pulled Matt out of his trance-like state. He kneeled next to the tube and put his hand on the casing. Nothing happened. He bent over the panel of lights and pressed one of the small buttons, then another. The tube seamlessly unzipped, releasing some kind of gas.

Matt held a hand over his face. 'Jesus, what the hell was that?'

'Not oxygen,' Rebecca said, and sneezed. 'But we're still alive so it's not toxic. Maybe some sort of preservative?'

The tube collapsed to reveal a young man, no more than twenty, with olive skin and smooth features. His hair was long and oiled, with the long side-locks the Minoans wore. He didn't look any more than five feet tall. He groaned, and then coughed.

Matt leaned forward. 'Holy shit, he *is* alive.'

Rebecca placed a hand on the youth's shoulder. 'Take it easy,' she said softly. 'It's okay.'

The youth coughed again, his face wrinkling as if in pain. He crushed his eyes shut, and his lips moved.

Matt bent forward, listening, translating. 'He's asking if they've arrived in the Elysian Fields yet. That's the Minoan version of heaven.' The youth's lips moved again, and Matt's brow furrowed as he concentrated. 'He says: *we are the gift to the gods.*' He looked up at the others, grinning. 'This is the first time Minoan, real Minoan, has been spoken in 5000 years.'

'Great,' Alex said, and nodded to the youth. 'Now ask him how they speak to their gods. How do they calm them, sing to them? Hurry it up, Professor.'

Matt spoke in a soft but guttural tongue. The young man's eyes flicked open – they were the darkest brown and filled with confusion. He grimaced, his teeth clenching together.

Matt spoke the same words again, but a little louder.

Rebecca laid a hand on his shoulder. 'He's sick; we need to ease up. He's been asleep for –'

'I don't care,' Alex said. 'Matt, hurry.'

Matt's words became more urgent. The Minoan coughed wetly, then groaned. His eyes flicked open, wide and rolling, and his mouth opened unnaturally wide, releasing a piercing scream.

'Jesus Christ!' Casey Franks grabbed Matt's collar and hauled him back. Thompson did the same to Rebecca.

As they watched, the young man's body seem to inflate, his facial features became distorted, and his eyes turned milky. His cry of pain was abruptly shut off as first his face and then his body collapsed in on itself. In another few seconds, he was nothing but a foul-smelling mound of sludge.

Rebecca gagged, and Matt's mouth was hanging open in horror. 'What the fuck just happened?'

'Fuck me.' Thompson grimaced. 'Some sort of infection?'

Alex shook his head. 'That smell when we opened the tube – atmospheric gases. His body was saturated in them. Maybe he was being conditioned for another environment. The abrupt change destroyed him.'

'What?' Rebecca waved at the other tubes. 'So they can't live on Earth any more? All of them?'

Alex nodded. 'I think so. I saw it in the Magera's mind when we connected in the desert, but I didn't understand it then. The Gorgons were herding some other race of beings toward this big city, as though they were cattle. Looks like we were to be the next herd. Sam's right – it's a harvest; this entire ship is a livestock transport. These Minoans thought they were gifts to the gods, but they were basically meals on wheels, being transported home.'

Sam growled deep in his throat. 'Someone woke up Magera and it started to go about its business again. For all we know, this might be a scout ship – the first of many. If they like the samples, Earth might turn into their giant stockyard.'

'Fuck 'em.' Franks shook her head, her teeth grinding together. 'Blow the shit out of it.'

'Wait, what about the Minoans?' Matt said. 'There's thousands of them.'

'They're already dead,' Alex said. He turned to the SAS soldier. 'Plant the C-4, all of it. We'll use the grenades too for a bit of extra kick. Let's turn this abomination into atoms, and then bury what's left.'

*

On the surface, the mist moved toward the cave entrance, stopping at the Land Rover and the truck left by the Greeks. It hovered by them for a moment, and the nucleus at its center coalesced, darkening. The weeping was drowned out by another noise – a deep roar of fury as it sensed the intrusion below.

The mist swept toward the cave's opening, and the metal guardrail buckled, as though squeezed by monstrous hands.

Once it had entered the darkness, the mist vanished, and the creature within took on physical form and descended into the cave's stygian depths.

CHAPTER 36

Sam and Reece Thompson stacked the C-4 in two piles on each side of the door, along with the HAWCs' M33 fragmentation grenades. Sam had wired in the small silver tubes, each one amplified with HMX – a powerful nitramine chemical. Because of its high molecular weight, HMX was one of the most potent explosives around, with a lethal shockwave many times that of standard compact military impact devices. Simply put, they were a small package with a huge blast.

Sam turned. 'Boss, time?'

'Sixty minutes.' Alex set his watch. 'Mark.'

Sam coordinated the timer and stood. 'We're outta here.'

Alex looked up at the enormous rockwall above the massive orb. 'This blows right, it'll take out the entire wall and bring down about a mile of rock.'

Sam nodded, hands on his hips. 'It'll work. And even if the blast doesn't kill these things, they'll be sealed in about a billion tons of stone. Better than Constantine's urn.'

'How much time have we got?' Matt asked.

'Plenty.' Alex looked at his watch. 'Fifty-eight minutes. But I wouldn't recommend any more sightseeing, so let's move it.'

Rebecca had her arms folded tightly across her chest. 'I wish there was a way to save the Minoans. We'll be killing them as well.'

Franks spat onto the cave floor. 'You must've skipped the part where the poor sap turned to mud right before our eyes. Like the boss said, they're already dead, lady.'

Rebecca fumed. 'There must be a way to save them. We should at least bring a medical team in to –'

'To what? To get turned to stone by that monster?' Franks leveled her steely gaze at the scientist. 'Boss knows what he's doing.'

Sam looked around the cave. 'Anyone seen that little Greek asshole?'

Matt snorted. 'He's probably halfway home by now, dragging a Santa sack full of gold.'

'He better not try something stupid when we're buggin' out.' Franks held a scope to her eye, scanning the stone steps in the far distance.

Matt shook his head. 'I think the gold was a priority. Doubt he'd hang around to take a few pot shots at us.'

Franks snorted. 'If there's one thing you can count on, it's greed'll win out every time.'

Alex nodded to the HAWCs to form up around Matt and Rebecca. 'If the Greek gets in our way, he'll be staying down here with the Minoans.' He glanced down at the chasm. 'Those dog things are watching us – I can feel them. Like most pack animals, they'll be waiting for a straggler to become separated. So we all stick together.' He looked at Matt. 'Try not to look wounded.'

Matt gazed into the chasm's dark depths. 'I don't know if I can run ... if we need to.' He gave Alex a weak smile. 'And my head's killing me.'

'Dehydration,' Alex said. He turned Matt's head and looked at his neck. 'Glands are up – might have been something in their saliva. Good news is, you're alive. Just take it easy. We don't want that wound to start bleeding again.'

Matt raised his eyebrows. 'Worried about me, or leaving a blood trail?'

Alex could see the fear in his eyes. 'Don't worry, we'll be fine. We're not going back into the chasm.' He gave Matt what he hoped was a reassuring smile and then turned away.

He could feel the huge animals in the darkness watching while remaining out of sight. But now he began to sense something else – the creeping feeling of desolation and fury he had felt in the Turkish desert. Magera was approaching, returning to her lair, and it would be a hundred times worse than what was watching them hungrily from below. Their time was fast running out.

'Just stay close to me. Home soon, Prof,' Alex said and stepped onto the narrow ledge that would take them back to the village.

*

Sam's eyes moved from Alex to the paved street. He'd noticed the HAWC leader's eyes shining silver in the darkness, and he seemed to be on high alert. They were moving quickly now – Alex had picked up their pace. No one spoke, and the silence seemed to swallow even the sound of their footsteps.

Alex held his fist up, and froze. 'Halt.'

Sam brought his rifle up and followed Alex's gaze, but didn't see or hear anything. He returned his eyes to the street. 'What you got, boss?'

'Ambush.' Alex exploded into activity, pushing Matt and Rebecca to the ground, his movements so quick that it was hard to follow him. 'Stay down.'

Two soft gunshots spat from the line of buildings ahead. One struck the ground where Matt had just been standing; the other kicked Alex's head back.

More shots rang out, and the group scrambled for cover. Thompson returned fire, while Casey Franks herded Matt and Rebecca into a space between two buildings.

Sam dragged Alex from the street as bullets whacked into his armored back, and tore Alex's helmet from his head. 'Shit.' The wound was a deep gouge across his temple, and looked like it had depressed some of the skull.

'How is he?' Franks crawled forward, but Sam waved her back. 'Cover our asses, soldier.'

Franks rolled away, coming to a stop on her stomach at the corner of the building. Thompson landed beside her, and both of them fired off several rounds. They pulled back as stone chips blew away from the building.

'I got three bad guys, all in tight,' Franks said. 'They're good. I'm betting our Russian friends have joined the party.'

'Use the laser on wide pulse – blow the shit outta them,' Sam ordered.

He put his palm over Alex's wound, causing Alex to convulse. Sam pressed hard to keep him down. One of Alex's hands reached up and gripped Sam's wrist. Sam felt the pressure and was thankful for the MECH's armor plating. Alex roared, a sound of pain and anger, and his body shook. Against his hand, Sam felt an unnatural heat emanating from Alex's skin. The wound's edges seemed to sizzle as the flesh knitted itself together.

Franks had pulled her KBELT pistol and ramped it up to a single ball of energy. She picked her objective and let the pulse go. It traveled almost at the speed of light to its target, and blew the front off the entire building. A figure darted behind the next building, firing back at her. Franks re-aimed, fired, and blew that house to rubble as well. The figure moved again. A grenade went off a dozen feet in front of her, and she pulled back just before she was obliterated.

'Damn,' Thompson said.

'Like I said, they're good.' She leaned back against the wall.

'We're better,' Alex said, using Sam's arm to pull himself to a sitting position. Blood dripped from his head onto his legs. He groaned. 'That hurt.'

'Easy, boss.' Sam held up a hand in front of Alex's face. 'How many fingers?'

'There are fingers?' Alex winced and put a hand to his temple.

Matt gave Alex a thumbs-up. 'Try not to look wounded.'

Alex nodded and wiped at the wound. It had already stopped bleeding and Sam could see the skin at the edges was pink.

Alex grabbed Sam's shoulder and dragged himself to his feet. 'How many are they?'

Sam nodded to Franks, who gave the report. 'We're pinned down. Three guns. Borshov's probably one of them.'

Alex looked at his watch. 'We need to get out of here.'

'I got someone coming out,' Franks said. She lay flat, aiming her rifle instead of the pistol. 'Gotta hostage situation.'

'Alex Hunter, you come out.' The deep voice with the thick Russian accent was unmistakable.

'Ah, crap.' Alex shook his head, trying to clear his vision. 'We have to do this now?'

'The big bastard's got hold of the Greek,' Franks said.

Sam snorted. 'So what?'

'They've got us pinned down,' Alex said. 'We need to get out of here, and this might be the only way to do it.' He grabbed Sam's arm. 'I can finish this, right now, but I need cover – don't want another head shot. Be ready to make a run for it.'

'Are you kidding?' Sam said. 'Even if your body repairs it-self, that pain you're feeling is probably due to your brain just taking a freaking hammer blow. Boss, you can't take on Borshov right now. Even at your sharpest, it'd be a risk. Sure as my grandmother's Irish, that big bastard will have something up his sleeve.' Sam stepped in closer and nodded toward Matt and Rebecca. 'One more thing: you go down, they're dead. We're all fucking dead.'

Alex's eyes looked lifeless. 'There are no absolutes in our job, Lieutenant.'

Sam recognized the use of rank. He let go of Alex and hoisted his weapon.

Alex motioned over his shoulder to where the Russians were taking cover. 'Borshov can keep us pinned down until the roof caves in on us. Or he can pick us off one by one while we're trying to protect the civilians. Either way, we all die.' He looked straight at Sam. 'We'll give him what he wants. *I'm* the diversion. While I'm out there, get ready to move.'

*

Borshov grinned at Alex as he stepped out from the cover of the building. He was holding the struggling Greek up in front of him, a knife at his cheek. Alex could hear the man whimpering. He knew the Greek was as good as dead. He'd played this game with Borshov before; no one ever got away.

'Tell your men to put their weapons down,' he said. 'They shoot, you all die.'

'I tell my men no shoot you. You do the same, *da?*'

Alex kept his eyes on Borshov's. 'Already did. It's just you and me now.'

'Good.' Borshov grinned. 'We are men of honor.'

Alex moved sideways, looking briefly to where he knew the two Spetsnaz had concealed themselves. He could see the barrels of their guns pointed at his HAWCs. They obviously thought Borshov didn't need their support. The Russian looked bigger and bulkier than ever. He wore a lumberjack shirt with red and black checks; combined with the thick beard it made him look like Paul Bunyan. All he needed was a big blue ox. His face was red; the heat must be stifling for him in the heavy clothing.

Alex pointed back to the orb. 'I've set charges. We need to get out of here, or we're all dead.'

Borshov shrugged. 'Not your problem any more.'

'I'm here. Let the others –' Alex stopped, remembering how Borshov had killed a HAWC in Chechnya, right in front of him, tormenting her, then hanging her by the neck so she slowly strangled – all for his own amusement. The man had no compassion, no soul. He was the embodiment of ruthless brutality. Never had Alex wanted to kill someone so badly.

'I'm here,' Alex said again. He crushed his hands into fists, feeling the armored biological material pop from the strain. His shoulders hunched and a rush of chemicals flooded his system. The fury welled up, and with it a demand for blood – Borshov's. Alex's jaws clenched as he strained against the beast within him, waking now. He was determined to maintain his self-control until his team was free. Also, he knew the big Russian was up to something. His word was meaningless. There would be an secondary ambush somewhere – of that Alex was sure.

'No guns,' Borshov said, shaking the Greek man. He whimpered again, his eyes on Alex, imploring. 'Just fists, *da?*'

Alex shook his head slowly. 'No guns. Just you and me.'

Borshov made a deep-chested rumbling sound that could have been a laugh. He grabbed the Greek's head and jerked upwards violently, tearing it from its shoulders in a fountain of blood. Borshov flung the head away, and it made a soft sound as it landed in the center of the street. Alex heard Rebecca vomit behind him.

Borshov tossed the limp body aside, grinning. He was splattered with blood, streaks of it running down his bristling beard. He half-turned to say something in Russian to his men, laughed, and then tore away the lumber shirt to expose the hyper-alloy technology attached to his body. It was a MECH suit, like Sam's, except just the upper-body framework. Borshov rolled his huge shoulders and the bars and strapping moved smoothly, meaning the nerve implants were also in place.

He grinned and shrugged. 'You stronger, now I stronger too. So now we see, *da*?' He held up his fists in a boxer's stance and planted his legs. 'Come, come.'

'No time for this, boss,' Sam called. 'Just say the word.'

'Ah, shit.' Alex looked at his watch, then back at Borshov. 'Let everyone else go, then you and I can settle this.'

Borshov shook his head. 'Won't take long. Everyone must see.' He nodded toward Tony's head, the eyes wide, a rictus of pain still deforming the features. 'I want your head. I take it home.' He tapped his face, just next to his ruined eye. 'I remember who did this.'

The first time Alex and Borshov had fought, Alex had been soundly beaten, then shot and left for dead. The second time, it was his turn – he had beaten the shit out of the big Russian, and left the man buried below tons of rock under the Antarctic ice. *This time will be the decider*, he thought. *One of us will die.* He hoped it wasn't going to be him.

Borshov started to circle him, slowly. The MECH was only attached to his upper body; his legs were under his own power. Even though the massive trunk-like limbs were like columns ending in size eighteen boots, they wouldn't be as fast or as powerful as the rest of him. Alex also noted his head was exposed – he now had two points of attack. *Time to end this.*

He charged, moving so fast that Borshov looked frozen in time. But the MECH suit, operated by microprocessors, acted at an even greater speed, reacting to Borshov's nerve impulses, fired off by the brain at over 100 miles per second. As Alex leaped at him like a missile, Borshov's massive fist smashed downwards to bat him away like an annoying fly.

Alex got to his feet, and shook his head. His ears rang from the pile-driver that he'd just collided with. Borshov was a big man, even bigger than Sam, and with the suit's capabilities added in, it was like fighting a lightning-fast bulldozer.

Borshov made a fist in the air, his hand sheathed in hyper-alloy plating. 'Pretty good, huh? Gift from *your* scientists.'

Borshov circled one way, and Alex circled the other. The Russian had his hands up, fists clenched in an old-style boxer's stance. He nodded. 'Try again, Mr. Arcadian.'

Alex did, coming fast, jinking one way, and then leaping the other, pulling back one arm as he rocketed toward the Russian's exposed face. He knew one blow with all his strength would end it. Even a glancing punch should stun Borshov long enough to give Alex time to wrench free the suit's implants, turning it into an anchor dragging him to the ground. Not even Borshov could fight for long while supporting all that extra deadweight.

Once again, the MECH suit reacted faster than Alex could move. Borshov caught Alex in midair, his long arms holding the HAWC at a distance. One armored glove compressed around Alex's throat, while the other made a huge fist. Alex braced for the impact, knowing a sledgehammer would have been more merciful.

Borshov held the fist back, grinning behind his black beard, savoring the moment. He squeezed harder, cutting off Alex's air supply. Alex gripped at the Russian's forearm, feeling the bars and titanium plating shielding it. He raked at the metal, pounded at it, his frustration fueling his anger.

Alex felt like his body was on fire. He roared his fury, and grabbed at the armored forearm, squeezing with all his strength. One of the support struts began to bend, and there was a ping as rivets separated.

But before Alex could finish the task, Borshov rocketed his fist forward. It connected just above Alex's eye. The world spun, and stars exploded across his vision. The bullet wound that had just knitted closed burst open, spraying blood over Borshov's chest.

Alex wanted to slip into unconsciousness, but another part of him was never going to let that happen. *Weak,* it hissed at him. *Get out of the way.* The voice was full of scorn. It didn't care if Alex's team was safe, or whether he was mortally wounded. All it cared about was sating its desire for blood and revenge.

Alex ground his teeth, not just fighting against Borshov's grip now, but against the demon rising in his mind. He needed to maintain control. If his team was to escape, he had to keep Borshov occupied, and draw the attention of the Spetsnaz. He couldn't afford to forget strategy and tactics and brawl like an animal.

Borshov brought his fist back again, his arm having completed its arc from the punch, ready to deliver a backhand as it returned in the opposite direction. Alex's legs drew back and he kicked out hard into Borshov's gut. There was plating over his torso, but the impact was enough to rock the big man backward and loosen his grip on Alex's throat.

Alex felt part of his biological armor suit rip away as he dropped, rolled, and then staggered to his feet. He heard Rebecca and Matt screaming their support, and his fellow HAWCs calling advice and tactics. The words were garbled, meaningless, drowned out by the Other One's voice in his head.

Borshov looked over toward Rebecca and grinned. 'Another woman. Maybe you like to watch her die as well?' He raised his fists. 'Come on. Stop running. Fight.'

Alex circled, looking for an opening. Borshov was growing impatient, obviously thinking he had the HAWC's measure, with victory only minutes away. The big Russian lunged and Alex backed up. He lunged again, and Alex danced back out of his reach. Too late, he realized the Russian had herded him into a small lane between two buildings, a dead end. Alex felt his back strike the wall – no further to go. He glanced down to see more broken swords, bones, and skulls – evidence of another last stand by a group of Constantine's soldiers.

The trap was what Borshov had been waiting for – he charged. Alex used the wall to spring at the huge man, flying at him like a human spear. Borshov lunged, incredibly fast, but Alex expected it and twisted away, striking out at the Russian's head as he moved. Borshov's shoulder jerked up in defense, but Alex's blow, delivered with all his extraordinary strength and the extra weight of the biological armor-plated gloves, exploded titanium tubing and the hyper-alloy plating from the Russian's upper arm.

Borshov's other arm flicked out, its hammer-like fist thumping into Alex's back. Alex went down, but got back to his feet and turned, smiling. Pain didn't matter any more.

Borshov rolled his shoulder. The movement was slower, and some fluid spurted from a severed tube. He pointed a finger at Alex. 'You still fast, huh?' He reached down to pick up a broken sword, hefted it, and spun it in his hands. The iron was green-coated, and only about a foot of the blade remained. He grunted his approval, and waved the sword back and forth. 'Soon I be like you. We have your scientist – the smart man who made you. By now he has told us everything.' He shrugged. 'No more Arcadian secrets. Soon be hundreds like you, maybe thousands.'

'You're not home yet,' Alex said.

He moved sideways, his eyes never leaving Borshov's. The big man slashed the blade back and forth, his eyes darting down to the ground momentarily, then he grinned and leaped at Alex.

Alex stepped back to brace himself, preparing to take the charge head-on. But instead of stable ground, his foot stumbled on a skull at his feet. Borshov had positioned him right over it. Alex fell backward as the big man leaped, coming down with the broken sword held in both hands. Alex reached to the side and grabbed a bronze shield, lifting over his face. The clang of metal on metal was loud in the huge cavern.

Alex batted Borshov off him and rolled away, bringing the shield up. He looked across to see Sam's gun up and pointed at Borshov. But Alex knew Sam wouldn't fire until the outcome was clear. Come hell or high water, Sam would stand his ground or die.

'Thirty minutes,' the big HAWC yelled.

Alex had two options – spend his last few minutes fighting the huge Russian, or be buried alive and condemn his team to the same fate. *Fight or die*, the voice in his head whispered. 'Fight or die,' Alex whispered back. He turned, bracing himself as Borshov rushed at him.

Alex held the shield up again, and Borshov's blow created a fist-shaped dent in the thick iron. The next moment, Borshov had ripped it from his hands. Grinning, he brought both hands together and the ancient steel crumpled like a soda can.

'No more flying away, little HAWC,' Borshov said, and charged like a bull.

Alex saw the Russian had a long machete tucked into his belt. *So much for no weapons*, he thought. He was outweighed almost two to one, which meant no matter how strong he was, he was on the wrong side of any mass times velocity equation. He needed other tactics, he needed something else. If he couldn't increase his mass, he needed to increase his speed, his strength and ferocity. He knew he had another weapon, but one locked away in its mental prison. Perhaps that *something else* he sought was there all the time, just waiting to be released... from within.

Borshov arrived. At the last moment of impact, Alex turned sideways, moving in past the Russian's outstretched hands by a hair's breadth. Automatically, Borshov's arms closed around him, the machine sensors allowing him to move faster than he could ever have hoped to by himself. Alex knew he was no match for the suit's super-assisted weight and power, but he now had what he wanted – he was in close.

Now, the voice in his head screamed, and Alex felt the familiar sensation of being wrenched in two. The ancient village, the heat, the darkness, his HAWCs, Matt and Rebecca – all went away, leaving just Borshov, the enemy.

A grin of triumph split the Russian's face as he began to compress Alex within his grip. Alex grinned back, then swung his head forward, smashing it into the bridge of Borshov's nose, breaking the already battle-scarred snout.

The Russian snorted blood and squeezed harder, and Alex felt the titanic pressure begin to bear upon his spine. Instead of slowing him, it made him more furious. He swung his head into Borshov's face again and again, hammering the squashed nose into a mess of cartilage and bloody pulp. In so close, he couldn't swing his arms for a long punch, but he could use close-quarters combat techniques – his thumbs, the tips of his elbows, his teeth. Though Borshov's upper body was like an armored bulldozer, his face was just flesh and bone. Alex swung at it again, gritting his teeth as his biological armor and also his spine began to crack. One of the Russian's brows split, running blood into his good eye.

Before we die, we'll make him pay. The voice didn't care about victory or death, just about the brutality of the battle. Alex head-butted again, and again, ripping his elbows back and forth, over and over, until Borshov flung him away.

The big Russian wiped at his face, trying to clear blood and gore from his eye.

Alex got slowly to his feet, his teeth bared, choosing the next point of attack. He was about to charge in again, when a sensation like a wall of ice smashed up against his spine. He crouched and spun, his senses on high alert to a new and more terrifying danger.

CHAPTER 37

'I got a shot,' Franks breathed as she sighted along the barrel.

'Negative on the shot,' Sam said quickly. 'Boss ordered us to sit tight.'

Sam kept an eye on the two Spetsnaz, who were undoubtedly doing the same to him. But that wasn't what transfixed him, instead it had been the two bloodied titans coming together in all their savage brutality. It reminded him of a ferocious dogfight, but with fists, boots, steel, and strength many times above those of mortal men.

Though Borshov was the enemy, and a monstrous adversary in the MECH suit, what worried Sam the most was Alex and the way he had changed – he had once again becomes the thing that was loosed in Italy, the being that even Alex referred to as the *Other One*.

Sam gritted his teeth as the two men smashed into each other again and again. Alex used every part of his body as a weapon, his eyes round and furious. Sam doubted that he remembered or even cared that the cavern was set to come down in mere minutes. The big HAWC knew he might be forced into an invidious choice – what if Borshov went down? Would the Other One be sated, or in its blood lust, turn its ferocity onto others? What would he then do against Alex? What *could* he do?

Sam gripped his gun and looked up at the millions of tons of rock overhead – maybe the cavern coming down might save them all from themselves.

Thompson lifted his head. 'Reid... *Reid!* We're going to have to move. Got to get Rebecca out of here.'

Sam cursed, but knew the SAS man was right. 'Okay, but you two need to be the shields – take all the heat from Borshov's men.' He turned to Franks. 'Get the civs out. I'll stay and cover the boss.'

Franks' lip curled and she looked as if she was about to challenge him.

Sam's voice went up a notch. 'Do it, soldier.'

Behind him, Sam heard Matt suck in a deep breath. 'Oh no, no, no. *Look!*'

Sam turned to where Matt was pointing. A mist was form-ing up at the far end of the street. 'For fuck's sake ... right now?' He pulled the helmet visor down over his eyes. 'Go to visor shields, people. Matt and Rebecca, blindfolds on. Looks like we got a visitor.'

Sam grabbed Alex's damaged helmet from the ground and moved to the corner of the building, hoping to get a chance to toss it to him. He prayed Alex, *the real Alex*, would take it.

*

Alex heard Sam call to him, and he spun in time to catch the helmet out of the air. He held it aloft for a few seconds as he used every one of the techniques that Marshal had taught him to control his dark side. He knew that if he could release it, then he could also restrain it – he was in control, not the other way around.

Blood spurted from Alex's nose, as a hammer-blow of pain struck from inside his skull. The cage swung shut – he won.

Clarity returned in an instant, and he knew immediately what the danger was. Without a second thought, he jammed the headgear over his head and snapped the visor down. Immediately the world turned to an artificial landscape – a high-graphics computer game, where everything looked real but wasn't quite right.

Borshov watched him, his face screwed in confusion. Behind the big Russian, the cloud formed up. Alex could hear it weeping. He wanted the man dead, but wanted to do it himself.

'It's Magera,' he called out. 'Better shut your eyes, asshole.' Then he turned and sprinted toward Sam. 'Get 'em moving.'

Sam roared instructions. Casey Franks dragged Matt and Rebecca, now blindfolded, to their feet and pushed them out into the street. Sam and Thompson ran alongside them, using their large bodies as shields against the Spetsnaz. As Alex had expected, it was unnecessary, as Borshov's agents concentrated their firepower on the solidifying figure rising up behind their commander.

Borshov spun and the figure grabbed him by the throat. Alex heard him groan as Magera compressed the MECH suit's armored collar around his neck. Words hissed from between his teeth: '*Mohctp stragoi.*' Alex didn't know what the Russian meant, but guessed it was something to do with 'monster'.

Borshov struck out, making contact with Magera but seemingly without effect. He struggled and jerked, but neither his own brute strength nor the MECH suit was a match for the being that gripped him. It slowly lifted him from the ground, and Alex heard the powerful suit's hydraulics humming with the strain. He knew the strong alloys were probably the only thing keeping Borshov in one piece now.

Its tentacles grasped at Borshov, slithering and writhing as though each had a mind of its own. Alex could see that the bulbous ropes were tipped with sucker pads.

Borshov's men sent more bullets smacking into Magera, but it didn't release its grip on its prey. It turned its terrible gaze on them, and Alex saw their faces first go blank, then twist in pain and horror. What looked like thick vomit poured from their mouths. One of the men struggled to his feet, clawing at his neck, but his movements soon slowed. A golden vapor escaped his lips, flying toward the Magera. It opened its large mouth and inhaled it.

Borshov screamed. He screwed his eyes shut as the creature brought his face close to its own, and struggled furiously, fighting for his life. The hideous face seemed to elongate toward him from within the mass of writhing tentacles. Borshov seemed compelled to open his eyes, and the Gorgon was revealed to him in all its horrifying glory.

Borshov's eyes went wide. He coughed and then gagged. A thickened paste of soft stone exploded from his lips and spilled down his beard, solidifying as it hit the air. Borshov stopped struggling. Gradually his face became pale and lined with fissures. He was trapped in a stone prison made of his own skin and bone. The Gorgon drew him in close, opened its mouth impossibly wide, and inhaled, sucking out his essence.

In those slitted alien eyes, Alex saw a hell that contained the souls of millions. He remembered all the Minoans in the ship, stacked up like firewood, and realized they were food. This was how the monster fed, consuming some essence from within a human being, leaving the body a lifeless block of stone.

He glanced at his team, already halfway up the steps that led to the cave's main entrance, and then down at his watch. Seven minutes left – barely enough time if the collapsing wall brought down the entire tunnel system.

He looked back to Magera and saw that its head was turning ... to him. Pain needled the center of his head, and fragments of static washed across his visor screen. The damaged helmet wasn't working at full capacity. He turned to run, but couldn't. Pain bloomed in his skull. It was too late.

*

Sam brought up the rear of the group. Matt and Rebecca were still blindfolded so their progress was slower than he'd have liked. Sam glanced back down at Alex, and saw that he was staring at the Gorgon, unmoving.

'Shit, no.'

The only positive to the situation was that Magera also seemed frozen in place. Borshov's body, now nothing more than calcified stone, and the heavy machinery of the MECH suit hung about the creature's neck like an anchor.

The sound of weeping rose, then was drowned out by a shriek of fury. As Sam watched through his visor, the Gorgon started to dissemble into mist again, and he had an impression of huge scaled hands grabbing at Borshov and tearing him and the hyper-alloy framework to pieces.

Magera was now free to descend on the frozen Alex.

Sam roared, 'The fuck you will!' He stepped to the edge of the steps, preparing to leap the more than a hundred feet down to Alex.

'Don't,' Franks yelled, and tried to grab him.

'Franks, get 'em up and out,' Sam said. 'That's an order.'

Franks' face twisted in disbelief. 'Like hel...'

Sam leaped into space, and landed like a colossus, shattering the street's paved surface and sinking about six inches into the rock. He went down on one knee, but the MECH suit absorbed the impact, and he was immediately up and sprinting toward Alex.

Magera descended on Alex, the hideous face forming up beneath the writhing mass of tentacles.

As Sam picked up speed, he saw the shattered remains of Borshov and his suit, and knew he stood little chance against the Gorgon. But sacrifice had its own strategic value. He was traveling at around fifty miles per hour now, with the locomotive force of a truck. He dropped his shoulder and launched himself at the huge figure, striking it mid-center and knocking it back twenty feet.

Sam rolled and came up fast, turning to Alex. Franks and Thompson were already there, dragging the HAWC leader away from the Gorgon. For once, Sam was glad Franks was so strongheaded. Alex was still unmoving, but he wasn't dead, and he hadn't been turned to stone.

Magera rose up like a column of dark smoke, then solidified, screaming her rage. Her focus wasn't on Alex any more.

'Game time,' Sam said. He gritted his teeth, pulled both his gun and knife, and charged again.

*

Casey Franks pulled Alex's damaged helmet off and slapped his face, hard. 'Boss, you still with us?'

He opened his eyes, sat forward and immediately threw up. 'My head.' He looked one way, then the other. 'Where's Magera?'

'We need to get you up and out of here,' Thompson said, putting his arm under Alex's shoulder.

Alex pushed him away and rubbed his eyes. 'If the Gorgon's free, we'll never make it.' He pulled on his helmet again, and turned in time to see the monster smash Sam aside. 'And we're not going anywhere without Sam.'

Matt was suddenly beside him, blindfold off, his computer resting on one knee. He tapped some keys. 'We got something we can try.'

A discordant, grating tune emanated from the computer; it sounded eerily alien. Matt jacked up the volume just as the Gorgon glided toward Sam.

Sam lowered his head, holding his ground, but Magera stopped and turned toward Matt.

'Don't look at it,' Alex said urgently. 'Keep your eyes covered.'

Matt turned away, but kept tapping at the keys, making the tune louder again.

'It's not working,' Rebecca said. 'It's confusing it, but not putting it to sleep.'

Sam raised his gun and fired. The bullets did nothing other than attract Magera's attention.

'We need to get out of here.' Thompson dragged at Alex.

'We'll never make it,' Alex said, getting to his feet. He saw Borshov turned to stone, the obliterated MECH suit. There was no way he'd let his second-in-command suffer the same fate.

'It wants me.' Alex had felt the thing's pleasure when it almost had him in its grip just a moment before. Perhaps it was his enormous strength or the furious being inside him, but whatever it was, Alex knew that he had given it nourishment beyond anything it had felt in countless millennia. 'Then I'll give it what it wants.'

Alex ran toward the Russian's remains, picking up the long silver machete and swinging it at Magera. Ten feet out, he leaped in the air, blade high, and brought it down with all his strength on her neck. The blade bit deep, but didn't sever the head as Alex had hoped. Instead, the huge head turned and its mouth dropped open. The wail that emanated from it bounced around the huge cavern like a hurricane of madness and fury. Light poured from the wound.

Alex raised the sword again, but before he could move, the pack of Cerberus hounds appeared, slinking between the buildings, their armored hides catching the glow of the flaming lakes of oil, their eyes as red as fire.

Alex turned, ready to defend himself from the new threat. Against a few of these huge beasts he and Sam had only just survived – a pack of them would tear him to shreds.

But instead, Alex felt himself grabbed and lifted and a force far stronger than his own demanded his attention. His helmet was ripped free, and then it was as if the world went away – there was no more sound, or sight, or heat or any other sensation, but the dreadful attraction of the Gorgon's gaze.

Alex turned his face away, crushed his eyes shut, and gripped the huge arm that held him. He fought, but he was an insect compared to its colossal strength and slowly his head turned back. He screamed and raged, thrashing in the creature's impossible grip. The Other One's fury exploded to the surface to struggle in unison, but it too was quickly subsumed. Alex's eyes were opened, and he looked.

He hadn't known fear for longer than he could remember – no man or beast had ever made him tremble or hesitate. Probably because death held no horrors for him anymore, and pain was something that was endured and overcome. But this feeling dragged at his soul and then tore it from him. Once again the images of the humid world were flashed into his mind. The sense of millions of years of invading, harvesting, and enslaving countless populations for food and slavery, and a determination that the Earth would be next.

A cold crept over him; first in his fingertips and then his toes. It moved inexorably along his limbs. Alex knew what was happening to him, as his body became immobile – the shouts of his comrades, the Cerberus, his own mind and body didn't matter – all that was left were the eyes of the hellish creature that slowly pulled the energy from him.

A flash of movement in his dimming periphery was the huge pack of the Cerberus, now picking up speed, mouths hanging open, powerful jaws ready. The ground shook under their combined weight as they charged. Alex would be spared this fate after all – by death.

The beasts struck hard, taking the larger figure of the Gorgon to the ground.

Alex was dropped and forgotten. He lay shuddering as if in a fit, and felt his team grab and drag him away. He felt cold, and weaker than he'd ever felt in his life.

He managed to hold up one creaking arm. His vision was blurred, like looking through a curtain of fine gauze, but he could just see that his hand was bare, the glove having been lost. The limb was now white, and as he watched, dust fell from his fingertips. He guessed his legs were the same.

'Can you hear me?' Matt asked as he lifted Alex's head a fraction.

Alex tried to nod but couldn't. Instead, he parted ash-dry lips. 'Leave... me.' There was a small puff of dust and he wasn't sure the words were heard. He summoned up every ounce of remaining strength he had. '*Leave... me... now!*'

Alex knew they were out of time, and also knew he was no longer all flesh anymore. He was already dead, and if they stayed, they would be too.

'Shit, this is bad.' Matt turned to Rebecca, grimacing.

Franks stepped in close and lifted him, bringing her face close to Alex's. 'Don't you fucking dare.' She shook him for a second, and then dropped him to shoulder her weapon as she turned to Thompson. 'We carry him.'

'Wait, look,' Rebecca said.

Alex continued to watch his hand. A line of healthy color was creeping up from the wrist to the fingers. His vision slowly cleared, and suddenly the heavy weight on his chest lightened. He made a fist several times and blinked.

'Amazing; he's healing,' Matt said, sitting back on his haunches.

'Get him up.' Franks pulled Alex roughly to his feet.

Alex nodded, leaning on her for a few seconds. 'I'm... okay... I think.' He looked across to the Gorgon, still in its titanic struggle with the pack of Cerberus. Its massive hands tore at their heavily plated limbs, ripping heads off and flinging them away. But their sheer weight of numbers prevailed. More appeared and threw themselves into the fight.

'Maybe they were the Gorgons' previous cargo,' Franks said.

'Before they found us,' Rebecca whispered.

Alex turned to see Sam making his way around the melee, then sprinting to join the others. 'Three minutes,' he yelled to Alex. He grabbed Matt and Rebecca, threw them over each shoulder of the MECH suit, and headed for the steps.

'Go!' Alex yelled to Thompson and Franks. He knew the female HAWC would never let him carry her, so instead he shoved her hard and fast in the middle of her back, pushing her up the first few steps. He staggered at first, but then picked up speed.

Thompson scrambled behind them. Alex looked back to offer him a helping hand, but the SAS man simply pointed to the high cave mouth. 'Keep going,' he yelled.

Behind them, the Gorgon had thrown off its remaining attackers and was making its way toward the stone steps.

CHAPTER 38

They barreled along the mosaic tunnel, Sam crushing 5000-year-old pristine images under his large boots. The tunnel got narrower, and he had to stop to let Matt and Rebecca off his shoulders. Matt kept one hand on the huge HAWC's back, and with the other held onto Rebecca, which meant Sam could still pull them along at great speed. When they came to the flowstone wall, Sam didn't stop; he exploded through it like a bulldozer.

They crossed the drained pond and headed for the metal steps, with no time to catch their breath. Their plan was for the Gorgon to be trapped by the rockfall, not to follow them out.

Sam led them up the metal steps, his feet clanging heavily on the steel. Matt and Rebecca were right behind him, followed by Casey Franks and Alex. Matt turned his head as he climbed and saw Reece Thompson emerge from the flowstone tunnel, his face beet-red. He looked up at them, his face resolute, then he sucked in a huge breath and simply ... stopped.

Like a gush of foul air, a dark cloud spewed from the cave behind him and enveloped him. It coalesced, and solidified, and then huge scaled hands ripped his helmet from his face. Thompson's mouth dropped open, and his eyes became rounder than Matt had thought was humanly possible. And then he screamed, with such fear it made Matt's legs go weak.

'No, Reece!' Rebecca stopped and put her hands to her head.

Matt grabbed her and pulled her on. He saw Alex pause by the railing, as if contemplating leaping over it, but in the next second Reece Thompson shuddered and turned bone white. Magera sucked in his life force, and finished its meal by ripping the petrified husk of his body into a thousand fragments. It was obvious its rage wasn't going to be satisfied by simply draining the intruders.

'Move, dammit.' Alex's face was furious.

They were more than halfway up when Matt chanced another look over his shoulder. Magera's solid form had started to dissipate into the dark cloud again, and Matt knew the mist would be able to move at a speed that could outpace even Sam and Alex.

'Incoming,' Casey Franks roared. She pounded up the steps, then turned to fire uselessly at the dark mass hundreds of feet below them.

Alex looked at his watch. 'What the hell happened to –'

As if in answer, there came a massive hammer blow from deep in the ground. It sounded like a million volcanoes erupting, accompanied by the grinding and cracking of millions of tons of rock.

Matt saw that the entire cave system was being sucked into a giant void opening up beneath them. The stairs began to bend and then collapsed, as if the darkness was reeling them in on a length of rope. Huge stalactites fell from the ceiling like monstrous daggers, and walls split open.

Rebecca stumbled and fell. Alex sprinted past, gathering her up. He pushed at Matt. 'Move it, Prof.'

Matt didn't need to be told twice. He ran, his heart hammering with exertion and fear.

Vast underground wells burst their confines, pouring millions of gallons of water and debris toward them, turning the cave into a maelstrom of collapsing stone and surging whitewash.

Sam was first out into the daylight, followed by Casey, Matt, then Alex and Rebecca.

They slowed, but Alex urged them on. 'We need to get higher. This whole area's going to collapse.'

They ran hard for another ten minutes, up to a bluff overlooking the cave entrance. Matt's body gave out and he fell to his knees, gasping. He looked back and gasped. The caves were gone. In their place was a huge black hole, rapidly filling with surging, muddy water.

Alex stared into its depths, and Matt knew he was searching for anything living coming to the surface. But there was nothing.

Matt rolled over to lie on his back. He heard Rebecca whisper, 'Reece.'

'He saved us,' Alex said. 'He knew what he was doing. Bought us an extra thirty seconds – the difference between that thing swallowing us and getting out. He was a good man.'

Rebecca nodded, and wiped away tears. 'The Gorgons, the Minoans, the ship – it's like it all never existed.'

Matt sat up. 'No one will ever believe it did. Probably a good thing. Some people are better off not knowing what really lurks in the dark.'

Alex finally looked away from the surging water. 'No one must ever know about it. We don't want anyone going searching for the ship, or the Gorgon. For all we know, it could be waiting down there for someone to dig it out again.'

*

On the flight home, Alex sat apart from the others. For once there was a calm in his mind – no screaming devils calling for bloodshed; no Other One in the dark corners of his consciousness, straining at its mental chains, waiting for the opportunity to take over. He dropped his head back against the seat. He was looking forward to continuing his treatment with Alan Marshal. For the first time in years, he felt in control. Though he doubted the furies within him would ever be fully laid to rest, he knew that he was learning to master them. He smiled and opened his hands, then squeezed them into fists, feeling the strength run through him. He felt good. He felt like he had something to offer at last, something to live for.

He thought of Aimee and Joshua, remembered how the boy had seen him in the trees and waved to him. Somehow his son had sensed the connection with the strange wild-eyed bearded man hiding in the forest. He smiled. Now he had something to hope for.

Sam collapsed into the seat next to him with a thump. He'd removed the upper-body MECH gear, but he still overflowed into Alex's space. Unlike Alex, Sam's wounds would take longer to heal. Just about every inch of his body was covered in a bandage, stitched or daubed with iodine.

Alex grinned. 'Hey there, Frankenstein.'

Sam snorted. 'Just another day at the office.' He looked hard at Alex. 'So, good to be back?'

The big man was probably the closest thing Alex had to a brother. He nodded. 'Yeah. It felt good.'

'Damn right it did.' Sam punched him in the shoulder. 'Good to have you back, Arcadian. You're home.'

Alex grunted and leaned forward to look out the window. 'Nearly home.'

CHAPTER 39

Colonel Jack Hammerson read the Magera report and shook his head. 'This goddamn world will never cease to amaze me.'

He closed the folder and fed the hardcopy version into a shredder. The online version he allocated to deep storage in the underground information silos beneath USSTRATCOM.

He picked up the next folder, and pulled at his lip as he read its contents. It was a report on a covert surveillance operation on a private citizen. He looked at the photograph of the mother and child. He knew the woman well, but she wasn't what interested him. With her was a child, a boy, less than two years old. He studied the face, the gray-blue eyes, piercing, serious. The next shot showed the boy holding up one end of a ride-on car with another kid in it. The child was lifting their combined weight with one hand.

'Like father, like son,' Hammerson said. He flipped the folder onto the desk and rubbed his eyes, then sat back in his chair and stared up at the ceiling. 'Ah, Aimee – there are no secrets left in this world any more.' He sighed. 'So, now what do we do with you, and Joshua?'

*

The interrogation rooms beneath the Kremlin were for special guests only. They were tiled and insulated, containing the screams that frequently emanated from within, and making them easy to hose out.

President Vladimir Volkov looked down at the man strapped to the gurney. A metal spike extended from his nostril, with wires leading from it to a box that sent a mild electrical current into the area of his brain between the hippocampus and amygdala. Captain Robert Graham twitched, and babbled nonstop, even though his lips were parchment-dry. The doctor pulled up one of his eyelids to examine the rolled-back orb. The captain showed no physical response to the touch.

'He has told us everything he knows about the Arcadian treatment and the subject,' the doctor said. 'He has no more secrets.'

Volkov grunted. 'Get the information down to the labs. I want the treatments duplicated and commenced immediately.'

'It seems they didn't have much success,' the doctor commented. 'Only one Arcadian out of over a hundred experiments.'

Volkov shrugged. 'That is still one in a hundred. And we have 10,000 volunteers waiting in our gulags.'

'And Captain Graham?' the doctor asked. 'He will never function normally again. Disposal?'

Volkov's mouth turned down momentarily. 'No, keep him alive. Let his brain empty completely. Who knows what other useful information he may have stored in there.' He stripped off his gloves and dropped them to the floor. 'So, now we make our own Arcadians.' He grinned, wolf-like. 'And in Russia, everything is bigger and better.'

AUTHOR'S NOTES

Many readers ask me about the science in my novels – is it real or fiction? Where do I get the situations, equipment, characters or their expertise from, and just how much of any legend has a basis in fact? In the case of the Gorgon, there are numerous mythological and religious stories, some dating back to the Neolithic Age, of men being turned to stone, of snake goddesses, and hideous monsters living in an underworld.

The Gorgon

The word 'gorgon' derives from the ancient Greek word γοργός, meaning 'fierce, terrible and grim'. Another derivation is from the Greek word *gorgos*, which means 'dreadful'. So it is an ancient word, as old as Zeus himself.

One of the earliest images of a Gorgoneia – a figure depicting a Gorgon head – dates from nearly 3000 years ago, and appears on a coin made of electrum (a natural alloy of gold, silver and other metals) discovered during excavations at Parium. Images with a Gorgon head were also found in the Knossos palace on Crete, dating from a thousand years earlier. A Lithuanian–American archeologist, Marija Gimbutas, argued that the Gorgon mythology extended back to at least 6000 BC, citing a ceramic mask from the Sesklo culture as proof. In her book *Language of the Goddess*, she also identified the genesis of the Gorgoneion in Neolithic art and jewelry.

Minoan jewelry found on the island of Mochlos in Crete shows the figure of a female goddess with a monstrous writhing head; while other Gorgons are portrayed with clawed feet, wings, fangs, tusks, flashing eyes, large teeth, and sometimes a protruding snake-like tongue. In Virgil's *Aeneid*, written between 29 and 19 BC, Gorgons are said to live at the entrance to the Underworld, dwelling in eternal darkness. In more modern times, the Gorgon's likeness has been immortalized by artists including Leonardo da Vinci, Peter Paul Rubens, Pablo Picasso, Auguste Rodin, and Benvenuto Cellini.

Medusa

Medusa is the most famous of the Gorgon creatures. She, along with her sisters Stheno and Euryale, were the daughters of the sea Titans Phorcys and Ceto.

Many versions of the myth have Medusa, the youngest sister, as a beautiful maiden with long silky hair, said to be extremely wise but very vain. She and her sisters all served as priestesses to the virgin goddess of wisdom, Athena. However, the sea god, Poseidon (Neptune), desperately desired Medusa and raped her inside Athena's temple. Athena blamed Medusa for Poseidon's attack and for defiling her place of worship. As punishment, she transformed the three sisters into hideous beasts with scaly skin, dragon wings, and hair formed of dozens of coiling snakes. As further retribution, the Gorgons were so horrifying that any man who beheld them was instantly turned to stone.

Medusa and her sisters grew to become vicious monsters that took great pleasure in torturing their victims. Perseus was given gifts by the gods – winged sandals from Hermes, a helmet of invisibility provided by Hades, and Athena's silver shield – to help him kill Medusa. Perseus crept up on the sleeping Medusa by looking at her reflection in his shield, cut off her head, and presented it to Athena, who placed it in the center of her aegis, the protective shield she wore over her breastplate. Perseus escaped Medusa's enraged sisters thanks to the winged sandals of Hermes, and by wearing Hades' helmet of invisibility.

The Medusa tale reaches back even further than classical Greece. She also appears in Libyan images, with her hair sometimes resembling dreadlocks, and was worshiped by the Libyan Amazons as their serpent goddess. Her name there is derived from the Sanskrit word *medha*, and Egyptian *met* or *maat*, meaning 'wisdom'.

Medusa's face is usually shown screaming, or staring with unblinking eyes. Her tongue sometimes protrudes like a snake's and her head is often surrounded by a halo of coiling snakes. The Medusa image was frequently used to guard and protect, up until the Christian era. Even after that, her face continued to appear on columns, doorways and gateways, signifying her role as the guardian of the threshold between the realms of the living and the dead, between the temporal world and the Underworld.

The Medusa is an ancient icon that remains one of the most popular and enduring figures of Greek mythology. She continues to be recreated in pop culture and art today. Her face is carved into a rock at the popular Red Beach in Matala,

Crete; is used as the logo for the famous fashion brand Versace; and even appears in some Greek bank vaults as a talisman for luck and protection.

The Basilica Cistern (Sunken Palace)

The Basilica Cistern, or Sunken Palace, is the largest of several hundred ancient cisterns that lie beneath the Turkish city of Istanbul (formerly Constantinople, and before that, Byzantium). The Basilica Cistern is located 500 feet southwest of the Hagia Sophia on the historical peninsula of Sarayburnu. The name derives from a large public square on the First Hill of Constantinople, the Stoa Basilica, beneath which it was originally constructed. The Great Basilica was built between the third and fourth centuries during the Early Roman Age as a commercial, legal, and artistic center. Ancient texts indicated that the Basilica had gardens surrounded by a colonnade and facing Hagia Sophia. According to ancient historians, Emperor Constantine created the original structure, which was later rebuilt and enlarged by Emperor Justinian after the Nika riots of 532 AD, which devastated the city.

The underground structure is enormous, even by today's standards, and historical texts claim that 7000 slaves were involved in building it. The cathedral-sized cistern is an underground chamber of approximately 105,000 square feet, capable of holding nearly 3 million cubic feet of water. The ceiling is supported by a forest of over 300 marble columns, each thirty feet high. The Basilica Cistern has undergone several restorations since its original construction, the most recent in 1985, when 50,000 tons of mud was removed, and a platform built to replace the boats that once used to take tourists through it.

In 1963, before the platform was built, the Basilica Cistern was used as a location for the James Bond film *From Russia With Love*.

Located in the north-west corner of the cistern are two columns that stand on blocks carved with the Medusa's face. The origin of the carvings is unknown, though it's been suggested the blocks might have been brought to the cistern after being removed from a building of the late Roman period. Architects believe the blocks were placed sideways and upside down to form the best support for the columns; however, legend has it that the blocks are oriented sideways and inverted in order to negate the power of the Gorgons' gaze. Many Byzantium-era sword handles and small pedestal columns were engraved with the Gorgon's head upside down, to deflect the power of her gaze while still enjoying its protection.

The Greek Underworld

Hell is viewed by many religions as a place of torment, often for eternity. However, religions with a cyclic history often depict hell as an intermediary state between incarnations, such as between life, death, resurrection or reincarnation. It is usually located in another dimension, above or below us, and sometimes entered through a volcano's crater, a cave, or even below the sea. It is sometimes portrayed as crawling with demons that torment those who live there, and ruled by a supreme being, a god of death, such as Nergal, Hel, Enma, Satan, or Hades.

The Greeks had a rich mythological underworld – a place where souls went after death – described variously as being at the far ends of the ocean or beneath the depths or ends of the earth. It was considered the counterpart to Mount Olympus, and filled with darkness in opposition to the kingdom of the gods, which was filled with light.

In Homer's *Iliad*, the underworld, Hades, is a dark, damp and moldy place buried inside the depths of the earth. The dead cross a river to get there, must pass through gates guarded by the monstrous many-headed hound Cerberus, and present themselves for judgement before King Hades. In the *Odyssey* (a sequel to the *Iliad*), Hades is described in even greater detail, and is now located at the end of the Earth, on the far western shore of the massive dark river Okeanos, beyond the gates of the sun and the land of dreams.

Hesiod's *Theogony* describes Hades as lying at the end of the flat disc of the Earth, beyond the River Okeanos and the land of evening. Hesiod also introduces the Islands of the Blessed, a paradise realm reserved for the great mythological heroes.

Charon, the ferryman of the dead, first appears in the epic poem the *Minyad* (attributed to Prodicus the Phocaean, date unknown), punting souls across the Akherousian Lake in a skiff. Here, the dead are often described roaming across fields of asphodel (a pale-gray plant that is edible but virtually tasteless, regarded by the ancients as a food of last resort).

In most versions, life in the underworld is full of shadows, without sunlight or hope; a joyless place, where the souls of the dead eventually fade into nothingness. Few mortals escape back to the land of the living, with two notable exceptions – Hercules descended to Hades to rescue Theseus (and also capture the giant hound Cerberus). But in Greek mythology, there were few mortals like Hercules. It takes an exceptional person to undertake exceptional adventures – such as Captain Alex Hunter, the Arcadian.

Sauromatians – the Snake People of ancient Russia

The Sarmatians or Sauromatians were an Iranian people whose territory covered the western part of greater Scythia (modern southern Russia, Ukraine, and the eastern Balkans) from about the fifth century BC to the fourth century AD.

Archeological evidence suggests that Scythian–Sarmatian cultures may have given rise to the myth of the Amazons. Graves of women have been found in southern Ukraine and Russia, with the women dressed for battle. Their bones showed signs of deep wounds, meaning these woman didn't just dress for battle, they also fought.

The Greek name Sarmatai derives from the shortening of Sauromatai, which is associated with the word 'lizard' (*sauros*). The Greeks compared the Sauromatians to lizards because of their reptile-like scale armor, created by slicing horses' hooves into discs and lashing them together. They also carried dragon standards, and had sharp teeth and small, lively eyes.

The Sauromatians started to decline in the third century, finally disappearing in the fourth century due to the incursions of the Huns, Goths, and Turks.

Stone Man Syndrome

How does someone turn to stone; become a living statue? The condition is still largely a mystery today, so it is any wonder that the ancient Greeks, Cretans, Minoans, Iranians, and dozens of other races came up with all manner of legends to account for this bizarre affliction?

In the seventeenth century the French physician Charles Patin described a case of a woman who was 'turning to wood', which was actually the uncontrolled growth of bone.

The woman had an incredibly rare condition that caused her flesh, cartilage, tendons, and organs to slowly ossify. In 1736, British physician John Freke described a youth with strange rock-hard swellings all over his back. The disease was named myositis ossificans progressiva, which means 'muscle turns to bone'. The name was officially changed to fibrodysplasia ossificans progressiva (FOP) in the 1970s.

Though fibrodysplasia ossificans progressiva is the medical term, the condition is commonly referred to as stone man syndrome. It is extremely rare, affecting one in two million people. A mutation of the body's repair mechanism causes tissue to become ossified when damaged. In many cases, injury causes a joint to become permanently frozen by rapid new bone creation. When the new bone is surgically removed, the body replaces it with even more bone, and the more rapidly the disease progresses.

The best-known case is that of Harry Eastlack (1933–1973), whose condition began at the age of ten. By the time of his death from pneumonia shortly before his fortieth birthday his body had completely ossified, and he was only able to move his lips. Eastlack donated his body to science, in the hope that scientists might find a cure for this little-understood, terrible disease. His preserved skeleton is kept at the Mütter Museum in Philadelphia, and has been an invaluable source of information in the study of FOP.

Why does a healthy person's body turn on itself like this? Evolutionary biologists have theorized that higher mutation rates are beneficial in some situations, because they enable organisms to adapt more quickly to their environments. For example, bacteria that is repeatedly exposed to antibiotics can have a much higher mutation rate than the original population, developing into a stronger strain. However, there doesn't seem to be a logical explanation for FOP. It's believed to be caused by a molecular misfire, a major system error in the

402

human body. Something causes the body's wound repair system to malfunction, gradually converting tendons, ligaments, and skeletal muscle into sheets of armor plating. The sufferer becomes a prisoner in his or her own body.

Stone man syndrome is one of the rarest conditions known to humankind, and one of the body's enduring mysteries.

ACKNOWLEDGMENTS

As a kid I believed in magic. Now as an adult, and seeing the way professional editors work their dark art, I believe in magic all over again. Thank you to Nicola and Tara – your work is a mix of good ideas, good judgement, and magic. Also, thank you to Pan Macmillan's Momentum's entire formidable team, and especially Joel and Mark, who turn my words into a book.

JAN 2016

CPSIA information can be obtained at www.ICGtesting.com
Printed in the USA
LVOW11s1657120815

449844LV00004B/769/P